The Shattered Gates

Book One of The Rifter

GINN HALE

Blind Eye Books

blindeyebooks.com

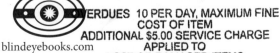

The Shattered Gates
Book One of the Rifter
By Ginn Hale

Published by:
Blind Eye Books
1141 Grant Street
Bellingham, WA 98225
blindeyebooks.com

Edited by Nicole Kimberling
Cover art, maps and all illustrations by Dawn Kimberling

First print edition November 2012
Copyright © 2012 Ginn Hale

ISBN 978-1-935560-23-4

This book is dedicated to Jemma, Philipp, Ian, and Hieu. I look forward to the stories of your many and great adventures.

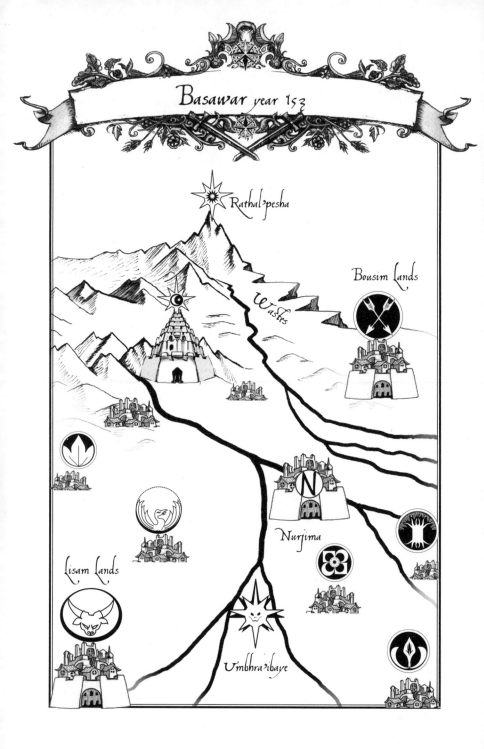

Basawar year 153

Rathal'pesha

Bousim Lands

Wastes

N

Nurjima

Lisam Lands

Umbhra'ibaye

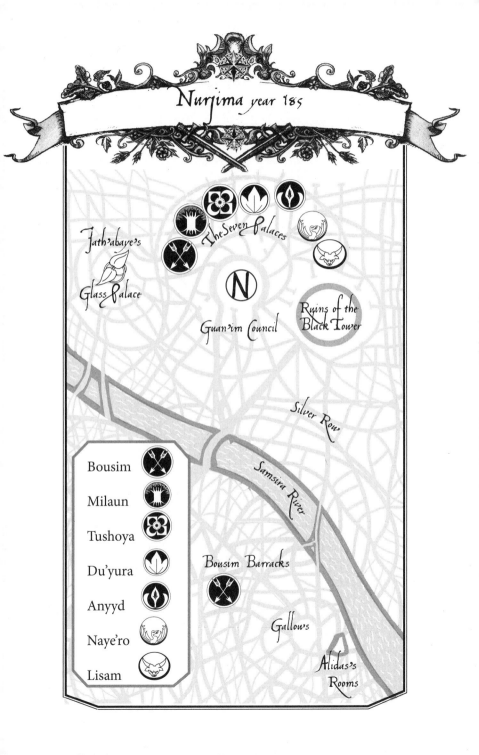

Nurjima year 185

Jath'abaye's
Glass Palace

The Seven Palaces

Guan'im Council

Ruins of the
Black Tower

Silver Row

Samsira River

Bousim Barracks

Gallows

Alidas's
Rooms

Bousim
Milaun
Tushoya
Du'yura
Anyyd
Naye'ro
Lisam

CHAPTER ONE

The letter wasn't addressed to John. The return address, however, was his. Not that he had sent the letter. He would never have mailed anything off without a ZIP code, and he certainly wouldn't have wasted postage attempting to contact "The Palace of the Day in the Kingdom of the Night."

But his roommate, Kyle, would have.

John frowned at the yellowed parchment envelope and the gothic letters scrawled across it. A blood-red droplet of sealing wax clung to the back of the letter like a wad of chewing gum on the underside of a school desk. As John turned the letter back over, he noticed faint watermarks on the envelope. Crescent moons.

John could almost see the mailman rolling his eyes as he tossed the letter into the mailbox along with a heap of bills, sale flyers, pizza coupons, and a glossy new underwear catalog.

He wandered back to the kitchen sink, pulled the trashcan out, and dropped the flyers and coupons into the mire of orange peels and coffee grounds. He paused a moment to consider the catalog.

Tanned men in an assortment of absurdly small briefs grinned up at John from the pages. What little clothing the models displayed was tawdry and over-priced. Still, he lingered on a spread of muscular bodies until their waxed chests and fixed gazes reminded him too much of store mannequins. Then he dropped the underwear catalog into the recycling bin and returned to the mysterious letter.

He turned the envelope over, feeling the uneven mass of the enclosed contents. It felt small and heavy, like a key. John traced the hard outline, almost embossing the shape into the sealed envelope. It was definitely a key. A house key. Probably the key to this very house.

He hadn't seen his roommate for two weeks, not since the awkward night that they had recognized each other through the crowd of half-dressed men roving the Steamworks bathhouse. John could still remember Kyle's expression, how it had shifted from something like appreciation to horror when he seemed to realize that John was staring back at him. Then Kyle had disappeared. Just vanished, as if he'd only been a trick of the dim light, and John hadn't seen him since.

Which was fine, John supposed. He was a private man himself, and he could understand the desire to keep one's personal life secret, but rent was due tomorrow.

John gazed at the envelope, feeling the weight of it in his hand. It would have been like his socially awkward roommate to work out some weird way to return the house key without actually having to tell John face to face.

With an absent push from his foot, John shoved the trashcan back beneath the sink.

Assuming this was Kyle's house key, Kyle's half of the rent was going to be hard to scrape together. And if it wasn't Kyle's key? John shook the envelope and considered how he would explain opening his roommate's mail.

Kyle obviously hated any kind of intrusion into his privacy. When he had first moved into the house, he fitted his bedroom door with a heavy iron padlock that looked like a prop from a pirate movie. Nothing of Kyle's decorated the living room, kitchen, or hall. No books, photos, posters, CDs, or tapes. In the bathroom, the only hint of his presence was a red travel toothbrush and a bar of soap. Oddly, the soap was still in its paper wrapper and had been from the first day that he moved in. He kept his dishes and food in a locked cupboard, protected from the bad influence of John's packages of instant noodles and peanut butter.

Sometimes John would look at Kyle and simply could not understand how he functioned.

Returning to the letter, John studied the wax seal. He supposed he could use a heated razor blade to slice through and then stick the seal back down with glue. Immediately, John imagined Kyle holding the letter few inches below his sharp nose and taking in a strong, suspicious whiff. It was the kind of thing Kyle would do. Freezing the letter might weaken the seal. Or John could try cutting the top of the envelope itself and then gluing it back up. He would have to carefully line up the edges—and there was still the problem of the lingering smell of most adhesives.

"Screw it." John ripped the letter open and dropped the key out into the palm of his hand.

It was not the house key.

It looked like the key to Kyle's room: gold and decorated with moons and etched with some faint script.

John stared at it for a few moments, trying to figure out why Kyle would send anyone the key to his room. He supposed that he might as well read the enclosed letter since he had already opened the envelope. Maybe it would offer him an insight into Kyle's strange appearance and odd behavior.

For a moment, he wondered if he really wanted to know more. There was a certain ease to simply not knowing what Kyle was thinking while watching him slink up the stairs, dressed in a heavy black leather coat, carrying lethal-looking knives and a bundle of cloth as long as a human arm. John wasn't sure if he was prepared for a deeper insight into Kyle's inner workings.

But he was so puzzling that John couldn't help being fascinated by him.

He wasn't bad looking. He stood nearly as tall as John but with a leaner musculature. His dark eyes and full mouth softened his otherwise sharp, angular features. He would have been handsome if weren't for the scar that sliced out from either side of his mouth, back almost to his ears. How did a guy get a scar like that? And that scar was only one of several that cut across Kyle's body like red interstate lines on a road atlas. Then there was his long, black hair and the tiny black symbols tattooed across the backs of his hands and his eyelids.

Who, in his right mind, got his eyelids tattooed? How did he ever get a job with tattooed eyelids? For that matter, what did he do for a living?

He claimed to be a milkman, but John didn't believe him.

And what about the two black-bladed knives he always carried? What about the sword?

John decided that the weapons alone might justify reading this one letter. He pulled it out and unfolded it. The entire page of parchment was blank except for a single word.

It said: "Don't."

CHAPTER TWO

The night wind slashed through the black branches of the trees, ripping off spring blossoms and young leaves. It swept over Kahlil, tugging at his braided hair and whipping through the folds of his coat. He drew in a deep breath. The bristling energy of the rising storm filled his lungs. Heavy violet clouds churned overhead.

A low reverberation cracked across the sky. It could have been thunder, but Kahlil knew it wasn't. The smell of gunpowder suddenly hit the air. If they were lucky up in the convent, the rain would break before the fires could spread. Not that he had the luxury to worry about the nuns. He was still a long way from safety himself.

Kahlil bolted from the cover of the trees. He leapt across an irrigation channel and sprinted for the apple grove. His pack rocked against his back, settling uncomfortably against his scabbard. Behind him siege mortars roared again, and he heard a crash as the timbers of the temple gate exploded. The smell of burning wood rushed over him on a warm wind. With it came the quick cracks of line after line of artillerymen opening fire.

"It's not them guns that kills ya," a soft voice whispered from his pack, "an' it ain't they bullets neither."

"It's the holes that kill you more than either." Kahlil only mouthed the words, not needing to give them voice when speaking to the bones.

Nestled safely inside his pack, the bones gave out a silent laugh.

Kahlil picked his way between the black trees. The overhanging branches of the apple orchard blocked the distant light of the burning convent. Above him, the first soft patters of rain began to fall. Soon the wet ground would make it hard to keep up his pace and his footing.

"Runnin' dead, down a hill," the bones whispered, "smokin' temple at you back."

"Little ghost caught a chill, rode it out inside a sack," Kahlil answered silently.

Again he felt the tiny shaking motions of mirth. Skeletal fingers petted him through the heavy leather of his pack and coat. The icy sensation pierced down to his bare flesh.

At the edge of the grove, an open expanse of road wound up toward the convent. A few yards further on, Kahlil saw a match flare briefly as one soldier offered another a light for his cigarette. They stood close, protecting the flame from the rain.

For a moment their faces were illuminated, expressions soft and relaxed. The chinstraps of their helmets hung loose. Their rifle barrels pointed over their shoulders, still strapped to their backs. Their coats looked crisp, probably still staining the shirts below with new red dye. Probably neither of them had seen action yet.

"Two only," the bones whispered. "Cut they throats and share they smokes with me."

Kahlil shook his head.

"Idiot," came the response. He felt the weak impact at his back as a bony little fist swatted him. "They shoot yous up against a wall someday."

"They could call every red ant in their army down on us," Kahlil mouthed.

"Look out. There's one behind yous."

Kahlil turned slowly, keeping his body close to the trunk of a tree. The sky glowed dimly behind the tangled black silhouettes of branches and trunks. The soldier paced in and out of the trees' cover. He didn't bother to hide his patrol. None of the Fai'daum forces were expecting trouble this far down the hill.

Their siege mortars, godhammers, and experienced soldiers were all deployed against the convent walls. Down here fresh recruits were only catching first impressions of war: distant screams, faint enough to mistake for insect sounds, and the thick scent of smoke. From here the vast walls of the Umbhra'ibaye were just black silhouettes, outlined in yellow flames.

As the patrolling soldier tromped forward, Kahlil noticed the pale dog that followed him. The big yellow animal kept low in the shadows and moved cautiously, catching scents and pausing to listen. Its eyes glinted in the dimness of the surrounding grove. The dog stopped and bent its head down, drawing in a deep breath of the moist ground.

"I smell bones," the dog growled.

Tiny finger bones clutched at Kahlil's shoulder blades.

The soldier turned back.

"Bones?" the soldier asked.

Kahlil's hands dropped to the hilts of his knives.

"Oracle bones." The dog lifted its head and drew in a deep breath.

"Are you sure?" The soldier stared down at the patch of earth as if he expected to see some sign of the scent.

"Kills it now!" the bones whispered.

He closed his eyes, concentrating on the cold, deadly space that ran beneath the warm, living world. With a flick of his wrist, he opened a seam and slipped into the Gray Space. From the distant gunfire to the tiny buzz of night insects, every sound went dead. Absolute silence enfolded him. Kahlil opened his eyes, and the shadows and rambling, wild branches of the surrounding trees returned to him. But now they were only pale gray forms. The ground and sky alike assumed the colorless flatness of mist.

Kahlil slid his knives from their sheaths. The blades were black as chasms cut from a starless sky. Then he threw himself forward. The misty forms of overhanging branches split and scattered as he plunged through them. Trees blew aside in wisps.

The soldier turned, frowning slightly, scanning the darkness. Perhaps he felt a chill move over him. Perhaps his eyes focused momentarily on Kahlil as he dropped out of the Gray Space and drove his knife into the soldier's throat.

Kahlil released the hilt immediately, and let his black curse-blade corrode the soldier's flesh.

He lunged for the dog. It sprang to his right and then leapt for his throat. He twisted aside but not fast enough. The dog slammed into him, knocking him to the ground. Searing teeth sank into his shoulder, jerked back, tore through his arm. His shoulder screamed as skin and muscle ripped.

The dog's eyes glowed brilliantly, and Kahlil felt the slithering sickness of a witch's curse wriggling from her lips into his torn flesh. He drove his second knife into the dog's neck. A hot gush of blood poured over his hand as he forced the blade across the animal's throat. The dog's jaw clenched down into his shoulder, as the animal choked on blood and half-formed curses. Then it went silent and suddenly collapsed on top of him.

He dragged in a deep breath, steeling himself against the pain of his bloody shoulder and then shoved the limp weight of the dog off his body. He lay still, listening for the sound of more soldiers approaching. But he heard no one.

The sharp jab in his back reminded him of the bones. He rolled onto his side. The pack wriggled. Then the bones slithered free, crawling along the ground on intricately carved forearms and narrow ribs. Countless incantations had long ago been etched into every bone, binding a soul and its power to the ivory remains. Gilded holy symbols and sacred spells crowned the child-sized skull. It lolled slightly to the side, hanging on the copper wires that held the small skeleton together.

The bones spread their tiny fingers and gripped the dog's corpse. Carefully, they felt their way through the thick fur up to the open gash of the throat. Then the bones dug into the wound, climbing into the dead body.

The damp ground and soft patter of falling rain soothed Kahlil's skin. He curled his hand over his bloodied shoulder and waited while the bones put on their new animal body. At least he wouldn't have to carry them anymore. That was good. He tried not to think of anything else.

"Layin' on a ground, sleepin' in a stable, wake up an' run while yous is able." The words rolled over him with a strong animal smell.

Kahlil looked over. The dog bared its teeth in a feral smile. The wounds in its throat knit closed as he watched, leaving only a stain of blood behind. The dog stretched and yawned.

"Sleepin' in an oven," the dog whispered, "sleepin' in a pan."

"Sleep through a war," Kahlil replied silently, "wake up a dead man."

The dog snorted at the response. "Yous gotta move, or them ants'll eat yous live."

"I know, I know." Kahlil forced himself up to his knees and then struggled to his feet. Moving slowly and deliberately, he retrieved his knives, then took the dead soldier's coat. Deep burning pain flooded from his shoulder down through his right arm. The witch hadn't completed her curse, but the remnants of her profane words still twitched in his open wound. He didn't bother to slide his injured arm into the coat but just pulled it over his shoulders. The wet wool felt like something dead draped over him. It smelled worse.

When he and the dog strode across the road, the two soldiers on patrol farther up just waved, mistaking him and the bones for the dead bodies they had left behind. Kahlil returned the gesture with his left arm. Then the two other men returned to their conversation. Kahlil walked carefully, mimicking the dead soldier's disinterested, ambling pace. He continued down the road a few yards and then crossed into the uncultivated woods on the other side.

He continued walking slowly, pacing himself, holding off his exhaustion and pain with a steady focus. He concentrated on each step. When his legs weakened and he stumbled, the muscular body of the dog pressed against him. He steadied and kept walking.

The woods thickened, and the sky slowly grew lighter. At some point Kahlil noticed that the soldier's coat had slipped off. He didn't bother to look for it. Suddenly, the dog stopped. Kahlil stumbled forward a few steps in a daze; then, his hand brushed against a smooth stone surface. Relief washed through him.

A ring of huge marble stones rose up from the forest floor like yellowed teeth. They reached to the treetops. At their center was a pool. The dog padded between the two closest stones, and Kahlil followed it into the water.

The inner faces of the stones shone as if they had been polished. Clear reflections rolled and broke across the water's surface as Kahlil waded to the deep center where the dog waited. The water lapped around his waist. Beside him, the dog paddled, holding its head above the surface. Sluggish ribbons of blood floated out from its fur.

"Hurrys up, or yous gonna have a drown puppy whens yous gets there."

Finally, he drew his sword. It was heavy and plain. Only the single black image of an eye marked the pommel. Kahlil threw his weight onto his left arm and drove the blade down through the water and into the earth below him.

"Here is your son, holding his key. Open these doors before me." He turned the sword in a half circle, twisting it like a key in a lock. The weight of water and silt flowed against it. Then, suddenly, it sank straight down into the waters.

Kahlil clenched his eyes shut. The Prayerscars over his eyes seared white-hot lines into his darkness. He pushed the air out of his lungs and dived down into the waters after the sword.

He sank fast and farther than the pool should have reached. His lungs burned as suffocating pressure closed around him. He felt no up or down, no sense of forward or back. Lost in the crushing light, Kahlil concentrated on that single thread that guided him, even across worlds. He felt muscle and bone and a heartbeat stronger than his own—and it drew him like filament landing a fish.

Blurred images of walls and stairs, pipes and electrical wires whipped past him. Then, suddenly, he broke the surface. He opened his eyes, and for a moment, he floated there, his face and chest rising up until he found himself lying on a wooden floor, gazing up at the familiar ceiling overhead. His sword jutted out at an angle from the bare light fixture in the ceiling. Cracks radiated out from where the blade had driven in.

Later today, he should pry his sword free and buy some spackle.

The dog stepped over him and jumped onto his narrow army cot.

Kahlil pulled himself up and flopped onto his side. His shoulder hurt, but in a numb way, as if his body was too tired to process the pain any longer.

He just lay there.

From the floor below, the sounds and smells of mid-morning began to penetrate his senses. The strong aroma of coffee drifted up to mix with the scent of wet dog that filled his room. A radio fuzzed through snippets of gospel, serious news voices, and flares of rock music. At last, the dial settled on an overly excited sports announcer. Some team somewhere had won something. A minute later, the radio went off abruptly. Bad news, he supposed.

Kahlil caught the sound of footsteps pacing the kitchen. He easily pictured John, striding through the room, his strong frame almost too tall for the ceiling fan, the breeze from its overhead blades tousling his disorderly blond hair. Then Kyle remembered him wearing only a white towel, glancing back over his tan, muscular shoulder and catching Kyle's guilty gaze.

What a dangerous and foolish chance that had been, and yet it had seemed impossible to resist.

He wondered how much time had passed since then. Even with the key, he couldn't perfectly control the Great Gate. Between the two worlds, hours, days, weeks, even years slipped by.

The distinct sound of papers flopping into the yellow trashcan below the sink reassured him that he'd returned to the same home he'd left. That would be John sorting through the mail. Kahlil wondered if anything had come for himself and then smirked at the ridiculousness of that thought. Nothing would ever come for him, not until it was time to end the world.

Chapter Three

"Don't."

John stared at the letter for several moments. He held it up to the light, hoping that there might be something more written on the creamy paper. Maybe a secret code in lemon juice, like the one he and his brother had used back when they were Boy Scouts. He turned the paper over, inspected the edges, and held it up to the light again.

Nothing.

He slumped down onto his cheap plastic chair and tossed the letter into the pile of bills on the kitchen table. He shoved the curly mass of his blond hair out of his face. So, he'd spent the last ten minutes convincing himself that he had a right to open his crazy roommate's mail, and this was all the payoff he got.

"Don't."

How disappointing.

Well, at least it hadn't been a picture of some porn star with his own face pasted over hers. He poured himself a cup of coffee. It was the cheap stuff, acrid in the mouth and hard on the stomach, but it was better than nothing. He took a slug and scowled.

If Kyle did not show up soon, how was he going to scrape together enough money for rent? Sell something? He didn't have much.

He scanned the kitchen. The faded, old Victorian cupboards revealed a box of peanut-butter granola, a little pile of coffee filters, and a single foam cup of instant noodles. The total value, he supposed, was maybe a dollar. The stale granola and ramen noodles had been in the house when John moved in a year ago.

Probably more like twenty cents.

He could always volunteer for one of the scientific studies at the university. One of his fellow graduate students had mentioned a sleep deprivation trial that paid daily. But John rebelled at the thought of being so closely observed and monitored. He supposed that he was almost as bad as Kyle when it came to maintaining his privacy. Maybe that's why they made such good roommates.

Then John remembered running into Kyle at the Steamworks bathhouse. Had it really been so bad that they had seen each other? If Kyle hadn't disappeared, maybe they could have laughed it off together. Or maybe their mutual knowledge could have become something more. There had certainly been desire in Kyle's eyes before recognition burned it away.

John wasn't sure if he liked that idea or not.

Also it was beside the point. Right now John needed rent.

He strode past the carved staircase into the living room. He gazed at his possessions. Not much: an old DVD player and a 12-inch television, which couldn't be configured to work with any remote control unit in existence. Not surprisingly, a number of supposedly universal remotes were piled up beside the television like sacrifices to an indifferent god of technology.

Both the television and the DVD player shared a rickety plywood-and-brick structure that served as John's entertainment center. Stacks of ecology textbooks slumped on the remaining shelves in no particular order. John glanced through the open door to his bedroom. His futon was the only thing of any value in the dim room. Maybe seventy dollars. John frowned at the hopelessly compacted futon and the disheveled bedding. It gave him a slightly sordid feeling to stare into his bedroom and contemplate money. He sensed that this wasn't a resource that decent people ever resorted to considering.

The gently aged architecture of the house itself didn't add any sense of respectability to John's endeavor. While the house wasn't in the best repair, the natural luster of the wood floors and detailed moldings reflected an enduring craftsmanship. Deep care showed in the perfection of the tall, smooth walls, and the carefully turned rungs of the staircase. The obvious devotion that had produced the house carried an almost moral quality. It radiated a simple goodness.

John's possessions suffered from the comparison. From his CD player to his running shoes, every item seemed conceived with an eye for quick satisfaction and disposability. Nothing accrued value. It all just fell apart.

John returned to the kitchen for a refill of coffee. Unwillingly, his gaze drifted from the cracked white cup in his hands to the substantial stack of bills on the table.

Money was such an ugly thing. It made people consider actions that they knew they would despise themselves for later—actions like begging their friends for loans. John scowled. He hated having to ask for anything. Money was the worst, though. Just the idea of it made him feel pathetic, like a kid who couldn't make it in the grown-up world. He'd had enough of that when he had been a kid.

The real problem with asking his friends for a loan, though, was the fact that most of them were broke. Usually, only John earned a steady income. He couldn't imagine many of his acquaintances amassing four hundred dollars, much less lending it out. Their universal poverty pretty much stranded John on the moral high ground, whether he liked it or not.

Upstairs, the toilet flushed.

John almost dropped his coffee cup. He heard the water pipes rattle, wheeze, and then subside as the pressure built. Then the sound of the shower hissing into life drifted down.

It had to be Kyle. He must have come home in the middle of the night, and John hadn't heard him. A rush of relief flooded through John. As strange as it was, he almost felt giddy with expectation, his trepidation about their meeting at the Steamworks vanishing with the prospect of financial relief.

As John reached out to straighten the stack of bills, he noticed the page of creamy parchment paper lying there. He'd forgotten about the letter and the key. He reached down into the pocket of his robe and looked at the key again.

The honest thing to do would be to give Kyle the letter and the key and apologize. He would probably be mad. He would have a right to be mad—possibly even furious.

John didn't think he had ever seen his roommate angry. He wondered just how mad a guy like Kyle could get. Immediately, he considered Kyle's collection of scars and also his ever-present knives. Would Kyle actually stab him for opening his mail? John glanced at the padlocked cupboards and frowned.

The key went back into the pocket of his bathrobe. He picked up the letter and its envelope and stuffed them into the recycling bin, beneath the underwear catalog. After he shoved the trash back under the sink, he rinsed his hands. When he turned around, Kyle was descending the stairs.

Usually Kyle moved well, employing a fluidity of motion that sometimes seemed almost too easy. John wasn't sure what exactly gave him that impression. It was a tiny thing, and after watching Kyle for just a few moments, the impression always faded from John's consciousness. It was like the slightest lingering accent that could only be caught for brief instants.

Today, Kyle's ethereal grace had been somewhat subdued. John's strongest impression was that Kyle seemed to have made an attempt at normalcy. His heavy coat and knives were nowhere to be seen. He wore dark gray work pants and a white sleeveless T-shirt. His long black hair hung in damp strings down his back. Even the scars covering his arms and at the edges of his mouth seemed paler and less obvious. His one disturbing feature was the thick bandage that engulfed his right shoulder.

"I didn't know you'd gotten back." John decided not to ask about the bandage, where he had been for two weeks, or their near encounter at Steamworks bathhouse. Confronted with the reality of Kyle, his curiosity folded.

"You might have been asleep." Kyle stopped at the kitchen table. He looked down at the bills and for a minute, John had the irrational thought that Kyle could somehow tell that the letter had been sitting right there.

John said, "I was just adding up the expenses."

"Nothing's overdue yet, is it?" Kyle picked up the electricity bill and looked at it. He turned it over slowly. He didn't appear to be reading the balance so much as studying the bill itself, as if it were an interesting artifact. After a moment, he placed it back on the pile.

"The water bill was due last week, but I paid it ..." John shoved his hands into the pockets of his robe out of habit. His fingers brushed across the metal surface of the key. He pulled his arms back up and crossed them over his chest. "And, you know, rent is due tomorrow ..."

"Oh, I've got the money for you." Kyle dug into his pocket with his left hand. He held his injured right arm close to his body. "How much was the water bill?"

John watched him pull out a thick wad of bills. They looked like hundreds. Hundreds of hundreds. John stared at the money. It was like something from a cartoon. Real people just didn't wander around with thousands of dollars in loose bills crammed into their pants pockets.

Kyle counted out the rent then glanced up at John questioningly. "How much for the water?" he asked again.

"Ah, it was fifty-four bucks total, so your half ..." Exactly how much money did he have there, John wondered. He couldn't even guess. Two inches of bills, maybe three? Maybe the bulk of it was fives and ones, and Kyle was just attempting to impress him by wrapping a hundred dollar bill around them.

Kyle frowned. "I don't have any smaller bills on me right now."

John could feel his mouth opening slightly, preparing to form the words, *"Where did you get all this cash?"* Instead he said, "I think I have some twenties. Maybe I can break one of the hundreds."

Kyle shook his head.

"Why don't I just give you a thousand? I think that should cover my half of the rest of the bills." Kyle dropped the money down on the table.

"A thousand." John repeated the number just to say something. It was too much money, obviously. Even adding in Kyle's half of the water bill, there would be a lot of money left over. Something like five hundred dollars.

That was enough to pick up a new pack and better supplies for winter camping, possibly even a GPS. Or, it could go into his Jeep repair fund. He could use a new pair of pants. If he just bought new socks, he could throw out his old ones and forget about washing them. Hell, maybe he'd actually buy something from that stupid underwear catalog.

He forced himself to stop his fantasy shopping spree. He couldn't just take the extra money. Kyle hadn't even seen how little he owed. Not one of the calls on the phone bill was his. The electric bill was tiny, and so was the gas. And John definitely didn't deserve to take anything from Kyle. He'd just stuffed his mail in the garbage.

"I don't think your half adds up to that much," John said.

"I'd rather pay too much than too little." Kyle shrugged, and then winced as he moved his right shoulder.

"But that's way too much." John glanced at the money. All the bills looked crisp and new.

"Don't worry about it." Kyle's tone was disinterested. He looked at the coffee pot. Again that expression of abstract interest flickered over his features.

"I can't just take your money," John insisted.

"No?" Kyle looked up at him.

"No."

"All right, then you can pay me back." Kyle started to shrug again but then stopped himself. "Why don't you take me out to breakfast, and we'll call it even?"

"Breakfast? We're talking about something close to half a grand."

"I eat a lot. If it really bothers you, leave a big tip." Kyle smiled, and John realized that the other man was enjoying this argument in some perverse manner.

"Okay, fine. I'll take you out to breakfast," John stated flatly.

Kyle broke into a grin. "Great. I'll get my coat." He turned and almost skipped up the stairs.

John stared after him.

Did he think he was going to get solid gold eggs? A priceless diamond omelet? He had to know that John was just going to take him to the crappy diner where he and his friends hung out. He could eat until he was sick, and it still wouldn't add up to five hundred bucks.

The Shattered Gates

This was something that some insane, Howard Hughes type did. Something befitting a knife-wielding freak who had to pay people just to sit in the room with him.

Suddenly, John's thoughts came to a crashing halt. That was it, wasn't it?

Kyle wasn't paying five hundred dollars for breakfast; he was paying five hundred dollars to have John take him out.

As John gazed up at the empty staircase, his entire body began to fill with tense premonition of the monstrous social horrors sure to come.

Chapter Four

It was the air; he always noticed it when he came through the gateway. The air here floated around him, feeling thick, almost liquid. Breathing here felt like drinking. Exotic, rich flavors rolled over his lips. Scents clung to his skin like seawater.

Kahlil drew in a breath. His lungs tingled with the heady suffusion of oxygen. It felt like enough to last him hours—just this one breath. But he wanted more. He loved tasting everything in the air: cologne, cleansers, human sweat, pollen, insect pheromones. The next breath would taste of hot asphalt, tobacco, wild flowers, and the distant ocean. The profusion of scents attested to the vibrancy of life here, so different from his own world of Basawar.

It delighted him even now as he stepped through the door of the diner, and the smell of a perpetual breakfast engulfed him. The odors of bacon grease, fried eggs, black coffee, and cigarette smoke hung like a yellow fog over the brown booths and Formica tables.

Kahlil watched John's expression change as he scanned the customers. John disregarded the cluster of teenage girls sharing one order of French fries. He ignored the two old men in denim overalls, as well as the line of strangers sitting at odd intervals along the counter. He paused as he caught sight of a booth far back, and then frowned at the blond woman who waved at him.

The woman was pale, her hair more white than yellow. Her eyebrows almost faded into the translucent expanse of her delicate face. Her tight, clingy clothes emphasized the fractional curves of her slim body. The image of a green-eyed kitten warped across the tiny expanse of her baby blue T-shirt.

An equally slender, dark-haired man slumped in the booth next to the woman. He looked like a remnant from an old film noir, dressed in black pants, a white shirt, and suspenders, his once slicked-back hair now hung in disheveled strings. He sagged against the padded seat like a corpse that had been propped up there. His eyes barely opened as the woman jumped up and waved at John.

"Hey, Toffee," the woman called out, "we were just talking about you. Come join us."

"Toffee?" Kahlil asked quietly.

"Nickname. John Toffler. Toffee." John's expression looked as if this was an old pain that he had learned to live with. Kahlil found it amusing. It was such a small burden.

It struck Kahlil as odd that either of the two people in the booth would be John's friends. There was a striking disparity between their physical appearances and John's that implied opposing life-styles. Where these two seemed tiny and nocturnal, John's build was tall and muscular, almost intimidating. His sun-bleached blond hair and deeply tanned skin blatantly displayed the weeks he spent outside.

"I'm here with someone, but I'll catch up with you guys later." John started toward an empty table across the room.

"You can both join us." As the woman got up, Kahlil stared in awe at her shoes. Like golden altars supporting her tiny feet, they were absurd and exquisite at once, exactly the kind of thing that no woman would wear in Basawar. He felt an inexplicable warmth toward the woman for owning such shoes.

She rushed to John and, catching him before he could sit, wrapped her arms around his waist. "Come on, I promise we won't embarrass you in front of your new boyfriend."

"He's not—" John began, but the woman turned to Kahlil. She held out her hand.

"I don't think I've met you before. I'm Laurie." She smiled, and Kahlil noticed the plastic barrettes shaped like ducks hanging limply in her hair.

"Kyle." He shook her hand.

Her pale eyebrows shot up. "Not Kyle the roommate?"

She glanced back to John for confirmation. Kahlil didn't miss the flicker of horror that passed over John's face as he nodded in acknowledgment.

"Yes, I believe that would be me." Kahlil smiled.

"So we meet at last." She peered up at him. "You really do have tattoos on your eyelids! I totally thought Toffee was lying about that."

"He wasn't lying." Kahlil bowed his head and closed his eyes, allowing her to see the Prayerscars clearly.

"Cool. They're eyes." Laurie moved closer to him, and he caught the very faint scent of beer and pine trees.

"Didn't that hurt?" Laurie asked.

"A little."

"Yeah, right. I would totally be screaming if they even came close to one of my eyes with a tattoo needle. I swear to God. I almost fainted when I got my ears pierced." She casually glanced at Kahlil's bare ears. "So do your scary tattoos have any special meaning?"

"I don't believe so."

"You don't believe so. That's kind of evasive." She grinned but didn't pursue the question. Kahlil warmed to her further for that.

"So do you mind if I'm really nosy and ask if you're single or not?" She seemed to be joking, but he wasn't sure.

"We really need to sit down and order, Laurie," John broke in. "And somebody should take Bill home." He pointed back to the booth where the pale man had collapsed onto the tabletop.

Laurie waved her hand as though she were brushing Bill's inert, sprawling form aside. "He just needs some coffee. Come on, you guys can help me bring him back to the land of the living."

Laurie grasped Kahlil's arm, tugging him back toward her booth. He allowed her to pull him along, and John followed behind.

"Come on," she said. "I've been wanting to meet you for ages, but John obviously doesn't want to share you."

"Maybe he just doesn't want to share you," Kahlil replied.

"Not in this lifetime." Laurie cocked her head slightly. "You know what I'm talking about, don't you?"

"I might." Kahlil started to shrug, then stopped himself, remembering his shoulder. The yellowpetal water had numbed the pain, but he didn't want to start bleeding through his bandages and clothes in the restaurant. John would never take him anywhere else again.

"So, what do you think of it?" Laurie asked with a teasing smile.

"Does it matter what I think of it?" He still marveled that desires of this kind could be discussed aloud here in Nayeshi, even in this sideways manner. The freedom to speak aloud made him almost giddy. He stole a quick glance at John and noted the flush coloring his tanned cheeks. Briefly he held John's gaze, and it seemed that something like interest lingered there, despite his obvious embarrassment.

But Kahlil warned himself against becoming caught up in this illusion of freedom. Someday, word would come from the Black Tower, and all of this would end in blood or ruins.

"Of course it matters what you think. That matters the very most." Laurie's voice dropped into a stage whisper.

"I believe my actions will speak for my thoughts on the subject." Kahlil smiled, knowing that neither John nor this woman could comprehend the truth of his words.

"Really?" Laurie returned his smile like a conspirator. "I thought that something like that might be going on. John never tells anyone anything, but I know when there are birds and bees in the air."

The conversation reminded Kahlil of talking to the bones. Everything alluded to something else. One word might mean another thing completely. "Sword" could be "a key." "A key" could be "death." They were like riddles. But where the bones spoke in riddles because their lives depended on deception, here it was a matter of harmless amusement. Kahlil could enjoy it, though John plainly did not.

He said, "No. We are not going to start talking like spies in a bad French film. We're just going to eat and talk, like normal people."

"You really can be a whole lot of no fun sometimes, Toffee." Laurie stopped at her booth and said to Kyle, "I have no idea how you put up with him."

"I didn't do anything ..." Bill cracked an eye. He looked at John and then to Kyle.

"Oh hey, Toffee." Bill's voice was rough. "We missed you at the mountain party last night, man." Slowly, he pulled himself fully upright and scooted over to make room for one of them beside him. Laurie took the space with a little bounce as she sat.

For a moment, both John and Kahlil remained standing, obviously waiting for the other one to sit first. It simply went too much against his instincts to allow himself to be blocked into a seat between a wall and John. If he had to get to his feet quickly, he didn't want to negotiate any obstacles. He stepped back slightly.

"After you," Kahlil offered.

John frowned at him but then acquiesced. Kahlil seated himself next to John.

"Bill," Laurie flipped a strand of his hair back from his face in an easy manner, "this is Kyle."

"The roommate Kyle?" Bill asked.

"Yep." Laurie was beaming like she'd discovered a treasure.

Bill squinted across the table. "You do have tattoos on your eyelids. I really thought Toffee was lying."

"Yeah, that's what I said." Laurie leaned past Bill and picked up the two laminated menus. It was a small act, but it struck Kahlil as conveying a great intimacy. Bill made no attempt to shift back and Laurie didn't seem to care if her body brushed against Bill's chest. Laurie straightened and handed out the menus.

"The special is this super-nasty chili thing," Laurie said.

"It's puke." Bill yawned. "Don't order it."

"I've been trying to steer clear of puke lately, so I suppose I'll pass on the special." John opened his menu, careful to keep to his half of the bench, physically restrained as he always was in the public company of other men. In private, he could be very different, though even then Kahlil had noted that John maintained a level of self-restraint, as if he unconsciously knew that something dark and powerful lay dormant within him.

"I'm going for the Denver omelet with sausage and some fake-ass maple syrup for my grotesque, meat-dipping pleasure." Bill pushed a string of his hair out of his face and smiled in a slightly suggestive way.

Kahlil looked over the bright photos of impossibly shiny fried eggs and fluffy stacks of golden pancakes. He flipped the menu over. The oatmeal, listed under the à la carte items, was not pictured. So far he had never found a single menu that did picture its oatmeal. He had no desire to eat oatmeal; he just wanted to see what it looked like.

The smell of strong, sweet perfume preceded the arrival of their waitress. She was an older woman with unnaturally red hair and big, doughy breasts packed into a frothy white blouse. She put two additional glasses of water down on the table.

"So is this gonna be everybody this morning?" she asked.

"Yep." Laurie offered her a charmingly pretty smile. The waitress smiled back.

"Coffee all around." The waitress didn't actually ask; she made a statement, to be refuted or accepted in silence. Encountering no objection, she turned over the brown coffee mugs and filled them.

"Sweet nectar." Bill picked up his cup and slurped the coffee.

Laurie ordered an item titled "Toast à la Français Superbe," which, from the picture, seemed to be a stack of French toast with a poached egg on top. She hesitated when the waitress asked if she wanted real maple syrup, which cost extra, or the regular stuff.

"Get the maple syrup. I'm paying." John didn't wait to see Laurie's delighted smile, but simply addressed the waitress. "I was thinking of having the special ..."

"No," Bill hissed. "You'll die."

"I'll have the eggs Benedict." John handed his menu to the waitress.

The waitress turned to Bill with a slightly sour look. Bill ignored her condemning expression and ordered an omelet, sausages, and syrup.

Then it was Kahlil's turn.

"I'll have the steak and egg breakfast." Kahlil relinquished his menu to the waitress.

"E. coli," Bill whispered.

"The steaks here are all cooked well done." The waitress ignored Bill and Kahlil went on with his order.

"That's fine. I'd like my eggs over hard."

"Toast?" the waitress asked.

"Wheat," Kahlil answered quickly.

The waitress nodded. He felt a certain satisfaction in having finally mastered the ritual interrogation of ordering a breakfast in this world.

Ten years ago, the baffling barrage of choices had been far more than he could contemplate or prioritize. White, wheat, rye, sourdough, over hard, over easy, scrambled, boiled or poached—he knew all the options now. And he was experienced enough to know that he liked his eggs cooked hard, even though he loved the way the words "sunny-side-up" sounded.

Kahlil realized his thoughts were drifting. He was exhausted and hurt, and he should have slept the entire day away, but he had wanted to see John. He had needed to see John smile and laugh and be kind.

In his own world, Kahlil saw such ugly things. He had done such hateful things. But here, it was different. This world was immersed in perfumes and abundance. Here, it was easy to be generous. There was so very much that giving could be painless. Goodness could seem inherent to all life. Here, even a being like John, a Rifter, a destroyer of worlds, could be a thoughtful, quiet graduate student.

"You know," Laurie announced, "normally I can just look at somebody and get a reading right away, but you're different."

"A reading?' Kahlil asked.

"Laurie's psychic," John explained, though his tone conveyed absolutely no conviction.

"Madame Laurenza Luciana mystifies even the most skeptical of men," Bill put in.

"Yes, I read that on the latest flyer." John looked amused.

Laurie smiled. "We added it especially for you."

"Well, I am often mystified by your clientele," John said.

"You're a witch?" Kahlil asked. It would be natural for witches to be drawn to the company of a Rifter. Alarm prickled at the edge of his awareness.

"I'm a psychic." Laurie corrected him. "It's not a religious thing. It's just my job. I tell fortunes and do palm readings. Mostly at the mall."

"I see." Kahlil relaxed again. Petty fortune telling was the field of the wishful. Witches dealt in blood and bones.

"So, can I try reading you?" Laurie leaned across the table and smiled sweetly at Kahlil. "I think I may be seeing true love in the future." She winked.

"Do as you like," Kahlil told her, suppressing a laugh at the absurdity of seeing anything in his future.

Laurie closed her eyes. She drew in several quick breaths and exhaled quickly, like a diver preparing to suppress his sense of oxygen deprivation. Kahlil held himself very still. The trick of breathing made him wary. He watched intently as Laurie opened her pale eyes. Her pupils were wide and black as bullet holes. She sat perfectly still, staring into the empty space between them.

"Well?" Bill asked after a few more moments. He started to say something more, but John silenced him with a motion. Bill took a quiet sip of his coffee. He squinted again at Kahlil. All three of them waited.

Laurie's small mouth compressed slightly and her eyes remained wide. Her skin was going blue. She was beginning to suffocate.

Beyond death lay the bones.

Somehow, without training, she must have learned that. Kahlil wondered how far she would dare to go. She was still a creature of flesh, so not too far, he guessed.

Suddenly, he felt something brush against him, very softly, almost like a breath of air. An old, musty scent washed over him. Kahlil recognized the smell, even as weak as this was. He couldn't allow her to go any further. He flipped the tattooed backs of his hands up, pretending to simply wrap his fingers around his coffee cup.

Laurie jolted back with a little cry that was half-hiccup, half-yelp. Her mouth opened wide, but she couldn't seem to inhale. Bill slapped her back. Laurie coughed violently and gasped.

"Laurie?" Bill leaned over, rubbing her back. He looked wide-awake now.

"Is she choking?" John sat forward.

"No." Laurie coughed again and then grabbed her napkin. She held it to her mouth and spat into it. She wiped her lips and crumpled the napkin.

"I'm okay," Laurie whispered. A little flush of pink came into her cheeks.

"I just ... I don't know, I guess I sucked in a bug or something. I feel like such a geek."

"You scared the crap out of me," Bill said.

"Oh no, you're not crappy anymore?" Laurie smiled. She looked up at Kahlil. "Sorry. I guess you think I'm a total flake now."

"No, I don't think anything like that," Kahlil said. John gave him a pointed look, but Kahlil didn't know why.

Then the waitress arrived with their food. Every other concern dissipated in the face of the warm dishes and bright little packets of jelly.

Kahlil enjoyed comparing the way people ate.

Laurie was shy at first, still seeming to feel self-conscious after her coughing fit. But, slowly, she relaxed. After a few minutes, she stabbed her fork into one of the pale curls of chilled butter, sweeping it playfully over the mounds of her French toast as if it were a skier. Bill was more animated about playing with his food. He dunked his sausages in his syrup while making little drowning noises. The two of them seemed well suited to each other.

John, on the other hand, seemed to approach his meal like a dissection. He expertly manipulated his butter knife and fork to excise the ham from beneath his eggs. He cut and shifted his English muffins, also separating them from his eggs. It struck Kahlil as particularly telling that John would choose a complex dish and then break it down into its components instead of simply ordering the separate items.

"Do you always chew your food so thoroughly?" Laurie asked Kahlil.

"Always," John answered for him.

Kahlil frowned. He didn't remember eating in front of John before.

"That time you ate the green apple," John said, as if it were a famous moment in their history together.

"During the electrical storm last fall?" Kahlil wasn't sure why John would remember anything about that night, though he himself recalled it vividly. Violent bolts of thunder and lightning had cracked the black sky. One burst blew out the electricity. He had barely been conscious. His entire body had ached with bruises and cuts. He remembered feeling ravenous and nauseous at the same time.

He had staggered through the darkness down the staircase, and John had off-handedly said, "Welcome home" and offered him an apple. Even now he remembered the sharp, sweet taste bursting his mouth as his teeth cracked through the crisp flesh. He had eaten it, forgetting for a moment about the blood collecting in the bandages beneath his clothes.

"He ate the entire thing," John went on, "stem, seeds, core and all."

"I was starving." Kahlil sliced thin strips from his steak. The foods here were so pungent that normally he could only manage them in the thinnest pieces. The apple had left his mouth tender for days, but he hadn't regretted it.

"Yes," John shifted in the booth so that they almost faced each other, "but you didn't rush. You must have chewed every bite thirty or forty times. It took forever."

"Twenty times," Kahlil said.

The conversation lapsed into perfect silence. That little pulse of quiet always told him that he had said or done something so out of step with this world that no one knew how to react.

"I'm just kidding," Kahlil said. "I don't actually keep count or anything. I just had this crazed old uncle who always made me chew everything a million times. It turned into a habit, I guess. I don't even know when I'm doing it."

The stillness at the table evaporated instantly. Laurie laughed and Bill nodded. John finished the bite of egg that he had scooped onto his fork.

"My grandma used to brush her hair one hundred strokes every morning before she'd get up." Bill squeezed more catsup over his omelet.

"Your grandma Ruby. She was kind of nutty, wasn't she?" Laurie asked.

"Yeah." Bill nodded proudly.

"One time John went to Bill's house, and Bill's grandma made John stand in the bathtub with a rubber hose tied around his waist," Laurie told Kahlil.

"She was really worried that he'd be struck by lightning." Bill drank a little more of his coffee.

"To be fair to her, John was actually struck by lightning once." Laurie paused thoughtfully. "That was up at Rawley Lake, wasn't it?"

For an instant, Kahlil thought he saw pain flicker through John's expression. He wondered what John remembered from that moment, when two worlds had touched, and the Oracles had lanced an invisible bond into John's flesh and bones. Had he seen their hollow eyes and carved bones? Had he glimpsed beyond them to see Kahlil, whose blood had forged the bond?

Then John simply shrugged.

"No." Laurie frowned. "No, it must have been Emerald Lake, because you were up on the rocks ..."

"To be perfectly honest," John said, "I don't actually remember, what with the thousands of volts coursing through my brain at the time."

"It was Emerald Lake," Laurie decided. "That lightning bolt just came smack down out of the blue."

John frowned, and for a moment Kahlil was sure that some recollection of the Oracles' writhing bones and bare skulls must still haunt him.

"According to the prevalent scientific theory," John said, "lightning doesn't actually originate out of the blue. It's a convergence of positive charges in the clouds with negative charges in the earth. The two meet around 150 feet in the air and what people actually see as lightning is the return stroke shooting back down."

Bill narrowed his eyes at John. "You're actually a robot, aren't you?"

"The politically correct term is Synthetic-American," John replied flatly.

Both Laurie and Bill dissolved into giddy, sleep-deprived laughter. John looked on with a pleased smile, and Kahlil got the feeling that he didn't really understand the people of Nayeshi all that well.

"Oh, speaking of strange phenomena." Laurie straightened and leaned toward John. "We saw the weirdest thing last night while we were up on the mountain."

"Oh?" John asked.

"Yes. It was incredible. You wouldn't believe it." Laurie bounced slightly in her seat.

"And it was?" John asked.

Laurie opened her mouth but didn't say anything for a moment. She frowned.

"You're not going to believe it," she said at last.

"I told you he wouldn't." Bill shook his head.

"Maybe you should tell me, and then I can say if I find it believable or not," John suggested. He reached past Kahlil for the coffee carafe and refilled his cup.

"No." Laurie grabbed John's hand. "You have to see it for yourself. Maybe you'll be able to explain it—I don't know."

"I was going to go up and check the run-off levels this afternoon anyway," John said. "If you two want to ride up with me, you can point out the unbelievable thing."

"That would be cool." Bill nodded. "I kind of want to revisit it just to make sure it was what I thought it was. I mean, the entire night was so weird. Very cool, though. There was this bird ..." Bill went on at length about the silhouettes of owls and the twisting and swirling branches of the pines. The way human figures jumped and writhed around the red bonfire as the night wind rose and howled across the mountain. Laurie added a few details to Bill's enraptured descriptions.

John listened. He was good at listening. He rarely interrupted and kept his comments to those encouraging monosyllables that assured a speaker of his interest. John sipped his coffee, but kept his attention on Laurie and Bill.

Kahlil liked the fact that people in this world were not without wonder at its beauty.

He listened to Bill and Laurie while he slowly ate the succulent slices of his steak. The warmth of food and the pleasant sound of the surrounding conversation soothed him. He closed his eyes. It felt so good to close his eyes. He felt the muscles in his back and neck relax.

Laurie glanced at him and smiled in a kind way.

"You look beat, Kyle."

"I had a restless night."

For a second time, John gave him that perplexing look.

"I guess you don't want to come up the mountain with us, then?" Laurie looked hopeful.

"You could sleep in John's jeep on the way up," Bill offered.

"No, but thanks for the invitation. I'd love to go some other time. Right now I've got too many things to do." Kahlil glanced to John. "Do we have any spackle?"

"I don't think so. Why?"

"I was just curious." Kahlil shrugged, and a sharp pang bit into his shoulder. The yellowpetal was wearing thin. He needed to get back home.

He started to say his goodbyes but was interrupted by the purely social protests that Laurie offered. Before she agreed to let him leave, he had to promise to go with Laurie and Bill the next time they went up the mountain. Bill pointed out that he should go with John, since John was the one who stayed up there for weeks on end. After that, there came a series of brief digressions on a variety of subjects from John's ecology thesis to faking Bigfoot prints, to the massive fungal mats that linked thousands of trees throughout miles of forest.

"I really do have to go." Kahlil started to rise; to his amusement, Bill and Laurie both waved at him in perfect synchronicity.

"Hey, Kyle," John suddenly called to him. "I should be back around six or so ... There's something I ought to tell you about." John didn't go on, but something in his expression seemed both tender and guilty. Kahlil couldn't help but remember John's naked back and then his glance over his shoulder. His expression then had been the same as now.

"I'll be there," Kahlil assured him.

"Great. I'll see you later tonight."

Kahlil walked home slowly, enjoying the morning sun, basking in the residual enjoyment of meeting John's friends. Maybe he would go to the mountain with them the next time they asked. It was such a dangerous temptation, to abandon his watch from inside the cold of the Gray Space and to join John in the warmth and vibrancy of this world.

It was noon when he finally reached the house. The dog had come downstairs and gotten into the trash. Kahlil scowled at her. Then he saw the letter and the torn envelope, and his nascent hopes died in a single word.

Chapter Five

"You know, Toffee, he seemed pretty nice." Laurie leaned back in the passenger seat of John's jeep. She pushed her shoes off and dangled her bare foot out of the open window.

"Yeah, when I first saw him, I was thinking he was some fucking vampire or something. But you know, he was okay." Bill chewed thoughtfully on a red licorice whip he had purchased from the rickety little gas station where they'd stopped two hours before. John spared it a quick glance and then shook his head.

On either side of the single-lane dirt road, dark walls of old forest rose over them. Deep green shadows and shafts of hard light fell across the road like a camouflage, disguising deep ruts and fallen tree limbs. Neither Bill nor Laurie showed any tension as they rounded the sharp curves in the road and bounced over the rough terrain. John supposed they simply trusted his skill and enjoyed the ride, as was their privilege as passengers.

"He didn't really say much about himself." Laurie took a drink of her soda. "Usually guys who look like that are all about telling you how tough they are and how bad they've had it. He was pretty quiet."

"That's what everybody always ends up saying about serial killers, isn't it?" The last thing John needed was Laurie playing matchmaker. His relationship with Kyle was strange enough already.

"Yeah," Bill said. "You could be living with the next Ted Bundy."

"He didn't seem like a serial killer," Laurie said.

"You don't live with him," John replied.

"Come on, you wouldn't live with a guy if you really thought he was a serial killer, would you?" Laurie asked.

"Have I mentioned how much I appreciate the fact that he's never been late with the rent?"

Bill seemed to feel the sudden need to vindicate himself. "When we lived together, I was only three weeks late once. Maybe twice."

"You were only three weeks late on the months you actually paid," John said.

"And that's why you guys don't live together anymore," Laurie broke in quickly. "And that's not even what we're talking about. Rent money wouldn't be enough to make you live with a murderer."

"No," John admitted.

In a way, he wanted to think unkindly of Kyle. Then he wouldn't feel so bad about taking his money and opening his mail. But it was an unfair tactic, and he knew it. As soon as he got home, he had to own up to Kyle and give him the key. He had been meaning to come clean with Kyle over breakfast—maybe even mentioning their near encounter at the Steamworks bathhouse— but then they had run into Bill and Laurie.

"He could be a drug dealer, though," Laurie commented.

"No one ever calls him. No one visits him. He doesn't seem to have any connections at all," John replied.

"Maybe he's a warrior-priest from some kind of weird sex cult like in *Erotic Coven II*," Bill suggested.

"You know, it doesn't matter how many times you work that movie into conversations. We are not going to rent it," Laurie told Bill.

John had, in fact, already seen much of the movie while Bill had lived with him. It had been difficult to avoid due to the sheer number of times Bill had watched it.

"Hey, I'm making a valid point this time," Bill said. "*In Erotic Coven II*, there's this exorcist guy who's got these tattoos all over his body. They're kind of like Kyle's." Bill leaned forward between the front seats.

"And?" Laurie took one of Bill's licorice whips.

"And when the naked demonic chicks attack him, the tattoos whip off him like ribbons." Bill grinned. John recalled the scene vividly and wished that he hadn't. Bill continued, "So these thick black ribbon things tie the demon chicks up spread-eagle and, you know, do them."

"The tattoos have sex with the women?" Laurie asked, nonplused.

"Yeah, they get all thick and … It's a lot cooler than it sounds," Bill finished.

"I bet." Laurie turned her attention to John. "So do you have any idea how Kyle got that scar across his mouth?"

Bill flopped back against his seat and opened another package of candy.

"I don't know." John down-shifted as the road swung into a steep downgrade. He was only half-listening to the conversation. The summer storm had blown down more branches than usual. As they drove farther into the bush, he had to swerve to avoid several huge shards of yellow stone that partially blocked the narrow dirt road.

"I wish I could have gotten a clearer read from him," Laurie said. "For a minute I had this flash … An orchard or something. Lots of trees and flowers. And then this terrible pain. It was like teeth or something, ripping into my shoulder. Then it was gone." She twisted in her seat to address Bill. "Do you think Kyle might have some kind of latent psychic force field?"

"Do you have any idea how flaky that sounds?" John asked.

"It does sound a little like some *Star Wars* reference," Bill commented. "The force is strong with that one."

"There is another," Laurie wheezed in an impersonation of a sickly Yoda. She turned back to face the front. "That's the problem. All these cheesy movies come along and pretty soon there isn't any way to describe a genuine experience so that it doesn't sound like some knockoff from a B-rated film. You know, I should get to sue George Lucas for rights to the Force. I am way more in touch with the Force than he is."

"Sweetie," Bill leaned in between the front seats, "you are the Force."

"Damn right I am." She smiled. "Can I have a Sugar Baby?"

"Sugar for my baby." Bill shook several of the tiny brown candies out of their yellow package and handed them to Laurie.

John couldn't figure out where these splintered yellow boulders had come from. They didn't resemble the dull gray rock that he was accustomed to seeing after landslides, and they were distributed much too randomly. They looked like they had dropped straight out of the sky.

He took a tight turn and had to slam down on the brake as a column of gleaming yellow stone suddenly jutted into his sight. The jeep skidded along the dirt road, then stopped dead. Laurie made an alarmed peep at the sudden stop while Bill and his candies flew off the back seat and smacked into the front.

"You all right?" John asked.

"Bill?" Laurie leaned over to him.

"I lost my moon pie," Bill replied. "I think I'm okay."

"Where the hell did this boulder come from?" John backed the jeep up.

"That's what we were trying to tell you about at the restaurant this morning." Laurie pointed at the column of stone. "They just showed up last night."

"Brought down by a mudslide, maybe?" John wondered. He leaned forward in his seat and studied the column. It was nearly as tall as the jeep and unnaturally symmetrical. Its surface gleamed as if it had been polished. John couldn't see any traces of slide. No rubble or washouts.

"They were just here, right after the rain let up. Like mushrooms," Laurie said.

"I found my moon pie," Bill announced.

"This is really strange." John carefully drove the jeep around the column.

"We started finding them just before sunrise. There's an entire circle of them up at the wolf rock."

"It's like a big yellow Stonehenge." Bill sat back and, this time, buckled his seat belt.

"So they just popped up out of the ground?" John asked.

"Well, not exactly. They didn't pop," Laurie said. "It was more like they just were there. Kind of like they could have always been here, and somehow we just never saw them before."

"That boulder was not sitting in the middle of the road last week," John stated.

"I know. I'm just trying to explain how it felt. I mean, there wasn't any noise or anything. They were just there."

John didn't find Laurie's answer particularly satisfying, but he didn't have any other.

He kept driving, but slower now and much more intently. He was familiar with this tract of land. He knew the curves and turns, the drops and inclines. But now it had altered, and the sensation was like coming home to discover all his furniture shifted around by ten or twelve degrees. It wasn't much, just enough to make him feel estranged.

"So how did you meet him?" Laurie asked after they had been driving several minutes in silence.

"Who?" John was thinking about the stones. They had looked like marble, and that was very unusual for this area.

"Kyle," Laurie reminded him.

"He answered my ad."

"You finally took out a personal ad?" Laurie sounded delighted.

"No, my ad for a roommate."

"Sorry." Laurie sipped more of her soda. "I got all excited for a minute there."

"Yeah," Bill said. "I'd love to see what Toffee would put in a personal."

"Reserved, secretive type is looking for other to hold out on." Laurie grinned.

"Must be grim," Bill added.

John frowned. "I'm not grim."

"You're no barrel of monkeys," Bill replied, "but then, I've never really thought that a barrel of monkeys would be all that fun. There they are, crammed into this tiny space full of excrement and other monkeys."

"So," Laurie went on, "Kyle answered your ad, and then?"

"He had enough to cover the month Bill hadn't paid and a deposit. That was that."

John turned off the main road onto a steep upgrade consisting of two wheel ruts. The previous night's rain kept the usual cloud of dust from stirring up in his wake.

"What does he do for a living?" Laurie asked.

"Sexorcist," Bill supplied.

"He's a milkman."

Several moments of quiet followed John's reply. He himself hadn't known how to respond when Kyle had told him. It was the kind of profession that he'd thought hadn't survived past the fifties. He had wanted to ask about it or say something thoughtful, but nothing came to mind. And there was also the fear that he would ask a small, meaningless question and then have to listen to a long and involved explanation of an industry that he simply didn't care about. It was a singular profession, being at once unusual and at the same time uninteresting.

And that was if Kyle really was a milkman. If he wasn't, John wasn't sure he wanted to know where all those crisp hundred dollar bills came from.

"Milkman," Laurie repeated. "Really?"

"So he says," John answered.

The road angled steadily upward, and slowly the air grew cooler. Most of the leafy, deciduous trees were behind them. Here, evergreens grew in close walls. They perfumed the air so that even now, in summer, John thought of Christmas.

"He didn't seem like a milkman," Bill said at last.

"No." John pulled off to a flat shoulder and parked.

"He seemed more like a serial killer or a sexorcist," Bill said. "Or a serial sexorcist."

"Bill, hand me my pack." John wished Bill would stop saying "sexorcist." He particularly didn't like having the image linked with Kyle. He had to live with the man.

Bill struggled to lift John's dark blue backpack. John leaned into the back and pulled it over the seat.

"That thing weighs a ton," Bill commented. "What do you have in there?"

"Love." Laurie pulled her shoes on. "He's weighed down with love."

"And water, among other things," John said.

"What are you going to do, build a swimming pool up here?" Bill asked.

For a second, John considered explaining the contents of his pack—a radio, flashlight, water filter, lightweight Mylar blankets, army knife, first-aid kit, matches, rehydration salts, and more. But that would only lead to a painful attempt to convey the importance of first aid and adequate preparation this far from civilization. It was exactly the kind of textbook lecture that brought out Bill's strongest juvenile-delinquent tendencies.

"Yes, I'm hauling a pack full of water up to fill my personal swimming pool." John got out of the jeep, pulled his pack on, and started up the mountain toward the wolf rock.

He glanced back to see Laurie and Bill wandering after him. Laurie had taken her shoes back off after a few steps over the uneven ground. The pockets of Bill's jacket bulged with Hershey bars and Lil' Debbie snack cakes. Neither of them looked like they belonged out here. John stayed ahead, but not out of sight. He didn't want to lose them, but he also didn't want to listen to them.

He wasn't like Bill or Laurie, who both could talk endlessly about nothing. They were the kind of people who were uncomfortable with silence. John was just the opposite.

Conversations, even with his friends, tired him. Struggling to comprehend someone or to be understood made him aware of how disconnected he was from other people.

It was different when he said nothing. In wordless calm, the rest of the world flooded the silence. Just like now: the cool wind whispered through pine branches, songbirds trilled over their territories, a startlingly brilliant blue jay cackled and flashed its wings above him.

The air smelled sweet, still humid from rainfall and infused with wildflowers. Old pines shot up, their musky branches spreading out, cutting the bright blue sky to tiny fragments. Between them, thin streams of light trickled down, filtering through oak and maple leaves in a pale, green radiance.

In the quiet, John noticed what he would have otherwise missed—the small tracks of a deer, droplets of rain still clinging to a spider's web, the intent gold gaze of a jet-black crow.

In the past, he had tried to point out these details to his friends, but something was always lost in the inevitable ensuing conversation. He seemed only able to maintain his delicate appreciation in solitude. Words fell short of capturing how the open air, the forest scent, and animal sounds washed over him, washed through him. He couldn't convey his feeling of immense intimacy and reverence to anyone else.

The sensation was strongest here, where he knew the land well. There were even times—when he pressed his hands down past the fallen leaves and decay to the dark, rich earth—that he almost sensed something reciprocal, a warmth beneath his fingers, a soft pressure, like an animal arching to be stroked. He never mentioned it to anyone else. It was too private, too absurd, and too deeply touching. But, sometimes, he sensed that the very earth felt his affection and in some way returned that sentiment. He guessed that this was what it was like to fall in love with a lifelong friend.

Today, John only had to pause a moment in the silence as the wind rolled over him to know that something was wrong. At his feet lay small shards of that polished, yellow marble. More of them lay partially hidden under the litter of fallen leaves and mud. John knelt to pick one up, then recoiled as an irrational repulsion shot through him. He could no more bring himself to touch the stone than he could have reached out to grasp a dead body. John drew his hand back, bewildered, then stood and continued to work his way up the mountainside.

The wolf rock was a large, granite outcropping that, when they were both seven, had struck John and Laurie as looking like a gigantic dog, howling at the sky. At the time, the two of them had lived in a state of almost hallucinatory fascination with wolves and with a series of books called The Wolf Riders. Both of Laurie's German shepherds had been dubbed wolves, as had cars, bicycles, and several couches. Anything the two of them could sit on had pretty much been fair game, including this particular extrusion of granite.

Its gray mass still jutted out from the side of the mountain. But where it had once dominated the terrain, now an arc of cracked and splintered yellow marble monoliths rose over it. One even erupted through the side of the wolf rock itself. Huge marble fragments were strewn about the base of the upright stones.

They all boasted the same highly polished surface, but some also seemed to be etched with a filigree. In certain places, the etchings resembled a flowing foreign script; at other points, they looked like a series of symbols. John moved closer but didn't touch any of them. One stone lay flat on the ground in the very center of the arc. The etching over its surface was thick and shot through with fissures. John leaned over and stared down at what looked very much like a series of moons surrounding a small keyhole.

It struck him as familiar. He fished into his pocket and pulled out Kyle's key. It looked like it might fit.

A weird, unreal feeling came over him. For the first time in his life, he had the idea that he might be dreaming, that this entire morning could be some exceptionally vivid illusion. But the earth beneath his feet was too real. It just would have been so much easier for him to accept if it were a dream. He might be able to enjoy himself, instead of feeling slightly sick and stupid.

He heard Laurie trudging up the incline, talking.

"See, what did I tell you? It's freakier in the daylight."

John glanced back to see Laurie and Bill picking their way between the shattered stones.

"Yeah," Bill said. "It seems kind of screwed up to see the same thing when you're tripping and when you're sober. These rocks are huge."

"So what is it?" Laurie asked John.

"I don't know." John gazed down at the keyhole again. His hand closed around the key.

Bill crouched down beside him. "Well, what do you think it is?"

"I told you, I don't know."

Laurie sat down on the other side of him. She leaned over the stone's etched surface. "You know, that kind of looks like a keyhole."

"Yeah, it does." Bill leaned forward as well. "That's kind of cool and kind of creepy."

"Do you have any more Sugar Babies?" Laurie asked Bill. He dug through his pockets, then shook his head.

"You ate them all?" Laurie asked. "You had, like, ten packs."

"I left them back in the jeep." Bill squatted down and then lay back against the ground. "Man, the sky looks beautiful today. Calling in to work was definitely the right thing to do. You just shouldn't have to work when it's this nice out."

"We should camp out tonight." Laurie smiled and leaned back on her arms beside him.

Neither of them were rational thinkers, John realized, so they couldn't be as shaken as he was by the sight of these stones. Both Laurie and Bill believed freely in a multitude of ludicrous and fantastic things. It made them unfazed by the outright impossible. After all, huge, inscribed monoliths appearing from nowhere weren't all that exotic if you already accepted the idea of angels from other planets manifesting as household pets and leading the way to a higher spiritual resonance. If that was the reality you lived in, then this was an almost pedestrian occurrence.

Still, all of Laurie and Bill's other beliefs were just that—faith without evidence. Their cat had never actually floated through the house telling them to resonate. But these stones were solid. Very real. And John noted that neither Bill nor Laurie had touched the yellow stones either.

"So, what do you think it is?" Laurie asked him again.

"I really don't know." John stared at the circle of moons. It was a common symbol. But was it just coincidence that the identical design appeared on the envelope of Kyle's letter? It probably fell well within the realm of probability. The key almost felt like it was burning in John's hand.

"Yeah, but what's your theory?" Laurie flicked a bug away from her face.

"I don't have one," John answered. He wished he could just think quietly for a few minutes. If he could just get a feeling for all of this, he might be able to figure his way through it.

"Could it have been buried, and some kind of earthquake pushed it up?" Laurie looked slightly distressed.

"No. That would have pushed everything above it up and out of the way. The marble wouldn't have passed straight through the wolf rock." John nodded his head in the direction of the granite outcropping.

"Jesus!" Bill suddenly sat upright. "I didn't notice that last night."

"Oh, poor Wolfy!" Laurie lifted her hands to her mouth reflexively. "It looks like it's been speared."

John opened his hand just a little and studied the key. It was dull gold and warm against his palm. A moon marked one side. He turned it over. Tiny lines of flowing script etched the other side. He had to find out if it fit. If it didn't, then he'd feel stupid and gullible for a few days and if it did… He didn't know what then. But at least he had to try it.

Laurie glanced over to him.

"What do you have there?" she asked.

"A key." John slowly rocked forward and held the key over the keyhole. It looked perfect.

"I don't think your house key is going to fit," Bill said.

"It's not my house key," John said.

John lowered the key directly down and felt it slide perfectly into place. He had known it would. Somehow, he had felt an absolute assurance of it.

"Oh my God," Laurie whispered. "It fits."

John crouched there, staring at the key and the stone.

Laurie asked, "Do you think something will happen if you turn it?"

"You've got to," Bill said. "You can't just stick a key in and then not turn it."

A key opens a door, John thought. That's what would happen. Some door, somewhere, opens. Then what?

"Go ahead." Laurie moved a little closer to him. "Bill's right, we've got to try it."

"All right then," John said.

John turned the key. It moved easily. He could feel something slide and click inside the stone. He held still. Laurie and Bill leaned over with him.

Nothing happened.

"Damn it," Bill said.

Laurie frowned.

"Maybe it's broken or—" The rest of her sentence split into a squeal as the ground dropped out from under the three of them.

A sudden crushing pressure enveloped John in a wall of blinding whiteness as if he had plunged into a pool of blazing water. He squeezed his eyes shut against the brightness. His lungs burned. He struggled to swim upward. A desperate hand clutched at his arm. He felt another body bump into his side. He caught hold of them and kicked hard.

They had to get through this. They had to get air. John kicked upward. The weight of both Bill and Laurie dragged him down, but he had gotten them into this, and he couldn't let them go.

Then suddenly a gust of dry, cold wind rushed over John. He opened his eyes and dragged in a breath. Laurie lay on his right and Bill on his left. Both of them gasped in the thin, frigid air like dying fish. Banks of snow loomed up on either side of the three of them.

John sat up and stared out over the empty white land and bare black trees. The pale sky met seamlessly with the snow-covered mountains.

He looked at his empty hands. He had lost the key.

CHAPTER SIX

Kahlil turned a shard of yellow marble over in his hands and thought that the day was only getting worse.

He had come home to find the key missing, his sword shattered into dull gray splinters, and trash strewn all over the kitchen floor. The trash shouldn't have bothered him, but it had. Perhaps the scattered garbage had struck him as too much of an omen of how the fragile domestic comfort of the last ten years would soon end. He'd cleaned it up but it hadn't made him feel any better.

Then he had gathered his weapons and ammunition from the locked kitchen cupboard; he had put on his heavy coat and he'd gone up the mountain to find John.

He pocketed the yellow stone and stalked through the trees. He felt sick and ugly, deciding which one of John's two friends he would trade for the key and which one he would kill outright. The witch would have to be killed, he decided. He couldn't take a chance with her.

He hated the thought of murdering a woman only a few hours after she had held his arm so warmly and smiled at him without a hint of malice. It was too easy to imagine her expression of happy surprise at his arrival. He could see that expression lingering on her face for a moment too long, as if she were unable to comprehend how his knives could be tearing through her flesh. She wouldn't understand. She wouldn't know anything in her last moments but pain, horror, and confusion.

No. In this world it didn't matter how he killed a witch. She wouldn't be skinned down to her bones afterwards. He didn't need to keep her skull intact. He could simply put a bullet through the back of her head. That, at least, would be fast. She wouldn't see him. She wouldn't know anything but the instant of impact. It would be over before she could even realize it. That was the only kindness he could offer Laurie.

He couldn't be so good to Bill or John. Particularly not John. But he promised himself that he wouldn't make either of them suffer for long. He would be quick. He had accepted it. It was all he could do.

But now more yellow stones glinted from beneath the leaf litter.

Kahlil turned a small shard of polished yellow marble over in his hands, then dropped it back down to the forest floor, where it landed next to a brown candy wrapper. Pieces of the gateway were scattered across miles of forest. An entire half of the arc had erupted from the mountain rock like new teeth bursting through a barren jawbone. The term "damaged" didn't begin to describe what had happened.

"Damaged" implied some hope of repair. This was utter destruction, and he understood what it meant. It had been the same reason that his sword, the key to the gateway, had been splintered. The priests weren't taking any chances should he fail to destroy the Rifter. They hadn't just locked the door behind him; they had eradicated its very existence.

But that didn't explain this. Kahlil crouched down and continued to stare at the stone in front of him. The circle of moons he could understand. They were the symbols of his order. The words written around them were archaic but familiar. Like words to a nursery rhyme, he recalled them as reflex, without trying: "Behold the doors of the God's Kingdom. Behold the Gates of Divinity and Desolation. The Kingdom of the Night. The Palace of the Day." The prayer went on and on, just as he would have expected.

But this keyhole made no sense. It wasn't even the right shape. It wasn't in the right place. It simply shouldn't have been there.

The dog sat down next to him. She lifted her head, following the flight of a bird. She looked intent, and for a moment, it was hard to imagine that she wasn't a just a dog. Then she glanced back down to the stone.

"The Rifter has his-self a key an' he makes his-self a keyhole," she said. "Opened it right up an' goes through."

"This is bad." Kahlil scowled at the keyhole.

"For them on the other side." The dog yawned. She seemed oddly content with the situation.

"The Rifter has crossed through to Basawar," Kahlil said, just to make sure that she did understand. "He'll destroy it."

"Tears it in two, that's what the Rifter do." She nodded her cream-colored head.

"We can't stop him or warn anyone because they've crushed the gateway," Kahlil added. "And even if I could cross, I couldn't kill him because I don't have the deathlock key. He does."

"So them thats locked you away, gots themselves hell to pay." She stood up and took a deep breath of the rich air. "I wants to chases me a fluff-n'-flicker, little tree-beastie."

"It's called a squirrel." Kahlil looked down at her. "Doesn't this bother you?"

She shook her head and then leaned her soft muzzle against Kahlil's leg.

"When theys cut the meat from me," she whispered, "when theys pierced me with knives an' ties me in red ribbons— then I screamed. I cried likes the whole world died. Not now. Now I tastes wind full of sweet bird meat. I runs where I likes, an' I pisses on a tree. An' thems that would can't do a thing to me. They brought they bad end. They got they Rifter revived."

Closing her eyes, she let out a deep animal sigh. Kahlil could feel her entire body relax against him. "Not a thing you can do abouts it now. We both free now."

He shut his eyes and sat still, a patch of sun slowly warming his back. He could hear animals, birds he supposed, making noises in the trees. The air, as always, tasted as strong and rich and exotic as a dream.

He did not belong to this world, a world that was too good for him. He was not like the bones. He had not already given everything up for his own home. He had no right to lay claim to the richness and luxury of this world while what was left of Basawar was torn to pieces.

Kahlil had been entrusted to watch over the Rifter: to find him in this world and protect him until it was decided if the Rifter would be needed or not. If he had been needed, then Kahlil would have brought the Rifter back and released him like an apocalypse over Sabir's red army of Fai'daum. If the Rifter was not needed, then it fell to Kahlil to destroy him.

It had been simple, only the matter of the single word "Don't" and the tiny key that opened the Rifter's death. And he had missed it.

He stroked the dog's head. When the order had come, he had been in the orchard, carrying her on his back. He had saved her, but at the cost of his whole world.

She deserved this life, the warm sunlight, the pungent scents and lush tastes. He didn't.

Kahlil opened his eyes.

"I have to go," he said. "I have to try to stop him."

"Don't," she whispered.

"I'm sorry, little sister." He stroked her head, ran his fingers over her soft, warm ears. She gazed at him and then slowly pulled herself up.

"Doors all closed," she said. "No words yous can say to opens them again."

"There's still one way." Kahlil drew his longest knife.

A small, involuntary whimper escaped the dog. The same kind of knife had been used to lay her open once. She took a step back from him.

"It's not for you," Kahlil assured her.

She sat back down but didn't come closer to him.

He didn't have his sword or the key, but the blood of a witch flowed in his veins and, offered in sacrifice, it might awaken the shattered gates one last time.

If he used his blood and the bond that linked him to John, then he might be able to follow him. But there was no certainty. He might bleed to death here on this hill or, worse, be torn apart and scattered across two worlds and countless ages. If he died, then it would be what he deserved for his failure. But he had to attempt his redemption.

Kahlil set the knife down on the stone and pulled off his coat. Stripping the bandage from his shoulder, he pulled the wound open again to start the blood running. His hand trembled as he picked up his knife again, but he forced himself to keep it steady. He sliced it quickly down his right arm, opening a wide furrow. A sharp pain rushed up in the blade's wake. Hot rivulets of blood ran along his arm. He could hear the dog whimpering, but he didn't look at her.

Closing his eyes, he concentrated on finding John—feeling that gentle pull as constant and strong as his own heartbeat—and following him back to Basawar.

At first the images were faint. Black branches faded in and out, as if coming to him through fields of static. Steadily, as his pounding heart pumped more and more blood from his wounds, the image became clearer. He could feel a searing cold wash over him. White masses of snow flurried against a pale sky. He pushed the air out of his lungs and threw himself into the shattered gate.

Everything went silent. Agony sheared through his body. His mouth opened, releasing a mute scream. His vision seared to an intense white as if he were staring straight into the sun. He couldn't look away. He couldn't stop it. He burned and writhed, as though he were being dragged apart in a hundred different directions.

《《《

He hardly sensed his impact against solid ground. His mouth was full of snow and blood. It tasted like rusting iron. He lay on his back in a snowbank between rows of brick buildings.

He got to his feet and walked to the mouth of the narrow alley, his body moving almost of its own accord. Pain tore through him, but he didn't make a sound. He clenched his jaw tight and drew in deep, cold breaths through his nose. His head pounded, and the ground seemed to lurch beneath his feet. He realized that he wasn't sure what it was that he was looking for and, more worryingly, he couldn't quite recall who he was.

He stared down the row of brick buildings. A hazy gold glow radiated from above as a gas streetlamp ignited. Another lit up, and then another, all the way down the long, winding street.

Jarring noises from carriages, and street hawkers ringing bells and shouting, came at him. He smelled roasting nuts for a moment. Then the strong scent of blood that clung to his body engulfed it.

His right arm hurt, he realized. It hurt badly. The skin was slashed open and scarlet ribbons of cold, congealing blood dripped down from his shoulder to his fingers.

What a mess.

He was sure that seeing his own damaged arm should have horrified him. But oddly, he felt as if he had almost expected it. That struck him as strange until he noticed the knife in his other hand.

There was something decidedly sinister about all of this.

For an instant, he thought that he knew how he had come to be in such a beaten state. Then the thought simply dissolved, leaving him with the knowledge that at one time he had known how this had happened. He had done something.

Or—no! There was something he had to do. Something important.

He had a pack, he realized. Of course he did. He'd known that.

Gingerly he slipped it off. The leather of the pack was tattered and faded. It smelled like dog. Inside he discovered a heavy coat and a pistol in a shoulder holster. There were also bullets—an absurd profusion of bullets.

What had he been doing?

Something wrong. He was suddenly sure. He had done something wrong, and it had made him sick with himself. He'd missed a letter, and someone else had read it. He'd killed thousands of people. He'd killed a dog.

No, he'd saved a dog.

Yes…. He could picture himself patting a yellow dog. She liked him. He had not killed her; he'd saved her life. She'd been in a fire or something. He felt slightly relieved. He didn't want to be the kind of man who murdered animals. That told him something, didn't it? That must make him a decent sort of person, right?

He contemplated the pistol and the bullets again.

Maybe he hadn't killed a dog, but he was sure that he had committed murder. It wasn't just the knife and the gun that told him so. He felt the certainty of it suffuse him.

Little slivers of memory flicked through him. The wet heat of another man's blood running down his hand. The feel of resistance as his black knife pierced flesh and scraped bone. It all came back too easily. If he had been a decent man, he would have been re-pulsed by these things. But he wasn't. The only emotion he could summon was resignation: he was obliged to perform a duty that no one could know about. Everything he did and everything about him had to be kept secret.

He had lied about his name, his occupation, where he had been, what he had done, how he came in, how he went out. He had lied in two languages and to every person he met. What he liked, what he hated, what he believed, what he desired, every detail had been a fabrication. He had lied enough to create an entire other man. And that man told lies as well.

Of course there had to be two of him, one for each world: Nayeshi and Basawar.

So, where was he now?

He squinted up at the scratchy, chalky sky and then gazed out at the wooden carriages and dull green tahldi pulling them. These were not the images he would have expected to see in Nayeshi alongside the interstates and strip malls.

Then this had to be Basawar. Probably the city of Nurjima.

A repulsed, nauseated feeling welled up in him. He had come home.

Kahlil remembered Nurjima. Or he thought he remembered it. But once he began walking through the streets, he discovered that the city in his memory and the one surrounding him were not the same. They resembled each other, like twin sisters, seemingly identical but subtly different.

Older, narrow streets still spoked out from ancient plazas, marking the obsolete boundaries of the first tiny villages that had since grown into a huge city. Old roads collided like wrecks of wagon wheels, while newer thoroughfares dissected their arcs into modern grids.

The rolling ground and the course of the frozen river that cut the city in half were exactly as he remembered. Even the lines of the bare, black trees seemed the same until he noticed the pale green buds of leaves. They should have been white.

He thought the mistake could have been his own or a matter of his injured eyes. Maybe he misremembered. Or perhaps the trees had been replaced since he had last been here. It had been ten years. The trees had been young.

He let it go and continued walking. He didn't have the strength to waste, wondering over trees or tiny, altered details like shop signs and street names. He noted them and ignored them. He didn't stop. He didn't dare to. And he didn't look back. He didn't want to see the trail his own blood studded across the white snow. He needed to find a temple. The priests there would know how to tend his wounds.

He staggered past people. Most of them seemed to be going home for the evening. An older woman with a child pulled away from him as though he were contagious. Men in dull blue hats and long coats simply checked their pocket watches or straightened their cuffs as he passed by.

No one offered him any assistance, not even answering his requests for the time or for directions to the Black Tower of the Payshmura.

Finally he found Blackbird's Bridge, one landmark he could remember. But when he looked out from the height of the bridge, he found the hazy, brown skyline disorienting. There appeared to be two yellow-tiled domes of the Gaunsho'im Council. One stood, as Kahlil remembered, in the north of the city, near the Seven Palaces. The other shone far south of the first, where the old Execution Grounds had been.

The Gaunsho'im must have built a second Council Hall. He couldn't imagine why, but he didn't understand half of what the Gaunsho'im did. They were the rulers of noble families, and they answered for their wastefulness to only themselves. If they wanted a second Council building, that was their concern. Construction of new buildings could be expected, even in times as bad as these. So long as the Gaunsho'im met their yearly tithes to the church, they could build as many tributes to their own importance as they pleased.

Kahlil stared down over the Seven Palaces and then past them. He saw long, gleaming roofs with tiles that shone like faceted crystal where none had stood before. To the west, clusters of dull, redbrick buildings piled up against each other. When he had last been here, only a scattered shantytown stood close to the riverbank. The additions didn't bother him so much. It was the one absence that frightened him.

The massive Black Tower should have shot up from the north point of the city like a black blade piercing the heavens. But it was nowhere to be seen. It wasn't a structure that could be missed. It had dominated the skyline, with huge cords of metal twisting up to a single, gleaming point. Its shadow alone should have sliced across the city in a straight, sharp stroke.

Kahlil stared and squinted and turned in a circle, but still couldn't find the tower. How could it be gone? He sank down to his knees, suddenly gripped with a sick fear.

He knew.

He couldn't remember, but he knew. Somehow he had allowed this to happen. He had failed foolishly and terribly. He supposed it was only fair that now he had nowhere to go, no one to care for him.

His eyes stung and burned, and he closed them. It would do him no good looking for a tower that no longer stood. He struggled to remember what he had done wrong. Without knowing, how could he make it right?

The chill of the snow soaked through his heavy pants. The night grew darker and colder. Now that he had stopped searching, the pain of his injuries began to cut into his awareness. He pulled both arms in close to his body and tucked his bare hands into the pockets of his coat.

He had no idea what to do now. Where could he go?

Then the fingers of his left hand brushed across something soft and rectangular. Frowning, he drew a worn leather wallet from his pocket.

His memory was bad, but he was sure that he didn't own a wallet. He was pretty certain that wallets like this didn't even exist in Basawar. He opened it and found only a torn photograph inside. The young man in the picture wore the expression of someone who thought that his picture had already been taken. The camera's flash had made his blond hair look too light and his eyes too dark. His eyes were actually sky blue. He was taller than he appeared in the tiny photo, and his voice was soft and low. This man was important to him. He was the reason Kahlil had come here. He was what Kahlil had done wrong.

Kahlil had failed to kill this young man. The knowledge simply opened within him. He'd killed many men, but he had let this one escape. He started to crumple the photo, then stopped himself. He didn't want to crush it. The photograph didn't show it, but the young man had a kind smile. The thought startled Kahlil. Then came a flood of confused memories.

He recalled drinking mulled wine with the man, and the two of them smiling like conspirators. He felt the warmth of the man's living body against a cold winter night, the smell of his skin and hair, the man whispering his name.

Kahlil felt like he might cry. He wasn't sure why, and it embarrassed him. He closed his eyes again and waited for the feeling to pass. These weren't things he had done. They couldn't be. But they felt as strong and powerful as true memories.

This just had to be a matter of confusion. Something was wrong with his head. He wasn't quite himself yet.

He slipped the photo back into the protection of the leather wallet, tucked it into his pocket, and gazed down over all the roofs of the city. There had to be some place he could go. Not too far to the west, he noticed the blurs and colors of crowds moving through the streets. Many seemed to be filtering into the same buildings. Kahlil squinted and shifted his head slightly to catch a clearer image. At last he made out the shapes of big placards hanging over the doors. Taverns, whorehouses, and public baths. There appeared to be a few cheaply decorated theaters as well. Kahlil guessed from the look of the neighborhood that the actresses probably did little more than remove their costumes for pennies.

He made his way there as quickly and directly as he could. Without any money, he needed to go where other men did—and where he would blend in, even with his bedraggled appearance.

Pausing before a tavern that bore the emblem of a fat, white weasel, he picked up a fistful of snow and washed the blood from his hands and cheek. His heavy coat hid his other injuries. As he rinsed his hands, he frowned. The sight of his clean, bare, left hand particularly disturbed him. The black Prayerscar that should have been there had vanished.

Inside, the tavern was crowded and dimly lit. The heavy, warm air hung low, weighed down with the smells of men's bodies, mutton grease, and lamp smoke. The tables were small and crowded around a tiny, raised stage.

A plump, dark-haired girl, dressed in a few swathes of cheesecloth, stood on the stage singing. She stared out, her face lifted a little higher than any patron's gaze as if she were not quite aware of their presences. Kahlil didn't know the song, but it was pleasant. Men made up most of the patrons. Some kept quiet, listening to the singer, but most conversed with each other. Their low voices produced a deep, steady rumble over which the girl's melody drifted.

Kahlil found an empty table and crumpled onto a seat like a flour sack slipping from a sure grip. The force of will that had kept him moving through snow and cold evaporated before the comfort of warmth and a place to rest.

For a few minutes he leaned on his left elbow, eyes closed, balancing on the edge of unconsciousness. The warmth surrounding him soaked through his coat, easing his muscles. The smell of meat and beer washed over him. His stomach felt raw as it gnawed at its own emptiness. He hadn't been hungry like this in years. He needed food, and for that he would need money.

He slowly surveyed the men surrounding him. He didn't waste time taking in their faces or figures. All he looked for were their coin purses. He didn't see any hanging from the men's belts, but that made sense. Only he and the other priests at Rathal'pesha had worn coin purses like that. In Nurjima, men kept their money in their coat pockets. He remembered noticing that habit the first time he had come here, when he had been sent to bow before the divine Ushso, the head of his order. He had received his Prayerscars then.

Again he glanced down at the bare back of his left hand and noted the absence of a Prayerscar. Kahlil scowled at his own untrustworthy memory. It seemed so perfectly real.

He had been barely twenty, and he had knelt naked in the huge chamber while black-robed priests chanted over him. He had closed his eyes, pride bursting through his chest at being Chosen.

First there had been the soft, stroking sensation as the priests painted black ink over the backs of his hands and across his eyelids. Then the ink had begun to burn into his flesh like acid. He had wanted to scream, but he had remained silent. At last the priests had washed his hands and eyes with blessed waters and balms. The pain had faded, but the burns had only grown darker until they had become jet black. And then he became Kahlil.

Again he observed the back of his hand, rubbing it as though the Prayerscar was somehow hidden. Though chapped and red at the knuckles, his skin showed no trace of black. Just as Nurjima had no Black Tower, he had no Prayerscars.

He couldn't have just made them up. No, they had been real. He felt certain.

Something had happened to his head when he'd crossed between the worlds. His body had been injured, and so, apparently, had his memories. But he was blessed even if he had no Prayerscars to show it. He carried in his body witches' blood and Parfir's own bones, and he could prove it to himself right now.

He picked a man at random, a big fellow with a yellow beard and meaty hands. The man sat at a small table ten feet or so from Kahlil. Other patrons crowded in close at nearby tables, jostling each other as they shifted and gestured. Kahlil guessed that a few tugs might not be noticed. He lowered his gaze to the blond man's dark brown coat, focusing his concentration on the man's bulging pocket. Then, casually, he lifted his left hand up close to his mouth and flicked his first two fingers apart.

A shock of biting pain shot through his fingers and bolted through his arm. The sensation startled Kahlil. It shouldn't have hurt just to open the Gray Space. It was only traveling through that caused injuries. But then he was already wounded and weak. The force it took to open the space must have been too much strain. His body didn't want to obey him.

Still, he didn't allow the rift in the space to close. Setting his teeth, he clenched his jaw against the groan that almost escaped him. Steadily, he tore the space wide, and the contents of the man's pocket began to fall into his hand.

There were coins and a banknote. Then a fat gold watch spilled out. The watch chain, however, seemed to have caught on something. Kahlil closed his fingers around it and gave a tug. The bearded man suddenly looked down to his coat and then to a slim man sitting at the table next to him.

Kahlil released the watch and let the space snap back closed. At the same moment the bearded man jammed his hand into his own pocket. He felt for the coins and banknote and found neither. A look of rage came over him.

"You thief! You think you can steal from me?" he shouted at the slim man next to him. "I'll damn well kill you!"

The other man barely had time to look up before the bearded man hammered a fist into the side of his head. The slim man fell, and the bearded man kicked him hard, knocking over chairs.

The other patrons drew back as the bearded man continued cursing and kicking the slim man. The singer went silent and stepped back from the edge of the stage. The slim man curled up, attempting to protect himself while the much bigger bearded man stomped at him furiously.

"I'll kill you, you light-fingered fucker!" The bearded man's face had gone red with anger.

Kahlil pushed himself up to his feet. He knew he was going to regret this, but he couldn't let the man on the floor take a beating for him. He shoved his way past the other tavern patrons and grabbed the bearded man's shoulder.

"Stop it," Kahlil said.

"Go to hell!" the bearded man roared, and Kahlil could smell the sharp tang of wine on the man's breath. Then he swung his fist up to smack Kahlil aside. Reflexively, Kahlil ducked and drove his own fist into the bearded man's nose. A hot gush of blood spilled across his left hand.

The bearded man staggered back and then threw himself at Kahlil. Out of the corner of his eye, Kahlil saw the bloodied, slim man being lifted from the floor by two other patrons. That was good.

Then he crumpled to the ground beneath the immense weight of his bearded opponent. The man's thick hands locked around his throat. Kahlil twisted beneath the man's bulk, but his left arm was pinned tight. His right arm lay stretched out against the wooden floor, but Kahlil could hardly make it move. The pain was simply too great. And now he couldn't breathe.

For a moment, out of pure animal reflex, he fought for air, spitting and gasping. The bearded man leaned over him, tightening his grip on Kahlil's throat.

"No man alive fucks with me, boy," the bearded man whispered. He grinned, and Kahlil saw that blood from his nose had dripped through his blond mustache and into his mouth.

Kahlil clawed at the man's chest with his left hand. His fingers only gripped into the man's coat. His lungs ached. This man truly intended to kill him.

The little air in Kahlil's lungs felt dead. His lips were numb, and a pulse of blackness edged in over his vision. Then Kahlil felt a desperate, burning force suddenly flash up from deep within him. A surge of power and rage scorched out from his bones. His muscles felt molten. His skin was like fire.

The pain of his injuries seared away to vapor.

He relaxed. Without thinking, he flicked the fingers of his left hand apart. Instantly an edge of Gray Space tore open. Kahlil pushed the edge of it up into the bearded man's chest. His hand slid into the hot, wet cavity of the man's body as easily as if he were slipping on a glove. With a flick of his hand, he slid the edge of the Gray Space upward, using it like a razor.

The bearded man hardly had a moment to look astonished before his body split open from sternum to jaw bone. His blood, steaming hot and nearly black with oxygen, gushed from the gaping wound. The bearded man spilled onto Kahlil, who lay still pinned beneath his massive bulk.

He couldn't sit up; he couldn't move. He felt sick and exhausted. It was all so familiar.

People stood all around him. Their faces appeared soft and distorted, as if he were peering through warped glass. His eyesight was getting worse, he thought. It seemed much darker now, nearly black. He could discern only indistinct shadows of movement above him. Someone laid a hand on his shoulder.

"It's going to be all right," a man whispered close to his face. Farther away, someone else laughed.

Then a vast darkness, like a new door into a space he had never crossed before, opened up and swallowed him whole.

CHAPTER SEVEN

Flurries of snow rolled up in little curls as a sudden wind swept down from the distant, gray mountains. Clouds hung low over the sharp, white peaks. Weeks ago, John had designated the ragged mountains as his marker for north. Sunrise and sunset confirmed that much, even though his compass swung in slow circles, never committing to a single orientation. A compass could easily break, but the solar system was another matter entirely.

And yet when John studied the night sky, he found it alarming. The few evenings that stars pierced through the clouds, they burned brightly. But neither he, nor Bill, nor Laurie, recognized any constellations, though Bill and Laurie gamely offered suggestions.

"Those six there," Laurie had pointed up to a far corner of the night sky, "they remind me of fireworks."

"Yeah, and that one looks like a beer bottle." Bill's voice always sounded strained now. Both the cold and the thin air scourged his lungs, making him struggle for breath. Even so, Bill couldn't stand to keep silent. "I think it's tipping to pour beer over those four stars there. I'm going to call them the sorority sisters."

A few days earlier Bill had christened the same cluster "the hot dog," but all of the constellations were so unfamiliar that it was easy to forget which was which. Some nights John almost convinced himself that he recognized the stars of the southern hemisphere in the scattered lights: the crow, the keel, and perhaps the centaur. Other nights they seemed to spread above him in utterly alien configurations.

Either way, he had long ago abandoned the notion of using them for any kind of navigation. Nights were too cold for travel anyway. When John ventured out to hunt among the stands of bare, black trees and deep drifts of snow, he always turned back toward their shelter while a few hours of light still remained.

In his travels he'd discovered that the land to the east flattened out into a plain and then suddenly dropped into a steel-gray chasm as if the entire world just ended there. The jagged cliffs were treacherous even in the light of the day. Buffeting winds swept up, and banks of icy fog often hid sheer drops. Occasionally, John glimpsed a rolling, black sea far below. Birds soared up the gray cliffs, riding frigid, salty winds.

John caught small birds when he could. They were scrawny things, plumed in thick layers of dishwater-colored feathers and smelling faintly of bad fish. They tasted better than they smelled— but not much.

Bill always cooked them with one hand clamped over his nose.

The weasels were much better, both for their skins and their meat. Plus, John found their behavior fascinating. Sometimes, even after he had trapped enough to feed the three of them, he would remain out in the snow, letting frost color his beard and watching the white creatures come out to play. The first time he had cut one open, he had noted the fine, red lining of its egg sacks. He hadn't said anything to either Bill or Laurie. He had wanted to be sure that he was right. But over the next week, he had caught enough female weasels to be sure.

John deliberately waited to approach them with his suspicions, until one afternoon when the air grew warmer and didn't seem to bother Bill's lungs so much.

He ducked through the tiny entrance of their snow-packed shelter, carrying the body of one of the weasels. It took a moment for his eyes to adjust to the dim surroundings inside. The shelter would have been even darker, if it hadn't been for the silver Mylar John had stretched over the frame of black branches before he had insulated the entire structure with thick walls of snow. The Mylar caught any light that seeped in through the entrance and reflected it throughout the low space.

Laurie and Bill sat close together, sharing Bill's black jacket for extra warmth. Next to them lay John's silent radio and his nearly empty first-aid kit.

"Hey, Toffee." Laurie frowned slightly, but her face had already grown so thin that the expression looked ghastly. "You look serious. Is something wrong?"

"These weasels." John held the soft, dead creature in his hands. "I think they're monotremes."

"Which means what?" Bill asked. The silver light inside their shelter exaggerated the permanent blue tinge of Bill's skin.

When they first arrived, Laurie had also experienced shortness of breath. Like Bill, she had blackedout whenever she moved too much. While she had adapted in a few weeks, Bill never had. Even now, if he exerted himself, Bill was likely to faint.

Fortunately for all three of them, the thin atmosphere didn't trouble John. If it had, they would have frozen to death before they could have even exhausted Bill's supply of Hershey bars.

"A monotreme," John explained quietly, "is a very primitive, egg-laying mammal. They're only found in Australia and New Zealand. As far as I know, the only living examples are the echidna and the platypus."

"So what are you trying to say here?" Bill raised an eyebrow. "You think we're in Australia?"

"No." John frowned. "We're obviously not in Australia." He wasn't sure how to explain without sounding overly dramatic and possibly panicking the two of them. It was a difficult thing to accept.

"So ...?" Laurie encouraged him.

"I think we may not even be on Earth." John just said it.

"Yeah," Bill agreed. Laurie gave a small sigh.

"You already knew?"

"We did," Laurie smiled at him, "but we didn't want to freak you out. You're not the kind of guy who can just accept something like this on intuition. You have to give yourself time and proof."

Bill nodded then asked, "So where did you think we were—before you came to this conclusion?"

"I didn't know." John shrugged, feeling suddenly stupid. "I just started looking for evidence to tell me."

"Well, this is a huge thing to have happened," Laurie said. "I mean, I don't think the shock has really set in for me. Don't feel bad."

"Yeah, man," Bill said, "if we had been in Australia, you would have been the one to get us out. Me and Laurie would have been trying to mind-meld with kangaroos and saying, 'Wow, alien life is so weird' and shit like that."

John just frowned down at the white weasel. Its toes were delicate, pink, and almost human. He could barely see the fine webbing between them.

"So, do you think you might be ready for something else freaky?" Laurie asked.

John didn't feel ready for anything, but he didn't want to say so. He nodded.

"Okay." Laurie dug into the pocket of Bill's jacket and pulled out a singed twig. She held it out in front of her and closed her eyes. John stared at the twig and then glanced back to Laurie. Her pale brows knit together in concentration. Her lips pressed into a hard line. Nothing happened.

"Damn it." Laurie's eyes popped open. "I almost had it."

"Just relax," Bill told her. "Try it like you did last time."

"Okay." Laurie closed her eyes again and blew the air out of her lungs. She grimaced absurdly as she concentrated. Bill leaned close to her, attentive as a gymnastics coach of a young Olympian. John watched too, feeling uneasy and unready for anything to happen, but at the same time hoping that something would.

There was nothing. Then John caught the faintest scent of burning. A wisp of smoke drifted up from the surface of the twig as a tiny red ember began to glow through the wood. The ember spread like the cherry of a cigarette and then flickered into a small flame.

Laurie pulled her eyes open and gasped for air, as if she had just broken the surface of a lake after a deep dive. She slouched against Bill, still breathing heavily.

John blew out the flame before it filled the confines of their snow-packed shelter with smoke.

"Pretty cool, huh?" Laurie smiled.

"Very cool," Bill told her.

"Could you always do that?" John inspected the end of the burnt twig.

"Maybe." Laurie leaned in against Bill, and he pulled his arms around her. Bill's blue-white hands looked like cut ice against the black jacket.

"I never tried as hard as I did here," Laurie said. "You know, that first night when the matches were all wet and the wood was wet, and you just kept trying to get a fire going?"

John couldn't forget it. He still had nightmares of looking up and seeing Laurie's entire body, pale as wax, shaking uncontrollably. He remembered Bill lying on his side, huge white flakes of snow accumulating in his black hair as he struggled to draw in a breath. He had seen them dying as the sky grew darker and colder. Snow had fallen, thicker and faster. He had wanted to cry, but instead he had kept on striking the wet matches. He'd never felt so helpless or so worthless in his life.

"That night," Laurie went on, "I kept staring at the wood and wanting it to burn so badly. I could almost see the spark. But it wouldn't happen. I'd see it every time you struck a match. I was almost holding my breath—"

"You were holding your breath," Bill said.

"Yeah, I must have been. We figured out that holding my breath makes a big difference. I don't know why, but there's something about that moment when I feel like I'm going to suffocate—if I can just keep focused, then I reach this intense force. It's really kind of scary. It feels like I'm dying. Like it's killing me. But you know, that night I was already dying, so I guess it didn't make such a big difference. All of the sudden, I felt this power burn through me. It felt like it was searing up from my bones—coming up from really deep. And then I lit the fire."

"She's been practicing since then," Bill said.

"I'm still pretty shaky with it," Laurie added.

John didn't know what to say. It all seemed so unreal.

"Maybe this is why we were brought here," Laurie said. "Maybe Kyle was some kind of messenger who meant you to get that key and bring us here."

"Maybe," John replied. He couldn't imagine what possible use he, Bill, and Laurie could be out in this frigid wasteland. But just at the moment, he had no faith in his ability to judge reality. He didn't know if he could rule anything out.

In the weeks that followed, Laurie grew more adept at lighting their fires. Bill cobbled together decent meals from the small animals and bitter, blue-gray berries that John foraged. Little else changed. Snowstorms came and passed. If there was a purpose to their presence in this frigid world, none of them recognized it.

John often returned to the area where they had first arrived. He always looked for the glint of a dull gold key in the masses of snow. He didn't know what he would do with it if he found it, but he kept searching anyway. He couldn't give up on finding a way home.

Today, he didn't discover the key. He found something else.

He knelt down next to streaks of vivid red blood, spilled across the snow. He studied the outline of a tall, prone body that had crashed deep into the white drift. A set of tracks led away from the impression. They marched north toward the mountains. But, curiously, no tracks led up to the imprint. It was as if a body had just dropped from the sky, struggled up, and staggered away.

John guessed from the size of the impression and footprints, that it had been a man, maybe as tall as he was, and probably injured.

At the horizon, storm clouds were gathering, and late-afternoon shadows lengthened. If he followed the tracks, he could be caught in a storm and lose his way home when darkness fell. But if he waited until tomorrow, the tracks would surely be lost under fresh snowfall.

John raced northward. The strange figure's strides were long—almost as long as his own. They led straight north, through thick stands of trees and across a frozen stream.

John noticed the way the sky was changing from its usual pale blue to a sooty color. The wind grew colder and whipped up powdery snow. He bowed his head, protecting his eyes from the wind, focusing on the few feet of ground directly ahead of him.

He had already gone too far to get back before night.

In an odd synchronicity, John noticed a growing distance between the footprints as the man stopped walking and began to run. Whoever it was, he seemed to know where he was going and wanted to get there quickly. John wondered how far he was behind the other man. Although the blood appeared bright and vivid, that could be deceptive. When the air was this cold, blood would remain fresh for nearly a full day.

Suddenly, the tracks turned to the west. John glanced up and, despite the dim light, saw why immediately. The land fell off sharply to a wide, ice-encrusted river. He thought he could see moving water at the very middle, but he wasn't sure. It certainly didn't look safe to cross.

John followed the tracks farther west than he had ever gone before. Stands of bare, black trees became more common. And a new smell suffused the air. John had been running so hard that he hadn't been thinking about it, but now it had grown strong enough that he couldn't miss it. It was the smell of fire and roasting meat. The smell of habitation. Just that scent gave him a surge of strength. He ran faster.

He could see warm, yellow firelight glowing between the bare branches of the trees. A feeling a joy and hope flooded him. He found himself thinking of things that he hadn't dared to let himself miss. A room of his own. A warm bed. A bath.

John broke out from a cluster of trees and stopped. Instantly, he pulled himself back into the cover of the woods. He dropped low and peered out, horrified by what he had seen. He had reached a cobblestone road. At uneven distances along the edge of the road stood huge metal poles with the bodies of men hanging from them on chains. Some of the bodies were only charred remnants; others were still writhing, gagged and burning alive.

CHAPTER EIGHT

The cold invaded. It devoured every other sensation until his body felt like a frigid expanse surrounded by darkness. Incrementally, the thought struck him that it shouldn't be dark and he shouldn't be lying still. People died this way—sleeping in soft drifts of snow, blanketed beneath layer after layer.

He had to open his eyes. The cold would kill him if he didn't open his damn eyes. He couldn't let himself fall asleep. John jerked himself upright and stared numbly around.

Instead of an open expanse of snow, he found himself gazing at the silver Mylar interior of the shelter. Afternoon light poured in from the small entrance and reflected across the metallized plastic, lending the cramped, low space a golden luminosity.

Laurie and Bill both looked up from tinkering with the hand-held radio. In the soft light and deep shadows, they both appeared hollowed and far too thin. Laurie's hair hung in dirty, blond strings. Patchy, black tufts of beard darkened Bill's chin. They were dressed in a bunchy mix of their old, stained clothes and strips of dried weasel hide. They looked like famished poster children for some Siberian relief campaign.

How could he have failed to notice how fragile and ravaged they had become in the last months? He'd just gotten used to it. He supposed he looked just as bad.

"I don't think it'll be too hot now." Bill picked up a silver thermos and handed it to Laurie.

Laurie smiled at Bill, very sweetly, as if he had said something touching. She took the thermos and turned to John.

"Hey, Mr. Frostbite." Laurie crawled over to him. She unscrewed the thermos and handed it to him. His fingers were still too clumsy to grip the steel surface. He held the thermos between the flats of his palms, like a child who had not yet mastered the dexterity or proportions of the adult world.

The warm broth scalded his chilled lips as he drank. It tasted like weasel meat. The heat of the liquid burned down into his body. It was good. He hadn't realized how starved he was until now.

"How are you feeling?" Laurie placed her hand against his forehead. He had to suppress the urge to jerk back from her touch. Her thin fingers felt like brands searing into his skin. The pain faded, as his skin warmed beneath the heat of her hand.

"Better." The word came out in a dry whisper.

"You look better," she said.

John closed his eyes. He was so tired. He felt the thermos slip from his hands and then the brush of Laurie's bony fingers as she caught it.

"Don't go back to sleep, Toffee. Stay awake for a little while, okay?" Laurie shook him gently.

John forced his eyes open again.

"How did I get back here?" John asked.

"You ask that every time you wake up," Laurie said.

"You just staggered out of the middle of that fucking blizzard, like a big, old abominable snowman," Bill said. "That was three days ago. Maybe four. I lost track of time when it was really blowing out there. It could have been day or night."

"We thought you were going to die. You were like ice." Laurie's eyes suddenly misted, and she pressed her lips tightly closed.

"I'm fine," he assured her. He would have said it even if he were missing his legs just to keep her from crying.

"Yeah," Laurie forced a smile, "but you look like shit."

"You just said that I looked better."

Laurie didn't say anything. She just reached behind him and pulled the blanket up around his shoulders.

"You looked worse than shit before." Bill scowled at the radio. Slowly, he turned the dial through frequency after frequency of static and then switched it off. He stood as much as the low ceiling allowed and walked over to John with the radio.

"I don't want to sound gay or anything, 'cause, you know, that's your bag, but I'm really glad you're not dead, man." Bill sat down next to him.

"Thanks, Bill ... I think."

"Anytime." Bill gazed at the radio. "You know, I can't really remember how that stupid radio commercial for the Beer Barn went. In a really retarded way, I kind of miss it. You'd think I'd miss something else, you know, like NPR news or the college radio station."

John tried to think back, but his mind was still fuzzy from the cold. There had been some little sound effect in the jingle, he recalled.

"It went, 'Beer Barn! Beer by the bucket!'" Laurie sang. "'Beer Barn! Everyone else can—' and then there was that angry 'moo' over the words, 'fuck it.'"

"Yeah, I miss the beer-cow's moo," Bill said, then amended. "Maybe I just miss beer."

"I think we all miss beer. I could certainly use one now." John's voice still sounded dry and raspy.

"Forget about boring old beer. Now we've got exciting weasel broth, made with real weasel!" Bill gestured toward the thermos. "It's warm and weasel-licious."

"You make it sound too good to resist," John replied flatly.

He was beginning to feel a little more alive. It didn't take all of his concentration just to stay awake. He lifted the thermos to his mouth. The steamy scent drifted up to him. The smell of meat, he thought.

Suddenly the clear image of bound bodies writhing in flames rushed up to him, unbidden. With it came the rich smell of roasting flesh and the sound of shrieks muted beneath bundles of oil-soaked rags and the sight of shadows dancing and jerking across the white snow as the flames crawled over them.

Nausea washed through him as he caught a second whiff of the broth. He passed the thermos back to Laurie.

"What's wrong?" she asked.

"Are you gonna hurl?" Bill pawed desperately around for some kind of receptacle.

John swallowed back the bile in his throat. "No, I'm fine. I just ..." He felt so sick just thinking about it. He pressed his eyes closed, desperate to push the memory back. He needed it to recede into the mundane recollections of trudging through snow, setting traps, watching the northern horizon for storm clouds. But now that he'd remembered the images, the smells and sounds wouldn't leave him.

"Toffee?" Laurie's voice rose sharply in alarm. Her hand gripped his shoulder too tightly.

"What's wrong?" Bill sounded scared.

He couldn't fall apart on them. They needed him to pull himself together. He was the one who always kept it together.

He said, "I'm all right. I was just a little woozy for a minute."

"Do you want some more broth?" Laurie started to lift the thermos, but John pushed it gently back.

"Not right this minute. I need to tell you guys about what I saw. Before I got caught in the storm, I was following the tracks of a man."

"A man? You mean another human being?" Laurie hadn't looked so excited since they had both been in the third grade, when she had genuinely believed she would receive a pony for her birthday.

"Who was it?" Bill asked. A tiny flush colored his pale cheeks.

"I don't know. I just found tracks."

"But they were human, right? It was a person?" Laurie asked.

"Yes," John said. "It looked like he just dropped out of nowhere like we did, but he seemed to know where he was. He went straight north, no wandering or circling."

"Oh God, he might know what's going on, or how to get out of here, or ... I don't even know. I'm so excited! " Laurie grinned.

"And you followed him, right?" Bill watched John carefully, as if he suspected that this was not good news.

"I followed him for most of the day, north, up to a river bank, and then west." John forced his voice to stay even. "I reached a pave-stone road. I could see the cobblestones where wheels had plowed aside the snow. The ruts didn't look like they came from cars. They were more narrow and spaced farther apart." John knew why he was obsessing on the tracks. He didn't want to think any further.

"Motorcycle tracks, maybe?" Laurie asked.

"More like a cart." In John's mind, cocooned bodies thrashed desperately as flames rolled over and burned through them. The noises they made were muted and deformed by agony. They came out strangely, like the shrieks of birds. Like small animals dying.

"I didn't look too closely at the tracks. I think there were only two."

"And?" Laurie asked.

Bill said nothing. John met his eyes and in that moment, a message seemed to pass between them. Bill tensed, waiting to hear the rest of the story.

"There were poles along the sides of the road, like flagpoles with chains at the tops." John couldn't stand to look at either Laurie's or Bill's face. He dropped his gaze down to the packed bark floor of the shelter. "There were people manacled to the chains. They were hanging from their wrists and wrapped up in layers of cloth. Kind of like mummies, I guess. And they were all on fire."

John couldn't go on. He could hardly form coherent sentences.

For a moment there was only silence, then Laurie whispered, "Were they—they weren't alive, were they?"

John nodded.

"Did you try to get them down?" Laurie asked.

"No. I ... There was some kind of accelerant in the wrappings. It made the heat intense enough to burn through parts of their bodies before they were dead. Their limbs were dropping off. I couldn't stop it."

Laurie stopped asking questions.

"So," Bill said, after a few more seconds of silence, "I'm thinking we should avoid that area."

"I think that would be a wise decision." John straightened. "We should probably try to hide our presence here as best we can."

"I really thought ..." Laurie held the thermos between her hands like it was a captive bird. "I really wanted this whole thing to be something good."

"I'm sorry," John told her.

"It's not your fault. I'm just dumb and flaky, that's all." She sniffed and then pushed her stringy hair back from her face. "How do you think we can make ourselves less obvious?"

Having a question to answer made John feel better immediately. It offered him a sense of control and knowledge. He didn't know where they were, but he could begin to make maps. He didn't know whose trail he had followed, but he could make sure that his own tracks were hidden from now on.

After that night he hunted more carefully. He found himself once again digging down to the cold earth and touching it, growing familiar with it, not just as an amusement, but because he depended on this land now. He needed to know in a breath if the least detail was out of place. If a stranger crouched in the dark stands of trees, or if men lay in waiting behind the drifts of snow, he had to sense their presence before they sensed his.

Their need for fire troubled John the most. Smoke was too easy to spot; its scent carried too well. Bill and Laurie now marched a mile south of the shelter and cooked under the cover of the trees. For each meal, they had to haul the supplies and raw food out and then carry everything back. It was exhausting for Bill, who could hardly breathe, but he didn't complain. None of them wanted to risk their lives for convenience.

Steadily, the snowdrifts grew wetter, and the air, even at night, turned warmer. John saw changes in Bill and Laurie and even in himself. All their voices quieted, their hair grew long and wild. They often sat silently, listening to sounds of the night outside their shelter. An animal tension infused their motions and gnawed at their sleep.

Whereas Bill had previously been slim, he now seemed wasted. His inability to either run or fight bred a desperate stillness in him. He could crouch against the dark trunk of a tree, small and perfectly motionless, becoming almost invisible.

Laurie's cheeks were chapped red, and cracked calluses marring her once delicate hands. Her body lost all traces of femininity. Thin strings of ligament and muscle barely covered the bones of her arms and legs. She had learned to hunt, but still hated to leave Bill alone. She watched over him constantly.

From the looseness of his clothes, John knew that he too had lost weight. The thick meaty feel of his body had been reduced to a hard leanness. Hunger and constant motion had eaten away the soft curves of his cheeks. He had become nearly as angular and weather-beaten as the bare, black trees. His beard was thick and shot through with white.

As the days lengthened, he begun spending more time out alone. He gave Laurie and Bill their privacy and the time to enjoy it, since he could give them little else. And sometimes, when they would curl up close to each other or kiss, John would feel desperately lonely. He preferred to be away at those times.

Always he wanted to return to the spot where he had lost the key and where he had first seen the man's tracks. Truly, a foolish temptation. He certainly didn't want to follow any more tracks to another scene of human immolation.

But he wondered if something might not appear there again. Maybe a door back home. So he approached cautiously. He no longer walked straight from one point to another. He circled, keeping to the stands of bare trees.

He was still a few dozen yards from the exact spot when he felt a sudden chill and caught a faint odor in the air. Something felt out of place. He remembered having the same sense the day he had come across the shattered yellow stones by the wolf rock.

John crouched down under the cover of the trees and concentrated. He scanned the expanse of white snowdrifts and the four dark patches where trees grew close. Then he heard something—a sound like a whisper. His attention whipped back to the closest drift of snow. He stared at the perfectly white expanse, and, as he did, the faintest gray shadow coalesced in the air. Instantly, it darkened, and a man suddenly appeared, suspended a few feet above the snowdrift, hanging in mid-air.

He knelt, his bare hands held up close to his chest, head bowed as if in prayer. His clothes were uniformly gray and heavy. The cut of his coat reminded John of photos he had seen of soldiers in World War I. He was a young man, maybe still a teenager, but well-built with close-cropped black hair and sharp features.

A second later the man and his shadow crashed together as the man dropped face down into the snow. The man immediately jerked himself upright.

"Jid! Jid korud'an!" The young man's tone and expression made it obvious that he was cursing. Kicking at the snow bank, he bent down and picked up his knit black cap. He scowled at it as he shook the snow off and then seemed to consider whether it would be warmer to put the damp cap on or leave it off. At last, he pulled it onto his head.

He looked simultaneously miserable and annoyed as he frowned down at the deep imprint where he had fallen. John followed his gaze and noticed the small red spatters of blood. The young man pulled back the coat sleeve on his right arm. John stared at the several narrow rivulets of blood, as well as the red welts that marked the man's skin. The injuries looked painful, but not deadly.

Seeming to come to the same conclusion, the man pulled his sleeve back down. He then scanned the horizon. When he caught sight of the mountains, his straight stance slumped a little. He curled his arms over his head, while muttering to himself, "Jid. Jid. Li'hir bai'an. Jid."

His tone, expression, and posture all struck John as the body language of a person who had completely screwed up. John felt a hesitant sympathy for him. If he had been bigger, or armed, then John would have felt too threatened to commiserate, but as he was, the man simply struck him as someone who was having a really bad time.

Then without any warning or reason, he looked at the trees where John crouched. At first he didn't see John. He just observed the trees with disinterest. Then he sighed and glanced down a little and his gaze met John's directly. They both stared in silence. The man's eyes were dark, the pupil and iris almost melting into one. He wore a fixed, startled expression.

Since John's knife was within easy reach, he waited to see what the man would do.

He glanced around, obviously searching for other men hidden in the stands of trees. When he saw none, he returned his attention to John. Very slowly, he lifted his hands away from his body.

"Vunan." He spoke very carefully. "Yura'hir li'ati ratim'at'iss."

He was obviously waiting for a reply. When John said nothing, the man went on, "Li'hir yura'ati ratim'at' sa?" he asked very clearly, his expression intent.

John knew that he had to respond. He didn't want to shake his head or nod, since he had no idea what, if anything, those gestures might mean to this man. He guessed that his best bet would be to say something. At least then the man might realize that John didn't speak his language.

John slowly straightened and lifted his own hands away from his sides.

"Hi." John found himself mimicking the man's very clear enunciation. "I have no idea what you're trying to tell me."

The man gaped at him as if a bird had just flown out of his mouth. It wasn't an expression of misunderstanding, but of disbelief.

"Ahab ..." For a moment, words seemed to fail the man. Then he asked, "How do you know those words?"

John knew he hadn't misheard. The other man had clearly spoken English. John guessed his own expression was a startled as the young man's. For a second, John had the terrible idea that he, Laurie, and Bill had just been lost in some isolated corner of Minnesota. But he knew better. They didn't burn people alive in Minnesota.

"You speak English?" John asked.

The man lifted his head as if in challenge. "I know all of the words. How can you know them?"

"I'm American," John replied. It was an answer, which, he realized belatedly, assumed a great deal of knowledge on the part of the man: that a majority of Americans spoke English, for example. Or even what America was.

"You are from that place?" the man asked.

"Yes. America. We speak English there." The conversation wasn't going as smoothly as John had hoped, but at least they were talking. "Do you know where it is?"

"In the Kingdom of the Night, beneath the Palace of the Day. With a gold key, through a gold doorway." The man watched

John's face closely as he spoke, as if he were uttering some kind of secret code.

"I have no idea what you mean by that." John decided to just be honest.

The man scowled.

"If you are from that place, then say what lies beside it," he said.

"Beside it? You mean its borders?"

The man nodded, and John took it for an affirmative.

"The Atlantic Ocean to the east; Pacific Ocean to the west; Canada, north; Mexico, south. Is that what you mean?" John asked.

"Atlantic, Pacific, Canada, Mexico." He recited the names and nodded his head. At last he asked, with great incredulity, "How can you be here?"

"I don't know. I just am." John didn't even consider attempting to explain. "Do you know how I could get back?"

The man shook his head. During the course of the conversation, his arms had slowly lowered back down to his sides. He took a few steps closer and John decided that he could afford to meet his new companion halfway. He was bigger, and he wasn't already injured. The odds favored him.

Up close, John could smell the wet wool of the man's coat. John guessed that he himself smelled much worse.

"Only the Holy Gateway can link the worlds," the man said, "and only Kahlil'im can cross it."

"Kahlil'im?" John was pretty sure that the Holy Gateway had to be something like the yellow ruin he, Laurie, and Bill had found in the mountains. "Who's Kahlil'im?"

"Maybe me. Others are training in Rathal'pesha hel vun'im'ati lafti'ya pom'an." The man didn't seem to notice that he had slipped out of English.

"I didn't really understand all of that. You were speaking ... What's your language called?"

"Basawar. The world and the word are one." The man smiled as he said this. He had a nice smile, the kind that New York advertising agencies would have loved to plaster all over cereal boxes.

"Yura'hir—" The man caught himself this time. "I'm sorry. I only speak these words in training. It's hard to remember."

"You're doing better than I would." John shifted uncomfortably. His feet were starting to get cold.

"You were saying that you are Kahlil'im?" John reminded him.

"I may be. Someday." The man frowned at the crushed snowdrift where he had fallen. "I still must learn how to make myself go where I should and not to bleed so much." He touched his right forearm.

"A Kahlil'im must be teaching you, then?"

"A Kahlil," the young man corrected him offhandedly. "Kahlil'im means many; Kahlil is only one. There are no Kahlil'im left," the man went on. "The last was torn to pieces between the worlds. What I learn is from the priests who keep Ushmana'lam, the holiest books. They can read the words, but they ... " he paused, "they cannot do everything the words say."

"So there are no Kahlil'im left?"

"Issin," the young man said, then caught himself. "There are none."

"So there's no way to open the Holy Gateway?" John continued.

"None."

John noticed that the man spoke certain words with the same accent he had detected in Kyle. Now that he thought about it, John realized that the man resembled his old roommate physically as well. He wasn't as muscular or as tall, and he lacked tattoos and scars, but he could have passed for Kyle's younger brother. He had the same dark eyes and full mouth.

"There isn't some kind of key that would do it?" John hoped his leading questions didn't seem as obvious to the man as they did to him.

"A key is given to Kahlil," the man said, "but only Kahlil can use it."

So Kyle must have been a Kahlil. That explained the key that had come in the mail. The words 'ripped to pieces between the worlds' made John feel suddenly sorry that he hadn't treated Kyle better. He wondered if being ripped to pieces had been a direct result of his theft of the key, then stopped himself. He already had enough guilt about bringing Laurie and Bill to this wasteland. He didn't need Kyle's death on his conscience as well.

He asked, "So, do you have a key yet?"

"No, just a black blood knife."

"Does the knife open anything?" John knew he was grasping, but he supposed it was better to ask than not.

"Cuts," the man answered.

He shoved his hands into his coat pockets. For a moment, John thought he would produce the knife, but he didn't. He just kept his hands tucked into the coat's protection. John felt a chill across the back of his neck as the wind picked up.

"It's cold, and I have been gone too long. I must go home, or I will be whipped." The man started to walk north through the snow.

"Wait!" John followed him. "I need to know how I can return to my own home."

"Have you been gone too long as well?" He didn't stop, but he slowed enough for John to catch up with him.

"Yes, I've been gone for a long time now." John decided that he could afford to walk with him for at least an hour before he had to turn back to the shelter.

"You must miss your family." The man wasn't looking at John but at the mountains.

"I miss my home."

The man paused and studied John. He said, "I could bring you with me to Rathal'pesha, but ..."

"But what?"

"I think they would burn you."

A chill sank through John's guts.

"Why would they burn me?"

"Maybe you aren't from the other world. Maybe you're a spy for the Fai'daum. Maybe you're a witch. They can find reasons as easily as turning over stones." The man began walking again.

"I speak English. I know where America is. That convinced you that I was telling the truth, didn't it?" John asked.

"No," the man said, "I believe you because I want to. You seem honest to me, but Ushman Dayyid and Ushman Nuritam don't want to believe anyone. They don't want to believe me, and I have the God's own bones. They would burn you right away, and then you would never go home."

"Would you be willing to help me get home?"

"I might." Again the man looked up at the mountains. "I don't know what I can do for you."

"Could you come back here and tell me more about your world? That would at least help me not get myself burned." John kept doggedly at it. He could not let this resource go without a fight, for all their sakes.

"Will you tell me about yours?" the man countered.

"Of course."

"Good." The man smiled at him. For a few minutes they strode along quietly together, side by side. John knew he had to turn back soon, but he didn't want to. His hope of finding a way home rested entirely with this man about whom he knew next to nothing.

"Can I ask what your name is, or what I should call you?" John asked at last.

"Are you turning back now?" the man asked.

"I was thinking of it. Why?"

"Some traders only exchange names with a new friend just before they part. Then, if their families have bad blood between them, it will not have ruined their time traveling together."

"I didn't know that," John said.

"I hadn't told you my name so that you would keep walking with me." The man glanced sideways at him. "It's good to have some company on such a long walk, but I shouldn't bring you any further. It won't be safe once we reach the river."

"Well, my name is John." John held out his hand, and the man blinked at it. Then he seemed to remember something and reached out to grip John's hand firmly.

"I am Ushiri Ravishan'inRathal'pesha."

"I don't think I'll remember all that," John admitted.

"You only need to call me Ravishan. The rest is title and place. It is not who I am."

"Ravishan," John repeated the name. "Will I see you again?"

The man nodded. "I must go now, but I will try to come back in four days."

"I'll see you then. Goodbye." John gave him a brief wave.

"Tumah." Ravishan briefly lifted his hands to his chest and then turned and continued walking north through the little rises and valleys of snow. John watched until he disappeared into the dark line of the distant trees.

John turned back. He brushed the snow back over both his and Ravishan's tracks as he went. His body bristled with an excited energy, making him want to go quickly and carelessly. But he forced himself to be thorough, to cover his tracks and slowly wind his way back to the shelter. He couldn't afford to take chances.

A lot of things could go wrong in four days.

Chapter Nine

"Loshai," John said in response to Ravishan's gesture at the pale, blue afternoon sky. Ravishan smiled his cereal box smile.

The spring air was cool but not cold. The last of the snow had melted away, leaving the ground carpeted in pale, mossy leaves and grass shoots. White leaf-buds dotted the black branches of the trees above them.

They had moved their shelter to higher ground when runoff from the mountains flooded the lower lands. Water rolled slowly between the higher stands of trees and washed far out to the east, until it spilled down the steep walls of the chasm in an immense waterfall. West of their camp John had found a deep slow moving river, where the fishing seemed particularly good. As he often did, Ravishan had appeared from the thin air and joined him on the river bank. Today they indulged in an impromptu language lesson.

"Loshai'hir pesha'an sa?" Ravishan asked and John concentrated on his voice. John didn't want to hear the words as much as see the images they represented. He wanted to understand them, not in the slow manner of matching their meanings to English equivalents, but as words in their own right.

It was a difficult thing to do. The inflections and pauses of Basawar contained such subtlety. Sometimes John found himself listening to the language with the same uncomprehending appreciation that he had for pure music.

"Iss. Loshai'hir holima'an," John finally answered.

The sky is white?

No, the sky is blue.

It was such a simple exchange. John wanted to be better than this. He needed to be better if he ever hoped to get into the city of Amura'taye, much less reach the massive, walled monastery of Rathal'pesha and the key that would take them home.

If he could just find work in Amura'taye, he might be able to buy medicine for Bill, or at least food beyond what John hunted and the scraps that Ravishan secreted to them in his coat pockets.

Then there was the matter of the keys and the gateway. He had steadily learned, through his conversations with Ravishan, that the payshmura priests kept the keys somewhere in Rathal'pesha. There were maps to the gateways as well. Ravishan hadn't seen either, but he had overheard Ushman Nuritam talking to Ushman Dayyid about them.

"One more question?" Ravishan asked.

"One more," John agreed. They had been talking for hours. Ravishan would have to get home soon. He had already stayed out too late with John on too many previous days.

John pulled up the delicate piece of netting that Ravishan had brought him. Two nearly transparent, white fish flopped against the fine mesh. John pulled them free and dropped them into the reed basket with the others. They were tiny fish. All of them together were hardly enough to feed him alone.

"Yura'hir li'ati pashim'um sa?" Ravishan smiled sleepily and yawned as he asked the question. He loved slurring his words or disguising them to challenge John.

"Yura'ati pashim'um sa?" John asked thoughtfully. He could see the pleased gleam in Ravishan's lowered eyes at stumping him.

"Sa?" Ravishan prompted.

"Du." John nodded. "Li'im pashim, pashim'sho." Yes, we are friends, great friends.

Ravishan broke into a grin at the answer. It pleased him when he could confound John, but it delighted him much more when John succeeded.

"Laman'Jahn'hir, domu'ya," Ravishan complimented him, not only affirming John's progress, but adding a scholar's honorific to his name. It struck John as quite an exaggeration. However, Ravishan seemed to take great pleasure in addressing him as Laman. John guessed it was the same kind of humor that fueled the widespread phenomenon of three-hundred-pound giants nicknamed 'Tiny.'

"Li'hir renma'ya." Ravishan leaned back against a tree and closed his eyes.

John knew from Ravishan's posture as much as his words that Ravishan was tired.

His right arm was wrapped in white bandages, and soft, blue shadows hung beneath his eyes. He breathed slowly and deeply, as if he were falling asleep. His lips parted slightly, and his hands hung limp. When he relaxed completely like this, John became acutely aware of how attractive Ravishan was. And also how very young he seemed.

John knew that he was only five years older than Ravishan, but those five years made a great difference. At seventeen, Ravishan was physically close to adulthood. He stood nearly as tall as John. His body was muscular and graceful from years of training in the monastery. Only a little of the softness of boyhood remained in his face.

Yet his affection was so strong and uninhibited, it seemed very childlike. By nature, Ravishan was friendly and outgoing. So much so that, at times, John had to remind himself that Ravishan probably had no idea of how flirtatious his behavior might seem. More than likely he was like this with any adult who showed him kindness. His long smiles and lingering gaze were simply the affectations of a lonely teenager. And he showed traces of adolescent rebelliousness as well. For one thing, he loved slipping away from his practices to meet with his new, secret friend.

"I don't want to say I am a milkman." Ravishan spoke without opening his eyes.

"What?" John didn't really see the significance of the statement.

"Ushman Dayyid and Ushman Nuritam say that when I cross into the other world, I must say that I deliver milk." Ravishan scowled. "Why can't I say that I'm a soldier? Or a wandering scholar? Why should we all say we are milkmen? I'd rather be something different, something interesting, like a—" he paused, thinking, "—like a pope. I might say that I am a powerful pope."

John struggled to keep from laughing.

"No one would believe you if you said that you were the Pope."
Ravishan sighed.

"Milkman is so boring," Ravishan said, but offered no other argument.

"It's a job that no one will ask you about because it's boring." John knew that well enough. He hadn't asked Kyle about his work.

It was strange to think of Kyle now that John knew he had been one of the Kahlil'im. John remembered the scars on Kyle's arms and glanced at Ravishan's bandages. Some of the cuts had been administered by the priests in a bloodletting ceremony that supposedly drained impure desires from the body and allowed the sacred bones within to take greater power. Other wounds came from Ravishan's attempts to jump between spaces.

When he disappeared from sight, he submerged into a soundless, gray world. It allowed him to move at blinding speeds through solid walls and over rivers. But it came at a cost. There was abrasiveness to the Gray Space. Ravishan had once described it as so cold that it seemed to burn and had said that it was filled with slicing edges that cut in and out. At times, it sliced through his flesh and left tiny blisters on his skin.

Ravishan always proudly pointed out that, because of his great skill, his injuries were far less than those the other boys in training suffered. Three other ushiri had been blinded; another two had died when they materialized inside solid objects.

That was only traveling through the Gray Space within one world. It was nothing compared to passing through the white agony that filled the space between worlds. Ravishan only knew of it through the priests, and they only knew from the writings of the Kahlil'im who had gone before. It blinded and burned and sliced bodies to ribbons. Without the sacred gateways and the keys that opened them, even a Kahlil would be killed crossing between worlds.

As Ravishan had described the dangers, John had thought of the gash across Kyle's mouth and his constant bandages. And he had wondered what Kyle had done while they lived together. How many times had he crossed between worlds? And what had he done when he realized his key was gone?

John never should have taken that key. Never.

"I don't want to be boring to them," Ravishan interrupted John's thoughts. "I want them to talk with me, like you do."

"The people of my world?" John asked.

Ravishan nodded.

"I don't think you're going to be boring to anyone even if you try," John assured him. "You're going to be pretty exotic looking. Once you receive those Prayerscars, you'll have to try hard just passing for normal in my world, trust me." Not for the first time, John considered telling Ravishan about Kyle. But he wasn't sure how Ravishan would take it. John knew that stealing Kyle's key wouldn't come across as a good thing, no matter how he worded it.

He and Bill and Laurie all depended upon Ravishan's good will for their survival in and eventual escape from the world of Basawar. Ravishan brought them clothes and food, and he'd told no one about them. Also, Ravishan would have access to a key someday. So far, that seemed to be their only hope for returning home. For now his friendship was too important, and too new, to burden with unpleasant revelations.

Ravishan sighed again and then said, "I just don't want to say I'm a milkman."

"Maybe you just don't want to obey Ushman Dayyid," John suggested.

"Maybe," Ravishan said. "I'm tired of him. He shouts at me when I do what he wants, and if I can't do what he wants, he shouts louder."

"Sounds like he's frustrated."

"Vun'hir wahbai," Ravishan murmured.

"He's an asshole?"

"You understood that?" Ravishan asked.

"Perfectly." John smiled.

"Domu, Laman'Jahn, domu." Ravishan grinned. "Soon you will know all of the profane words."

"It's the small triumphs that make life worth living."

A noise from farther back among the trees alerted them to the presence of others. They went silent and peered into the shadows. Even now that Bill and Laurie wore the clothes Ravishan had brought from Rathal'pesha, John instantly recognized them. They were much more slender than the few shepherds that John had seen. And they moved more cautiously, as if the knowledge that they were trespassers in this world had suffused even their muscles.

"Tumah, Vur'Loshai. Tumah, Vun'Behr." Ravishan greeted both of them with his hand raised in peace.

Ravishan had given them all Basawar names. He called Laurie, Loshai. Bill, Behr. And John's name had shifted to Jahn.

Laurie waved. Bill made a little shrugging motion, as if he were too tired to raise his arm, which might have actually been the case.

"Tumah, Ushiri Ravishan." Laurie mimicked Ravishan's gesture. Bill said, "Hey."

"What's up, my man?" Ravishan strode to Bill and held out his palm for Bill to slap. Today Bill only batted his fingers weakly.

"I feel like crap." Bill sat down beside a tree and rested his head on his knees. Laurie knelt down next to him and rubbed his back.

Ravishan frowned and crouched down beside them.

"Behr," Ravishan said, "your breathing still troubles you?"

"Yeah, same old story." Bill lifted his head. "So what have you two been up to?"

"Just talking," John said. "Trying to fish."

"Any luck with that?" Laurie asked.

"I caught a few." John tapped the reed basket with his foot. "Nothing compared to the weasels though. Those little guys can really swim."

"Weasels?" Ravishan looked up at him. It was rare for him to not know a word, but it did happen from time to time.

"Ganal'im," John supplied.

"Sa? Ganal'im Nayeshi'hir sa?" Ravishan asked.

"Iss. Hel shir'ro ganal'im," John pointed out over the water where the white weasels splashed and dived after fish. "Weasel shir'ro ganal, iff otter shir'kin ganal."

"Could we please speak English, today?" Bill broke in before Ravishan could ask more.

"Sorry," John said. He hadn't really noticed when he had stopped speaking English.

"Thanks." Bill leaned his head back down against his knees.

"Do you want me to take you back to the shelter?" He had carried Bill before, when Bill just couldn't move without beginning to choke. That had been back during the coldest days of winter. John had hoped that the warmer weather would make things easier for Bill.

"I'm sick of the fucking shelter. I just want to be somewhere else." Bill closed his eyes. "I want to go home."

Laurie wrapped her arms around him and he leaned into her. Their small bodies were almost lost in the folds of their gray wool coats.

"We're gonna go home," Laurie said. "We'll have pizza and macaroni and cheese and beer and hot showers—and we'll watch movies."

"Any movies I want?" Bill asked.

"Any movies you want."

"Even—"

"—*Erotic Coven II,*" Laurie finished.

"You're the best, you know that?" Bill said.

"Yeah, but I'm glad you do too." Laurie kissed the top of his head.

"I don't think I even care about stupid *Erotic Coven II* anymore," Bill said. "I just want to breathe. I just ..."

"I know." Laurie pushed his hair back from his face. "It's gonna happen. I promise."

"Behr," Ravishan had to crouch down to get his face as low as Bill's, "when I become Kahlil, I promise that I will return you home. I'm sorry that I brought you here."

"You didn't bring us. We—" Laurie cut herself off when she saw John's expression. "It just happened."

"That's how it would seem to you, but I prayed to Parfir for an entire year. I asked him to bring me a new teacher." Ravishan glanced up at John. "I begged him to bring me someone who would help me."

"Well, we've certainly been a lot of help for you so far," Bill said.

"You have," Ravishan said. "Before you were here, I dreaded every day. I only thought of the pain." He touched his bandaged arm lightly. "When I thought of crossing through the gateway, and when I imagined the pain of it, I nearly cried. I'm ashamed of myself now, but then I even thought of running away."

"You still get injured when you cross," John said.

"It doesn't seem so bad," Ravishan replied. "Now I can't wait to wake up and practice my skills and bring you things and talk with you out here. And now I know that I will be Kahlil. You are my sign that these little cuts aren't for nothing. Someday, I will return you all to your home, and I will defeat the Fai'daum in my own world." Ravishan smiled, one of his truly handsome smiles. He seemed to glow with belief and happiness.

It was this kind of pure enthusiasm, John thought, that inspired the Children's Crusades in the Middle Ages. Only someone young and inexperienced could so completely and easily give himself over to faith and sacrifice. Ravishan wanted to believe this, and he would believe it. He had not yet learned that a coincidence could be just that, or worse, that adults around him might use his faith for their own needs.

"You know," Laurie's voice was soft, "when we first came here, I knew it had to be for a purpose."

"You were brought for me," Ravishan said. "I'm sorry that you've had to suffer, but I give you my word that I will take care of you."

Laurie's smile was nearly as childlike as Ravishan's. "I knew there was a reason for all of this."

Ravishan straightened. He looked up at the sky and frowned.

"I have to return to Rathal'pesha. Ushman Dayyid will expect me early today since I was late yesterday." He began to lift his hands in peace then paused. "Behr, I will see if I can find a medicine for you. There is a drink that our healer, Hann'yu, gives us when our lungs are torn. I'll bring it two days from now."

"Thanks, Ravi." Bill raised his hand in the symbol of peace. "Tumah."

Ravishan smiled and returned the gesture to all three of them.

"Tumah," he said, and then he closed his eyes and was gone.

John waited a few minutes in silence. He didn't know why,

except that he couldn't quite believe that Ravishan had simply gone. Some superstitious part of him worried that atoms of Ravishan still lingered in the air, listening and watching.

"You shouldn't encourage him to take responsibility for us being here," John said at last.

"What do you mean?" Laurie asked.

"I mean that he has enough problems in his life. He doesn't need to think that he did this to us on top of everything else."

"How do you know he didn't?" Laurie asked.

"Because I was there when we went through that gateway. I was the one turning that fucking key, and I'm the one who lost it." John didn't raise his voice. Instead, he stepped closer to Laurie. "I did this to us, not him."

"How can you be so closed-minded after everything that's happened?" Laurie demanded. "We don't know what brought us here, and we don't know why. Maybe Ravishan does."

"She's got a point, man," Bill said.

John glared at Bill. "Ravishan did not bring us here. He's just a teenager."

"Children can have tremendous psychic energy, John," Laurie said, "particularly teenagers. A lot of people believe that the conflicted energy in a troubled adolescent can even create—"

"This isn't some tarot reading at a strip mall!" John cut her off. "This isn't some New Age feel-good movie."

"Hey—" Bill began.

"Shut up," John snapped. "This is a place where they burn people alive. This is a place where they cut the shit out of Ravishan and whip him for disobedience. He could be killed for what he's doing for us. We have no right to make him take total responsibility for us!"

"I didn't say he had to take total responsibility," Laurie shot back, fire in her eyes, "but we don't know why we were called here. Maybe we were the answer to his prayers."

"Or maybe we were fucking around with something, and it just happened," John replied. "Maybe Ravishan should have run away, but now he thinks that he has to stay and suffer to save us."

"How can you be so negative?" Laurie demanded.

"It's called realism," John replied.

"It's pretty negative realism," Bill put in.

"Look," John shoved his hair back from his face, "I don't care what bizarre ideas you choose for your own life. I don't care what you say when you're helping your beautician clientele decide what hair color resonates with their higher powers. I don't give a damn about that. But this is Ravishan's life. If he needs to get the hell out of that monastery, then he should be able to. We shouldn't be stopping him."

Laurie didn't say anything. She just stared at John like she was about to cry.

"You know, John, you can be a real asshole when you've got a crush on a guy," Bill said. "I never noticed that before."

"That has nothing to do with this—and I do not have a crush on him. He's a kid," John snapped.

"Yeah, whatever." Bill shrugged. "Laurie and I should probably get back to the shelter and start dinner."

Bill struggled to his feet. Laurie got up quickly and helped him. John suddenly felt like an ass.

"I'm not trying to—" he began, but Bill cut him off.

"It's okay, Toffee. We get it. Nobody is gonna feel good about anything ever. Don't worry."

"I didn't say that," John said.

"No," Bill said. "You don't need to say anything more. We stupid flakes can only take so much of your super-smarter-than-everyone-else Realism. We're just gonna go back home and pick our butts like we always do."

"I didn't say you were picking your butts," John said.

Laurie made a weird noise like she had been crying and then laughed. Her hair hung over her face. She wouldn't look up at him.

"I'm sorry," John said. "I am an asshole. I'm just really worried about Ravishan."

Laurie pushed her hair back. Her eyes were red, but there weren't any tears.

"It's okay. You're right about pressuring him." She sniffed and wiped her nose. "But, you know, sometimes it really hurts when you won't even consider what I have to say. You just put all of my beliefs down like they didn't mean anything."

"I know. I'm sorry." John knew this was all he could say. He couldn't make himself say that he was wrong.

"So, are you staying out tonight, or are you coming home?" Laurie asked.

"I'm staying out."

One of the strong points of their friendship had always been that they could be apart for a long time and still remember each other and their fondness. Until now they had never had to test their friendship under the opposite circumstances. Eight months in one tiny shelter was more than some marriages could endure. They needed time apart.

"Here," John grabbed the reed basket and handed it to Laurie, "you should have these tonight."

"Thanks," Laurie said. She and Bill started back through the trees.

John lay back, concentrating on the feel of the ground beneath him. It didn't have the strong, rich smell of the earth he was used to. The soil of Basawar seemed emaciated by comparison. It responded to him with eagerness and desperation, rolling up under his fingers, curling close to his body. He traced the slight rise and fall of the earth as if he were stroking the skeletal ribs of a hungry dog. He knew that this was where his sense of reality came from. If he were honest with himself, that was just as absurd as any of Laurie's beliefs. Still, he felt it so keenly and so very personally that he could neither question this communion nor share it with anyone else. This was his private faith.

Overhead, thin black branches arched up against the pale blue sky. Even on clear days like this one, the skies of Basawar were never bright blue. They, like the soil, were drained, exhausted. They reminded John of the bleached remains of dying corals or of cut flowers, all their vitality and color bleeding away into a vase.

John frowned at his own morbid turn of thought. Bill had been right about his negativity and about his feelings toward Ravishan as well. John did feel a stirring of attraction toward him. But John had no intention of allowing that pang of desire to affect any of their lives. He was just lonely—and Ravishan…

John considered the way Ravishan smiled, how radiant he seemed when they walked together or stood close. In another man, John would have found those glances and smiles flirtatious, but he refused to believe that Ravishan could be knowingly seducing him.

Life in the monastery had deprived Ravishan of normal human affection, and so he probably had no idea how easily his responsiveness to John's attention could be misconstrued.

But John would never allow himself to cross that line. Never. Not only was Ravishan just a kid, but also far too much depended on his continued generosity to risk alienating him with the complexities of adult desires.

John closed his eyes, feeling tired of this foreign place.

In his own world, when he felt this miserable, he could lose himself in the richness of the earth. It seemed to nourish him just with a touch. He tried to recapture that sensation. He relaxed and spread his fingers into the ground. A sense of motion rushed over him. He could feel his hands holding the dirt, his back pressed into the ground. But within his mind there came a dreamlike sense of whipping over the ground like a breath of wind.

He rushed out to the east, skipping across the surface of the water. He felt the rending break of the chasm walls as they dropped for miles straight down to a cold, dark ocean. The black walls of the chasm hurt him, like the edges of an open wound.

John flinched from it, and suddenly he was rushing north. He whipped over the soft shoots of grass and grinned as they tickled him. He swept up and dived between the thick stands of trees. Then he seemed to break out into a clearing.

Huge walls, cut from the face of a mountain, stretched up. He rushed over them, sweeping across terraced steps of farmland, bent men and women pushing seeds into the soil, and heavy-coated sheep. He swept over another wall into a maze of cramped, narrow streets. Men on heavy bicycles crowded the thoroughfares, and the scent of cooking fires filled the air. The smell clung to John, and he went higher, rising over hundreds of steep steps that wound up to the peak of the mountain.

With a surge over a last tall, white wall, he dropped down into an open courtyard. Dwarf trees twisted up from alabaster planters. Latticed walls of pale stone wound along pathways. The air smelled of incense and pine.

Without even considering, John knew that he gazed upon Rathal'pesha, the monastery of the white mountain.

A figure in dark gray robes sat beside one of the dwarf pines. The figure looked up, and John saw that it was Ravishan. He smiled and then lowered his head again in prayer.

John felt a deep relief to see that Ravishan had gotten home safely.

Then he opened his eyes and found himself lying on his back, staring into the dark night sky. He must have fallen asleep hours ago, he realized. He'd been dreaming.

John started to rise, but stilled when he heard unfamiliar voices. There were men in the woods, a little to the north of him. John could see them by the light of their fire. Twenty or more, dressed in rust-red coats, armed with rifles. They sat in a circle, a few of them facing out into the darkness, keeping watch.

They were being addressed, it appeared, by a large yellow dog.

Chapter Ten

John lay still in the darkness, watching and listening. Behind him the slow-moving waters of the river lapped quietly at the muddy bank. Just a few yards ahead of him, the shadows of men and trees jumped and flickered in the firelight. A gentle wind brought the scent of wood smoke to him.

The dog paced around the fire, moving among the gathered men. Her thick yellow coat bristled and relaxed as she spoke. Her voice was rough, but feminine like that of a chain-smoking blues singer. Her eyes caught the firelight from time to time and seemed to glow out into the darkness of the woods.

He wanted to understand what was being said, but he could hardly believe what he was seeing. He would have thought that years of talking animals in pet food commercials and other advertisements would have inured him to the strangeness of it. But those animals were manmade manipulations. This was a genuine dog. Speaking.

He watched as her lips curled and parted with the perfect flow of Basawar words. She was definitely speaking. The dog barred her teeth and the last of her sentence came out in a low growl.

John turned his head to gaze up into the dark night sky. He couldn't look at her and think about the foreign words at the same time. It was just too much for him to manage at once. He concentrated on the smoky barroom voice.

"Ashan ..."

That meant brothers.

"Shir' rashan'ati rashiadu'hi ..."

We must kill ...something unclean? No, John thought ...soldiers ...guards.

She went on speaking as he tried desperately to follow her.

John knew he was missing words. He dug his hands into the warm soil. Grass shoots seemed to curl around his fingers like they were returning his grip, gentle and assuring.

He had to know if these people would kill him; if they were moving toward the shelter. He had to listen the way he listened to Ravishan, hearing the language like music, feeling the meaning, simply knowing.

He closed his eyes and forced himself to relax as he did in his exercises with Ravishan, letting the words wash over him.

"Ashan," the dog said, "we will not waste ammunition in warning shots this time. Take the guards down right away. I want clean shots to the heads or through the hearts. We don't have the time or spare ammunition to fuck around." A low growl carried through her last words.

"Daru, you and Saimura will come in from the back," she went on. "Your objective will be to take the ushiri candidate alive. Kill anyone else, but Sabir wants that boy alive. You understand?"

"Perfectly," came the response.

"Good. The rest of us will keep the way open for you. Since the group is traveling with a fucking ushiri candidate, we'll need to watch out for the real thing. Look for the braids. If you even think you've got a Payshmura ushiri or ushman in your sights, put a bullet straight into his head. Don't pause. Don't think about it. Shoot. Got it?"

"Got it." The response came in a hushed unison from some twenty different voices.

"Good." There was a brief pause for a sound almost like a yawn. "This is the Bousim family's private convoy we're taking on."

"Priest-sucking noblemen," a young man spat.

"Well-armed noblemen," the dog growled. "Their guns are going to be better than ours, they'll be mounted, and the guards will be professional soldiers. Real rashan'im."

"Do they have the new guns?" a different man asked.

"Yes." The dog sighed heavily. "Our friends in Nurjima say the Bousim family purchased five hundred of the new breech-loading carbines. So, we can't count on having much time to hit them while they're reloading shots. We need to take them down before they even get their guns up."

"That's why you had us hauling scrap iron and blasting powder in the packs. We're mining the Holy Road under their feet, aren't we?" It was the same young man who had asked about the guns. He sounded pleased.

"Yes, Saimura. Let's hope the blasts blow them up the Thousand Steps to Heaven's Door." The dog's voice was low and amused. John heard other quiet laughs. She continued, "The Bousim convoy should be this far north by morning. We'll need to have the mines in place before then. Let's get unpacked and get to work. Saimura, Daru, you two sleep. I want you rested for tomorrow."

"You got it, Ji," an older man's voice responded. Daru, presumably.

"I'm already asleep on my feet." Saimura's voice was now familiar to John.

Afterward, he heard the rustling of thick cloth and the low rasps of heavy pieces of metal. He opened his eyes and looked over toward the men who ringed the low-burning fire. Their silhouettes melted in and out of each other as they reached and passed objects between themselves. They spoke, but too softly for John to discern.

The dog continued to pace. When the wind picked up, she lifted her head and inhaled deeply. She swung her head toward John and stared into the darkness, sniffing. John's breath caught in his chest. He didn't exhale, fearing that she would smell it. After a moment, the dog turned away and drew in the scents coming from the north.

John didn't doubt that she had caught the scent of him, but perhaps his smell had not struck her as belonging to a man. John imagined that if he had had a bath in the last seven months she would have discovered him immediately. But, as was, he hadn't been near soap or a fire and those were two of the most distinctively human scents.

Dressed in weasel skin, with fish blood, soil and grass staining his hands and hair, no trace of civilization clung to him. He smelled only of his surroundings, but the same wasn't true of Laurie or Bill. They both cooked with fire and the perfume of wood smoke clung to them always. If Laurie came out to get him, the dog would doubtless notice her right away. There was also the problem of what would happen if any of the men came down closer for water.

He doubted that these men would have any qualms about murdering him. It was obvious from their conversation that they were already committed to killing a good number of people. The fact that they had to be explicitly told when they were expected to keep someone alive seemed particularly telling.

They outnumbered John and they were armed with rifles and explosives. He possessed only his hunting knife and a sharpened stick that he used as a fishing spear.

John considered the wooded land in front of him. The trees weren't close enough to offer reliable cover. And he was sure that the dog would see him if he stood up. That only left the stream behind him. Its slow flow would take him south, closer to the shelter. But it would make for a terribly cold trip.

Carefully John rolled onto his stomach and pushed himself backwards. His feet slid across the cool mud and then slipped into the cold shallows. Water seeped into John's boots and soaked into his pants. Slick, clammy mud slithered into his shirt and clung to his arms and chest. His body slipped further back into the water with a soft gurgle. He caught his breath as the frigid water rolled against his groin and stomach.

The stream's current caught his legs and hips, tugging gently at him. It washed up over his back and sent involuntary shudders through the muscles of his arms. Icy water splashed against his face. He clenched his jaw to keep his teeth from chattering.

John dragged his hands over the muddy floor. He numbly grabbed the smooth stones and fine webs of tree roots. He rolled to his back, keeping his face above the shallow water. The sky above him looked endlessly black and the stars seemed far too bright.

The current pulled him slowly away from the scent and flickers of the fire. As he drifted away, a wild idea came to John. It was almost crazy, but if it worked, he might be able to get them into the town of Amura'taye.

John floated and thought until he knew he was beyond even the dog's earshot. Then, clumsy with cold and shaking, he pulled himself out of the water and stumbled back to the shelter. The slightest breeze prickled his skin and set his teeth chattering.

Even after he ducked inside the insulated warmth of the shelter, the shivering and chattering made his explanation to Laurie and Bill come out with starts and jumps of vibrato.

John stripped off his wet clothes as he talked. Laurie silently handed him the weasel skin pants she had been sewing for him. John pulled them on. One leg was much longer than the other, though neither reached John's ankles.

Bill held the flashlight up, lighting the piles of their bedding and discarded winter rags as John dug through them. When John glanced back at him, he noticed that Bill had pulled his blanket around himself more closely, as if just looking at John's chilled body made him cold.

"A talking dog?" Laurie asked at last. "You call me a flake and then come back and say you saw a talking dog?"

"I didn't actually say you were a flake," John said. "Bill said that."

"Don't try to pin it on me." Bill only poked his face out of the blankets.

"You implied it." Laurie pointed at John's bare chest.

"Look, I can only say I'm sorry so many times." John picked up a scrap of cloth and realized that it was a remnant of one of his two sweaters. He pulled it on. The arms were missing but it covered his chest.

"Saying you're sorry once more isn't going to kill you." Laurie held out one of her own filthy but dry socks. John reached for it only to have Laurie pull it back from his grasp.

John sighed.

"Fine," he said. Laurie had always been like this as far back as the second grade.

"I'm very sorry." He held out his hand for the sock.

"Very, very sorry?"

"Yes." John frowned. He really wasn't in the mood for this.

"Maybe very, very, very sorry?" Laurie waved the sock at him.

"I am sorrow incarnate," John growled. "I have no other name."

"Ooh. That's a good one." Laurie relinquished the sock.

"I think the other one is here somewhere." Bill shifted around in his blanket, then produced a second sock. "You can apologize to me later about something else."

"That's very kind of you." John forced his feet into the small socks. Despite the holes in the toes and heel, his feet felt immediately warmer. He pawed through the clothing for something to use as a coat.

"Why are you getting dressed now?" Bill asked.

"I'm going to go down the road and find the Bousim convoy those men were talking about."

"Don't you mean that the dog was talking about?" Laurie asked.

John shrugged. That fact seemed too absurd to reiterate, particularly now that Laurie looked so smug.

Bill said, "I don't know if getting involved is the best idea."

"It may not be," John admitted, "but I have to at least warn them."

"Wait," Laurie's pleased expression disappeared, "you're not going out now? With a bunch of gun-toting killers out there?"

"I'm not going out to meet up with the killers," John said. "I'm going in the opposite direction, south, to the convoy they're planning on ambushing."

"Why?" Laurie demanded. "Nearly drowning and freezing to death wasn't enough for one day?"

"I just got wet and cold," John said. "Someone in that convoy is being admitted into Rathal'pesha as an ushiri."

"Ushiri?" Bill asked. "Isn't Ravi an ushiri or something?"

John nodded. "A priest training to become Kahlil."

"That still doesn't mean you have to go running to warn them in the dead of night," Laurie said.

"It'll be too late by morning." John tried to pull on the coat Ravishan had brought for Bill. It was too small to get his shoulders into. He stripped it off again. "This convoy belongs to the

Bousim—the noble family that rules most of the north. If I can help them, then they could definitely get us into Amura'taye. We can get out of this shelter."

"What if these guys don't care if you were nice and warned them?" Laurie asked. "Weren't you just yelling at me for forgetting that this is a place where they burn people alive! Wasn't it those Payshmura priests and their Bousim friends that did that?"

"Ravishan said that the men they burned were Fai'daum—" John began but Laurie cut him off.

"And that means what?" Laurie held up her hands questioningly.

"They're an organization of bandits and robbers. They have some kind of grudge against the Payshmura priests and the nobles who support them. They've been known to slaughter pilgrims and burn down churches."

"Maybe because the priests keep burning them alive," Bill muttered.

"Maybe," John agreed. "I don't know and it doesn't really matter."

"Yeah? Well, how do you know that these guys aren't going to think that you're one of those Fai'daum when you come running up to them?" Laurie demanded.

"Because I think the men I overheard were Fai'daum. If we could prevent them from being successful, then I think that it would prove that we have no affiliation with them. We have a lot better chance of being allowed into Amura'taye if we can do that."

"It doesn't matter what I say, does it?" Laurie asked. "You're going to go no matter what, aren't you?"

John picked up his hunting knife and tucked it into his belt.

"I think it would be the best thing I could do for all our sakes. We need a better shelter and better food and we need to find a doctor for Bill. Plus, Amura'taye is at the foot of Rathal'pesha. Ravishan wouldn't have to travel so far to meet with us."

"It won't do us much good if you just get killed," Laurie said.

"He won't get killed," Bill said quietly.

Laurie scowled at Bill, who simply shrugged in response.

"You're not going to get yourself killed, right?" he asked John.

"No," John said flatly.

"That's supposed to prove something?" Laurie demanded.

"Sweetie," Bill reached out and caught her hand, "he's a big boy."

Laurie frowned but let Bill pull her back into his arms. Bill kissed her and Laurie sighed.

"You're both stupid male idiots," Laurie murmured. Bill kissed her again.

John picked up his boots and tugged them back on. They were still wet, but they were better than nothing. He frowned at his ragged coat. If he wrung the water out of it, it shouldn't be too bad. The heat of his body would probably warm it up soon enough.

"Should we come with you?" Laurie asked.

"I don't think so." It was a polite offer, one that Laurie had to know he would decline. They all knew it. John moved faster on his own. He also spoke Basawar the best of all of them.

"I should be back soon but if not ..." John couldn't think of anything that either of them should do if something happened to him. "Tell Ravishan what happened. He'll probably have heard something at Rathal'pesha."

"Be careful, okay?" Laurie said.

"Yeah, if it gets sketchy just come back," Bill advised.

"I will," John assured her. "I'll see you both soon."

He picked up his coat and ducked out of the shelter. Outside, a cool night wind rolled over him. Anticipation and fear surged through his body, making his heart pound and his blood rush in hot pulses. So much could go wrong, but so much could be gained. As he made his way down to the road, the black shadows of the woods seemed full of possibility and for the first time in months he felt real hope.

CHAPTER ELEVEN

The Bousim convoy wasn't hard to locate. Dozens of lanterns beamed between the black tree trunks like beacons. The two coaches and three wagons were festooned with bright lanterns. Light glowed across the black lacquered surfaces of the coaches and glinted over traces of gold filigree. Reflections also gleamed along the lengths of the gun-muzzles and sharp bayonets of the uniformed men riding alongside the carriages and wagons. John counted thirty riders, but he knew he probably missed a few.

The animals harnessed to the carts and carriages and being ridden weren't horses. John didn't know why he had thought they would be. They looked more like deer or antelope. Sharp horns spiraled up from their heads. When the light caught their hides, John saw that they were a greenish tone of gray. A few of them were marked with pale dapples on their faces and hindquarters. He remembered Ravishan telling him that men in Basawar rode tahldi. He had to assume that these were tahldi.

The drivers of the carts and carriages were dressed in thick coats and wore wide brimmed hats. They hunched in their seats. One man looked like he had slipped into a doze. In contrast, the uniformed riders surrounding the carts and carriages held themselves with a militaristic tension that was hard to read. John couldn't know if their alert stances and straight backs were evidence of discipline or apprehension. Their silence, too, might have been a code of conduct. Their expressions were set, almost blank, but their eyes moved constantly, searching for motion in the surrounding night.

Rashan'im, John thought. Cavalrymen like these were called rashan'im. They served in noblemen's private armies.

John crouched in the underbrush at the roadside, half blinded by the brilliance. The convoy proceeded forward at a slow pace.

After watching for a few minutes, he decided that the least threatening approach would be the best. He certainly didn't want to leap out from the woods and get himself shot before he could say a word. It would be wiser to let these nervy men come across him in the open. John crept back farther into the woods. He turned north and sprinted ahead of the convoy. Then he walked out onto the open road to wait.

Months of staying under the cover of the trees and keeping away from the Holy Road made this sudden exposure feel unnatural. He caught himself moving slightly to the side of the road, where the shadows of overhanging branches offered him greater camouflage. He made himself stop and move back out to the center of the road.

Everything was dark. The slight shadows cast by a faint moon and distant stars hardly impacted the surrounding blackness. But to John the subtle differences between the black trees and the dark sky seemed glaring. He could pick out the shapes of leaves on the tree branches and individual stones in the cobbled road. It was probably the result of living so long without light, he reasoned.

John watched the steady approach of the luminous convoy. He could make out the exact shapes of the coaches. Their lanterns burned brightly into his eyes. John rested his gaze on the sharp silhouettes of the rashan'im.

The two men at the lead looked older than John, somewhere in their late thirties or early forties. One was clean-shaven; the other had a thick black beard. Both wore their dark hair clipped very short. The bearded man looked like his nose might have been broken at one time. The other had softer features and a more angular build.

John noticed the small steely insignias that decorated the chests of their coats and the backs of their gloves. Two crossed arrows. The same insignia decorated the carriage doors.

John found it odd that he could clearly see these men while they, still intently staring around them, had not yet noticed him. He wondered if it was just that he knew where to look and what he was looking for. These mounted soldiers didn't know what they should expect to see. John was pretty certain that none of them were expecting him.

Suddenly the clean-shaven rider at the front pulled his mount up short and gave out a call. The entire convoy ground to a halt behind the front riders. John heard muffled whispering voices from farther back. A shadowy head popped out from the window of one of the coaches and then was jerked back in.

"Tumah." John held his hands out in the gesture of peace that Ravishan had taught him.

The clean-shaven rashan lifted his short rifle and took aim at John's chest. All the words John had rehearsed as he had raced through the woods now crashed in a jumble of fear. The formal greetings and proper titles that he had previously decided on seemed dangerously long-winded now.

"I mean you no harm," the Basawar words came to John in a rush.

"Move aside, dog! The Bousim house has neither the time nor patience for your filthy begging." The bearded man addressed John in the derogatory form normally reserved for animals.

Anger flashed through John and for a moment he considered obliging the highhanded demand and letting them just march on to their deaths. It was a terrible and petty urge and John ignored it.

"I am not here to beg, sir." John straightened and lifted his head so that he looked straight into the other man's face. "I live in these woods and I have come to warn you that there's a trap ahead of you on the road."

The clean-shaven man lowered his rifle, just slightly.

The bearded man, obviously the one in charge, continued, "Very well, dog. You may speak. Tell us about this trap."

Again the man's tone grated at John, but he ignored it. He was in no position to demand to be addressed with human respect. He wasn't the one holding a gun.

"I overheard men planning to attack the Bousim family convoy. They said something about taking the ushiri candidate captive."

"What else?"

"They're mining the road. About three leagues north of here, I think. They didn't say where exactly but it has to be this side of the river bridge. After that the woods get too thin to offer any cover. They're expecting you to reach them by early morning."

"How many of them?" the bearded man asked.

"Twenty, I think."

"Their weapons?"

"Rifles and knives. Maybe some bows," John provided.

"What are you called, animal?" the bearded man demanded.

"Jahn," John said his name the way Ravishan did. Only after he had spoken did he realize his mistake. Both the riders ahead of him smirked. The word 'jahn' referred to blond hides, like the coat of the dog he had seen. It would be the kind of name a pet would have, but not a man. It was like saying he was named Spot or Blackie.

"Well then, Jahn," the bearded man leaned forward in his saddle and smiled, revealing crooked teeth, "you're a good boy to have run all this way to warn your masters, aren't you?"

Several of the riders laughed out loud at this.

"It's what any decent man would do." John put an extra inflection on the word man.

"A little better." The bearded man's expression grew serious. "It's a rare man indeed who travels through the godless night all alone just to deliver a warning to strangers. It sounds a little like something out of a child's book, doesn't it?"

"That's right." The clean-shaven man sobered as well. "Some nights devils dress in saints' skins."

John's lip curled at the response. He hadn't expected these men to throw their arms around him and thank him for his trouble, but this tone of accusation was outright offensive. He'd been terrified, nearly frozen, and had just run through half the night for these men's sakes—for just the chance to enter Amura'taye. He certainly hadn't come just to be insulted.

He said, "Look, I've warned you. You can believe me or not. I don't give a damn." He started for the cover of the woods but froze when he heard the distinct sound of a gun being cocked.

"That's no way to speak to your betters, dog."

John turned back, meeting the bearded man's gaze and refusing to flinch despite the gun aimed at him. The bearded man regarded him, and then with a smirk, he lowered his rifle. The clean-shaven man seemed surprised but made no comment.

"You want a reward for this, don't you?" the bearded man asked.

John didn't trust his voice not to betray his anger, so he nodded. "What is it?"

"A little money and sponsorship into Amura'taye." John kept his tone flat. "I want entrance for myself, my sister and her husband."

The bearded man nodded thoughtfully.

"And if this trap of yours is a ploy? You'd expect to take some kind of punishment, wouldn't you?"

"A ploy?" John couldn't imagine how warning them could be a ploy or how this man might think it would serve John. So far all he'd gotten were insults and firearms pointed at him.

"You wouldn't be the first Fai'daum to draw a guard off with claims of a threat. And you wouldn't be the first beggar to pretend to be a hero for a handout."

"I'm not Fai'daum and I'm not a beggar," John stated.

The bearded man lifted his rifle slightly as if toying with the idea of shooting John. For one delirious moment it struck him as almost funny to think that if he got shot Laurie would really have something to gloat about. But irony lost all amusement as John gazed down the silver-gray barrel and contemplated the reality of being killed.

The bearded man seemed to come to a decision. He looked to the clean-shaven man. "Pivan, take twelve men, and our Jahn here, ahead. If you find Fai'daum, kill them. If you don't, then kill this dog."

"Not finding them won't mean they aren't there," John began to protest.

"No, but I imagine that you'll be a motivated guide for my men this way." The bearded man smiled at John again, showing his craggy teeth.

Pivan signaled to the rashan behind him. A minute later, John was hauled up onto a big tahldi behind a youthful-looking rider with wavy brown hair.

"I'm Alidas," the young man said. "If you fall, you will likely be trampled. Try to stay on." Then he made a slight motion with his legs and animal beneath them raced ahead in high, fast bounds. The motion was nothing like riding a horse. John gripped the cinching strap at the back of the saddle for dear life. A distinctly seasick feeling rose in his stomach as they soared up and then dropped with every stride.

"They should be in the woods." John tried to keep his voice even despite the jolting leaps. "On the right side."

None of the riders made any reply but Pivan's gloved hand flashed up and he formed some sign. John noticed the way the silver crosses on his glove caught the dim moonlight. Immediately, the riders reined their mounts up into the woods. They formed a loose line, Pivan and Alidas riding at the front. John gripped the strap desperately and leaned out a little from Alidas' back, attempting to survey the surrounding woods.

Everything seemed different when he didn't have his feet on the ground. The angles were all wrong and he wasn't used to moving at this speed. The black branches and underbrush blurred past too quickly. His knuckles ached from the tension of his grip, but he still concentrated on the woods ahead of him.

"A little to the east of that cropping of trees there should be a rise. It will give us a better view," John whispered.

"Which trees?" Alidas asked.

"Just ahead on the right." John pointed and then quickly returned his hand to the cinch strap.

"I see it now," said Pivan. He moved slightly on his mount and the animal instantly responded, bounding toward the thicker outcropping of trees. Alidas followed his lead and the other men fell in behind.

No one spoke. The riders communicated only by hand signals, moonlight sparking off the silver crosses on their gloves. Pivan swung his hand out and all the riders stopped. Witnessing these riders' skill and discipline, John understood why they would feel assured enough to send twelve men to face twenty.

The night sky grew lighter, changing from a dull charcoal to the color of concrete. Far in the distance, John spied a human form leaning close to a tree. The moment he saw one, he began to notice others close to the road. Most crouched in the underbrush, their rust-colored coats fading into the dull branches and leaf litter.

"There," John whispered. He pointed to the nearest man. "You see, I wasn't lying. They—"

The rest of his words were knocked out of him as Pivan gave a sudden gesture and the entire force of riders charged ahead.

Alidas' body shifted in front of John as he reached to the side of his saddle, and in one swift practiced motion, brought up his rifle and fired. One of the shadowy men ahead of them jerked and fell to the ground. A thunder of shots cracked out from all sides.

The Fai'daum scurried behind trees. Some fell. A few turned with their own guns and fired return shots. None of the rashan'im fell. They fanned out, crashing through the underbrush and trampling the men on the ground.

Alidas reined his mount after three men who had broken from the cover of two fallen trees. Fine branches slapped at John's face as they charged through the dense woods. The smell of black powder filled the air. Alidas fired again, the crack of the gun deafening. A red burst of blood erupted from the back of one of the running men's heads and he crumpled to the ground. Alidas fired again but then John only heard a metallic snap of an empty rifle.

Alidas cursed and urged his mount forward faster. Two men still ran ahead of them. The tahldi sprang ahead, raking its horns across the nearest man's back. The man gave out a cry of pain and jumped to the side. As he did, Alidas slammed the butt of his rifle into the man's face. Hot blood spattered up across John's cheek.

The man fell and the tahldi sprang with its full weight onto his chest. John heard the man's bones snap beneath them. A horrified nausea washed through John as he glanced back and saw the bloody mass of the man's body. He looked like the spattered remains of a crushed insect, arms and legs twisting out from a mulchy red ruin.

Alidas took no notice. He urged his mount forward after the last man. John stared at the Fai'daum man's back. He didn't know if it was right or wrong but he couldn't keep himself from wishing that this one would escape. As the man wove between bushes and branches, he gave a soft cry and John recognized his youthful voice. Saimura.

They bounded over a charred stump, landing only a hand's length from Saimura. John could see his young, terrified face clearly. The mount swung its horns but Saimura lunged aside and sprinted toward a thick crop of trees.

"Jid!" Alidas cursed and reined his mount after Saimura.

Just let him go, John thought.

But he knew it wouldn't happen. All around him, he caught glimpses of the same brutality. Half hidden by tree branches and distance, other riders impaled men, shot them, trampled their fallen bodies. The smell of gunpowder and the sound of screams filled the woods.

Alidas loaded his rifle and took aim at Saimura's back. John considered bumping Alidas. But he was pretty sure that Alidas would kill him for that offense. John wanted to close his eyes but found he couldn't. He stared at the young man, knowing that this slaughter was, in part, his doing.

Just as Alidas fired, Saimura's ankle caught in some knot of hidden roots and he went down. The bullet missed him. He struggled to his feet, but his leg wouldn't hold him. He fell again.

"This time you stay down," Alidas whispered. He lifted his rifle and took aim again.

John saw a motion from the left, very close to them, something bright and moving fast. Then the tahldi shrieked and reared. Alidas' rifle fired up into the branches of the trees. John rocked back. His fingers slipped from the straps and he hit the ground with a sickening snap.

The air smacked out of John's lungs and a hard pain exploded up his back. Only the rush of panicked energy gave him the strength to roll up to his feet and away from the flailing hooves of the rearing animal.

The dog had it by the throat. As her jaws crushed through the mount's flesh, dark blood welled over the dog's muzzle. The tahldi thrashed desperately, trying to shake the dog off. Alidas swung like a doll in his saddle. His rifle went flying and landed near John's feet.

Suddenly, the dog was thrown aside. A geyser of blood sprayed from the mount's neck and it collapsed with Alidas half pinned beneath it. The moment the dog hit the ground, it turned and sprang for Alidas.

"No!" John grabbed Alidas' rifle and took aim at the dog. She stood over Alidas' limp body, growling, her eyes on John.

"Just go," John said softly. "Get out of here."

The dog barred her teeth. Blood so dark that it was nearly black glistened across her entire face.

"I'll kill you if I have to," John told her.

Slowly, her eyes still on John, her teeth still barred, she backed away. John kept the rifle trained on her until she at last turned and fled into the deep shadows of the western woods. The empty rifle dropped from John's hands. His arms shook with shock. He wondered how badly he'd been hurt by the fall. Definitely not as badly as Alidas.

John knelt down over the fallen rider to check his pulse and breath. Alidas was alive, but not conscious. There was blood all over him, but John thought it was his mount's. The tahldi lying on top of Alidas' left leg was a mess, its head connected to its body by only by a stretch of tendon and a flap of skin.

John touched the ground. It was soft and moist. A thick layer of half-decayed leaves and twigs covered the actual soil. He dug fistfuls of dirt and leaves from around Alidas' pinned leg and then pulled him out from beneath his dead tahldi. The leg looked bad, twisting at the wrong angle below the knee.

John stripped off his coat and tucked it around Alidas' inert body. He didn't trust himself to attempt to splint the leg. He'd probably do more harm than good and there had to be some kind of physician in Amura'taye. For now he just needed to keep Alidas warm and safe.

Distantly, John heard gunshots and the sound of a tahldi screaming, but it was so far from him that it could have been a bird call. Even with the growing morning light, he couldn't see any of the other riders. He guessed they each chased their own chosen quarry, as Alidas had.

John sat down beside Alidas, exhausted and shaking. His eyes burned and his back ached. He'd been up the entire night. But he knew he was trembling from more than simple exhaustion.

He'd never seen brutality like this. He hardly knew how to react. Intellectually, he knew that this battle would have taken place whether or not he had warned the Bousim convoy. Still, he couldn't keep from feeling responsible for the carnage surrounding him, for Alidas' hopelessly mangled leg.

More gunshots cracked through the woods.

If John hadn't warned the Bousim convoy, then perhaps Alidas would not have been injured; but then again, maybe he would have been killed. John pulled the rifle close and leaned his head down on his knees. He would stay with Alidas until Pivan came searching for his surviving rashan. He didn't think that there was anything more he could do. Just wait.

His eyes were drooping closed when he heard a hushed moan behind him. Turning back, John realized that he had forgotten completely about Saimura.

The young man's chestnut hair was tangled with dirt and rotten leaves. Mud streaked his tattered, reddish coat, pants and bare feet. He had his hands wrapped around his right ankle.

As John pushed himself to his feet, the young man looked up at him and went pale. His brown eyes were wide with fear. The moment he caught sight of the rifle in John's hand he drew out a long hunting knife. He didn't hold it toward John. Instead, he turned the blade to his own throat.

"Don't," John whispered to him.

"I won't burn on your Holy Road," Saimura said.

"Saimura," John said his name and the man almost dropped his knife. "Don't hurt yourself."

"How do you know me?" Saimura asked.

"I just know," John answered. He certainly wasn't going to tell the truth.

"Are you a friend of the revolution?" Saimura lowered his knife.

John could see that Saimura was so scared that he would believe almost anything, if it meant that he would live.

"There are too many people who might overhear us." John crept closer to him. "You have to be quiet and just trust me."

"Are you Sabir's—"

John cut him off with a small shake of his head.

"Let me see your ankle."

Saimura watched in silence as John investigated his injury.

The ankle was swollen and hot, but Saimura could rotate it and also flex his toes. John guessed it wasn't broken, just badly sprained. Either way, Saimura wasn't going to be able to move with any speed for a few days at least. John wrapped the ankle with strips of weasel hide that he cut from his pants.

His pants were already a wreck anyway.

"You're going to have to hide here until night. After that you'll be safe. Just keep south of the river," John whispered to him.

"They'll see me here."

"No," John assured him, "I'll hide you. You just have to stay very still and very quiet, all right?"

Saimura nodded.

It wasn't hard to do. Saimura was slim and already covered in leaves and mud. John dug out a hollow under a split tree where the fallen trunk and branches would mask Saimura's shape. Once Saimura was settled in, John spread leaves over him.

"Sleep if you can," John told him. He didn't dare say anything more. Pivan's riders might find him at any moment. Both he and Saimura would end up dead if they were seen having a conversation.

John walked back to where Alidas lay, pale against the dark ground. He was probably as young as Saimura. John checked his pulse again. It felt strong.

When he glanced to where Saimura was hidden, he saw nothing but scattered leaves and dead black branches. He didn't allow himself to look back again. He tried to just forget that Saimura was even there.

The morning light grew stronger. It hurt John's eyes after so many hours of wakefulness and dark. He heard the sound of hooves pounding against the soft ground and felt the vibrations as riders grew closer. Pivan was at the lead. John counted only seven other riders, then he noticed that several men rode together.

Four animals lost, John thought, and at least three men wounded. He wondered if that would be considered a triumph or not. He supposed it depended on how many of the Fai'daum men survived. Not many from what he had seen.

He felt sick.

Pivan reined his mount to a stop and dismounted. In the morning light, John could see that the rashan's coat and uniform weren't black but deep green. He strode toward John, glaring, but as he caught sight of Alidas wrapped in John's coat, his expression softened. He crouched down beside his young rider.

Up close, in the morning light, John could see the deep lines that etched the edges of Pivan's eyes and mouth. They lent some character to his soft features. John didn't know whether he liked that character.

"What killed the tahldi?" Pivan asked.

"A dog tore out its throat." John was so tired that he had to speak slowly and take care to only use Basawar words, not English.

"That was no dog," Pivan said. "That was Ji Shir'korud, the demoness of the Fai'daum." Pivan gave Alidas' fallen mount a cursory once over. He seemed to observe the furrows of dirt where John had dug Alidas out from under the animal because he immediately glanced at John's mud-encrusted hands. "Why didn't she kill Alidas as well?"

"I held her off." John lifted Alidas' rifle in explanation.

Pivan nodded. "If you had left him to die, I would have hunted you to the ends of the shattered earth."

If he hadn't been so tired John supposed he would have been either angered or worried to receive another threat in place of gratitude. As was, he found it somehow funny.

He was struck with the delirious idea that Pivan only knew how to communicate via threats and John wondered if Pivan would have asked someone out in the same manner.

If you don't go out with me, I'll hunt you down to the ends of the shattered earth.

John smiled.

"Do you think I'm joking?" Pivan demanded.

"No," John murmured, "I'm moved by your commitment to the relationship."

Pivan looked deeply confused by this and for a moment John thought that he had responded in the wrong language. But his words had all been Basawar. Then he realized that Pivan was the kind of man who didn't know how to deal with humor.

"His leg's badly hurt. The bones will need to be set," John said, to give Pivan a solid crisis to respond to.

"I'll take him." Pivan reached over and very carefully lifted Alidas into his arms.

"Come," Pivan called to John, as he carried Alidas to his waiting mount. "We are expected in Amura'taye."

CHAPTER TWELVE

The ride into the walled city, Amura'taye, at the foot of Rathal'pesha passed in delirious waves of exhaustion and sudden bursts of fevered wakefulness. John clung to the back of a rider. He watched the terraced farmlands and herds of heavy-coated sheep blur by. The women working the fields in their rough wool dresses seemed familiar to him. When they passed through the huge gates of a second wall, John suddenly thought he had been here before. Then he remembered that he had dreamed of these narrow city streets. He had smelled the thick smoky cooking fires. He knew that there would be crowds of men in the streets, a few of them riding dull gray bicycles.

The sound of little bells chiming from street vendors was new. And for the first time, he noticed that stone bridges arched over some streets, connecting the upper stories of massive stone buildings. Armed men looked down from the bridges.

As they continued traveling, John drifted in and out of consciousness. One moment he thought that all the buildings on the road looked rundown, brick tenements and shops with cracked doors. Dark, cramped alleys seemed to wind aimlessly between structures. Filthy goats and half-dressed children ran through the streets. Some of the older children ran alongside the riders, begging for coins. The riders ignored them and their tahldi swung their sharp horns if any child came too close.

John felt his head droop and his eyes close for what seemed only a matter of seconds. When he looked up, he noticed that the buildings lining the cobbled road were large, more ornate, and often surrounded by gleaming walls of latticed stonework.

Through the gaps in the walls John caught glimpses of painted doors depicting pastoral scenes and waterspouts shaped like birds or fish rising from tiled roofs.

When they stopped at last, it was before a large two-story building with a green-tiled roof and carvings of flowers bursting across the polished wooden doors. A motif of crossed arrows repeated all across the stone walls surrounding the main building, its vast courtyard, and the outlying buildings.

John almost fell off the tahldi; he was so tired and sore. He blindly allowed a man to lead him to a narrow room on the first floor. There were no windows or decorations in the room, only a small bed but that was all that mattered to John.

Later he woke long enough to devour a hot, nearly flavorless, broth. Pivan asked him about his sister and brother-in-law.

"Loshai iff Behr." John gave their Basawar names and roughly described where they could be found. They would know to claim that they had come from the isolated western region of Shun'sira to pray at the foot of Rathal'pesha. Ravishan had practiced the words with them all in case any shepherds or hunters came across them.

John fought to keep his eyes open as he spoke to Pivan.

"I should go with you." John attempted to rise, but Pivan laid a gentle hand on his shoulder.

"No. You need rest. Your back was badly injured and you're fevered. Don't make me beat you down." Pivan spoke in a firm, fatherly tone. And John thought that he truly must have had a fever, because he found Pivan's kindly threat comforting. He laid his head back down against the cool mattress. He would get up in a moment, he thought, and seconds later he fell into a deep sleep.

After a full day's sleep, Pivan woke him to tell him that his sister and brother-in-law had arrived and that Lady Bousim had requested that they break their fast at her table.

"Lady Bousim?" John stumbled slightly over the woman's formal Basawar title. Pivan frowned at him slightly.

"I don't know that I'm ...prepared to meet such a person," John replied.

"We have baths for that," Pivan responded, and not for the first time, John wondered how much he miscommunicated with his shaky grasp of the Basawar language.

Maybe Pivan suspected something of the same nature, because he sent a servant boy along with John to make sure he found his way to the men's bath where Bill waited.

Inside, morning light poured through the crude panes of the rock crystal skylights overhead. The light gleamed across the white-tiled floor and reflected in the large mirrors mounted on the stone walls. Several benches stood near the mirrors but otherwise most of the small space was occupied by a huge, white marble tub. Wisps of steam rolled up from the hot waters piped into the tub and the air was filled with the humid, mineral scents of hot springs.

Bill perched on the edge of the tub, naked and in good spirits. He greeted John with all the asthmatic enthusiasm he could muster.

"I can't believe that I'm actually excited to be taking a bath with you," Bill said, smirking.

"Likewise," John replied.

"Well, who wouldn't be thrilled to get a glimpse of this awesome body?" Bill flexed his arms and John gave a laugh. It did really frighten him to see just how emaciated Bill had become. John could easily count every one of his ribs and the vertabrae of his spine.

But things would get better now, John assured himself.

As he stripped off his clothes, the muscles of his shoulders and back ached. A quick glance in the mirror showed him deep bruises still darkening from blue to purple and several red scrapes.

"Man, your back looks like a big, ugly blueberry pie," Bill said, then frowned. "No, maybe more blackberry pie. Wait, I got it! It's black-and-blue berry." Bill grinned and then dunked under the hot water. He bobbed back up, leaned back against the white stone, and sighed, breathing easier than he had for some time.

John slid into the water slowly, taking time to adjust to the heat after so many months of relentless cold. Finally, he eased down and began to wash the filth off himself. Bill scrubbed at his own body, and rafts of mud and dirt floated off them both.

The water was much deeper at the center of the tub and John dunked his head. At the far end of the tub, a drain carried the fouled water away.

At last, John hauled himself out of the water and onto a bench. Steam from the bath crept over the mirrors, making John's reflection look muted, as if lost in a deep fog.

His long blond hair looked like a smear of butter. His back, as Bill had noted, was mottled with bruises. Red scrapes gouged across his ribcage.

At least he was clean. That alone made him feel much better. Free of mud and blood and sweat, he felt as if he had somehow become more human. He supposed it was simply the sense of rejoining civilization with its beds and baths and its rituals of hygiene.

Of course, those rituals varied from civilization to civilization. And John realized, as he studied the line of small instruments on the marble stand before him, that he was not familiar with those of Basawar.

The serving boy who had taken Bill's and his clothes away had left the tray of shining tools along with towels.

John picked up a long silvery one. It looked like a very sharp butter knife or perhaps a scalpel. There were also several things that looked like shaving brushes. Why there was more than one, he didn't know. An assortment of nasty looking little picks and tweezers lay along side several round, flat tins.

John unscrewed the lids of two of the metal tins. One contained a white powder. The other brimmer with what looked like wood shavings.

"So, what do you think they did with our clothes?" Bill was working soap into his hair. The white lather slowly darkened to brown as he massaged it through. A mass of leaves, mulch and twigs had rinsed out of John's hair. He'd had to use a bristled brush to get all the dried blood and mud off of his body. His skin still felt slightly raw and tight from the experience.

"Burned them," John replied.

"You think?" Bill asked.

"I hope." John unscrewed the other two tins. One was filled with a rough dark red powder. The other was full of clear goo. John sniffed it. It had no scent.

"So, what's all that?" Bill asked after he'd rinsed his head a third time.

"I don't know," John said.

"Any guesses?" Bill leaned back against the marble and caught his breath. It took a lot out of him to go without air, even for the short time it'd taken to rinse his hair. John waited until Bill's breathing slowed to normal.

"Most of the men I've seen here are clean-shaven so I'm thinking that some of these have to be for that. This blade, probably." John held up the silver knife. Its razor edge caught the soft light and gleamed.

"What about shaving cream?" Bill frowned. "I'm not all over the idea of shaving with some knife and a bar of soap."

John set the knife back down and inspected the rest of the brushes, picks, tweezers and tins. He wondered how inexplicable the contents of his own bathroom would have been if he hadn't known what they were meant for.

"So?" Bill prompted from the water.

"I don't know," John said.

"Try one," Bill suggested.

"Try one how?"

"I don't know." Bill shrugged. "Taste one, maybe?"

"They're not food."

"How do you know?" Bill asked.

"Because the boy who brought them in said they were for our bath. And that we'll be having the honor of eating in the Lady Bousim's company after our baths," John said.

"You understood all that?" Bill looked impressed. "I kind of got the idea that we were supposed to use them to eat some woman in the bath."

"Eat a woman in the bath?" John asked.

"Yeah, well, your version does sound a lot less weird, but mine's much more sexy." Bill pulled himself weakly from the water and sat on the edge of the marble tub. John tossed a towel to him.

"The kid didn't say what any of this is supposed to be for?" Bill poked one of the long curved picks.

"I guess anyone from Basawar would know." John picked up one of the fine brushes. He ran it across the palm of his hand. The bristles were far too soft for brushing hair. He put it back down.

"I wonder how Laurie's doing?" Bill pondered.

"Better than us, I hope." John shrugged.

"I bet she got her stuff figured out in a few seconds," Bill said. "She always knows what all the stuff is in those baskets of soaps and crap. Maybe it's a woman thing."

John guessed that Laurie was doing the same thing they were. Hesitantly, he poked his finger into the tin of clear goo. It felt slick and almost oily. Some kind of pomade, he wondered. Or maybe it was a skin cream or possibly an ointment? It could be anything. John wiped his finger off on a towel.

"Salad dressing?" Bill suggested.

"You're just hungry, aren't you?" John asked.

"Starving," Bill admitted. "I haven't eaten since yesterday afternoon."

"Well, I'm pretty sure this isn't a salad dressing." John screwed the caps back on the tins. Bill absently ran his fingers through the long strings of his patchy black beard.

"So," Bill said, "what are we going to do?"

John shrugged. "I suppose we just sit here and wait. If we can look like we lost track of time in conversation, there might be a chance that one of the servants will try to hurry us along and maybe give us some clue."

"Yeah, I guess that's a good idea." Bill finished drying himself off and then wrapped the towel around his waist. The fluffy white cloth engulfed his emaciated pale body. "I was actually thinking more about what we were going to do in a broader sense. You know, how are we going to live with these people? I mean, we don't even know the right way to wipe our asses—"

John cut him short with a raised hand. Out in the hall, he heard floorboards creak, as if someone was approaching or just stepping away from the door. They both sat in silence listening, though John could tell from Bill's expression that he had no idea what he was listening for.

There was nothing. It might have just been one of those noises that old buildings made as they settled. Still, it made John instantly aware of how vulnerable they were. How careful they would need to be. They weren't alone in a shelter anymore. A vast household of servants and guards surrounded them.

"We have to speak Basawar," John said softly. "As long as the three of us are here, we're going to have to remember to only speak in Basawar."

"Even when it's just us?" Bill asked.

"Always," John whispered. He couldn't shake the feeling that someone might be listening to them even now.

"But I sound like some kind of retard." Bill scowled. "I mean, it takes me five minutes just to get a sentence out."

"You'll get better with practice," John spoke the Basawar words carefully.

"Easy for you to say, Mr. Show-Off," Bill whispered.

John refused to respond in English. "Behr, yura'ati vass'atdu Basawar hi."

"Du, Jahn," Bill agreed with all the enthusiasm of a sullen teen.

"It won't be so bad after a while," John told him in Basawar.

"Wahbai," Bill responded.

John might have been offended at being called an asshole if he hadn't known that it was one of the Basawar words that Bill knew and liked best.

From outside the door, John heard the creaking sound again, but this time it grew louder until it became the distinct sound of footsteps. A moment later, there came a light rap at the wooden door. John called for the person to enter and four men in sage green shirts, darker green vests, and black pants came in. The servant boy had been dressed in the same manner. Light yellow embroidered symbols of crossed arrows decorated the high straight collars of the men's shirts.

Before John offered them more than a greeting, they split into pairs and began grooming Bill and him. The oldest of the servants picked up the tin of goo and began to froth it with one of the smallest of the brushes.

Meanwhile, two other men began working the fine combs through John's and Bill's hair. They weren't rough, but they weren't gentle either. John supposed that their manner was professional.

Still, he would have been reassured by a little more tenderness. When one of the men jerked several hairs out from inside his nostril, John flinched back, barely suppressing a howl of pain.

Bill made a terrible choking noise as the same thing was done to him. The servants seemed unmoved. They had probably forced hundreds of other men to cry out under their ministrations. John briefly entertained the thought that their impassive professional expressions matched those that cold-blooded assassins always wore in movies.

One of the men picked up two of the viciously curved silver picks. John watched him in fascination and slight dread. The man fitted one pick over the other and then selected a small screw that John hadn't noticed before. He screwed the picks together. In a moment, John realized that the man had just fitted together a pair of scissors.

He combed and trimmed John's beard, then went after Bill's.

The old man at last seemed to have worked the goo into a huge white frothy mass. It looked almost exactly like shaving cream. Then, still frothing with the brush, he spilled a little of the red powder into it and then the wood shavings. John frowned.

The old man stepped up next to him and smiled widely.

John smiled back and the old man shoved the now pink woodchip-infused foam into his mouth. A flavor like stale cinnamon seeped over John's gums. The old man began scrubbing the foam against John's teeth with another of the brushes.

While the old man brushed John's teeth, another man went to work on his toenails and fingernails. Then the man began to trim away at the hair on John's body. John remained as still as he could, listening the clink and click of sharp implements far too close to his most tender areas.

He glanced over to Bill to see how he was managing. Bill looked like a cat being given an enema. John almost laughed.

After everything else, the shaving was quick, painless, and simple. The last tin, the one full of white powder, was worked into a lather and the sharp silver blade was used. Then it was done. The four servants packed up their tools and left Bill and him sitting there gleaming, naked, and dazed. It reminded John of stories of how people were found after alien abductions.

John thought of telling this to Bill, but he couldn't figure out how to say alien in Basawar. And Bill wouldn't have understood him anyway.

Bill opened his mouth as if to say something but then didn't.

A few moments later there was another knock. John called for the person to enter, though this time he was a little more hesitant. The servant boy who had brought them the towels poked his head in. He bowed slightly before fully entering the room. John closed the door behind the servant boy, since his arms looked too full to do it for himself.

"These are for you, sirs." The boy laid the stack of clothes down on the bench beside Bill.

Every garment was a shade of muted green, ranging between olive and sage. Beyond the color they bore little resemblance to the stiff, formal clothes that the house servants wore. These rustic garments were simple: pullover shirts, long underwear, and heavy pants. None of them had holes but they felt soft and worn in. Probably donations or secondhand goods. Most of the clothes were slightly too short for John and too big for Bill, but they were all warm and clean.

When the servant boy stepped out of the room to retrieve their boots, Bill leaned close to John and whispered, "We look like the Jolly Green Giant and his little buddy Sprout in these getups."

"Vass'hi Basawar, Behr," John whispered back.

"Du, du." Bill scowled at the reminder.

Once they had their boots on, the servant boy led them out of the bath and through the house. Aside from his own bed, John had seen very little of the place earlier.

The tapestry-insulated walls and stone archways seemed medieval and out of date when compared with the piping and mirrors in the bathroom. John noticed that there were sconces on the walls for torches. Iron chandeliers filled with unlit candles hung from the ceilings of the larger rooms. The strong smell of burning wood pervaded the building, and with it came the scent of animals, oil, tallow, and lard.

They ascended a narrow stone staircase, which brought them into a surprisingly small room. John had been half expecting some large feast hall full of rough-hewn tables, rush mats, and tankards of beer. He guessed the image had come to him from some half-remembered Robin Hood movie.

Aside from the drab tapestries on the walls and floor, the chamber was nothing like what he had expected. A small fire flickered and snapped behind a decorated screen. At the far end of the room, sharp morning light poured in through tall windows. A highly-polished, rectangular wooden table dominated the chamber. Dark wood chairs circled it. Silver trays of steaming meat and plates of bread and other foods covered the table.

Laurie, dressed in a simple olive shift and a dark green sweater, was already seated. She, like Bill, looked tiny in her loose-fitting clothes. Her long light hair shone white in the hard light.

The three other women seated opposite Laurie looked like plump dolls in comparison. Where Laurie's skin was red and chapped, theirs was creamy and smooth. Their breasts were full, as were the curves of their hips, unlike Laurie's body, which seemed as flat and sharp as an assembly of wooden planks. She resembled the table more than the women sipping from delicate bowls across from her.

The woman opposite Laurie was older, perhaps forty-five or fifty years old, while the two girls beside her looked barely out of their teens. All three of them had dark hair and wore it up in ornate, twisting braids. Little strings of silver beads hung from their hair and dripped down the pale green folds of their long flowing dresses. John didn't know what material their clothes were made from, but it caught the light and shimmered like silk.

"Tumah," John greeted the women and bowed the same way the servant boy had bowed to him in the bathroom. Bill followed his lead. Laurie twisted around in her seat and smiled at them. Her expression was one of both joy and desperation. John wondered how long she'd been waiting and how well she'd managed to field questions.

All three women stood. The one in the middle beckoned John and Bill into the room. Her hands were small with long white fingernails. Tiny silver chains hung like delicate manacles between the silver rings on each of her fingers. John guessed that she was the noblewoman whom the convoy had been escorting along with her son.

"Gentlemen, we are so glad that you have arrived. Please, won't you be kind enough to join us in our morning repast?" The lady spoke in the most formal form of Basawar, adding soft whispered honorifics and drawing each word out into the next so that she was almost humming.

John froze, momentarily overwhelmed by the lady's formality and poise.

Bill immediately deferred to John dropping back slightly.

All through the morning John had been silently preparing himself for another conversation like the ones he had easily managed with Pivan and other soldiers. Direct and to the point, more interrogations than conversations, really.

He'd guessed most of his responses would be limited to yes or no answers. The majority of his effort would have been channeled into listening closely to the questions, so that he made the right choice. He hadn't thought to expect formality, civility, or niceties. He wasn't sure that he was up to that level of language yet.

He felt one of Bill's bony fingers jabbing into his side, and realized that he had to respond to the lady's question.

"Thank you." John could hear the roughness of his words. "It would be our honor to join you."

He seated himself to Laurie's right. Bill took the chair on her left. John noticed the little movement as Laurie squeezed Bill's hand under the table.

"Rashan Pivan'ro'Bousim has told me that you are called Jahn," the lady said.

It took a moment for John to recognize Pivan's name in its full form. His rank of rashan, cavalryman, sounded a little like

Ravishan and for an instant John had been deeply confused. He tried not to let it show.

"Yes," he said, "I'm called Jahn. This is my sister Loshai and her husband, Behr."

"Sky and Honeybee. What lovely names." The lady turned to the younger woman on her right. "They go together, don't you think?"

"Yes, they certainly do. Perhaps it was fated that they should be wed." The young woman smiled, showing a little gap between her front teeth.

The lady nodded and then returned her attention to John.

"Your sister is so very proper. She wouldn't speak a single word in her husband's absence. She put all our gossiping to shame." The lady didn't look or sound entirely pleased.

John wasn't sure how to respond. He couldn't say that it was good, but he didn't think he should say that Laurie's silence was wrong either, since it was apparently proper. He decided to try and just sidestep it entirely.

"I'm sorry for having to ask this, but I'm not sure how you would like best to be addressed." John bowed his head slightly.

"That is difficult, isn't it?" the lady said. "If we were to hold ourselves to the holiest codes, you would not be here in my presence at all. But Rashan Pivan'ro'Bousim says that you may have saved my son's life, and also that you fought the Fai'daum demoness, Ji Shir'korud, for the very life and soul of Rashan Alidas'ro'Bousim. So it would seem that I am most deeply in your debt. I certainly could not bar you from my table. But what shall you call me?"

She sighed and lifted the small bowl in front of her to her mouth. The chains on her fingers clicked against the porcelain bowl.

As she drank, John became acutely aware of the smell of the food wafting over him. He hadn't eaten since the night before and then it had only been broth. Succulent slices of what looked like pork steamed in heaps on a silver platter in front of him. The distinct scent of fresh bread drifted up from golden rolls and there even seemed to be something like the smell of coffee in the air.

His stomach groaned.

The lady glanced up at him in obvious amusement. The two young women on either side of her put their hands over their mouths to hide their grins.

"I should decide before you are starved to death, shouldn't I?" The lady laughed but without making a sound. Her lips parted and the small tremors of laughter shook her chest but all that came out was breath.

John stole a glance to Laurie and Bill but the two of them looked as bewildered as he felt. John could only guess that noble-women of Basawar trained themselves to laugh mutely. He had seen groups of common women out in their fields cackling with laughter. It seemed to follow what the lady had mentioned earlier about Laurie's silence being proper.

"You may call me Gaunvur Bousim. Since I am the only one of Gaunsho Mosh'sira'in'Bousim's wives residing in this city, there shouldn't be any confusion," the lady decided.

John nodded. Ravishan had told him that wealthy men often took several wives, and that in aristocratic gaun'im households, each wife held a formal title according to the number and quality of sons she bore her husband. John didn't even try to remember the husband's full title and name; he just concentrated on the lady's: Gaunvur Bousim, Lady Bousim.

"It's an honor," John said.

"The honor is mine as well." Lady Bousim swept her hand out over the trays of food. "Please, eat all that you like. I only regret that I have such poor dishes to offer you. If we were in Nurjima, I would give you fruit and flowers from my husband's garden. Here, at the edge of the shattered world, I can only offer you this."

"This is more than enough," John assured her. "Thank you."

John took one of the empty plates and filled it with food. He wasn't sure if Laurie or Bill had followed much of the conversation, so he simply passed the plate down to Laurie. She passed it to Bill while John filled a second plate for her. Last, he served himself. The three women also ate, but much more slowly than any of the three of them.

At first John was so hungry and ate so quickly that he hardly noticed anything about the food that he devoured. But as the sharp pangs of hunger abated he began to realize how little flavor there was to the dinner fare.

Though it had obviously been roasted, the pale cutlets of meat were as tasteless as if they had been boiled for days. The bread was as bland as a communion wafer and the cheese tasted like thick slabs of unsalted butter.

Once his stomach no longer hurt, John didn't really feel the desire to eat more. Laurie and Bill seemed to be having the same problem. Bill chewed on a piece of bread with kind of expression that he normally reserved for tricky math problems. Laurie's plate was only half empty, but she was already cutting pieces of her meal into smaller and smaller bits as if she hoped to reach the atomic level and render them invisible free-floating particles.

Lady Bousim idly sipped from her bowl. Then she turned to the young woman on her right.

"Inholima, my dear, I have just realized that we have no more daru'sira to offer to our guests. Won't you go to my chambers and find my jars of tea so that we can make a little more?"

There was a momentary pause before the girl responded and John thought that she might refuse. Then she nodded and stood.

"Do be quick, my dear." Lady Bousim smiled at her as she left the room. The moment the girl closed the door behind her, the smile evaporated from the lady's face.

"Ohbi." She looked to the girl on her left but said nothing more. Instantly, the girl sprang to her feet and crept across the room to the door. She knelt down and, muting the slight creak of the doorknob with her hands, opened the door and peeked out.

John, Laurie, and Bill all watched her in silence.

She closed the door and rushed back to her seat beside Lady Bousim.

"She's out of hearing," Ohbi whispered.

"Very good," the lady said. "You hid the teas?"

"Yes, Gaunvur." The girl beamed.

The lady looked straight at John.

"The girl, Inholima, is my husband's spy. You must never trust her."

"All right." John didn't know what else to say. Whatever was going on in this household was already beyond him.

"Tell your companions this," the lady said to him.

"What do you mean?"

The lady leaned forward over the table, her dark eyes fixed upon John's face.

"I know what you are. I know that you speak the Hell-Tongue of the Eastern Kingdom. I had my servant boy, Bati'kohl, listen to you when you thought that you were alone in the bath. Tell them in your own language that they must trust none of my servants but Ohbi and Bati'kohl. Any of the rest will see them burned at the hands of the Payshmura." She all but spat the name of the priesthood.

John hesitated, suspicious that this might be some kind of trick to uncover them. But he couldn't see how he could make it worse since she already knew that they didn't speak Basawar. The genuine intensity in Lady Bousim's expression made him want to believe her.

He turned to Bill and Laurie and explained what the lady had said.

"We don't have much time to talk," Lady Bousim continued the moment John had finished, "but you must know that I am your friend."

"Thank you," John replied, "but why would you want to help us?"

"Because my great-grandmother was from the Kingdom of the East. She came here when she was just a child, before the Payshmura called down the Rifter from Nayeshi and had him tear that beautiful land to shreds." Her small hands tapped nervously over the porcelain bowl, clicking the silver chains against its surface.

John realized with some relief that the Lady Bousim did not, in fact, know who they were after all. He, Bill, and Laurie weren't from a lost Kingdom of the East. They weren't even from this planet. Ravishan had said that the Basawar name of their world was Nayeshi. Apparently, the Rifter came from the same place.

"My great-grandmother knew spells," Lady Bousim went on in a quick whisper. "She could call fire and bind the waters. She was a proud, beautiful woman—a free woman. Her hair was golden like yours. Only a little of her blood flows in me. I don't know her words of power. I speak only Basawar. I bow before the Basawar god in his temple and my hands are chained with Basawar wedding rings." Her expression turned sad and she clenched her hands into fists around the chains. "But I have never forgotten that I am descended from Eastern queens. I have never stopped looking for others like me. My people. I always knew a few of us had to have survived. Our home may be lost to us forever but we will never forget that there was once a great kingdom where there is now only that hideous chasm."

John felt a pang of sympathy for the woman. Her pained expression and voice alone would have elicited his compassion, even if he had not understood her words. Her eyes were bright with unshed tears.

She said, "I have prayed every night since I was a child that I would find you."

Laurie and Bill both looked to him for an explanation but John didn't want to interrupt Lady Bousim.

"Later," he whispered.

Ohbi held out a thin white circle of cloth and Lady Bousim took it and wiped the tears from her eyes.

"I'm so foolish," Lady Bousim whispered. "Inholima must not know that I've been crying when she comes back or she'll run to Rashan Pivan right away and tell him."

"How did you know that we were from the East?" John asked. He wasn't sure how well she would take the revelation that they weren't. If he could avoid telling her, he thought that would be for the best.

"I'm sorry to say that I didn't recognize you at all the night you brought warning to us on the Holy Road. When Ohbi peeked out from the carriage and described you to me, I thought you must have been some filthy peasant. You disguised yourself very well. But then Rashan Pivan came to me and told me that you, a ragged peasant, had stood against the demoness, Ji Shir'kurod. I knew you couldn't be a common man, so I sent Bati'kohl to attend you in the bath and to listen to you when you were alone among yourselves."

John had thought that he had heard someone outside the door.

"Bati'kohl brought me a piece of your raiments before he burned them." She slipped her hand inside one of her long sleeves and pulled out a small strip of blue Gortex.

Ohbi gave a small gasp as she saw it.

"I have never seen such a brilliant color in all the world," Ohbi whispered.

"You never will again." Lady Bousim turned the material through her fingers. "The great queens of the East are all gone and all that remains of their splendor is this scrap. My great-grandmother had gowns the color of the sunset and of violets. They all had to be burned when she went into hiding. Not a single thread could be saved."

"I'm sorry," John said.

"You're sorry for me?" Her expression verged on defiance, and then she smiled. "I think I am sorry enough for myself. You must not indulge me too much or I will have myself weeping again. And what do I have to cry over that you three do not have worse? Here you three are, starved and beaten from a lifetime of living at the edge of the world. Here you are among strangers whose language only one of you knows and whose customs are all wrong to you. And yet you are not crying. It makes me proud to see you and a little ashamed that my ancestors hid among the nobles when yours did not."

She pondered the scrap of blue fabric in her fingers and then handed it to Ohbi.

"Burn it."

The girl reverently carried it to the fireplace and then dropped it into the flames.

"Seeing the three of you together," Lady Bousim went on, "I knew at once that you were the children of Eastern mothers. Your golden hair, his blue jewel eyes, and Loshai." She gazed at Laurie like she was looking at work of art.

"Silver hair, pale eyes, delicate witch's bones," Lady Bousim said. "I might have known just looking at her. But I wouldn't have been sure. It was only when I saw the three of you together before me and Bati'kohl had told me that you spoke in a strange language that he had never heard before that I knew instantly who you are."

"Do you think others here know?" John asked.

"No, most of them don't even know that customs of the Eastern Kingdom have survived. That is how well the Payshmura destroyed us. Now, you see a fair-haired child and no one thinks anything of it, not even the child's own mother. She may have Eastern blood but it doesn't matter because her soul has become Basawar. It's pitiful."

"My lady," Ohbi returned to her seat next to Lady Bousim, "I'm afraid Inholima will be returning soon."

Lady Bousim sighed.

"I must not ramble during this little time we have left. There are things you must know." She turned to address John directly. "If Rashan Pivan'ro'Bousim asks you why you were out in the wastes, you must tell him that you were on your way to Amura'taye to beg the priests to pray for your brother's health. Rashan Pivan is a religious man. He will be pleased to know that you are as well. You will have to make sure he sees you going to the first step of the Thousand Steps and chanting prayers, but it's a small price to pay for his trust."

"I don't know any Basawar prayers," John interjected.

Lady Bousim gasped at John's revelation but then smiled.

"Of course you don't. How perfect you are," she said.

"My brother, Bati'kohl, knows many," Ohbi offered. "I can send him to Jahn with evening tea and he can teach Jahn what he needs to know."

"A good idea," Lady Bousim complimented Ohbi, then returned her attention to John. "You should only need to pray tomorrow. The day after that is the Opening of Heaven's Door. The steps will be cleared for the ushiri candidate."

"That would be your son?" John asked.

"Yes, unfortunately Fikiri was chosen. If he reaches Heaven's Door and passes, then we will all be stranded in this priest-riddled backwater. We will be expected to live out the rest of our lives here, praying for his success in reaching Nayeshi." Lady Bousim's lip curled in disgust. The silver beads hanging from her hair rang against each other like tiny bells. "But there is a good chance that my son could fail." Lady Bousim and Ohbi both appeared to be relieved by this thought. "Rashan Alidas'ro'Bousim was to be his attendant, but the man can hardly move now. Fikiri can't be sent without an attendant and the rest of the rashan'im are married men so they can't enter Rathal'pesha. In two days time, we will likely turn around and return to Nurjima. The three of you must come with me. I will see that you never go hungry again and you will teach me what my mother was afraid to. You will teach me the wisdom of our lost kingdom."

"Nurjima is a long way to the south, isn't it?" John asked.

"Yes, but it will do you no good to remain here at the edge of the shattered world. The Kingdom of the East will never return. It is rubble beneath the black sea."

"Nurjima is beautiful," Ohbi assured him. "The streets are lit with golden gas lamps and there are all the smartest and funniest people there. The theaters stay open until almost morning with actors and singers—"

"Ohbi," Lady Bousim cut her off gently, "they have only lived on the wastes. They don't even know what a street lamp is."

Ohbi looked amazed at the idea of this.

"Nurjima is beautiful," Lady Bousim told him. "There are people there who are open-minded and wise and they will help you if I ask them to. You must not be afraid."

John wasn't afraid—at least not of the prospect of street lamps. But the idea of leaving Amura'taye worried him deeply. The key to Nayeshi lay in Rathal'pesha, not Nurjima. And Ravishan was here as well and he knew what Lady Bousim did not: how to cross between worlds.

Still, refusing the lady's offer might insult her so badly that she would reveal their identities to Pivan.

Inholima's return saved John from having to give Lady Bousim an answer. She opened the door very quietly and quite slowly as if hoping not to be noticed.

After she poured them tea, she seated herself at Lady Bousim's right. Lady Bousim commented on how pretty her hair was and asked what she thought the lady should wear for the Opening of Heaven's Door.

As Inholima answered the question and the others that followed, the lady offhandedly excused John, Laurie, and Bill. She hardly spared them a glance when they left the room. She seemed utterly rapt with Inholima. The girl smiled shyly and blushed a little from the compliments and attention that the lady gave her.

If he hadn't known better, John would have thought that the girl was Lady Bousim's dearest companion, a girl whom she adored like a daughter. But he had seen how dead and cold her expression turned the moment the girl left the room.

John found her ability to mask her emotions both impressive and frightening. She had looked into his eyes with the same sincerity and sweetness that she now turned on Inholima.

"Behr and I need a little more rest," Laurie said the Basawar words softly and carefully. "We were up all night, traveling here."

"Do you have rooms?" John asked.

"We share one." Laurie's brow furrowed as she concentrated on her words. "It's across from yours."

"Did you understand much of what she said?" John asked in a whisper.

"Yes," Laurie leaned close to John, "I listen better than I talk. I'll explain to Behr while we're in bed. I don't think a spy will be able to sneak in there with us."

"I hope not. We should meet later."

"We'll come and get you in your room after our ..." Laurie frowned. "Short sleep."

"Nap," John supplied the word for her.

"I know that one," Bill said. He would have gone on but two maids came up the stairs, causing all three of them to lapse into silence.

Their rooms were on the first floor, at the back of the huge main building. They slunk through several large halls as well as the massive, steamy kitchen on their way. Everywhere John looked there were servants dressed in the green of the Bousim family.

Dozens of men and women stopped work to greet them in a welcoming ambush. Women offered Laurie their shawls and gave advice for treating Bill's 'thin lungs.'

The men were more reticent but they still wanted to know how long John and his family had lived out in the wastes. What had they eaten? What had the demoness, Ji Shir'kurod, looked like? Did she breathe fire? Did she speak in the tongue of men?

John answered most of the questions, while Laurie avoided saying anything by stepping behind John and feigning shyness. Then a hunched old woman began to probe Bill with unceasing questions about his condition. Bill did his best, shaking his head and nodding, but at last he simply began to cough violently.

John apologized and said they needed to get him to bed right away. And the three of them slipped out of the kitchen down the narrow hallways of the servant's quarters. Once they reached Bill and Laurie's door, John wished them both peaceful dreams. They disappeared inside together.

John turned to face the door to his own room.

He wasn't sure what he would do in that tiny, empty space, but at least he would be alone and be able to relax in solitude and silence. He'd grown used to living in the wilderness and here, with the sounds of servants chatting, the smells of fires and perfumes and the close confines of the stone walls, he felt overwhelmed. Almost trapped.

He needed to have a few moments when he didn't have to concentrate on each grunt and syllable of every person anywhere near him. He wanted just a little time to be alone and quiet.

And he wondered about Ravishan. The boy had an uncanny knack when it came to finding him. If he could be alone, Ravishan might simply step out of the Gray Space. The thought appealed to John in ways he could barely admit to himself.

John opened his door to find Rashan Pivan in full uniform standing next to his bed, waiting for him.

CHAPTER THIRTEEN

"You have spoken with Lady Amha'in'Bousim?" Pivan asked. He seemed amused by John's unhappy expression.

"I have," John replied.

"Aren't you going to come in?" Pivan leaned against the wall. The room was small and dark. It smelled slightly of John's own body, his sweat, and breath. The confines and the scent made it seem like a deeply personal space. The narrow single bed by its very nature implied privacy. Pivan, with his heavy coat and uniform, did not belong there.

John stood his ground. The two of them crammed into the tiny confines of the windowless room smacked too much of a debasing locker room encounter for John to enter.

"I was going out," John said. "I just wanted to see if my coat had been brought back to my room."

"Lady Bousim had it burned," Pivan said. "There are some old coats in the barracks that might fit you."

"I probably don't need one."

"Don't be an ass. If you're going out, you'll need a coat. We're half way up a damn mountain." Pivan stepped toward the door. "You can follow me to the barracks, unless you'd rather hide from me under your blankets?"

John wanted to tell Pivan to go to hell, but he knew better. He couldn't afford to offend anyone right now, much less a man who apparently had the authority to have him burned alive.

"Fine," John replied. He stood back from the door to let Pivan pass. It gave John a brief, petty pleasure to note that he stood a good six inches taller than the other man.

He followed Rashan Pivan back through the huge kitchen with its massive fires and meat spits. This time none of the servants said anything to him. They only bowed their heads as Pivan passed. John followed him through a side door and out into the crisp morning air.

The Bousim house was not just a single building but several structures surrounded by a stone wall. East, toward the front of the house, there were formal gardens, though now only a few squat spring starts poked up from the cold ground. Near the front gate, John also noted a line of short pine trees with wildly crooked branches. Small white cones nestled like birds' eggs in the midst of dark green needles.

At the back of the house stood several black brick buildings adjacent to a wooden corral, where six tahldi stood pulling dry grass from thick bales. In the light of day, John could see that the animals were the color of moss. Their long, spiraling horns gleamed glossy black. The animals responded to the sight of Pivan. Their heads came up, their ears pricked with excitement, and they nuzzled their noses out to brush his hand. Even after he passed their dark brown gazes followed him.

Pivan led John to the building across from the corral. It turned out to be a barracks. Men in dark green uniforms crouched around an iron woodstove in the middle of the big main room. Beds lined the walls. Canvas curtains, which could have been drawn around the beds for privacy, were tied back.

Several men lay in their beds. John recognized Alidas' pale face and curling brown hair. He slept, but two of the others seemed to be playing cards.

As Pivan led him past the rows of beds, John noticed that the uniformed men, like their tahldi, watched Pivan as he passed. John hadn't been sure of the animals' expressions but the men's faces shone with excitement and reverence. No matter what John thought of him, Pivan was clearly a good leader to his men.

Pivan made a small motion with his gloved hand and immediately a slim, swarthy young man jumped to his feet and saluted Pivan.

Pivan gave him a hint of a smile.

"Mou'pin, this is our good dog, Jahn. He needs a coat." Pivan frowned at John, taking in the poor fit of his clothes. "One that's big enough to cover him."

"From the storeroom, sir?" Mou'pin asked.

"He's too big to fit in a cavalrymen's coat," Pivan said. "See if you can't find a market somewhere in this backwater and get him something from there."

Pivan reached into his coat pocket and tossed Mou'pin a coin purse. "Don't go alone and don't take all damn day."

"Yes, sir." Mou'pin saluted again.

"Come on," Pivan said to John. He turned and led John back through a door at the far end of the room.

A bed and a dresser were shoved up against the left wall. A heavy wooden table and two chairs stood in the middle of the room. Next to the one small window there was a low shelf with a single leather-bound book, a dish of polished stones and a cloth decorated with the holy Payshmura symbols of the sun and moon.

"Your room or your commander's?" John asked.

"Mine." Pivan closed the door. "Rasho Tashtu is obligated to keep his bed in the great house, where he is close at hand should Lady Bousim call for him."

Pivan pushed out the chair closest to the door.

"Have a seat. We should talk."

"What about?" John asked.

"Sit down," Pivan repeated and this time John obeyed him.

Pivan removed his coat and threw it across his bed. Then he walked to the shelf and without looking chose one of the polished stones, a tawny colored one. He rubbed his thumb across its surface and then set it aside.

Pivan asked, "Are you a married man?"

"No." John hadn't expected that question.

"Have you ever been?"

"No." John recalled Lady Bousim saying something about the rashan'im all being married. All of them but Alidas, who was to have been her son's attendant up to Rathal'pesha.

Pivan nodded thoughtfully. He walked to the table and took the seat across from John.

"I imagine Lady Bousim treated you quite kindly when she called you before her."

"Yes," John replied.

"You're the type of man she is often kind to." Pivan put an unusual emphasis on the word kind. John knew what Pivan implied about Lady Bousim and he didn't like it.

"The lady treated my sister and her husband just as well as she treated me. She seemed compassionate to us all."

"I'm sure she did. Lady Bousim is immensely compassionate and she can be very charming when she wishes to be." Pivan leaned a little closer to John. "Back in Nurjima, there was a fair-haired young man who Lady Bousim felt such compassion for that Lord Bousim had him hanged. Another was shot where he stood in the lady's bedroom. Her compassion knows no bounds."

John began to open his mouth to say that nothing like that was going to happen, but Pivan cut him off.

"It is the lady's immense compassion that got her shipped out to this freezing backwater," Pivan spat. "And as much as I wish it were not the case, it is my duty and the duty of my commander to see that she does not leave this place. She has humiliated her good husband too many times."

"I don't see what this has to do with me," John said.

"It doesn't. Not yet. But it will if you stay in the lady's company. You clean up too nicely for her to keep away from you." Pivan's eyes moved over him slowly as if cataloging the changes that a bath and a shave had made. "You're young and well made. I would hate to have to hang you."

Pivan stood up and returned to the shelf. The morning light pouring in from the window cast hard shadows across his face, making his frown seem gouged into his mouth. Again, he chose a stone from the small silver dish. "They tell me that you came here to pray at the foot of Rathal'pesha. Is that true?"

"Yes. I wanted to pray for my sister's husband," John answered warily, discomfited by Pivan's suspicious change of subject.

"I'm not sure how such a sickly man managed to chain your sister's hands. Perhaps she didn't give him much of a fight." Pivan smiled as he said this. "But I can see why you would worry about his ability to care for her. Is that why you stay with her?"

"I stayed to help them both. Behr isn't just my sister's husband. He's a friend of mine." John didn't know if he'd actually answered Pivan's question, but it was all he felt safe saying. He knew very little about Basawar marriage rituals, except that men could and often did take more than one wife and that divorce was unheard of.

"But if they were protected? If they were assured of food and shelter?" Pivan came back to the table. "Then what would you do?"

"What would I do?" John repeated the question. Pivan regarded him calmly, waiting.

"I don't know. It's been so long that I haven't really thought about it. It may never happen." John didn't have to work to inject weariness into his voice. He spoke the truth. They might never find a way home. And then what? What would he do if they had to spend the rest of their lives here?

"But you don't have a woman waiting back in your village?" Pivan's voice broke into his thoughts.

"No," John said quickly. "I don't have anyone."

More truth. This conversation was turning out to be among the most depressing of his life.

Pivan nodded and then placed the polished stone down onto the tabletop between them. He performed the action so deliberately that John knew it must carry some great significance. But he had absolutely no idea what that might be. The white quartz was cloudy at the bottom and then grew more transparent toward the top. It looked almost like a piece of ice sitting in front of him.

Pivan said, "If I swore that I would provide for your sister and her husband and see that they would never be without shelter or food, would you be willing to leave them behind?"

"Behind here?"

"Yes." Pivan kept his eyes on the stone. "Young Fikiri'in'Bousim must have an attendant to accompany him to Heaven's Door. Alidas was chosen, but you've seen his leg yourself. He can't possibly climb the Thousand Steps."

Suddenly all of Pivan's questions made perfect sense to him.

"You're willing to take care of Loshai and Behr if I go in Alidas' place?" John asked.

"I have offered you my word," Pivan said. "Will you take it?"

John realized that physically taking the stone somehow symbolized his agreement to the proposition.

"You would have to live in Rathal'pesha as a priest," Pivan continued, apparently ready to argue against what he imagined was John's reason for hesitation. "You would leave no son after you, but your sister's sons will be safe in the Bousim house and they will each know what you did for them. Your name will not die with you."

None of what Pivan said mattered, beyond the knowledge that he would protect Laurie and Bill and that John would get inside Rathal'pesha. He would have access to the holy keys as well as Ravishan and his teachers. John's heart raced at just the thought of finding a way back home. Could it really be this easy?

"Lady Bousim will be furious," John murmured.

"She will be angry with me, not with you," Pivan said. "She doesn't need to know that you agreed to this. She can believe that I forced it on you."

"Could you do that?" John was thinking of the legal aspect but instantly he realized that his question could also be taken as a personal challenge, which of course Pivan did.

He smirked at John.

"I've broken demons. I could break you," he stated flatly. "But I couldn't give you the strength to climb the Thousand Steps to Heaven's Door. A man's whole will has to be behind that kind of work."

"What if my will isn't enough? What if I fail?"

"I'm a bad man to disappoint." Pivan smiled at him. "But I'm sure that Lady Bousim would be greatly pleased with you."

John nodded and then accepted the polished quartz.

"A wise choice," Pivan told him.

《《《

The next afternoon John found himself following Pivan through the narrow streets of Amura'taye. The last rays of afternoon sun cast long shadows and felt pleasantly warm on John's face. His new coat hung over his shoulder, giving off a faint odor of sheep. John didn't take much note of it anymore. Every man, woman, and child he passed on the streets was swathed in the scent of wool. It clung to their bodies and hair.

The very streets were full of the animals. Shepherds drove herds of sheep and goats past. A breed of tiny goats seemed to wander the streets in packs like feral dogs. Once or twice one of them charged John's shins, butting him and then leaping away. Often they left behind a little steaming pile of droppings. John took consolation in the fact that they missed his boots.

At last they reached the Payshmura shrine where John would practice the prayers Pivan needed him to know. John drew in a deep breath of the cool air. His head was still full of the prayers that Lady Bousim's servant, Bati'kohl, had taught him earlier that morning.

John found it a little ironic that Pivan would want to teach him one set of prayers so that Lady Bousim could have no objection to him, while the lady sent her servant to teach him another set of prayers to win Pivan's approval. Neither of them knew of the other's plans.

John kept it that way. He didn't even mention the bargain he had struck with Pivan to Laurie or Bill. It was the only way he could ensure that both Laurie and Bill were genuinely surprised when Pivan sent him up to take Fikiri to Rathal'pesha. Lady Bousim was observant enough that she would know from their faces if they had been part of the deception against her.

Dim lamps filled with sheep fat illuminated the simple wooden shrine. The flames popped and sputtered as the mountain winds swept through the flimsy wooden walls. An old man offered both John and Pivan their own warm clay cup full of daru'sira.

Unlike the pale, sweet tea he'd enjoyed with Lady Bousim, this was unadulterated, dark and bitter.

"It tastes like goat's piss, but it will make your voice strong when you call prayers on the steps to Heaven's Door," Pivan told him. John drank it. If nothing else, it kept him warm while he knelt before the rough stone statue of the god Parfir and repeated the prayers again and again.

After only an hour, his knees ached. Next to him, Pivan seemed unaware of any discomfort, his expression rapt as he whispered prayers.

Townspeople came and went, paying little attention to John or Pivan. Most of them simply bowed their heads before the rough stone statue and chanted their own prayers, then stood and departed. Many of them placed clay cups of goat's milk at the foot of the statue or left balls of rough yarn.

Their prayers, unlike the ones John repeated, were simple and often just pleas for better health or greater harvests.

"Parfir," Pivan whispered at John's side, "the earth is your flesh, the rivers your blood, the skies your breath. I honor your body with my own. I honor your soul with my own ..."

John joined in his prayer, gazing up at the stone figure of the Payshmura god. Years of soot and the deep shadows made it hard to see the statue's features clearly. But occasionally, when the lamp flames leapt high, John caught a clear view.

The stone was dark and rose up into a man's body, arms outstretched. In places his muscles seemed to melt into carvings of branches, flowers, and leaves. Lichen had colonized the figure and John thought that he saw birds moving up in the darkest corners.

John found it odd that the figure gazed downward and not up. He supposed he had seen too many pictures of Christian martyrs and saints staring glassily up at the heavens. It made a kind of sense that an actual god should be depicted looking downward at his mortal followers.

"Your flesh is my earth. Your blood is my river. Your breath is my sky. Your body, my world. Your will, my life ..."

John repeated Pivan's words more slowly this time, familiar enough with them now to be able to consider their meaning. Parfir embodied the land itself.

Peering up into the shadows, John noticed that Parfir's face had been more delicately carved than the rest of him. His handsome countenance wore a benevolent smile.

Oddly, the people who came in to pray didn't look at Parfir. Instead they, like Pivan, bowed their heads before him. Many closed their eyes. John thought it was too bad that they didn't look up. It might have reassured them to see that Parfir smiled over them.

That handsome smile made him think of Ravishan.

It had been two days since John had seen him. Today was the day that Ravishan had promised to bring medicine for Bill. Ravishan would be searching for them and they wouldn't be there for him to find.

A panicked feeling rushed through John as he tried to think of a way to send word to Ravishan. Nothing came to mind. He would just have to hope that Ravishan stayed sensible and didn't get himself in trouble looking for them. If he could wait one more day then John would be there in Rathal'pesha with him.

They continued repeating the prayers over and over until John's throat was rough. Then, at last, Pivan decided that they had done enough.

"Any more and I'll begin to regret that I didn't become a priest myself," Pivan said. Seeing his expression, John didn't think he was joking.

After the long walk back, John gladly dropped down to his bed. When he closed his eyes, he thought he could still hear Pivan whispering prayers.

CHAPTER FOURTEEN

The morning air was cold and the sky colorless as water. The sun had not risen high enough to burn away last night's chill and frost still clung to ceremonial stones and iron statues like prickly white lichen.

John flexed his fingers inside his fur-lined gloves to draw a little more feeling into them. He resituated the sheepskin of daru'sira that Pivan had given him, slinging it over his shoulder.

The Thousand Steps to Heaven's Door began at the highest point at the north end of the city. The steps themselves were unremarkable. Plain gray stone, they were only a little more narrow and tall than the steps leading up to the college library back at home. Each step taken alone was simple and unimpressive. But one look up the mountainside and their monumental scale became clear.

Carved into the face of the mountain, the steps rose like an immense scar. John craned his neck back, following the straight line of the stairs up to where they were lost from sight in the white wisps of clouds. The two huge iron statues of Parfir standing at either side of the first step seemed tiny by comparison.

"One thousand," John muttered. His breath came out in white puffs.

He glanced over to where Pivan stood. The tip of his nose and his cheeks were red from the cold but he didn't seem to care. Pivan's features were set in an expression of stern confidence. He gazed down the road behind them, only narrowing his eyes slightly as a distant group of men staggered drunkenly into his view.

"Maybe we should go to the house—" John began but Pivan cut him off with a shake of his head.

"You have to be here for him. Once the candidate arrives, he cannot wait. If you are not here for him, then he will have to go without you," Pivan said. "And Gaunan Fikiri'in'Bousim cannot make the climb without an attendant. Even I wouldn't be callous enough to force that on him."

"Well, he can't make the climb with an attendant if he's not here," John replied. "We've been waiting for an hour." Despite the thick socks and new, heavy boots, his toes had gone numb.

"These things take time." Pivan sighed and turned to John. "You remember everything?"

"The first and last step have to be his own. No food, only daru'sira to drink, and we have to be inside before the sun goes down."

"And the prayers?" Pivan asked.

John gave Pivan a look of sheer disbelief. He had done nothing but repeat prayers for two solid days: prayers obviously crafted for easy recall. They had a catchy kind of rhythm that stuck in his head even better than the Beer Barn radio jingle had.

He said, "Do you really have to ask that?"

Pivan gave a slight laugh, then said, "There is one other thing. It is a sacred word. It must be said when you reach Heaven's Door."

"All right."

"It should be Fikiri's to say but I don't know how much of a bad influence his mother may have been on him."

"He may not say it?"

"His voice might betray him or his tongue might be cursed." Pivan turned his attention down the road. "It's true what they say about her. She has Eastern blood and witch's bones."

Two days ago John would've had no idea what Pivan was talking about, but since then he had overheard numerous conversations about Lady Bousim. As he traveled from the Bousim pilgrimage house to the prayer shrine, he had listened to the stories and gossip spread and transform. The lady had grown from a willful wife who shamed her husband and allowed her silver wedding chains to tarnish into an Eastern witch. Stories of how she enchanted her husband, seduced priests, and even cast spells over her son abounded.

Pivan never started any of the rumors but he did nothing to stop them either.

"Lady Bousim wouldn't harm her own child," John said.

"No, but she would go to great lengths not to lose him. She loves the boy as much as her husband despises him."

John disliked hearing this. He hadn't met Fikiri but he knew that the boy was only thirteen, too young to be despised by anyone, but especially by his own father. John knew all too well how badly that mere idea could hurt a young man.

"You think I'll have to say the word for him then?" John asked.

Pivan gave a silent nod. John waited, but Pivan kept his lips pressed tightly closed.

"I can't say the word if I don't know what it is," John reminded him.

"It is sacred and divine. You must respect it, for it is Parfir's own tongue. You must only speak it when you are worthy of him in your body and soul."

"I understand," John replied too quickly.

"No!" Pivan rounded on him and for a moment John thought Pivan might strike him. "No, you can't understand. This is a bargain for you but for other men it is their calling. Parfir's will smolders within them; his word lights their souls and burns through them. This word was given to me by such a man. It was his last word."

John bowed his head. He knew better than to let Pivan see his face. Countless conversations with Laurie had made him wary of any person wearing that expression of fixed intensity and speaking with a strained, aching tone of conviction.

John didn't doubt that Pivan felt a deep reverence, but the best John could do was respect a spirituality he didn't share.

"I will give you this word for Fikiri's sake, because his mother should not be able to bar him from heaven." Pivan drew in a deep breath and closed his eyes, almost as if he were in pain.

"I-am-here-my-lord." Pivan slurred the English words together but John still recognized them. He was so surprised to hear them coming out of Pivan's mouth that out of reflex his head jerked up to make sure that it had been Pivan speaking.

An expression of relief swept over Pivan's features and he beamed at John.

"So, his word does touch you." Pivan closed his eyes. "Then this is his will."

John didn't trust himself to respond. Luckily a movement on the road caught his eye.

"Someone's coming."

Six rashan'im, including Mou'pin, rode their tahldi hard up the road. Dust and frost flew up beneath the animals' hooves and their fast breath rolled out in white clouds like smoke from a steam engine.

A terrified boy with short dark blond hair clung to the neck of Mou'pin's tahldi. His heavy black coat and hood made his skin look sickly pale. Tears streaked his face.

"Gaunan Fikiri'in'Bousim?" John asked. He was smaller than John had expected and seemed younger than thirteen.

Pivan nodded. "He has not yet entirely committed his heart to the priesthood."

"I can see that." John considered the Thousand Steps again. That would be quite a distance to drag an unwilling boy.

The distant pounding of the tahldi's hooves became a thunder. The riders surged up to the top of the road and Mou'pin reined in his tahldi beside Pivan. Grinning, he tossed Fikiri down to his commander.

Pivan caught the boy and set him on his feet directly in front of the steps.

"Today you are called to serve Parfir. Honor him and honor his house." Pivan shoved the boy forward but Fikiri resisted.

"She'll hate me if I go!" Fikiri cried out.

Pivan leaned down close to the boy and whispered, "I'll kill you if you don't."

Fikiri bolted forward, scrambling upward in a panic. Pivan straightened and then clapped John on the shoulder.

"He's all yours. Parfir help you."

John just started climbing.

The moment Fikiri caught sight of John behind him, he threw himself ahead with greater speed. He slipped and caught himself, and then gave out pathetic groans and sobs. He sprinted up the steps with reckless energy. John didn't try to catch him. He paced himself.

Twice he called out to reassure Fikiri that he meant him no harm, but his booming voice only seemed to further frighten the boy. After that, John concentrated on not falling down the frost-slick steps. As he went higher, the frost solidified into thin sheets of ice.

Steadily the air grew thinner and colder. Wind cut through John's coat. The first dull ache began to play through the muscles of his thighs and calves.

Behind him, Pivan and his rashan'im had receded to tiny shadows against the Holy Road.

Ahead Fikiri dragged his feet up one step, swayed, and then slowly negotiated the next. He glanced back at John and, seeing how much distance John had gained, again bolted forward. He stumbled up a few steps and then slipped down to his hands and knees, sobbing. He curled his arms around his legs and sat there in a miserable, trembling heap.

When John reached him, he knelt down and said, "I'm not going to hurt you."

Fikiri's face was red and wet from exertion and tears. His breath came in gasps and unappealing snuffles.

"I want to go home," Fikiri mumbled. He didn't lift his eyes to John.

"I know," John told him. They had that in common at least.

"Please, can we go home?"

"I'm sorry, but no." John slipped the sheepskin of daru'sira from his shoulder and handed it to Fikiri. "Drink some of this."

"What is it?"

"Daru'sira."

Fikiri met John's face for the first time. He seemed startled. He said, "You aren't Alidas."

"No, I'm called Jahn." John smiled, exploiting the innocuous nature of his Basawar name as best he could.

"I had a hunting dog called Jahn." Fikiri gave him a weak smile and glanced to the edges of John's hood, where strands of his blond hair hung against the black wool. "Are you a friend of my mother's?"

"I've met her. I'm the man who stopped your convoy on the Holy Road the night before you reached Amura'taye."

Fikiri looked at him blankly.

"You were in a carriage on your way here," John reminded him.

"I remember the train station at Nurjima but after that all I remember is the priest's voice, chanting prayers over and over ..." Fikiri trailed off. Tears began to dribble down his cheeks.

"Drink a little daru'sira. It'll warm you up," he told the boy.

Fikiri sniffed and sipped the drink and then handed the skin back to John.

"Do you think you can walk?" John asked.

Fikiri's mouth trembled. "Do I have to?"

"Yes, you have to." John felt like an utter asshole making the boy stand and keep going, but he needed Fikiri to get into Rathal'pesha. And anyway, Pivan wouldn't offer Fikiri much of a welcome if he caught him dragging himself down the mountain.

John helped Fikiri to his feet and let the boy lean on him as they continued climbing.

Icy mist from mountain clouds drifted over them, enfolding them in whiteness and cold. Sudden, sharp winds swept down, slicing through John's clothes and chilling the sweat on his back and thighs. Fikiri shivered constantly and wept intermittently. When the sound of his crying didn't drown it, John could hear the boy's teeth chattering against each other.

"They won't let us enter even if we reach Rathal'pesha." Fikiri sniffed. "They'll leave us out to freeze to death on the mountainside. There are prayers that have to be said and words—"

"I know," John told him. "I know the prayers and I know the words."

Fikiri halted as though riveted to the stairway.

"You know them?"

John shrugged and then began to chant the prayers.

A strange, dreamy expression spread across Fikiri's face.

John stopped chanting and said, "You see? It'll be fine."

"What did you say?"

"I said, it will be fine." John frowned at Fikiri.

"No, it won't!" Fikiri's lips began to tremble. "There are prayers and words that have to be said. I don't know what they are."

"I just told you that I know them."

"You did?" Fikiri's look of surprise seemed utterly genuine.

"Yes, I just said one of the prayers to you."

"You didn't say anything," Fikiri told him.

John began the prayer again, and once more the tension and fear drained from Fikiri's face. His arms hung limply; his eyes drooped nearly closed. A slight, sweet smile spread across his lips and he swayed with John's voice as if it were music. Then Fikiri began climbing. He took the steps with the rhythm of John's voice, moving with an ease and grace that he had previously lacked.

So that was the purpose of the prayers, John realized. Inducing this trance-like state was what the attendant did and why Fikiri needed one. There was no way he would endure the climb on his own will alone. Left to himself, Fikiri would have just sat down and cried until sunset.

John felt slightly guilty as he continued chanting prayers that compelled Fikiri to mindlessly climb the steps. It seemed like a sinister power to have over the boy and one that, as a decent person, he shouldn't use. On the other hand, they were making much better time this way and Fikiri wasn't crying.

John kept praying.

The words that had pervaded the last two days flowed from him. One prayer led into the next and the next after that. They repeated in a long cycle, the words pulling him onward.

John's climb wasn't a painless daze like Fikiri's. His muscles burned and his throat ached. He didn't dare to look ahead him. He didn't want to see the endless line of steps still before him. He kept his eyes on his feet.

There was snow now. Little patches of it filled the shadowed corners of the gray stone steps. Clumps clung to John's boots. John's legs felt like weights. The bruises across his back throbbed. Ahead of him Fikiri continued, oblivious to both fatigue and cold.

Suddenly, John felt something in the air. Something like a breath blown against his ear. It was a familiar sensation. It was the way the air seemed to tremble just as Ravishan appeared before him.

"Nahara'hi, muhli," a low voice hissed.

John instantly looked up, searching for the source of the threatening words. But only Fikiri stood before him, his dreamy expression fading as John fell silent, listening.

"Shir'im'hir inaye!" the voice came again.

John whipped around and looked down the steps. Still, no one. He looked farther ahead on the steps.

"Korud," a second low voice growled over them. "Shir'im'hir maht!"

A terrified whimper escaped Fikiri.

More voices joined in, hissing and growling in Basawar.

"Turn aside, unworthy filth."

"How dare you walk the Thousand Steps to Heaven's Door, hideous, ugly creature."

"Dirty."

"Sinful."

"Filthy."

"Piece of shit."

Fikiri collapsed to his knees, weeping and begging Parfir to forgive him, to spare him.

The voices swept over them, seeming to rise from the sky and stones. John narrowed his eyes. Sky and stones didn't speak Basawar or any other language. These were human voices, men's voices. The air shivered with the sensation of hidden spaces opening and slipping closed. It had to be the Payshmura priests.

"Fikiri." John crouched down beside the boy.

"I'll kill you," a voice whispered.

"Tear you to pieces," another hissed.

"Burn you alive."

Their words were like a swarm of insects slashing through the air. John could almost feel their words brush across his face. He could smell their breath.

"It's a trick, Fikiri. They're testing you," John told him.

Fikiri sobbed. "I don't want to die! Please! I don't want to die!"

"You won't." John placed his hands over Fikiri's ears.

"Go back."

"Give up."

"Turn aside."

John kept his hands pressed over Fikiri's ears and slowly Fikiri began to calm down. He looked up at John and then glanced from side to side as if he expected to be able to see if the disembodied voices were still there.

"Are they gone?" Fikiri asked.

John shook his head and slowly peeled one of his hands back.

"You will suffer."

"Burn."

"Bleed."

"Scream for mercy."

Fikiri's lips trembled.

"If it was Parfir," John said firmly, "could my hands keep his voice from reaching you?"

"Are they devils?" Fikiri whimpered.

"No." John found that he was almost shouting now.

"Run from me!"

"I am death."

"I am ruin."

"It's just a trick that the priests are playing to test you," John shouted over the threats and insults. "You must not listen to them."

"I will devour your flesh."

"Rot your bones."

"Eat your soul."

"I'm scared." Fikiri was trembling. "I don't want to die."

"You aren't going to die! Just look at me, Fikiri." John forced Fikiri to lift his head. "Just look at me and repeat what I say."

Tears dribbled down Fikiri's face but he didn't look away.

John shouted out the words of the prayers. And slowly Fikiri began to repeat them.

"Parfir," John led Fikiri as Pivan had led him, "the earth is your flesh, the rivers your blood, the skies your breath. Parfir, the earth is your flesh, the rivers your blood, the skies your breath. I honor you. I honor you. I honor you ..."

Slowly Fikiri's eyes drooped, his mouth relaxed, so that he was only whispering. He slumped into John's chest, still muttering the prayer.

John continued chanting. He carefully lifted Fikiri onto his back and then pushed himself up to his feet.

Angry, resistant pain shot through his muscles. For a moment John's legs trembled as if they might buckle. He stumbled, caught himself, and continued grinding the words of the prayers out. Slowly, he struggled up the steps. The hissed insults and whispered threats washed over him.

John ignored everything but the prayers and the steps. The weight, the cold, the pain—he refused to feel them. Staring down, he took gray step after gray step.

Gray step after gray step.

They seemed to go on endlessly beneath him.

And then there were only cobblestones beneath his feet. John lifted his head. A white stone wall rose up in front of him. It glowed a pale yellow in the early afternoon light. Only a few feet ahead of him, the last step stood before a broad iron door in the wall. The step gleamed brightly and as John drew closer he realized that it was made of gold.

John lowered Fikiri to his feet. The boy moaned and called sleepily for his mother.

"Wake up." John could hardly get a sound out, his throat felt so raw.

Fikiri opened his eyes. He looked like the nap had done him good.

He said, "The voices are gone."

John nodded and pointed to the tall white wall and the iron door.

"We've reached Rathal'pesha." John pulled the sheepskin of daru'sira from his shoulder and drank. The juniper-like bitterness felt good against his dry throat.

"You have to go through the door." John still couldn't get much more than a whisper out.

"But I don't know—" Fikiri began.

"The word you must say is I-am-here-my-lord," John told him.

Fikiri tried and failed.

"I-am-here-my-lord," John repeated. "Say it."

"I'yam herem'myl'ord," Fikiri whispered.

"That's great." John sipped more of the daru'sira. The burning in his throat cooled to numbness.

"I already knew the word," Fikiri confessed. "My mother will never forgive me if I go in."

"I'm sorry," John said.

He suspected that Lady Bousim might not forgive Fikiri for becoming a Payshmura priest. She despised the Payshmura absolutely, maybe even more than she loved her son. John entertained no illusion about parents and unconditional love. It wasn't fair to put Fikiri in that position. But then, life wasn't often fair.

And John had not climbed nine hundred and ninety-nine steps to turn around and walk back down.

For a brief, exasperated moment he considered dragging Fikiri to the door, kicking it open and hurling the boy through. Pivan had probably had something like that in mind when he had told John the holy password. But John was exhausted and the big iron door didn't look like it could be kicked open easily.

"Fikiri, you're going to go in there one way or another." John corked the sheepskin and swung it back over his shoulder. "You can either do it with pride and dignity or you can be thrown in on your ass, crying. Those are your options. Right now they are the only choices you have. So what's it going to be?"

Fikiri sniffed.

"Look," John said, "your mother isn't going to know how you entered Rathal'pesha. As far as she knows, I beat you up, tied you in ropes, and you fought every inch of the way. But the men on the other side of that wall are going to be watching. And they're who you're going to have to live with."

Fikiri wiped his eyes.

"What would you do?"

"If I were you?"

"If you were me," Fikiri said.

Shove the big exhausted guy out of my way and run like hell down the stairs, John thought in all honesty. But then, he wasn't Fikiri and he would never have allowed himself to be carried up the steps in the first place.

John said, "I'd walk in on my own two feet. I wouldn't let those priests think that I was unworthy of them."

"Are you coming in with me?"

"I am."

Fikiri straightened his shoulders and then turned to face the huge white wall. He strode to the door, called out the holy word, and then walked through as the iron door was pulled open before him. John felt a little proud of Fikiri as he followed silently behind him. At least he'd managed to pull himself together at the end, when it had mattered.

Just past the iron door, hundreds of gray-robed priests had gathered to greet the ushiri candidate. They lined the walkway leading to the Great Temple and cheered as Fikiri stepped before them. Others stood on the high battlements that lined the great white wall and cheered.

Most of them were grown men in their forties or fifties. The rest seemed to be spread between mid- and late-thirties. Only rarely did John notice a boy as young as Fikiri or even a man as young as himself.

The uniformity in their slim builds, soft features, and dark hair implied some common heritage. Pivan would have blended into their midst flawlessly. Fikiri's dark blond hair stood out. But at least his build was small and slim. Aside from the slightly sharper point of his chin and nose, his features resembled those of the men around him.

John, on the other hand, stood out among them as utterly foreign. Nothing he could do would disguise his greater height and muscular build. Months of hunger hadn't helped things either. The hard angularity of his face and body had only become more marked since he had been living out in the woods. With his bright blond hair and light eyes, John guessed that the priests, like Lady Bousim, would think he came from an Eastern bloodline.

Still, none of the priests seemed unfriendly toward him. As he trailed Fikiri, they smiled at him and seemed to be cheering him as well. One hunched old man caught his arm briefly and pressed a tiny yellow cookie into his palm.

"Strength for the attendant," the old man said and then he nudged John along.

The Great Temple rose up like a white mountain of its own. All the stone paths in the courtyard seemed to converge at the foot of its gray stone stairs and massive black doors. Arched over the doorway, silver moons caught and reflected the afternoon light. At the very top of the arch there was a single gold sun. It looked a little like the cookie John had been given.

Fikiri came to a dead stop at the foot of the Great Temple's stairs.

A group of men in black coats and gray cassocks stood at the top, forming a line before the doors. John recognized the silver emblems of moons marking the collars of their coats. They were ushiri like Ravishan. He scanned the line of men for his friend's face but didn't find him there.

An old, skeletally thin priest stepped forward. His hair hung past his waist in white braids. The skin of his exposed face and hands was finely creased and folded, like paper that had been balled up and then spread flat.

Another priest, a man in his forties, stepped up behind the old man and steadied him. Though the action was one of servitude, John didn't get that kind of impression from the younger priest's face. He towered over the older man. Thick black braids cascaded down his broad shoulders. His bearing and expression radiated pride and self-assurance. John immediately sensed that it was not the dark priest's obligation to care for his elder but his right.

"Candidate Fikiri, you have come a long way through hardship and danger but Parfir has reached out his hand and given you his protection." The younger priest's words boomed over them and John recognized his voice as one of those that had threatened and cursed Fikiri on the Thousand Steps to Heaven's Door. "Now, Candidate, come this last small distance and know his will."

The younger priest beckoned for Fikiri to ascend the stairs. Fikiri stole a glance back at John. John nodded and Fikiri went.

The old priest kissed Fikiri's forehead and then whispered something over his head while tracing a symbol in the air. John waited at the foot of the stairs.

Then the old man turned. The assembled ushiri pulled the huge doors of the Great Temple open. The dark-haired priest led Fikiri by the shoulders and directed him after the old priest as they walked into the Great Temple. The black-clad ushiri followed behind.

Then the gray-robed priests who had gathered below cheered once more. All around John priests in plain gray robes surged forward, hurrying into the temple. Some cheered; others sang bits of prayers. A few seemed to be sneaking little conversations back and forth between refrains of prayers. None of them bumped him or jostled him but neither did they stop to talk to him. John felt almost like they didn't see him at all.

Then a bony hand caught his arm—the old priest who had given him the cookie. His head was entirely bald and the wrinkles of his face so deep that they looked like they had been etched into him. His drooping eyelids nearly obscured his dark eyes.

"Ushman Dayyid is young," the old priest told him. "It's been too long for him to remember the last candidate who came to us with an attendant. Forgive him for forgetting you."

"I don't mind, really," John said.

"Come." The old man pulled him slightly toward the stairs. "Wine should be served to you. I remember these things even if these boys do not." He indicated another priest, who looked to be about sixty.

John allowed the old priest to lead him up the stairs, though after the third step John found that the old man was clinging to him for balance more than leading him. Other priests passed them. Some stopped, but the old man waved them on.

"Save us a place," the old priest told one of them and then waved him ahead.

"I have heard you are called Alidas." The old man smiled. "That's a southern name, isn't it?"

"I believe it is, but I'm not Alidas," John replied. "He was injured on the Holy Road and Rashan Pivan'ro'Bousim chose me to take his place. My name is Jahn."

"Really?" The old man's brows lifted high enough that John caught a clear glimpse of his brown eyes. "Because of your hair, I suppose."

John nodded.

"I'm Ushvun Samsango." The priest grinned and John smiled back. The old man had obviously outgrown the name and its meaning, 'swift runner.'

When they reached the top of the stairs, the heavy black doors were beginning to swing shut, all of the other priests having already entered. In a way, John hoped that he might have the excuse of being locked out to escape whatever strange and alien ceremony he might be expected to take part in. Then John saw the look of hurt on Samsango's face.

John rushed forward and caught one of the doors. It was heavier than he had expected and he had to strain to hold it in place.

"Truly, you were born an attendant," Samsango commented as he walked past John through the door. John followed him, allowing the door to swing closed behind him. Hundreds of gray-robed priests knelt on the stone floor. They filled the space like paving stones, enclosing the bases of stone columns and stretching from wall to wall. Only a white walkway leading from the doors to the huge altar remained clear. Samsango sat down beside another priest but shook his head when John moved to join him.

At the foot of a carved stone altar far at the front, Fikiri knelt before Ushman Dayyid. The old, white-haired priest sat in a high-backed stone chair, while the rest of the ushiri formed a half-circle behind him.

In the absolute silence of the huge room, the door slammed shut behind John. It sounded like a thunderclap. For a moment every man in the temple looked up to where John stood.

"Welcome, Attendant." Samsango's thin voice carried through the stillness. "You have traveled far and through danger ..."

"You have carried another's pain as your own," the old, white-haired priest took up Samsango's salutation. His voice was surprisingly strong and clear. He gazed at John as he spoke. For the first time, John got the impression that the old white-haired priest was actually aware of his surroundings. "You have offered your body and will and Parfir has brought his holy protection through you. You are welcome among us."

While the old white-haired priest spoke, Ushman Dayyid stared at John with a cold assessing expression, as if he were trying to guess his weight or deduce his occupation.

"Come sit here," Samsango whispered. His bony hand waved, barely reaching past a younger priest's shoulder. John stepped toward Samsango and the other gray-robed priests shifted and moved to make room for him. In a matter of moments, he was seated on the stone floor and the ceremony continued.

John was glad that he had practiced so many prayers because he ended up needing to recite most of them as the ceremony progressed. He had learned enough of the phrases and rhythms of the prayers to easily follow along in those he hadn't learned from Pivan or Bati'kohl.

The black-robed priests undressed Fikiri, exposing spirals and swirls of black script written across his pale skin. Slowly, they began to wash it off. John peered at the writing. He recognized the flowing lines and sweeping curves of the Payshmura holy script, but he couldn't read any of it.

As the priests scrubbed Fikiri's skin, Ushman Dayyid spoke of freeing Fikiri from the blessed bonds that gave his will, weight, and pain unto his attendant. John guessed that the markings were some kind of spell that had put Fikiri under the thrall of the prayers John had chanted. A year ago he would have found such a thought absurd. Now he simply accepted it.

As the writing washed away, Ushman Dayyid went on, his voice rising and falling through the constant drone of the surrounding prayers.

They bathed Fikiri in different waters and oils, each accompanied by its own prayer. Dayyid and all of the black-coated priests chanted blessings, passing what appeared to be bird's eggs to Fikiri and between themselves. And all the while John and the gray-robed priests kept up their steady cycle of prayers. The roughness returned to John's throat and when he could, he simply whispered the words.

At last Dayyid's deep voice boomed out through the chamber, calling out that Fikiri should live forever free from the desires and sins of the flesh.

"Let only the spirit of Parfir live within him. Let only the will of Parfir touch him," Ushman Dayyid proclaimed. Two black-coated priests pulled a gray cassock onto Fikiri and then slipped one of their black coats over his shoulders. Fikiri stood, looking pale and overwhelmed. He took the cup Ushman Dayyid handed him and drank from it.

A wild roar of cheers echoed through the chamber.

Then more wine was poured and the singing and music began in earnest.

Thinking on it, John realized that this was the exact moment when the holy ceremony transformed into a festivity. John followed the lead of the men around him, particularly Samsango. He sang along with his fellow priests and accepted the clay cup of wine they passed to him.

John didn't trust himself to drink much. He doubted that he could maintain his grasp of Basawar when drunk. Some English phrase was too likely to slip out. So he pretended to sip from his cup and politely declined any more. As the priests around him slowly broke off into conversations with each other, John kept reciting the prayers that Bati'kohl had taught him.

"Enough prayers," Samsango said to him at last. "You will still have plenty more to say tomorrow and the day after that and all the rest of the days of your life." Samsango wobbled a little and gazed down at the full cup in John's hand.

"Are you going to drink it?" Samsango asked over the dull roar of surrounding conversations. John shook his head.

John held the clay cup out to him. "Have it, please."

The ancient priest took the cup. "Not to your liking?"

"I'm too tired to drink." John had to raise his voice as a group of priests near them broke into loud laughter. "I'd pass out on the floor if I had much more."

Samsango nodded, drank John's wine, and then asked if there was anything he needed.

John replied, "A bath and a bed."

"You are too easy to please, Jahn." The old priest laughed. "It's just as well that you didn't ask for a woman since there aren't any here, but I had a good joke ready if you had."

Samsango told him the joke anyway. John failed to understand it but he joined the old man in laughing. At last, Samsango instructed John through a set of doors to the right of the altar where he could find the hot spring baths.

John washed and soaked and allowed the hot waters to soothe his bruised, tired body. When he got out, he found that, once again, someone had taken his clothes. A towel and gray robes had replaced them. Another little cookie sat in a clay dish beside the robes. It was bland but not bad. John ate it quickly and wished that he had been left a few more. Or better yet, a plate of spicy enchiladas.

He dressed and then simply wandered through the huge halls and over the raised walkways of Rathal'pesha. He traced his fingers along the curves and script-like lines of the latticed walls. The stone felt warm beneath his hands. Cool evening winds blew over him. Away from the party, the monastery was quiet and the solitude soothed him.

He explored the depopulated chambers and courtyards as if they were a ruin he had discovered. The silver dishes of polished stones set in alcoves, the tiny white flowers growing between the stones of the walkways, he took in the small, alien details with fascination.

Now and then, he noticed priests high up in the battlements on the walls, but they paid no attention to him. He passed below them in his simple gray robes just as any other priest might have.

John wandered through Rathal'pesha while the sun sank.

At last only the pale glow of the moon on the white stone walls illuminated the twilight darkness. He searched without thinking about it, without wondering what he was looking for. Finally, he reached an open courtyard and stopped.

He already knew that dark dwarf pines grew up from carved alabaster spheres throughout the courtyard. He had dreamed of them and seen the tree roots cracking into the stones' surfaces as if they were eggs. A surreal feeling suffused him as he observed the soft green moss growing along the edges of the white stone pathways. The air smelled of incense, wine, and pine needles.

A man in dark gray robes leaned against the alabaster base of one of the dwarf pines. He sat deep in a shadow, with his head cocked as if listening. The position offered John a clear view of his muscular throat and sharp jaw. The rest of his face was in shadow, his tall body hidden in the folds of his priest's robes. And yet John knew him at once.

Ravishan.

John had been hoping to see him all day, but suddenly he was glad he hadn't. The soft darkness and evening quiet seemed so much more suited to their meeting. Earlier, in the crowds of priests, their words would have been drowned under the roar of hundreds of voices chanting prayers and the cacophonies of gongs, bells, and drums.

John's first instinct was simply to walk out to him. But then he felt the familiar cold whisper of the Gray Space opening. Then there were words. A soft voice brushed through the air and wrapped around Ravishan.

"Rock a cradle cut from stone. Rock the baby, flesh from bone."

Ravishan lifted one hand to his lips and John felt him slice the air in front of him with a flick of his fingertips. Ravishan's mouth moved, but John couldn't hear his words. They slipped into the Gray Space, doubtlessly emerging somewhere miles away in the ear of the one they were intended for.

"Them that knows," the girlish voice whispered back to Ravishan, "says they is blind since the Bousim bastard is delivered live when his blood should be spill likes water on the stones."

He didn't know who Ravishan was talking to, but her words disturbed him. He didn't want to hear this—not now when he had just found some brief sense of calm. John retreated, and the hem of his robe brushed across the surface of an alabaster stone. It barely made a whisper of sound, but Ravishan turned immediately. His wide eyes looked entirely black in the darkness. His face caught the moonlight with the same radiance as the stone walls.

"Who are—" Ravishan began but then his jaw dropped in disbelief. "Jahn?"

Ravishan sprang to his feet, rushed to John, and threw his arms around him in a hard embrace. It startled John. He had never been a person who displayed affection so openly. He didn't even hug his own mother. And yet, at this moment it felt too good to resist. John wrapped his arms around Ravishan and returned his embrace.

The strength and heat of Ravishan's body pressed so close and the scent of his skin seemed almost heady. John felt his heartbeat skip in a wild rhythm as Ravishan's jaw brushed against the tender skin of his neck. It felt so good after nearly a year of physical isolation.

Too good, John realized. He caught himself before his relieved grip slipped into a caress. He stepped back, and hesitantly, Ravishan released him.

"How did you get here?" Ravishan's expression was a muddle of joy and disbelief. "I looked for you. I looked all that day and the next but ..." He trailed off, apparently in awe of John's clean-shaven jawline. "You look so different like this."

The apprehension John had felt while listening to the girl's sinister whispers wrap around Ravishan vanished.

"I came as the attendant to the ushiri candidate. I wanted to tell you but I didn't have any way to send you word." John leaned back against one of the alabaster stones and explained what had happened since Ravishan had last seen him. He left out helping the Fai'daum youth escape and Lady Bousim's confusion about where he, Laurie, and Bill came from. Otherwise, he told Ravishan everything.

"I'm sorry I couldn't find a way to tell you. I didn't want you to be punished for staying out looking for us. Were you?"

"Ushman Dayyid wanted to kill me but I told him that I had gotten lost and too sick to come back." Ravishan shrugged.

"He believed that?"

"After I threw up, he did." Ravishan grinned. "I ate a fistful of goatweed just before I came back to make sure that I would."

Ravishan leaned against the stone next to John.

"You look so ...handsome now," Ravishan said. "I feel a little nervous, like I'm just meeting you. I don't even know what I should call you. What name did you give them?"

"Jahn," John said, "I wasn't in a position to be too creative."

"But that's ..." Ravishan furrowed his brow. "It's my name for you."

"Well, now it's everyone's name for me."

"You deserve a better name," Ravishan said.

"I don't think I'd remember to answer to a better name." John smiled at how seriously Ravishan seemed to take the matter.

"But now everyone will call you Jahn."

"Well, what would you want them to call me?" John asked.

"I don't know." Ravishan lowered his gaze to where a knot of pine roots cracked through the alabaster. "Something else."

"Like wahbai?" John suggested. A look of horror washed over Ravishan's face at the idea of John calling himself 'asshole.'

"Or faud?" John suggested the word he was pretty sure meant something close to 'fuck.'

"No," Ravishan said quickly. "Don't call yourself any of those things. Not even as a joke. Ushman Dayyid would skin you alive for it."

"Then Jahn wasn't such a bad choice?"

"I suppose it wasn't." Ravishan reached past John to pull a spray of pine needles from the branch above them.

"So you saved the candidate's life?" Ravishan pulled one of the pine needles loose from the rest, and after a moment, let it drop to the ground.

"I don't know." John shrugged. "He was pretty well guarded. He might have been fine without my help."

"The Issusha'im Oracles foresaw his death." Ravishan shifted to face John, his hip and elbow resting lightly against the smooth alabaster. He leaned close, keeping his voice low. "But you stopped it."

"Maybe," John said. "Maybe the oracles were just wrong."

"The Issusha'im Oracles are never wrong." Ravishan let another pine needle fall.

"They just were, weren't they?"

"Only because of you." Ravishan studied his face and suddenly John felt aware of their close proximity. He could smell the sharp tang of pine on Ravishan's skin. Someone coming across them like this might get the wrong impression. Hell, John was starting to get the wrong impression himself.

Ravishan didn't seem to notice it at all. He leaned closer, smiling.

"No one in the Black Tower knows how the prophecy was broken, but I do." He poked the sharp point of a pine needle against John's shoulder. "You did it, my Jahn."

It would be wise to step back a little, John thought. Then he didn't.

"Up in the Black Tower, do they think that it was good or bad that Fikiri survived?" John remembered the words that had floated over Ravishan. 'His blood should be water on the stones.'

"Who knows what they think."

"But wasn't that what you were talking about when I got here?" John asked.

"You heard us?" The remaining pine needles slipped from Ravishan's hand but he didn't seem to notice.

"Not you," John said. "Your friend."

"Your ears are too sharp." Ravishan looked a little nervous.

"Who were you talking to?" John asked.

"No one." Ravishan dropped his gaze to the alabaster surface beneath him. It was an oddly shy response and John felt a sudden uneasiness at it.

He said, "It had to be someone. Do you have a lot of secret friends like me?"

"No." Ravishan shook his head. "She's just a girl at Umbhra'ibaye. We talk sometimes."

"A girlfriend?" John asked. It shouldn't have burned in his throat to say the word. He wanted Ravishan to look up at him, but he didn't.

"She's a sister, a nun." Ravishan drew a circle on the stone with his finger and then rubbed it away as if it could have made an actual mark. "We gossip from time to time."

John decided to let the subject drop. It had to be difficult for Ravishan, being a priest at such a young age. He had probably sworn celibacy before he had known what he was giving up. Now, who knew what desires he struggled with?

John could recall what he had been like when he was seventeen. Lonely, he thought, but unwilling to entrust another person with his affection. An oath of celibacy might have come as a relief to him. It wouldn't have saved him from unspeakable, awkward crushes, but it might have saved him from a few encounters he would have rather never endured.

It probably wouldn't have made that much of a difference. He had already developed his preference for the solitude of mountains and wilderness. He had already known to trust the soil and stone, things that never asked him how he felt or where he had spent the night.

He supposed he hadn't changed much, really. He'd gotten taller, graduated from college, and fallen into another world. Still, he remained the same.

Ravishan was probably nothing like John had been. Nothing like John was now. He'd been stupid to even think about it.

Perhaps sensing John's withdrawal, Ravishan continued, "I'm not like those old monks who whisper dirty things to girls. We were just talking."

"It's all right. I don't think there's anything wrong with it. I guess that you'd be in trouble if anyone else knew."

"Yes, I would."

"Then I won't tell anyone," John said.

Ravishan smiled such an honest, handsome smile that John shied, withdrawing further from his openly affectionate expression. It was one thing for him to find Ravishan handsome, even to indulge in a brief flirtation, but he would be worse than a fool if he allowed himself to believe that Ravishan returned his desire.

John forced himself to focus on much more simple desires, a decent meal and somewhere to sleep. Those were the kinds of things that he had a right to want. He straightened, stretched, and asked if he could get something to eat.

"Supper is already past," Ravishan said, "but I think we could sneak into the kitchen and have something from the cold cupboards."

"You haven't eaten either?"

"I couldn't and still claim to be sick."

Ravishan showed him to the kitchens. The rooms were vast and gloomy, but a residual heat radiated through them from the deep red embers of the roasting fires.

They made themselves sandwiches from old rolls and cheese and smoked goat meat. John had eaten lamb and mutton before, but not goat. The meat was tougher and its flavor stronger. Ravishan said it wasn't as good as dog but goats were cheaper and easier to raise. And they gave milk as well.

They talked about food. John started to say that dog wasn't eaten in his world and then had to correct himself. He asked about cats but Ravishan didn't know what one was. The closest thing that he could describe in Basawar was the ubiquitous weasel. Ravishan said they were good animals that laid delicious eggs and ate vermin. That didn't really sum up a cat, but John was too tired to be picky.

It was comfortable, easy conversation.

At last Ravishan led him to a room where he could sleep. He leaned so close that John could feel the heat of his skin through his robe and he wished John good dreams.

"For you as well," John replied.

After Ravishan withdrew, John lay awake in the darkness, still aware of exactly where Ravishan's chest had pressed against his own. When he at last slept, he dreamed of green forests and a home that he could hardly remember.

CHAPTER FIFTEEN

Kahlil sat up and glanced at the clock. Its small brass hands formed a tiny cross: it was a little past four in the morning. Outside, the full moon glowed in the white sky, illuminating a courtyard blanketed by newly fallen snow. Most of it would melt away once the sun rose. Everything was ephemeral this early in spring.

Kahlil gazed out through the narrow second-story window for a few more moments before finally getting out of his bed. He dressed quickly and then drew the heavy canvas curtain aside and walked to the big cast iron stove in the middle of the room. The wood had burned to embers, but those still glowed hot red. He held his hands up over the stove, catching the waves of heat in his palms.

All around him the other canvas curtains were still drawn, enclosing each of the men's beds in an illusion of privacy.

'You sleep alone, but I am not far.' Those had been the words of a prayer he had known once, or maybe it had been a song. Maybe it was something that had just occurred to him at this moment.

He didn't try to sort it out any longer. Over the past two years he had learned that if he pursued a memory it only twisted and broke into contradictions.

When he had first arrived he had believed that it was the 165th year of the Divine Ushsho'shokri, when in fact it had been the 183rd year. He thought he was a priest but his body held memories that no priest would entertain. He had thought that he was fighting to save the last Payshmura Stronghold at Rathal'pesha, but now he knew that the entire northland had been shattered and burned when he would have still been a youth.

He could open the Gray Space. He could step through stone walls and iron bars. And so he had believed that he was the Payshmura Kahlil and that he had traveled to Nayeshi. But when he looked for the Prayerscars that should have marked his body, all he discovered were the faint traces of a red Fai'daum tattoo dotted across his ribs. And no one he met had ever heard of Nayeshi.

Anything he believed about himself turned on itself and became a lie.

His memories were made up of shattered scents and images that would arise within him and then fade. Some of them would seem compatible, linking together a chain of a few days or even weeks; then, an absolutely opposite memory would surface. It was almost as if he were attempting to put together a single puzzle from the pieces of two different ones. Hopeless.

The single feeling that pervaded his sense of himself most was isolation.

He looked over the long rows of canvas panels. A rashan slept behind each one, a man who belonged with the rest of them. They had trained together and they rode their patrols through the Bousim sectors of Nurjima together. They knew one another's histories and lives. They were brothers, cousins, friends. They married each other's sisters and interlaced their lives in affairs and disputes.

Even the men who loathed each other knew each other. Often, they loathed each other because they knew one another too well.

But none of them knew him. None of them shared a past with him. He had arrived among them, wrapped in bandages, hidden by surgical dressings. He had healed behind the canvas panels while they came and went on their business.

Only Rasho Alidas had seen him then, and Alidas didn't ask questions. He wasn't a man who cared to know too much about the past. Only the here and now concerned Alidas, and Kahlil had learned to take comfort in his attitude.

It didn't matter who he might have been. That was not who he was now. He created himself each day and slowly built his own history.

He shifted silently in front of the stove.

Far down along the row of beds he heard low whispers. Then came the discreet noises of a man slipping from one bed and creeping between the panels to lay back down on his own mattress.

Everything would be in order by sunrise. Even the most passionate of the rashan'im were careful.

Or maybe they had just been secretly betting on the turn of cards? The white sky and the full moon offered light enough for that. Kahlil knew better than to trust his own instincts in the matter of illicit meetings. He was too lonely.

At the far end of the open hall, Rasho Alidas' door remained closed, but Kahlil saw the yellow light of a lamp spark up and seep out.

The door opened quietly and Alidas frowned out into the darkness of the barrack. His age showed in the weathered lines at the corners of his eyes and in the gray streaks winding through his curling brown hair. This year he would be fifty. Kahlil found him handsome in spite of that. His full southern mouth and high cheekbones lent him an air of youth and the leanness of his body added to that impression.

He hadn't pulled on his riding coat and his white shirt hung only half buttoned over his chest. He absently continued fastening his shirt closed as he walked, moving quietly despite the limited motion of his right leg. He started toward Kahlil's bed and then stopped, catching sight of him in front of the iron stove. He beckoned Kahlil inside.

Alidas' room was small and simple. It smelled like saddle leather and cedar soap. A dull glow of moonlight fell through the small window, illuminating the twisted white blankets on Alidas' unmade bed. The closet door hung open, revealing Alidas' spare uniforms, his lighter summer coat, and his spare boots. The adjoining door to Alidas' private bathroom was shut. Alidas' towel hung over the back of one of his chairs. His razor, mirror, and shaving tins sat out on his table.

For a brief moment, Kahlil caught a glimpse of his own face in Alidas' shaving mirror. It still seemed wrong to him that his eyelids were bare and only the corners of his mouth bore any testament to the wide scar that should have been there.

Kahlil closed Alidas' door behind himself. He took a seat in one of the two ornately carved chairs. Rather than taking the chair opposite Kahlil, Alidas leaned against the edge of the table. He avoided sitting in chairs, as it was often difficult for him to regain his feet smoothly. He disliked anything that brought attention to his bad leg.

"How was it last night?" Alidas asked.

Kahlil frowned and asked, "What do you mean?"

"All quiet in there?" Alidas leaned closer and tapped Kahlil lightly on the forehead.

"Oh," Kahlil shrugged, "I don't know. I slept well enough."

"Well enough." Alidas smiled as he repeated the words. "I suppose that's all a man can ask for. So, none of your bad dreams?"

"Nothing too bad."

"And your memory? Still the same?" Alidas asked.

"It's never the same," Kahlil replied. "That seems to be the problem."

"Yes, but it hasn't gotten worse?"

"No." Kahlil picked up one of Alidas' shaving tins. Even closed it gave off a deep woody scent. "Everything from the past two years is perfectly clear. It's just further back than that ..." Thinking of it gave him a feeling of uneasiness, as if he were trying to read through warped panes of glass. "Why do you ask? Afraid I'll forget your birthday?"

"No," Alidas replied, "I was just wondering if you've remembered any more of your old life. Family or friends who might help you out?"

"No." A feeling of frustration began to well up in him. He didn't want to be talking about this. He preferred not to even think of it. It wasn't like Alidas to bring it up. Usually, he got straight to business. Kahlil put down the shaving tin.

"So, what about the here and now? Who is my man this time?" Kahlil asked.

"It can't always be so simple." Alidas frowned at Kahlil's directness.

"You give me a name and I give you a corpse. What could be more simple?" Kahlil shrugged.

"This time I don't have a name. I don't even know when this man will show up for his execution." Alidas pulled his dark green jacket on but didn't button it closed.

"Another assassin?" Kahlil asked.

Alidas nodded.

"Belonging to whom?"

"I don't know." Alidas' brown eyes seemed to darken to nearly black beneath the shadows of his narrowed lids. "He might be in Gaunsho Lisam's hire, though it's hard to say. He may not be a professional at all."

"It's not some poor man Gaunsho Bousim imagines to be another of his wives' lovers, is it?" Kahlil asked.

"No." Alidas smiled. "I think you and I might be the only ones left alive if we started down that road. No." Alidas' frown returned. "My man in the Seven Palaces has heard that Ourath Lisam plans to have Jath'ibaye killed. It seems that he thinks he can seize Vundomu for himself."

Kahlil could see what caused Alidas to scowl. Jath'ibaye's reputation alone warranted concern. He was rumored to be a Shir'korud demon, a deranged Payshmura oracle and even an undead Eastern sorcerer. Some whispered that he slept with men. Others claimed he consorted with beasts.

What was known of him as fact was not nearly so perverse, but troubling all the same. He had served the Fai'daum during the war with the Payshmura priests. It was believed that his assaults had led the Payshmura to unleash the Rifter. The entire northlands had been devastated in just a few hours. Jath'ibaye had been one of the few men to walk out of the ruins alive.

Now he and his surviving Fai'daum followers held the fortress of Vundomu and all of the lands lying north of there. They owned coal and iron mines, as well as the taye fields that had once been gaunsho'im holdings. If there were any ruins left of Rathal'pesha or Amura'taye, those too were in Jath'ibaye's grasp.

For seven years after Rathal'pesha's fall, Jath'ibaye and his followers had beaten back each and every gaunsho's army. They had held the northlands and even threatened to advance in the face of further assaults. Finally, the Gaunsho'im Council had been forced to offer them a treaty.

In the twenty years since then, Jath'ibaye had become a gaunsho in everything but name. He retained his own army. He paid taxes and his great glass house was the eighth palace in the square of Seven Palaces. Once a year he even rode south from his lands to attend the Gaunsho'im Council.

"Gaunsho Lisam really thinks he'd be able to take the north if Jath'ibaye dies?" Kahlil looked up at Alidas.

"Who knows what he really thinks? He lies even to his allies. But he could take advantage of the confusion that Jath'ibaye's death would cause." Alidas picked up his razor and folded the sharp blade closed. "He's benefited in the past from chaotic situations."

"Taking rulership in the wake of his brother's death is nothing like seizing a foreign land," Kahlil said. "I've never met Jath'ibaye, but his people stood with him through the Payshmura's fall and the Seven Years' War. They've only grown stronger in the twenty years since then. I'd be willing to bet that they wouldn't take kindly to the assassination of their leader. And they won't give up their lands."

"It may not be Jath'ibaye's lands he wants," Alidas said. "If Jath'ibaye is assassinated here in Nurjima, his followers could place the blame on any of the gaunsho'im. The Bousim lands are closest to them."

"And the Lisam lands are the farthest south." Kahlil frowned. "Does he think that he can invade his neighbors while they're holding back Jath'ibaye's followers?" Kahlil's own face scowled back at him from Alidas' mirror.

"Either way there would be war in the Bousim holdings." Alidas sighed. "These young noblemen coming into power now, they don't know what it takes to wage real war. They've never even seen a battlefield. To them it's just a game."

Kahlil didn't know if his memories of battle were from the Seven Years' War in the north or some other conflict, but it didn't matter. He remembered battles. He remembered fires and hunger and driving snowstorms that stripped his will down to a struggle just to stay upright. He remembered the smell of wounds and pain that tore through him, even when he closed his eyes to sleep.

"It won't come to that," Kahlil said. "I'll take care of the assassin. Old Jath'ibaye won't even know that he was there."

Alidas smiled but only briefly.

"It won't be as easy as killing a wanted man in an alley," Alidas warned. "This assassin may be a member of Gaunsho Lisam's family or one of his friends. If you're caught murdering a nobleman, I don't know what I can do to protect you. Officially, the Bousim family won't even acknowledge that you are in their pay."

"So, I kill him and then I'm on my own?" Kahlil asked. The prospect seemed oddly familiar.

"I won't force it on you." Alidas didn't look at him. Instead he tightened the lids of his shaving tins and put them away.

"You couldn't." Kahlil shrugged.

"True enough," Alidas said.

"So what happens if I decline the offer?" Kahlil asked.

"Gaunsho Bousim has entrusted me with this duty," Alidas replied. "It will be done one way or another."

Kahlil sighed. He knew little about his life history, save that Alidas had been good to him. Alidas had taken him in and explained the world to him. He had listened while Kahlil muttered, hissed, and ranted in strange languages. Alidas had fed him and cared for him. And when Kahlil had recovered, Alidas had provided him with housing and pay.

What life he had now he owed to Alidas.

"I'll do it," Kahlil said.

Alidas smiled briefly. The expression didn't actually make him look happy so much as tired.

"I wish there was someone else ..." Alidas began. Then he folded his shaving mirror back into its case and returned it to the dressing closet.

"When will I go?"

"This morning, before the change of patrols."

"Sending me out on an empty stomach?" Kahlil asked. He didn't really care, but it was the only thing he could bring himself to complain about. He didn't want to leave. He had just begun to feel at home. Perhaps not with the other men, but with Alidas.

"I'll buy you something on our way to Blackbird Bridge." Alidas picked up his boots but didn't move to put them on. He just stood with his back to Kahlil. "You should pack your things."

Kahlil nodded. There wasn't anything for him to pack, but he understood that Alidas wanted to be alone. Kahlil returned the canvas enclosure and made his bed. He supposed it was the last thing he would ever do here.

CHAPTER SIXTEEN

From the distance of the Blackbird Bridge, the great palaces looked ornate and tiny, like silver foil charms that a child might have lost in the drifts of morning snow. The early sun glittered over needle-like spires and glowed across bright mosaic walls. Jath'ibaye's Glass Palace flashed like a faceted diamond.

The streets were still largely empty, save for few street vendors gathered in the plaza several blocks behind them. Occupied with preparing their carts and wares for morning business, none of them even spared a glance to the distant bridge where Alidas and Kahlil stood.

"Work has already been arranged for you," Alidas told him. "You'll be hired as a runner for the Lisam household. The position should offer you some freedom of movement."

Kahlil managed a nod. He didn't want to be doing this. "My name? Still Kyle?"

"Kyle'insira. It has a good southern sound to it, doesn't it?" Alidas' smile looked forced. Kahlil could see that he wanted their parting to seem easy and natural, as if he were going to just another job.

"It's not as southern as Alidas, but it'll do."

Kahlil lapsed into silence, staring out at the distant, gleaming palaces. He knew he should be going. His gaze shifted to the walled-off, barren land where the Black Tower had once stood. It was said to be cursed. Not even the gaun'im would build anything in its place. Looking at it sickened him and yet he continued doing it.

"So, how are the clothes?" Alidas' voice pulled his gaze away from the desolated land.

"They're good." Kahlil slid his hand into the deep pocket of the coat and again ran his fingers over the key that had been there when he had first put the coat on. There was something deeply comforting about touching a key and turning it through his fingers. It felt like a door key. Kahlil supposed that he found it familiar and reassuring because it implied that there was a place for him; a door that would open to him. He supposed this sensation must be one he carried with him from a time when he had belonged somewhere, when he'd had a home.

But he didn't have a home now and the key was meaningless if he didn't know what it was for.

"You know, there's a key in my pocket."

"I was wondering when you were going to mention that." Alidas smiled and this time it seemed genuine. "I rent a room on Water Street in the Redbrick District. It's the black door behind the bone carver's shop. If there's trouble, you can go there. It's not too pleasant, but it will give you a roof over your head and the people there aren't likely to ask any questions."

"Someone lives there?" Kahlil asked.

"In my rooms? No." Alidas shook his head. "I use the place from time to time for business that I can't conduct at the barracks."

Kahlilconsidered asking what kind of business Alidas conducted there but thought better of it. Alidas had already offered him more information than was prudent—certainly more than Kahlil would have expected.

Alidas said, "If you don't have anywhere else to go after you're done with all of this, then we can meet there."

"Thank you." Kahlil didn't know why he found the offer so deeply touching—perhaps because he never would have expected it, and somewhere deep in him, he had wanted something like this desperately. Just having this small key made the entire prospect of working alone against a gaunsho seem easier. It assured him that he hadn't been abandoned.

"You should get going," Alidas said at last.

Kahlil obediently turned and started down the bridge.

"Be careful," Alidas called after him.

"You as well." Kahlil didn't look back and doubted that Alidas did either. He started toward the Seven Palaces, the wealthiest district of Nurjima.

In the last two years, he had worked almost exclusively in the west bank slums, rooting out wanted men who hid outside of Alidas' legal authority. He had grown used to the squalor and the smell of open sewers. He was accustomed to working his way through the mazes of squats where northern refugees had been abandoned to their own means.

The genteel open spaces of the other half of the city struck him as strange. As the sun continued to climb, the shadow burned away to pale modulations in the light-colored shop walls and wide clean streets. Even the alleys were open and spacious. There was nowhere for a man to crouch, no trash or dark shadows to camouflage his form.

He wondered if he had always thought this way. Had he come from a shadowy slum or some dark, crowded place? The question didn't stay with him. It, like any thought about his past, was an idle fantasy. He could decide that he had come from the Kingdom of the Night if he liked; it made no difference now.

The streets were black and shiny with melted snow. He crossed two tracks running parallel down the center of the wide main street just before the huge yellow trolley whipped past. Its bright paint and shining brass fixtures glowed against the sedate beige bricks of the surrounding buildings.

He had read about the trolley in the papers, but at the time he had been thinking of other things. Now it struck him as fascinating. No tahldi pulled it and no coal engine powered it. It ran on the currents trapped in the unassuming black cables strung overhead. The cables looked so unimpressive, even a little ugly.

The trolley pulled to a stop at the top of the hill and a group of young women climbed aboard it. Then they and the trolley disappeared down the other side of the hill.

Nothing like the trolley existed in the west bank slums. According to the newspaper, the lack of trolleys and mechanical industry throughout all but the richest areas was due to Jath'ibaye's restriction on exports of iron from the northlands.

Jath'ibaye's actions mystified him. Why wouldn't a man engage in what would certainly be a profitable venture for him and his Fai'daum?

An older man and his three wives stepped out of a shop door directly into Kahlil's path. The light scent of daru'sira and honey wafted out behind them until a slim waiter closed the door. As the husband led his wives across the street one of the women glanced back at him. He grinned at her and she quickly averted her gaze.

He had been out in the world for years, he realized, but he had not been a part of it. He had not thought about it. He had been lost in the ruins of his memory. Living in the barracks and working for Alidas had given him structure. It had given him support and safety, and it had sheltered him from the rest of the world.

Now, he would soon lose the structure of the last two years. He would have to make his own decisions and direct his life. It should have been a terrifying thought, but instead Kahlil felt only excitement.

He didn't know why he had felt so disinterested and numb to the world for so long. Perhaps it had been a result of such deep injuries. But now he remembered that he had once loved making new discoveries.

Kahlil quickened his pace up the hill. He stopped at the top to briefly take in the Seven Palaces and Jath'ibaye's Glass Palace. This would be the last assassination he performed for Alidas. If he lived, he would be free. His future depended on what he did in the gated thoroughfares and aged buildings below.

The Seven Palaces of the Gaunsho'im were solid, huge structures. Even from the distance of this hill, Kahlil could tell that they'd been built in an earlier age when heavy walls and holy symbols alone could rebuff any assault. They came from a time before god-hammers, mortars, and grenades. The palaces formed a crescent around the smaller but more modern Gaunsho'im Council Hall. By comparison, the golden dome and slender white pillars gave the Council Hall the look of fragile modernity.

And then, just a little west of the Seven Palaces, there was Jath'ibaye's Glass Palace. It wasn't a single structure so much as several strung together by covered walkways. Many of the buildings looked like the gray brick barracks that Kahlil was familiar with. They wouldn't have been out of place in the Bousim military

compound where he had been living. But there were other buildings that Kahlil could hardly believe existed in Basawar.

They flashed and glittered in the light. The walls and ceilings
were made of thousands of panes of glass and the barest metal
supports. They seemed almost made of nothing and too fragile
to believe. He could see directly inside. The dark green forms of
trees and plants filled every space.

Why build houses of something so delicate as glass? Why house
trees indoors? Kahlil felt an intense urge to go there. He lifted his
hand, touching the edges of the Gray Space. It would be easy to
let himself in, but he wasn't his own man yet. The Lisam Palace
was where he was meant to be. He dropped his hand back into
his pocket and continued down the hill. Soon enough he would
travel wherever he wished.

《《《

Two weeks later, Kahlil thought that he might end up going
everywhere in the entire city before the month was out. During
the course of his work as a Lisam runner, he had already navigated
most of the streets and alleys of the wealthy North Shore, Silver
Row, and Five Fountains Districts. He had delivered notes, cakes,
hats, and velvet coats. Today, a cage of small white birds with vivid
red beaks was tied into the basket of his bicycle.

The battered bicycle that he had been issued made a series of
almost human moans as he pedaled it up the steep incline of Bakers' Hill. The birds chirped in response to each groan and squeak.

Suddenly ahead of him a form rocketed up over the top of the
hill. A spindly black silhouette of limbs and wheels arced up against
the pale afternoon sky and then plunged downward.

"Lisam runner! Out of my way!" the young man shouted from
his bicycle.

The runner came barreling down the hill, so fast that his taupe
uniform became a mere blur. Kahlil just barely caught a glance of
his flushed face and brown hair.

Kahlil swung out of the way of his fellow runner. The birds in
his basket shrieked and fluttered their clipped wings wildly. Kahlil
heard the other runner's laughter rising up from behind him.

It had to have been Fensal. Kahlil had seen him launch himself and his bicycle across gaps and down staircases. The sight was always accompanied by Fensal's weird laughter. It sounded half like happiness and half like a scream. A few times the laugh had been followed by a genuine scream and a crash. But Fensal always got back up and continued on his way.

Kahlil glanced back in time to witness Fensal zip in front of the Golden Trolley and swerve down another of Nurjima's steep hills. Doubtless, the wives and daughters of the gaun'im in the trolley had been horrified. Letters would probably be written to the city's two respectable papers.

"Once again the Lisam runners prove themselves a menace," Kahlil murmured to himself. Fensal would cut out the article and post it in their barracks.

"Kyle!" A woman up ahead flagged him down. Yu'mir had been the first person to befriend him in the Lisam household. She didn't stand out, particularly dressed in the tawny uniform of a Lisam runner. Her dark skin, brown eyes, and brown hair all seemed to melt into the dull umber of her wool coat. She had a plain face and unremarkable body that made her easy to mistake for other people and hard to pick out in a crowd. If Kahlil hadn't known she was a grown woman, he too might have mistaken her for a boy. Especially dressed in men's clothes as she was today.

"Vuran Yu'mir." Kahlil greeted her formally with a slight bow of his head. "What are you doing out alone and dressed as a runner?"

"House Steward Desh'oun sent me. There weren't any men free to escort me, so he thought that I would be safest if I dressed as a boy." Yu'mir frowned down at her oversized pants. "I was lying in wait for Fensal and for you as well."

"Fensal and me?" Kahlil asked. "Why?"

"All the runners are being called back." Yu'mir glanced down at the basket of his bicycle. The little birds chirped at her and held open their mouths, expecting bits of seed bread.

"They're really noisy," Yu'mir commented.

"They're hungry." He dug a few crumbs out of his coat pocket and tossed them into the cage. The birds quieted immediately and flitted to the floor of their cage to peck up as many crumbs as they could. "Why have we been called back?"

"Jath'ibaye." Yu'mir lowered her voice. "His ship was seen coming down the river past the west pier. He should be arriving at his Glass Palace any time now."

"He was supposed to still be three days away." Kahlil couldn't imagine how an entire ship could have moved ahead that quickly.

"Someone made a mistake somewhere up the river," Yu'mir said. "They were following the wrong ship. That, or Jath'ibaye switched ships in one of those little river towns. I'm sure someone's going to lose his skin for it."

"So, now what?" Kahlil was asking himself as much as Yu'mir. He hadn't had time enough to get to know all the Lisam house staff, much less guess who might be the assassin in their midst.

"Now the entire household's up in arms. There are invitations that haven't even been written that will have to be delivered and gifts that haven't been picked up. Everyone's got new rush jobs."

Kahlil continued up the hill, walking his bicycle so that Yu'mir could keep up with him.

"I'll return to the house as soon as I've delivered these birds," Kahlil said. With all the new work he wondered how easily he could slip away. He wanted to survey Jath'ibaye's security in advance, if possible.

"How much farther do you need to take them?" Yu'mir asked.

"The birds? Just over the hill," Kahlil replied. "How are you getting back to the house?"

"That ass Fensal was supposed to give me a ride, but he refused. He said it would dishonor my womanhood." Yu'mir scowled. "Does he think I can just get on the trolley like some nobleman's wife? And I'm dressed like this. The door guard will throw me on my ass."

"I'll take you back."

"Thanks." Yu'mir smiled at him.

Kahlil was about to say something more to her, but they had reached the top of the hill and the shine of the river far below caught Kahlil's attention.

Dozens of ships and fishing boats lined the river piers. Anonymous vessels that he had never taken much note of came and went. Now each seemed fascinating. Any one of them could be carrying Jath'ibaye. Any one of them carried the potential to alter his life forever. Just watching them, Kahlil felt his heart begin to race. His last job had finally begun.

CHAPTER SEVENTEEN

The Lisam Palace was vast and grand, but also cluttered by an overabundance of images of long-horned bulls, the Lisam emblem.

Kahlil doubted that anyone other than the Lisam noblemen and their breeders had ever seen one of the rare beasts alive. But certainly everyone in the Lisam Palace saw them in every other condition. They charged and menaced as statues; they glared out from shields and paintings. Bulls were carved into the furniture and over the doors. They reared up from the geysers in the courtyard fountains and stood on the gaunsho's table, cast in small butter molds and carved in ice. They were even stitched onto the shoulders of Kahlil's uniform.

After leaving Yu'mir near the servant's quarters, Kahlil made for the kitchen's backdoor. Inside, several women cooks stood glowering at a line drawing of one of the animals. Desh'oun, the house steward of the Lisam Palace, held the picture out in one bony hand and pointed to various areas of the bull's anatomy with the other.

The air of the kitchen was thick with the smell of roasting dog meat. A skinned dog carcass lay on the long wooden table. Carved bones had been tied to the dead animal's head and goat hooves had been sewn to the stumps where its paws would have once been. It didn't really look like a bull calf, but it at least gave that impression.

Wooden bowls of stuffing lay beside the carcass and the older gray-haired woman held a clay salt jar in her arms.

"It is a bull. It must have them." Desh'oun tapped the picture for emphasis.

"Can't we make this one a girl?" the youngest of the cooking women asked. Kahlil couldn't remember her name, but she was pretty with reddish hair and a wild pattern of freckles that spilled across her cheeks. The other two women's fingers were tattoed with marriage bands but hers were still bare.

"There are no girls," Desh'oun snapped. "They are only males."

"Then how do they breed?" the freckled woman asked. Her two companions lowered their faces to hide their smirks.

Desh'oun's usual tolerance had obviously been worn out. With an expression of pure anger he lifted his hand as if he would strike the woman. Instantly, all three of the cooking women cowered back. Kahlil started forward but Desh'oun dropped his hand down to his side. He drew a deep breath and exhaled loudly.

"You will prepare the roast exactly as it is shown here." He smacked the picture down onto the long wooden table. "And if you do not, I will personally come into your rooms while you sleep and butcher you like bitches for the gaunsho's breakfast."

All three women nodded and returned to the wooden table. They didn't look up or speak a word between them until Desh'oun had turned and left.

It wasn't like Desh'oun to threaten his staff for such a small joke. Doubtless, Jath'ibaye's early arrival had not only thrown all of the gaunsho's plans into disarray but also ruined all of Desh'oun's careful arrangements.

The smell of sweets and meat rolled over Kahlil and the scent reminded him of somewhere he had once been. The pungent oil and warm bread seemed to tug at a distinct memory. Kahlil closed his eyes, letting it come as it would.

There surfaced an image of brilliant yellow fried eggs, stacks of pancakes, and maple syrup. Also the voice of a man he liked and a pair of shoes that looked like golden altars.

"You, runner." One of the women's voices broke into Kahlil's thoughts. He opened his eyes and saw that all three of the cooking women were staring at him.

"What are you doing?" the freckled woman demanded.

"I was waiting for Desh'oun to leave." Kahlil stepped forward into the light. "I didn't want to catch his attention."

"That's wise enough. He's fit to swallow a live weasel," the freckled woman commented. She shoved a fistful of stuffing into the dog's gaping abdomen.

"He was almost fit to swallow you," the older, gray-haired woman said to the freckled woman.

The freckled woman's expression grew sulky. Kahlil recalled that Desh'oun usually bantered with her in a fatherly manner.

"It's probably because of Jath'ibaye's early arrival." Kahlil wandered closer. Behind the women, he spied wire racks piled with cooling pies and custards. These shared space with steaming loaves of bread and something nearly black that he didn't recognize. It all smelled good.

He'd been running emergency messages and dropping off parcels since noon without any break. The sky outside the kitchen windows was turning dull and dark. Spatters of black mud stippled his taupe pants.

"Don't even think of it," the black-haired woman said, catching the direction of Kahlil's longing gaze.

"You look as sad as a roast pup." The black-haired woman laughed.

"Shall we put you out of your misery and into the oven?" the freckled woman asked. "No, you look too stringy to eat."

Kahlil said, "I'd say Fensal is your man. He's got the right meat for a bull calf."

All three women snickered and Kahlil took a step toward the table. There was a little dish of pitted cherries only two handlengths from him.

"So, who's the roast for?" Kahlil indicated the dog carcass on the table, taking a casual half step closer to the bowl of cherries.

"You'd think it was for Parfir himself—" The gray-haired woman went instantly silent as she realized what she had said.

Since the destruction of the Payshmura, the name of Parfir was rarely called. His statues had been torn down, his worship outlawed by the Gaunsho'im Council. He was too dangerous of a god. Now, only old men and women ever slipped up and spoke of him or of his destructive incarnation, the Rifter.

"You think it will be for Jath'ibaye?" Kahlil went on as if he hadn't heard her and all three of the women seemed relieved.

"No," the black-haired woman answered, "Jath'ibaye wouldn't come here the first night he's arrived. Even if he did, he can't appreciate the refinement of meat this tender. He eats like all those northern peasants: goat and wild taye."

"Stringy things like you," the freckled woman teased him.

"Even he'd choke on the aroma of me right now." Kahlil shifted so that he was leaning against the edge of the table. The side of his right hand brushed the cool surface of the cherry dish. He continued, "So, can you tell who will be visiting the house just from what was told to the cook?"

"Of course. Desh'oun may not say who it's to be served to, but when he tells us how it's to be made, we know," the old gray-haired woman said. "This dog will be for Gaunsho Lisam himself. Cherry stuffing is always for him."

Kahlil frowned. All the other dishes had already been prepared and were nearly done. He could tell just from the heavy smell in the air. But this dog probably wouldn't even get into the fire for another hour. By then it would be well past the time for dining.

"Are you going to have it cooking all night?" Kahlil forgot about the cherries.

"Certainly not." The black-haired woman rolled her eyes. The other two shook their heads as if he were an idiot.

"It would be black as the Great Chasm by then." The freckled woman finished with her bowl of stuffing and glanced around the table. Then she noticed how close Kahlil was to the cherry dish. She snatched it away from him.

"These aren't for you," she told him.

"That's all you girls ever say to me," Kahlil replied.

The other two women laughed at the paler girl's reddening cheeks.

"So then," Kahlil looked back to the gray-haired woman, "how long does it take to roast a dog like this one?"

"Hoping to wait up for a scrap?"

"Could be," Kahlil said.

"With the belly cleaned out and the stuffing already cooked, it'll be done in six hours," the gray-haired woman replied, after a brief mental calculation. "A little past your bedtime I'd think."

"Sadly true," Kahlil conceded.

It was far too much for one man to eat. So it seemed Gaunsho Lisam would be having dinner guests at the unconventional hour of two in the morning. And it was obviously being ordered at the last minute. Perhaps Jath'ibaye's early arrival had forced Gaunsho Lisam and his conspirators to rush. If so, then it was quite a sumptuous meal Gaunsho Lisam was providing—the kind of thing that only other noblemen would expect.

"I suppose I should get washed up." Kahlil stepped back.

"Aren't you going to try for some of these?" The freckled woman held out the dish of cherries.

"No." Kahlil flicked his hand up and opened his fist so that she could see the palm full of cherries already there. "I wouldn't want you to think I only came round for the food."

Her shocked expression was perfect.

Kahlil fled the kitchen before the women could respond. He had just enough time for a short nap. Later tonight he would see how Gaunsho Lisam and his guests enjoyed their mock bull calf.

Chapter Eighteen

The night was never as dark as Kahlil expected it to be. The sky would darken to a dull slate but it never attained pure black. A darker night, a consuming blindness, existed within his mind. By comparison, the night sky over Nurjima was only a shadow.

Early on, Alidas had noted Kahlil's uncanny ability to see through the darkness. Kahlil supposed it was one of the qualities that had made Alidas decide to use him for hunting wanted men. He couldn't imagine what else Alidas could have seen in his beaten, half-mad condition that would have seemed worth saving.

Worth saving, but apparently not worth keeping.

Absently, Kahlil reached up to the base of his collarbones to touch Alidas' key, which he wore on a chain around his neck. At times, an unreasonable fear of losing it overcame him. Keys were small things, easily misplaced and easily lost. Just the thought chilled him.

It frightened him in a way that creeping through the forbidden halls of the Lisam Palace couldn't match. Here, there were only a scattering of night watchmen and soft dull shadows.

This tension was nothing compared to the cold horror that gripped him when he lay in bed, almost asleep, and the thought of losing the key washed over him. At these times, his fear seemed less like an emotion and more like poisoning. The scars all across his right arm would burn. And then, desperately, he would grip the key hanging from his neck. Slowly, the fear would drain from him.

Even now he caught himself stroking the key. The gesture had already become a habit. It soothed him just to touch it. His body relaxed as he traced the curves and edges of its form. The metal was always warm from lying against his bare skin.

His heartbeat quickened as the bright fire of a watchman's lamp reflected a dozen yellow flames across the mirrors. He dropped the key back into his shirt, slipped back behind a statue of a rampant bull, and held perfectly still.

As the watchman walked, the polished mirrors on either side of him lit up like torches, reflecting his single lamp into a blaze. To Kahlil's eyes the long hall was nearly as bright as it would have been by day. He could see the gold filigree etched into the faces of the mirrors, dull white quartz set into the eyes of the statues, and even the soft luster of the butt of the watchman's holstered pistol.

Kahlil caught his breath.

A moment later the watchman reached the end of the hall and marched down a staircase, the lamplight fading steadily as he descended.

Kahlil released the breath of air that had been growing stale in his lungs. He sped to the end of the hallway, to a different staircase that led up.

Whichever ancient Lisam gaunsho had commissioned this palace had obviously loved bulls, mirrors, and stairs. The center of the Lisam Palace itself was an immense structure of staircases and hall-like landings. It wound upward like a seashell. Smaller staircases branched out from it to the surrounding floors.

Looking down from the last, highest staircase, Kahlil could see the mosaic floor of the great hall at the very bottom level of the palace. Two red bulls locked horns across the smooth stretch of marble. Above him, he saw the last landing, then the carved beams of the roof and the long iron chains that supported the chandeliers.

Faint voices floated from the landing above. The men spoke with raised voices but didn't argue, and from their tone they were perhaps a little drunk.

Kahlil followed the voices to a set of heavy wood doors studded with iron nails. Yellow light seeped from beneath the doors as did the sweet, pungent scent of roasted dog with cherry stuffing.

Even this close, the voices of the men inside remained unidentifiable to him. One man in particular had such a low voice that only rumbles carried through the heavy wooden door, hardly sounds so much as vibrations.

There was no way around it; he would have to go inside.

He closed his eyes and made a quick motion with his hand.

First he perceived only the darkness behind his closed lids. Then perfect silence enfolded him. The rumble of voices, the small sounds of silverware, and the crackling of the fire all went dead. Pale gray forms rose up like mist. The red iron and dark wood of the door hung in front of him now in gray monotones.

Where the wood of the door had been darker, now it was the denser iron that stood out as nearly black in Kahlil's mind's eye. Kahlil's hands shone radiant white as he lifted them to the surface of the door. He could feel a kind of grain, not just in the wood but also in the iron nails. Forced in one direction it would divide cleanly. If the grain were forced in another direction it would splinter and tear against his flesh as he passed through.

When he had been a boy he had torn himself ragged and bloody, fighting against the grain of the Gray Space. It had taken him years to sense them. He remembered, very clearly, holding his hands in a bowl of still water and trying to feel the invisible bonds that held it together. Once, he had torn through the liquid in exactly the wrong manner. Hydrogen had ripped from oxygen and the oxygen had burst up in a sudden spout of flame.

Kahlil often wondered why, of so many of his memories, he retained this one so very clearly. The memory of his scorched fingers always came back to him just before he moved through solid objects in the Gray Space. It made him careful.

He flicked his fingers apart and stepped through the door as if he were a wraith.

The chamber wasn't small, but compared to the looming dimensions of the great hall and the ballroom, its lower ceiling and hexagonal shape lent it a feeling of intimacy. Tapestries of hunting scenes insulated the walls. Heavy curtains were drawn across the windows. Silk blinds, which would have served to hide musicians performing while guests ate, were folded and leaned up in the far left corner. The profusion of cloth gave the room a soft, quilted appearance.

Had he been able to feel heat from within the Gray Space, Kahlil imagined, he would have found this room warm, even a little too hot.

At the center of the room stood a heavy round table with four places set at it. Three of them were occupied by noblemen. The middle of the table was piled with food. The roast dog had already been sliced into cutlets and drizzled with gravy. Spiced bread, goat cheese, and tiny pickled weasel eggs were all stacked in dishes. There was fruit there as well, but it was difficult for Kahlil to recognize.

Deprived of scent and color, all of the food took on a lifeless quality. Kahlil couldn't find it any more appetizing than hunks of modeled clay. Human beings too seemed foreign, like animated dolls, when viewed from the Gray Space. There was no color to them, no warmth, sound, or scent. They ate, gestured, spoke, and laughed, but it all seemed mechanical.

Kahlil gazed at the three men. They were all noblemen, all gaun'im. Kahlil had seen their faces in the papers. In passing, he had read some small bit of information about each of them, though most of it had to do with what plays they had attended or whose daughter they had taken for a wife.

Viewed from the Gray Space, Gaunsho Ourath Lisam's curling red hair seemed dull. His full southern mouth looked like a deep gash. The gold Lisam seal, hanging from his neck, was nearly black. Kahlil guessed that his vest and pants were either the dull gold or dark brown that Ourath usually wore.

He poured himself some wine and then refilled the glass of the man seated to his right, Nanvess Bousim, who smiled and said something.

Kahlil frowned. He had not thought that any member of the Bousim family would be involved in Ourath's assassination plans. He wondered if Alidas knew.

Nanvess touched something on the table, a bundle of leather scraps. Kahlil stared at it but he couldn't tell what was inside. A knife, he guessed from the shape. It was obviously of some importance. Nanvess continually glanced to it.

Across from Ourath and Nanvess sat Esh'illan Anyyd. Younger than the other two men, his face still retained some traces of childhood. When he smiled, it was in an open, wide manner that lent him the appearance of a delighted ten-year-old. His body, however, was thickly built. His dark hair was shorn closely to his face and he appeared to be wearing a shoulder holster even to dinner.

Esh'illan said something and Ourath gave him an unamused glance before replying.

Kahlil scowled. He wasn't going to get very far if he couldn't hear them. He surveyed the chamber. The tapestries hung too closely to the walls for him to go unnoticed behind one. There were no chests or closets. But there were the silk blinds in the corner.

Kahlil walked past the table to the blinds. As he passed Nanvess, Kahlil noticed the man shudder. Movements from within the Gray Space often traced chilling trails through the air. Nanvess didn't seem to think anything of it.

Kahlil crouched down behind the blinds and then dropped out of the Gray Space. Immediately the colors, scents, sounds, and heat of the room engulfed him. Meat, lavender oil, gold silk, scarlet wine, laughter like a clap of thunder. There were also waves of heat: living warmth, humid breath, the blazing fire, and perfume lamps.

He could observe most of the room by peering between the panels of the screens. He had been right about Ourath wearing dull gold. Esh'illan, too, had dressed in gold and dark cinnamon. Nanvess stood out from the others in his dark green clothes. At least in that much he seemed loyal to the Bousim household.

"—dependable, when he's obviously late," Esh'illan finished his statement. Then he took the silver serving fork and piled several cuts of dog meat onto his plate.

Ourath frowned at Esh'illan.

"He isn't late. It's Jath'ibaye who has decided to arrive early." Ourath's voice had been the one too low to hear.

Esh'illan stopped cutting his meat. "Do you think it's for a reason?"

"Do I think what's for a reason?" Nanvess seemed to have been preoccupied by something else. His hand still lay atop the bundle of leather.

"Jath'ibaye's early arrival," Esh'illan said. "Do you think he suspects us?"

"If that were the case, would he come at all?" Ourath asked.

"He has to come." Nanvess spoke with a tone of calm assurance that Kahlil naturally tended to like. The slight trace of northern accent, too, seemed familiar and pleasant.

"It's a matter of pride," Nanvess went on. "Jath'ibaye needs the world to believe that he can walk into the middle of Nurjima, right into the Gaunsho'im Council, and we'll be too scared to do a thing about it. If he didn't come, then he'd be risking the chance of someone thinking that he and his Fai'daum aren't the great power they pretend to be."

Esh'illan blinked at Nanvess as if expecting him to continue. Nanvess just picked up his wine glass, swirled the red liquor, and then put the glass back down without drinking.

"Then you think he knows?" Esh'illan asked.

"What?" Nanvess frowned. "No. I simply said that Jath'ibaye would have to come here even if he did know that there was a trap awaiting him."

"But what if he does?" Esh'illan persisted.

Nanvess didn't reply. Ourath helped himself to another serving of black plums.

"Well," Esh'illan said quickly, "he's not taking me without a hell of a fight. I'll put a few bullets in that bastard before his demon bitch takes us down."

"The bitch moves faster than you'd think." Nanvess didn't look at the younger man.

"She doesn't move faster than a bullet, I'll bet." Esh'illan patted the butt of the revolver in his shoulder holster. "When Jath'ibaye comes for me, I'll be ready."

"He isn't coming for you," Ourath said. "He doesn't know of our plans or of our friends in the north."

Esh'illan ate a few bites of his cutlet. Nanvess continued worrying his bundle of leather scraps while Ourath opened his pocket watch and checked the time.

"So," Ourath closed his watch, "where is he?"

"Still at the docks, I heard." Esh'illan disengaged from his food. "They're saying that he won't come off the water until daybreak."

"Not Jath'ibaye," Ourath said. "Our man. Where is he?"

"He'll be here soon enough," Nanvess answered. "Any minute now."

Esh'illan stopped eating and said, "He's not going to walk through the walls again, is he?"

Nanvess lifted his head. He smiled.

Kahlil heard Gray Space rending. A sudden chill twisted down his spine.

"He's here," Nanvess said.

Kahlil shuddered as a wave of icy air hissed through the room. A flame arced up, the raw elements of the air igniting as they were ripped apart. Kahlil had rarely seen such brutal force used to rend the Gray Space. A noise almost like an animal scream tore through the still of the chamber.

A man in black robes stepped out from between the flames. His blond hair writhed around his face, caught in the churning wind of the two clashing atmospheres. The man swung his hands down. His fingers twisted through the Payshmura signs of sealing and death. Instantly, the Gray Space snapped closed behind him with a sound like rending iron and the flames died. Only a smell of ozone hung in their wake.

A deep, cold sickly feeling began to churn through Kahlil's stomach. He hadn't expected this, nothing like this.

The knowledge of opening the spaces had been one of the Payshmura's most guarded secrets. Only fifty men, secured in Rathal'pesha, were ever taught it. Of them, only a few ever surpassed the simple act of opening the spaces. Those who could move through the spaces were supremely rare.

With Rathal'pesha destroyed and all the Payshmura teachings lost, Kahlil had never thought for a moment that he would meet another man like himself. He was the Kahlil, from blood to bone. Until this moment, it had been his singular identity, not just his title but also his name. And now there was another.

Kahlil just stared at the man. He had no idea what he would do pitted against a man with skills like his own.

Nanvess rose to his feet.

"It's been too long, Uncle Fikiri." Nanvess embraced the older man. "Jath'ibaye has arrived early. One of my rashan'im saw him at the docks this afternoon."

"We know." Fikiri gave a brief, shallow smile. "He was poisoned. His people are bringing him to his Glass Palace for a remedy."

"Will he die?" Ourath asked. His low voice sounded like a purr.

"Not of the poison alone, but it will certainly aid his demise," Fikiri replied.

Though he, like Nanvess, spoke with a slight northern accent, Fikiri's features appeared Eastern. His dark blond hair and angular cheekbones seemed at odds with the slightness of his build. Kahlil guessed that he must have been a child of mixed blood.

He looked older than Kahlil—too old for his fit build, as if he'd been aged by far more than the mere passage of years. His red and swollen knuckles stood out against the tangled white scar tissue that criss-crossed the back of his right hand.

There was something familiar to Kahlil about that and about the man himself. He seemed like someone that Kahlil had seen before. Someone he had known? Maybe at Rathal'pesha?

Kahlil wasn't always sure that he had been there himself. But he had to have been. And so had this other man.

Fikiri Bousim: the name made Kahlil feel oddly cold, as if he were reciting the name of a dead man.

Fikiri stepped closer to the fireplace and held his hands up to the heat. As he moved, Kahlil noticed the faint remnants of embroidered silver moons at the collar of Fikiri's robes. In the illumination of the firelight, Kahlil could see that the robes themselves had been patched with other black cloth, particularly the right arm.

Fikiri turned back to his three companions. He glanced over the carcass of the dog and the half-empty dishes of plums and spice breads. At last his gaze came to rest on the bundle of leather beside Nanvess' plate.

"I found it just as you said." Nanvess had followed Fikiri's gaze. He stepped back to his place at the table and picked up the leather-bound bundle.

"My lady saw it in the hollows of her oracle's skull," Fikiri murmured.

Kahlil couldn't help but notice the slightly distasteful expression that passed over Esh'illan's face. He mouthed the words 'hollows of her skull' to himself and then shook his head.

"So, what is it that she saw?" Ourath asked. "We've been waiting quite some time to find out."

"Yasi'halaun," Fikiri's voice was almost a whisper, "the black knife of the Kahlil."

Nanvess carefully unwrapped the rags of leather.

"It was in one of our garrison storerooms wrapped up in the remains of a leather pack. I have no idea how it came to be there."

Kahlil stared as Nanvess slowly uncovered the gleaming black body of the knife.

It was his knife. Kahlil knew it the moment he saw it. He had been holding it when he had first come to Nurjima. But then there had been that fight and he had forgotten about his knife. He had forgotten about all the things he had brought with him.

Alidas must have stored them away. And now his knife was here in the hands of these men. The uneasy feeling in Kahlil's stomach ground into him a little more.

Nanvess lifted the black knife gently and turned it in the lamplight. It was as dark as night should have been; dark in a way that seemed to devour the surrounding light.

"Yasi'halaun," Fikiri whispered the name like a prayer. "The blade that drinks the blood of the god himself."

"Will it kill Jath'ibaye and his bitch?" Esh'illan frowned at the knife.

"In the right hands it could do much more than that," Fikiri replied. "It is almost a living thing. Fed on the blood of the powerful, this blade could become sharp enough to cut through the walls of the world."

"But it can kill Jath'ibaye?" Esh'illan repeated his question a little more forcefully.

"It will do everything we need it to do," Nanvess told Esh'illan. "Are you going to fret like a child-bride all night?"

"I'm not fretting. I just wanted to be clear," Esh'illan replied. "All this talk about living blades and hollow skulls rings a little too much of Payshmura mystics and all their gibberish. Look what that got them. A smoldering black pit. The Anyyd house isn't interested in toying with those kinds of forces."

"It's not as though we are attempting to summon the Rifter," Ourath replied smoothly. "We are practical men in a position to make great gains. And we're not talking about gibberish. We're talking about new lands. An entire of world of new lands."

Fikiri nodded. "With this blade and Jath'ibaye's blood we can open the gate to Nayeshi. My lady swears it."

The knot in Kahlil's stomach twisted.

Nayeshi. Kingdom of the Night, Palace of the Day, the Rifter's cradle. These three noblemen shouldn't have even known the name.

And this man, Fikiri, and his lady, they seemed to know too much and too little at once. They shouldn't have known that the yasi'halaun existed or that it could be blood-fed to open a Great Gate. They shouldn't have known of the Great Gates at all. But since they did, they should have also discovered that the Great Gates were delicate and deadly. Opened incorrectly, one could tear apart acres of land, ripping through stone and iron alike. A gate could swallow men alive and spit out bloody paste.

It took the combined effort of both the Payshmura ushman'im and the Issusha'im Oracles to control a Great Gate. It wasn't just a matter of spilling some Fai'daum leader's blood with the yasi'halaun and then opening one.

Watching them was like watching toddlers play with grenades. It had to be stopped. Not just the assassination, but all of this.

For a moment he considered simply lunging out and taking the yasi'halaun from them. He could slip into the Gray Space in an instant. But then so could this other man, Fikiri.

"To be honest," Ourath gazed at the black knife with a warm smile, "I'd do it just to be rid of Jath'ibaye."

"Being rid of Jath'ibaye is actually the point." Esh'illan, too, was looking at the knife, but his expression wasn't nearly so pleased. "I just think that we'd be better served by putting a bullet through his head, instead of using some little knife."

"It doesn't have to be one or the other," Ourath assured them. "I'm sure we could shoot and stab him. Possibly hang him if time allows."

"You think it's a joke?" Esh'illan demanded.

"No." Ourath pushed a ringlet of his deep red hair back from his face. "I simply think you shouldn't underestimate the power of the weapons we have at our disposal." Ourath glanced meaningfully from the black knife to Fikiri.

"I'm not underestimating them. I know they have real power. I just don't know if I trust all this sorcery. It seems as likely to kill us as Jath'ibaye, maybe even more so. After all, if it works so well, then why couldn't the Payshmura destroy him in the first place?" Esh'illan leaned back slightly and glanced up at Fikiri.

Fikiri returned the man's gaze.

"How well have your guns served you against Jath'ibaye so far?" Fikiri's expression remained dull, but the edge of bitterness that tinged his voice made him sound ages older than the men around him.

Esh'illan flinched from Fikiri's scorn.

"I don't give a damn so long as it works," Esh'illan muttered. "We need the iron in Vundomu."

Nanvess smiled at Fikiri. Ourath looked pleased. Esh'illan looked like he had swallowed a worm. He took a deep drink of his wine.

"So, it will be at the Bell Dance?" Esh'illan asked Ourath. Ourath nodded.

"You'll need this, then." Nanvess stood and held the black knife out to Fikiri. Fikiri slipped it into the empty sheath at his hip.

"The stones," Fikiri asked Nanvess, "did you find them?"

"What stones?" Esh'illan interjected.

"I moved them," Nanvess told Fikiri.

"Good." Fikiri nodded. "Then that leaves only one other matter—"

"What stones?" Esh'illan demanded a little more loudly.

Nanvess scowled at him.

"Jath'ibaye placed bewitched stones in our houses and in the Gaunsho'im Council Hall," Nanvess answered.

"In our houses?" Esh'illan looked from Ourath to Fikiri. "Why didn't you tell me about them?"

"They've been taken care of," Nanvess said. "We can't have meetings like this every time there's some small detail to arrange. It's suspicious enough as is."

"But I could have been informed," Esh'illan said.

"You have been," Nanvess replied. "Just now."

"What did they do?" Esh'illan demanded.

Fikiri sighed and said, "They respond to the presence of power like mine. They warned Jath'ibaye of any disturbance in the hidden spaces where I move."

"And that's all?" Esh'illan looked suspicious.

"That's all that matters for our purposes," Nanvess replied.

"I want to know—" Esh'illan began in annoyance.

"It's difficult to explain to men who have not practiced sorcery," Fikiri cut him off softly. "So I'll show you."

Fikiri lifted Esh'illan's half-full wine glass. He folded his chapped hands around the glass and pulled it against his chest. He pressed his eyes shut.

"Certain inanimate objects can be infused with a witch's will." Fikiri kept his voice soft and his eyes closed. "If he concentrates on them he can control them, even from a distance."

Fikiri opened his eyes. Then he handed the wine glass back to Esh'illan, who took it gingerly, as if he expected it would burst into flames. Kahlil half expected that as well.

This certainly wasn't a Payshmura teaching.

Fikiri lifted one hand up into the sign of peace. Slowly the dark red wine swirled up from the glass forming a replica of Fikiri's hand. Esh'illan gaped at the red fluid as its overly supple fingers curled into a fist in imitation of Fikiri's next gesture. Then the hand gave them a coy wave and splashed back down into the glass.

Kahlil guessed that his own expression mirrored Esh'illan's. He had never seen anything like that before. He had walked between worlds and carried the living bones of an Issusha Oracle on his back, but he had never seen this. It had to have been an Eastern teaching. He wondered what other skills Fikiri possessed.

Esh'illan gingerly sat his wine glass down on the table and then carefully nudged it away from his plate.

"So the stones in our houses," Esh'illan's voice was low, "could Jath'ibaye make them do ...that?"

"Possibly, but I doubt he would have," Fikiri said. "Tricks like that are tiring and rarely accomplish much. It serves Jath'ibaye far more to have wards."

"And they're gone now?" Esh'illan asked.

"He'd feel it if they were removed completely. That would have been a warning to him in itself," Fikiri replied. "Nanvess has shifted their positions so that there are gaps in Jath'ibaye's web. Chinks in his armor."

"The west garden at the Bell Dance will be his weakest position," Nanvess said.

"There's still his bitch." Esh'illan started to reach for his wine glass, then dropped his hand back down to the carved arm of his chair.

"He won't bring her to the dance if I ask him not to," Ourath said.

"If you ask him?" Esh'illan frowned at Ourath's self-satisfied expression.

"He's not a man without his weaknesses." Ourath's smirk split into a handsome grin.

"You're joking." Esh'illan's boyish face screwed up as if he'd swallowed a fly. "That's disgusting."

Nanvess laughed.

"You think it's funny?" Esh'illan demanded of Nanvess.

"I think it's no surprise that Ourath wants the man dead so very badly," Nanvess replied. Standing back from the others, Fikiri said nothing. The flat line of his mouth seemed to compress slightly more.

"That's disgusting." Esh'illan couldn't seem to stop grimacing. "You don't let him ..."

"Absolutely not." Ourath rolled his eyes. "I merely listen to his insane ramblings and look fascinated. He's pathetic, really."

"Keep talking like that and you'll have him crying his eyes out on your doorstep." Nanvess grinned.

"Maybe you should," Esh'illan said. "While he's bawling we'll just shoot him."

"Maybe you should just marry him and settle all our troubles on the wedding night," Nanvess suggested.

"He might like where I'd shove that black knife a little too much." Ourath laughed and the other noblemen did as well.

"I've seen him tear boys like you apart with his bare hands." Fikiri's voice cut through their laughter. All three noblemen instantly fell silent. The only sound in the room came from the tiny pops and snaps of the wood burning in the fireplace. Kahlil found that he was holding his breath, afraid that Fikiri would hear him exhale.

"Don't ever think that he's a joke," Fikiri growled. "He could kill any of you in a heartbeat."

Nanvess bowed his head. "I'm sorry, Uncle. We didn't mean—"

"It doesn't matter." Fikiri waved his apology aside. "I can't stay here much longer. Jath'ibaye will sense my presence. There is still the matter of this knife." Fikiri brushed his scarred right hand over the hilt of the black knife. "There was a man who brought it into the city and into the Bousim garrison. He needs to be found."

"Who is he?" Nanvess asked.

"The Kahlil," Fikiri replied dryly. "Who else would you think?"

"But—" Esh'illan began.

"Don't argue with me. I don't have the time or the patience for it." Fikiri looked directly at Nanvess. "Find him and kill him."

Nanvess nodded. "He'll be dead in a day."

"Good," Fikiri said. He lifted his hands to his chest. "I will see you again in three days. Be ready."

Kahlil felt the air suddenly shudder with building force. Soon Fikiri would be gone. Kahlil lifted his own hands, drawing his concentration and strength. Fikiri split the fabric of the room with a rending force. Again there came the sound of tearing metal. Flames and a sudden, chill wind writhed around his black-robed figure. Fikiri stepped into the ragged Gray Space.

If he could take him by surprise from behind, Kahlil thought he might have a chance. But he had to catch the man. At the very least, he needed to know where Fikiri and his lady hid themselves.

Kahlil followed far more quietly. He slipped through the Gray Space with only a whisper. The surrounding room faded to dull mist.

He couldn't see Fikiri, but he could feel where the other man had passed before him. The texture of the surrounding Gray Space was jagged and splintered and cut into Kahlil like needles of splintered glass.

Fikiri moved in huge bounds of space. He shot through the walls of the Lisam Palace and out over the open streets of Nurjima. His path cut through walls and buildings and then ploughed through the steep hills of the northern area of the city.

Kahlil plunged after him. The faint gray surroundings streaked past almost faster than he could discern them. He swept through the walls of a bakery, a bedroom, through trees and animals alike. Still, he found Fikiri's trail slashing out far ahead of him. He whipped through a heavy black wall and jerked to a halt.

Suddenly the misty images of the surrounding world had become a jumble of chaotic forms. Huge dark girders shot up through pale stone staircases. Walls jutted through each other at wrong angles and then folded into long, open hallways. Twisted pine trees grew up through a massive altar. Apple blossoms drifted down from half of a domed ceiling.

It was as if entire landscapes had been superimposed over and into each other. The Gray Space, too, felt thicker and twisted. Kahlil took a small step and immediately he found himself several feet behind where he had stood. With a step to the side he instantly found himself on one of the pale staircases. He skipped, like a scratched record, from spot to spot.

He turned slowly in a circle, trying to locate Fikiri's trail. But that too was disjointed and randomly etched through his surroundings. He took a step toward the nearest line of jagged splinters and instantly he was ten feet back from it, in the middle of a carved stone column.

This wasn't good.

The entire night hadn't been good, but this had to be the low point.

Kahlil didn't have any idea where he was or how he could keep following Fikiri. This place had to be some kind of trap. He was a little worried about where he would find himself if he left the Gray Space. At least while he was inside it, Kahlil couldn't be harmed by hurtling into a stone column.

Kahlil crouched down and scowled at the fractured lines of Fikiri's path. The marks resembled arcs of hanging frost, disconnected over the walls, stairs, towers, and trees. Kahlil studied it, trying to find a pattern. He tilted his head and his view snapped to a different angle, somewhere down near his knees. He jerked his head back up straight, feeling slightly sick.

A dull little bird fluttered up from the branches of a pine tree. A murky marine form darted from the shadows and swallowed it. The creature undulated up through the air like an eel swimming in deep water and coiled up into the branches of an apple tree.

This wasn't the place or the time to just throw himself after Fikiri. Even if he could work out the way, Kahlil realized, he would be entering Fikiri's world. And it didn't look at all familiar. There was also the strong possibility that, should he need to escape, he might have to pass through more spaces like this one.

He was going to have to challenge Fikiri in a place that he knew. It would have to be at the Bell Dance in three days.

Kahlil retraced his steps, skipping back across the staircases and hallways, until he reached the point where he had first stepped into this distorted collision of structures. He drew away from it into the evenly textured Gray Space that he was accustomed to.

Then suddenly something blazing hot snapped up around his leg. Kahlil looked down only to see a blinding white form. The air around him screamed as it was ripped open. Warm air and sound slammed into Kahlil as he was torn out of the Gray Space and thrown down.

He hit the ground hard.

A huge blond man towered over him.

"Did you think I wouldn't know you were here?" the man bellowed. He grabbed a fistful of Kahlil's hair and jerked him up. "I'll kill you—" A look of pure shock swallowed the man's expression of fury. He stared at Kahlil and his grip on Kahlil's hair went slack.

"You ..." the blond man whispered. His blue eyes widened. His lips parted slightly as if Kahlil had knocked the breath out of him.

Kahlil didn't wait for the man to regain his composure. He snapped open the Gray Space, plunged through the man's body, and out through the black wall behind him.

He was in Nurjima again. He recognized the orderly lines of buildings and the trolley tracks cutting through the street. Behind him there was the wall. Kahlil recognized it now. It had been constructed where the Payshmura's Black Tower had once stood. The heavy wall closed the ruins off from the rest of the city.

Kahlil turned and ran from it as fast as he could.

CHAPTER NINETEEN

He was dying. Blood poured from his chest. He tasted it in his throat. The blond man stared down at him. He'd had this dream before, only now Kahlil recognized the man's face.

It was Jath'ibaye, watching him die.

Then his eyes snapped open and he was awake. He groped for Alidas' key, and finding it still in place, his muscles instantly relaxed.

Thin predawn light drifted in through the small window above him. He lay in bed, staring up at a low wood ceiling. Canvas panels hung on either side of him. The heavy smell of other men pervaded the air.

It seemed that he was always waking up like this.

He expected to hear prayer bells, ringing low and deep, or the crack of tahldi butting antlers. Instead, there came the shouts of a paperboy calling out the morning headlines. He was in the Lisam house in the runners' barrack.

Kahlil's back was bruised and his right leg ached. He could hear other men around him getting up. Knees creaked. There were rough coughs and groggy yawns.

Outside the window, the paperboy continued his spiel. Kahlil heard the boy shout Jath'ibaye's name. Doubtless, the papers were announcing his arrival. Kahlil sighed. It was old news to him.

Kahlil rose cautiously, testing his weight on his injured leg. His ankle throbbed but it held him.

"Out of bed, lazy men, the world awaits!" Fensal hurled aside the canvas curtain that separated his and Kahlil's beds. His brown hair was wild and uncombed. He wore only a pair of half-laced underpants. He pounced onto Kahlil's empty bed and then swept apart the canvas panels on the opposite side and attacked the runner in the bed beyond Kahlil's. The other man was unfortunate enough to still have been sleeping.

Fensal hammered the other man with his pillow until the man feebly fought back. Once satisfied that the runner was awake, Fensal moved on to the next bed, eventually making his way around to all sixteen beds.

Kahlil didn't think there had ever been a time in his life when he had been as wildly energetic as Fensal. Of course, he couldn't remember most of his life, so he couldn't be certain. But he knew that even if he had possessed as much raw energy as Fensal, he wouldn't have used it in the same manner.

"Today is the day!" Fensal bounced up and down on a bed and then bounded to the center of the room. "Today, the streets will be packed with other runners. They will try to take our hills. They will clog our back streets and try to run us off the road. Will we let them?" Fensal struck a dramatic pose. "No, my brothers! We will run them down. We will crush them and pass them on every incline!"

Some of the runners clapped. Others laughed. Three or four howled in wild agreement, egging Fensal on.

"Remember," Fensal gazed out at the empty space above the door as if he were a saint receiving a divine vision, "Jath'ibaye's runners will be out there too, witnessing the battles, attacking the weak. We must not fail. For the honor of the Lisam house! For the honor of our beautiful machines! We will overcome all obstacles!"

Several of the youngest runners were already on their feet, enlivened by the speech. Fensal beamed. Kahlil clapped along with most of the older runners. Fensal bowed and then strode back to his bed. He picked his pants up from the floor and stuck his legs into them with the resolute expression of a rashan fastening his gauntlets.

Kahlil gathered his own clothes off the wall pegs above his bed and started for the bathroom, slightly favoring his hurt knee. The new bruises stood out clearly on his pale skin and it didn't take long for Fensal to notice the injury.

"You hurt your leg?"

"I fell."

"Did your bicycle take much damage?" Fensal asked.

"I wasn't riding it at the time."

"Oh ..." Fensal screwed up his face at the thought, as if it were an inconceivable event. "Well, that's good, I guess."

Kahlil turned back toward the bathroom.

"Be careful out there today," Fensal added from behind him.

He guessed that Fensal might someday grow up to be a decent leader for the Lisam runners; maybe in ten or twelve years, when he had mellowed. He certainly had enough love for the work and skill at it. Right now, he was still too inexperienced at reading the men around him. He could inspire them and impress them, but he rarely had any insight into the subtleties of their minds.

Fensal was no Alidas, but then maybe he didn't need to be. He delivered packages, not death sentences.

Kahlil shouldered his way in past the other runners into the bathroom and found an unoccupied washbasin. Steam condensed on the tiled walls. Kahlil splashed hot water over his face. A moment later his skin was cold again. Spring still hadn't warmed the morning air.

He opened his shaving kit. The razor would need sharpening again soon. Maybe he would have time to do it after the Bell Dance. The razor would probably keep its edge for three more shaves. Kahlil turned the straight blade in his hand, watching the light turn from a dull glow to a hard white gleam at the edge.

The razor wasn't important and for that reason Kahlil focused on it. The edge of his razor, the smell of the soap, the roughness of his towel—he concentrated on small things. Details.

The feel of the air this morning was cold and crisp with the sting of frost. The roads would be slippery.

Kahlil went through the motions of the morning—washing, dressing, eating, and taking his orders—in a sanctuary of minutiae. It kept him calm.

Terrible plans were in motion. Right at this moment Nanvess Bousim had men searching for him. His black knife, the yasi'halaun, had fallen into the hands of a sorcerer. In three days Jath'ibaye's murder would probably start a war. And worst yet, the Great Gates could tear the world to pieces.

The relative dullness of his razor didn't matter. It wouldn't save or destroy a single life, so Kahlil put the reality of it between himself and overwhelming dread.

The other runners at the table radiated excitement. They devoured mountains of weasel eggs and baited each other over their cycling prowess. Fensal worked them up with the promise of races later in the day. The runners swapped duties and negotiated routes to ensure that they completed their deliveries early enough to join the races against runners from other houses. The rare opportunity to challenge Jath'ibaye's runners elicited particular excitement.

"Nam's fast," Fensal was saying, "but I'm fearless. This year he's going to be tasting my dust all the way back to Vundomu."

Desh'oun wouldn't have approved of any of this. But then, he was far too busy to pay attention to the petty rivalries of the house runners. Meals had to be prepared and guest rooms readied before the Bell Dance. All morning Kahlil only caught a single glimpse of Desh'oun. The gaunt man had stalked past their open door and disappeared down a hallway. Yu'mir and another kitchen girl hurried behind him, their arms full of linens and bedding.

For the people around him this was a hard, exciting, busy day. Their disasters, if they had any, would involve burned meats or dropped packages or stains that might never come out.

For him, there were assassinations and blood-fed black knives. There was Nayeshi and the soundless corridors of the Gray Space. His life was so different from theirs. He couldn't imagine even attempting to explain it to them, much less commiserating.

Kahlil chewed his roll. It was almost too sweet. He stared down at his bread knife, and in spite of his efforts to avoid disturbing thoughts, Jath'ibaye's angry face came unbidden into his mind.

Kahlil knew that face. Even in the dark he had recognized it. It was face of the man who stood over him in his nightmares. It was the face in the photograph he had been carrying when he had first reached Nurjima. The moment Kahlil had looked up and seen the man, Kahlil had known he was Jath'ibaye.

And Jath'ibaye had known him as well. It had been the first time anyone in this world had looked at him with complete recognition.

He knew so little about himself that he found it disquieting to think that someone else could know more.

The knot in his stomach began to twist again. He wasn't going to be eating anything more. He needed to get to work. Only three days remained until the Bell Dance. He needed to report to Alidas. "I better get going." Kahlil pushed his plate aside and stood.

Fensal looked up from his meal. "You're clear on the new routes?"

"Red Row, Bakers' Hill, and Five Fountains." Kahlil picked up his coat and pulled it on.

"Perfect. Get done as fast as you can. The races will start at four up on Black Hill." Fensal grinned in pure delight.

Kahlil nodded and left. He'd already loaded his share of the packages into the basket of his bicycle and tucked letters into his satchel. He delivered them quickly. Fensal would have been proud, he thought, and a little astonished to see the unorthodox shortcuts he took.

Once the letters were out of the way he locked up his bicycle at a soup house and slipped into the alley behind the building. He closed his eyes and immediately the colorless, silent Gray Space opened before him.

Moments later he was at the black door behind the bone carver's shop. He could have simply passed through the door, but he didn't want to. Instead he stepped out of the Gray Space. The smell of the air in the cramped streets of the Redbrick District was choking compared to what he had grown accustomed to at the Lisam Palace. In the middle of the day few people were out on the street, yet the odor of the surroundings attested to their overwhelming presence here, human sweat and urine matched by the scents of animal carcasses and rendering vats.

People shouted between the narrow brick buildings. The low, deep pounding of work hammers throbbed through the air, and above that Kahlil could discern the high screeching of butcher saws scraping into bones.

Kahlil knocked on the door. After no response came, he took out the key Alidas had given him and let himself in.

He'd expected the rooms to be as austere as those that Alidas occupied in the Bousim barrack, but these were far different. The space itself was smaller and colder. Framed pictures of tahldi and their riders hung on the plaster walls. Most of the pictures looked old and faded and the only face Kahlil recognized in any of them was that of Alidas himself.

A red embroidered carpet covered the floor and the two chairs in the first room were large and padded with dull red cushions. The greatest difference, however, was the sheer number of books. There had to be hundreds of them, packed into bookshelves and piled onto Alidas' desk, even stacked on the floor.

Kahlil picked one up. The cover was tattered and stained but otherwise unmarked. Kahlil flipped it open and read:

Down the cold hill
Alone in the meadow
She waits for him still
An unknowing widow

Clearly a book of old southern poems. The next book in the stack turned out to be a history of the seven gaun'im families, containing a profusion of maps and line drawings of famous leaders. Beneath that lay a slim volume of medicinal plants. Kahlil had never heard of or seen many of them.

Most of the books on the shelves were older and a few that Kahlil flipped through had been dedicated to people other than Alidas. Kahlil guessed Alidas had gathered them throughout his travels as a rashan and bought most of them used.

The first room adjoined two smaller rooms: a cramped bathroom and a bedroom just large enough for a bed and a dresser. Kahlil sat down on the bed.

It felt good to get off his feet. He hadn't gotten much rest last night. Briefly, he entertained the idea of lying back and sleeping here. He knew it was foolish but he felt safe in Alidas' rooms. He could have easily lain back and napped until Alidas returned home.

But it could be days before Alidas arrived and he hadn't come here to sleep. He had to inform Alidas of Nanvess' involvement in the assassination plan as well as Nanvess' order to find and kill him. Kahlil frowned at the blank plaster wall. If the Bousim house wanted Kahlil dead, then Alidas' position could become difficult.

Still, he owed it to Alidas to inform him.

In the desk in the main room Kahlil found a pen, root ink, and paper. There were ledgers and what looked like a diary. Kahlil didn't disturb either, though they tempted him fiercely. If Alidas hadn't given him the key to his rooms, Kahlil might have read them. But something about the trust in offering that key made Kahlil want to be worthy of it.

He wrote a brief report of what he had seen the previous night in Ourath's chambers. He considered describing his encounter with Jath'ibaye but then decided against it. He'd only inform Alidas about Nanvess because that concerned Alidas directly. Kahlil set the note aside to dry.

On a second piece of paper he wrote:

I came by but you were out. I read a little in your book of poems. The one on page thirty-four was particularly insightful. If you read it, tell me what you think of it—Kyle'insira.

He lay the second note down on the desk in plain view. The ink on the first note had already dried so Kahlil folded it into quarters and slid it inside the book of poems. After that, he had no further excuse for lingering in Alidas' rooms so he let himself out. It was already afternoon. Fensal would be expecting him back.

Less than an hour later, Kahlil pedaled up to the kitchen courtyard of the Lisam Palace. The bicycle racks were almost empty. He locked up his own and then let himself into the kitchen's backdoor.

The heat and smell of roasting meats wafted over him. Most of the women working at the long wooden tables didn't bother to do more than glance up as he came in. They were far too busy, rolling out fine crusts and mixing fragrant batters. Yu'mir, though, caught his eye and beckoned him over. Flour dusted her brown hair and Kahlil thought there must have been some on her face as well. She looked terribly pale.

"Watch his hands. They're fast," another woman commented as Kahlil walked past. Kahlil glanced back and recognized the freckled woman from the night before. He winked at her and she gave him a playfully menacing look.

"You can flirt later." Yu'mir stepped forward and caught his arm. "Right now I need to speak to you."

Kahlil glanced down at her. He had spent so little of his life near women that at times he forgot how small they could be. Her hand didn't even enclose his wrist.

Kyle allowed her to pull him to the far side of the kitchen. The smell of blue leaf and other winter herbs was stronger here. He guessed that the locked cupboard next to him was full of precious spices. It was the coolest and darkest area in the entire kitchen.

"So, what's for—" Kahlil began but Yu'mir cut him off.

"Is Fensal holding his stupid races today?" Yu'mir whispered.

"Why?" Kahlil asked.

"Because Desh'oun has two packages that he wanted Fensal to deliver and I can't find him anywhere."

"I can't really say." Kahlil made his best noncommittal reply.

"He's out racing, isn't he?" Yu'mir's expression of annoyance shifted to anxiety. "Desh'oun will fire him if he finds out."

"Don't tell him then."

"There are still the packages," Yu'mir replied. "I can't just throw them away and pretend that they never existed. They're important."

Kahlil sighed. He supposed that they were important. Not to him. None of this mattered to him. But to Desh'oun and Fensal and Yu'mir this wasn't something that they just had to play at for the next three days. This was the reality of their lives. Nothing so consuming and immense as planned assassinations threatened them, but that didn't mean that they lived without crisis or trouble. Fensal loved and needed his work here at the Lisam Palace. Yu'mir obviously cared about what happened to Fensal.

"So I'll deliver the packages," Kahlil offered.

"Can you do that?"

"Easily. We switch routes all the time. I know where he keeps his seal of delivery. So long as you don't tell, I won't, and Fensal should be fine."

"Really?" Yu'mir suddenly smiled at him and Kahlil realized how truly worried she had been. Her eyes shone as though she was on the verge of tears. "Thank you, Kyle."

She gave his hand a squeeze. Her fingers felt soft and warm against his.

Making Yu'mir happy gave Kahlil an odd rush of pleasure. It felt good to do something kind for another person just for their sake, rather than out of duty or necessity. It made him feel like he might actually be a good man deep down.

"I have the packages locked in the spice chest." Yu'mir took out a small key and unlocked the cupboard. A strong smell of dried herbs wafted out as she opened the doors.

The packages were surprisingly small: a little box wrapped in white cotton and a letter. Yu'mir placed them in Kahlil's hands and said, "They're to be given to Jath'ibaye personally."

CHAPTER TWENTY-TWO

The panes of Jath'ibaye's Glass Palace reflected the amber glow of the setting sun. At twilight, the glass sheets caught the light so well that they seemed cut from the sky itself, lending the building an ethereal beauty. But the sharp barbs of the surrounding fence stood in stark contrast. Black iron pickets rose above Kahlil in a twisting wall of cast-iron thorns and heavy bars.

Although a number of the palaces were surrounded by fences of ferocious appearance, Kahlil had found most of them easily surmountable. Designs of curving claws and massive teeth often presented perfect handgrips and footholds.

Not that he normally needed to resort to climbing, but still, he couldn't keep himself from reaching out and lightly gripping one of the curving iron projections. It looked strong enough to support a man's weight.

Tiny sharp teeth stung his fingertips. Immediately, Kahlil pulled his hand back. Long sharp needles encrusted the top side of the iron thorn. Even the tentative pressure of Kahlil's curious touch had been enough to sink them into his flesh. He glanced down at the dark blood beading on his fingertips.

Obviously, Jath'ibaye wasn't fool enough to trust the safety of his palace to any purely ornamental menace. Kahlil supposed he should take some reassurance in that knowledge. Perhaps it meant that Jath'ibaye would be capable of deterring his own assassination.

He had certainly seemed strong and capable enough to do so last night. Kahlil suppressed a shudder of dread at the memory of Jath'ibaye's powerful grip. The previous night's encounter had not been exactly amicable, and he wasn't sure how Jath'ibaye would react to seeing him again. At the same moment, he felt a pulse of excitement. There had been such recognition in Jath'ibaye's face.

The man knew him and Kahlil needed to know how.

He curled his hand into a tight fist, allowing the pressure to staunch the tiny wounds—the last thing he wanted was to stain the white surface of the package he was to deliver—and then he walked his bicycle toward the great iron gate.

Surprisingly the gates hung open, though two sentries stood posted alongside them. The sentries' tanned and weathered faces made it hard to guess their ages, but neither had gray hair. Their coats were sewn from thick goat hide that might have been dyed bright red at one time, but now had faded to dull russet. Their boots were stained and dusty.

They suffered in comparison to the sentries at the Lisam palace, who wore gold, ceremonial swords, and bright badges of rank. These two men gave Kahlil more of the impression of conscripted goat herders than of men in a dress guard.

But their smooth, gleaming rifles shone with the same meticulous care that other dress guards reserved for their buttons.

It wasn't the uniform that made the soldier, he supposed.

"Lisam runner." Kahlil held up Fensal's soapstone seal.

The sentries examined the seal, looked him over, and told him he had to leave his bicycle at the gate. Then one of the sentries escorted him across the open stone courtyard and into the Glass Palace.

The first two floors of the palace weren't built from panes of glass, but from heavy stone. The massive entry doors were solid, black iron. In any gaunsho's palace such doors would have been a foolish extravagance. What iron they could bargain out of Jath'ibaye was always put to use for guns, engines, or new rails. It couldn't be wasted just hanging around as entry doors.

Inside, the sentry handed him over to a muscular auburn-haired man. He looked about Alidas' age, his crow's feet and smile lines lending him an air of experience rather than decline. Unlike the sentries, he wore a new, well-tailored suit.

From his reddish hair and expensive clothes, Kahlil would have guessed that he came from a refined southern family. But his speech destroyed that impression. His words compacted and split in the unmistakable cadence of a northern peasant. Kahlil recognized the accent from countless exchanges with the refugees, thieves, beggars and whores of the west dock slums.

"I'm Saimura, Jath'ibaye's steward." The man paused, peering at Kahlil closely. "Have we met before?"

Uncertainty shivered through Kahlil. He didn't really know the answer to that question, but he had no intention of saying so.

"No, I don't think so," he replied. "We runners are all over the city. You may have seen me somewhere else."

"True." Saimura nodded. "So you have a delivery?"

Kahlil took the small box and letter out of his satchel and offered them to the steward. Saimura made no move to accept them.

"They're unmarked," Saimura commented.

"They're meant for Jath'ibaye, but I'm sure it would be fine for me to leave them in your care. You are his house steward, after all." Kahlil gave his best smile.

"That's very trusting of you." Saimura returned his smile but without any enthusiasm. "But I'm afraid that Jath'ibaye insists on proper procedure. You can wait for him in the mist garden. It's relaxing there, and you look quite tired."

"Thank you," Kahlil responded out of habit. He carefully tucked the box and letter back into his satchel and followed Saimura out of the entryway through a wide whitewashed hall.

The darkening rays of orange sunlight poured down from the glass roof two stories above, coloring the walls peach and gold. Kahlil paused and looked up at the sky. At the dull dark center, he could see the faint curve of the crescent moon shining above him like the ghost of a smile.

Saimura glanced back at him and Kahlil hurried to catch the steward. As he walked, he caught voices coming from other rooms. Most of them sounded like Saimura, poor and northern. None of the walls, floors, or ceilings were decorated. Over the doorways, there was only a hand-painted design of two leaves, one red and the other green. The emptiness bordered on monastic.

He didn't know why, but the starkness of the surroundings evoked a weird nostalgia. Out of some forgotten habit, his right hand automatically folded into the Payshmura gesture of peace. When Kahlil noticed, he hid his hands in his coat pockets.

Saimura stopped in front of a door. It, like the others, was black iron, but it had been varnished far more heavily. Its surface gleamed in the fading sunlight.

Saimura asked, "Are you hungry?"

"A little, yes."

"Runners always are." With some effort, Saimura pulled the door open. "Go on in. I'll have some food brought for you. It may be a long wait for Jath'ibaye."

Beyond Saimura, Kahlil saw a profusion of greenery. Walls of ferns and wild ivy sprouted from massive planters lining a huge room whose floor was nothing more than a winding trail between raised beds teeming with lush foliage. He could barely discern the far wall between thick bodies of trees, whose branches reached up past his line of sight.

"There are some benches just down the path," Saimura said.

Kahlil mumbled his thanks, still gaping at the foliage. It seemed like Jath'ibaye had captured a forest and put it inside this one huge room.

Why would anyone, even an Eastern sorcerer, want to keep the outdoors inside?

Rich, scented air rolled over him, bringing to mind the intoxicating air of Nayeshi. He closed his eyes and took in a deep breath so saturated with life that he felt like it could sustain him for hours.

He opened his eyes and noticed Saimura grinning at him from the door.

"Breathe as much as you like. It's free," Saimura told him. Then he let the door drop closed. The latch slid into place with a heavy reverberation.

Locked in again. Or at least that was what Saimura had intended to do. Kahlil smirked at the thought of common doors and walls restraining him, but he remained. He certainly had no reason yet to disprove Saimura's confidence in the building's security.

He could escape through the Gray Space any time he wanted, but he chose to push ahead into this lush forest.

He strode deeper into the immense chamber.

Overhead open walkways arched from one side of the second story mezzanine to the other. A few lamps flickered up there, but otherwise only the last red and violet streaks of the sunset burned against the dark night sky. The white stone floor stood out against the surrounding black soil and deep shadowy foliage.

Kahlil found the stone bench Saimura had mentioned beside a mound of grayish goatweed, yellow bellflowers, and another scrubby plant he didn't recognize. Two slim chains hung down from the ceiling, supporting unlit lanterns. Kahlil was glad that they weren't burning. The evening darkness seemed to better suit both the surroundings and his mood.

He carefully avoided touching the goatweed, as he knew from experience that it gave him a rash, even if he couldn't remember precisely what that experience had been. It struck him as an odd plant to choose to cultivate, though dimly he recalled that its musky leaves could be used to induce vomiting. The roots, however, contained a deadly poison.

More evidence that Jath'ibaye wasn't exactly helpless.

He sat down to wait.

Somewhere, in one of the trees, birds called to one another.

Just ahead, there came a rustling of dark leaves, then a big yellow dog stepped out from between two bushes. Its hide was faded and graying, but its eyes gleamed clear gold. The dog met his gaze and Kahlil knew he had seen it before. He stared at the animal with the uneasy feeling of having slipped into a dream: a terribly wrong dream.

A dream in which this dog was his sister.

Her teeth had yellowed with age and her eyes gleamed wild gold. She told him that her true skin had been stripped from her bones and this hide was just a coat to keep her warm. She laughed and he could smell raw meat on her hot breath. Then her brilliant red blood was pouring over his hands.

He couldn't stop staring at it.

After a moment, the dog dropped its gaze from him and rustled back through the undergrowth, disappearing out of sight and hearing.

He put his head in his hands. He had thought he had finally overcome this kind of insane reaction.

The dog was just a dog. The world was full of them. It didn't mean anything. This one had probably escaped the kitchen kennel and was now wandering the household, lost. That was just what dogs did. He couldn't let the sight of one animal throw his mind into disarray. Otherwise he would end up the same confused, deluded mess he had been before Alidas had found him.

He wished this place wasn't so disconcertingly familiar. The leaf designs above the doors, the worn red uniforms, even the smell of the air, everything around him seemed like a fragment of one of his dreams suddenly made real. It awakened shattered bits of memories and nightmare images that he had thought forgotten.

His sister was not a dog. He felt absurd even having to tell himself as much. He didn't even know if he had a sister. Family and history both fell into the realms of conjecture. He didn't really know anything about himself.

But Jath'ibaye did. When Jath'ibaye had looked at him, his hard gaze had been bright with recognition. Last night, Kahlil hadn't dared to stay and see what judgment would come after that first moment of contact. But he couldn't stop thinking about Jath'ibaye's expression—or about the certainty that had flooded him the instant he met the other man's stare. They had known each other.

Had they been friends? Had they been enemies? Was Jath'ibaye, like Fikiri, another man who could claim the right to be called a Kahlil?

His gut roiled with a turmoil of questions, but for now he had to bide in patience. There was nothing to do but wait and hope Jath'ibaye would bring the answers.

About twenty minutes later a young, plump kitchen woman arrived. She lit the lantern above him and then gave him a tray of taye bread, goat cutlets, and steamed blue leaf. Kahlil ate the food and recalled that the Lisam kitchen women had said that coarse, simple food was all that Jath'ibaye ever ate—the kind of thing peasants lived on because they had to. Kahlil couldn't imagine anyone choosing this as their only sustenance. After he finished the meal, he pushed his dishes under the bench.

With every new detail Jath'ibaye seemed more and more strange and yet more familiar for his oddity. It felt right to Kahlil that Jath'ibaye should choose coarse food. He was suddenly sure that the man drank his daru'sira strong and bitter and that he licked his fingers when he ate pungent goat cheese.

High in the sky, he could see that dim stars had joined the sharp moon. He'd expected that with nightfall the air would grow chilly around him, but it remained warm and sweet. Who knew when Jath'ibaye would arrive? Maybe he wouldn't, and the steward would take the packages after all.

Kahlil smirked at the thought. All this worry, all his fear and hope, just to have the house steward hand him a sweetdrop candy for a tip and thank him for his trouble. That was how this would probably all end up. He guttered the lantern overhead and closed his eyes for a nap.

He didn't sleep, but he stretched his legs out and let his arms lie limp across his stomach. He listened to the sounds around him. Somewhere far off two men talked in low voices, a strange collision of northern and southern dialects. The words were indistinguishable but the tones rolled over him with soft calm.

As the voices drew closer, Kahlil cracked an eye. On the walkway above him, a lamp gleamed. Two men walked close, but did not touch. He knew them at once: Ourath Lisam and Jath'ibaye.

"You seem distracted this evening." Ourath's voice was tinged with concern. Light from the perfume lamp he carried glowed over his brown velvet jacket.

"It's nothing." Jath'ibaye turned from the lamplight to survey the greenery beneath him. Though his long blond hair was pulled back it still looked wild, as if it had been restrained in the midst of an escape. He wore clothes like those of his sentries: heavy and simple. But he carried no weapon that Kahlil could see.

"Winter seemed so long this year," Ourath commented.

Jath'ibaye turned back to Ourath but said nothing. Despite his age—Kahlil knew he had to be fifty at the least, older most likely—he appeared as young as Ourath, more powerfully built and much fairer skinned, but still so young.

Though it struck Kahlil that he should not look so very pale. He seemed almost ill. Then Kahlil recalled the poisoning Fikiri had mentioned.

"It's probably only a whim of the weather," Ourath went on lightly. "I'm sure that it will be warm soon enough."

When Jath'ibaye still made no reply, Ourath began toying with the handle of his perfume lamp. Steadily, he swung it from side to side, causing the chains holding the lamp to spin. The shadows surrounding him jumped and twisted into each other.

"Careful." Jath'ibaye caught the chains and slowly stilled Ourath's lamp. "You don't want to spill burning oil."

Those tiny silver chains had to be hot. They had to burn into Jath'ibaye's palm, but he didn't seem to notice or care. Ourath's full lips spread into a deep smile.

"I'm touched that you are so worried for me." Then he gave a theatrical pout. "Or are you simply afraid that I might burn down your little forest?"

"Whichever you like. Just don't do it again." Jath'ibaye released the chains. His voice conveyed the cold authority of a trainer disciplining a dog. Hardly the manner of the malleable effeminate Ourath had made him out to be during his secret dinner.

"I didn't mean to anger you," Ourath said softly.

"You didn't."

"Really? You seem angry."

Jath'ibaye looked at Ourath as if he were looking through him. "Would it please you if I were? Would it make this easier?"

"Of course it wouldn't." Ourath began to twist the lamp handle again but then stopped himself. "You know I want you to be happy."

Jath'ibaye said nothing. Then again, Kahlil supposed he might become quite taciturn himself had he just been poisoned.

Ourath sighed and said, "You're annoyed because I announced that you would be attending the Bell Dance, aren't you?"

Again, Jath'ibaye didn't respond, and now Kahlil began to wonder if his own questions would be met with the same stony silence Ourath currently enjoyed. He hoped not.

"I'm not asking you to attend because I want you to suffer." Ourath shook his head and his red hair gleamed like polished copper. "And inviting you certainly hasn't done my standing any good. But this is more important than a little social discomfort. If you do come, it will be the first real, meaningful, peaceful gesture since the truce. The Bell Dance is the night we celebrate the alliances of the noble houses. If you attend, I think it would demonstrate to the gaunsho'im that you respect their authority. They need to feel that you aren't just out to destroy them. You say that you want real peace between—"

"I'll go." Jath'ibaye cut him off. "Just don't expect a miracle to come of it."

"Thank you." Ourath gave another handsome smile.

Jath'ibaye simply turned again to stare down at the trees and greenery beneath him. Kahlil squinted up, trying to read his expression. Then he realized that Jath'ibaye returned his gaze. Jath'ibaye stood there, still and silent, looking through the darkness directly at him. A flush of embarrassment flooded Kahlil and he had no idea why.

Jath'ibaye's expression remained as closed as that of a marble statue, his pale eyes luminous in the night.

Kahlil felt his skin flushing hotter, an alarming reaction that he couldn't remember having since his awkward youth. In a sudden panic, Kahlil looked down at his boots as if they had become instantaneously interesting. Slowly, his cheeks cooled.

When he stole a glance back up to the walkway, Jath'ibaye was escorting Ourath across to the eastern side of the building.

"You can see the moon flowers blooming from here," Jath'ibaye said. "They originally grew wild in the southern lands but have died out in the last ten years. I've found them to have a good effect on soils that have been over-farmed."

Jath'ibaye went on describing the properties of weeds and bushes that had apparently died out in the south. The light of

Ourath's lamp grew dimmer. Kahlil strained to hear more, but Jath'ibaye and Ourath had moved too far away. He only caught the low rumble of Ourath's voice and then nothing else.

Kahlil stayed put, too shocked by his own reaction to move. It had been inexplicable, unexpected, and humiliating. He'd probably been as red-faced as a bride caught on the chamber pot.

Time passed, while Kahlil hunched in the darkness feeling juvenile and self-conscious. Even Alidas had never been able to provoke such a reaction from him. He had to be more exhausted than he had thought. Or perhaps it had been the result of being caught spying on two men in such an obviously private exchange.

Were they really lovers? Last night Ourath had both implied and denied it. Jath'ibaye had seemed cold toward Ourath. Though, in the end, he had given Ourath what he wanted.

Somewhere in the distance of the greenery Kahlil thought he heard leaves rustling.

"Runner." Saimura's voice broke into his thoughts.

Kahlil jumped up to face the man.

"Yes?"

"I'm sorry to have startled you. I wasn't sure where you were." Saimura squinted through the darkness at him. "I thought that Addya lit a lantern for you."

"She did, but I was feeling tired so I snuffed it."

"I see," Saimura said. "I came to tell you that Jath'ibaye has retired for the evening."

Kahlil didn't know whether to be relieved or disappointed. He supposed it didn't matter. "You'll want me to leave the package with you, then."

Kahlil reached for his satchel, but before he could dig the package out, Saimura stopped him.

"I won't be taking it."

Kahlil scowled. He wasn't actually going to be asked to come back tomorrow, was he? He wouldn't do it. He'd just throw the damn package away before he went through this again.

"Jath'ibaye requested that you be escorted up to his personal chambers and deliver the package to him there."

《《《

Jath'ibaye's chambers were plain, almost ascetically so. There was a fireplace but no fire. The bare stone floors and walls radiated the night chill. The only light came from an oil lamp on the table and the room smelled of bitter medicinal herbs.

On the wide bed a roll of bandages lay next to a scalpel. But as Saimura escorted Kahlil into the room, Jath'ibaye snatched both items up and secreted them away in a blackwood box at the bedside.

He stood immediately and welcomed Saimura with a quick smile. His blond hair hung loose, and this close, Kahlil could see how sun and weather had streaked it to white in places. He wore no coat now, just reddish work pants, and his white shirt hung open. Kahlil frowned at the white swath of bandages that encircled Jath'ibaye's broad chest. As if sensing Kahlil's attention, Jath'ibaye turned his back and buttoned his shirt.

"That was certainly fast," Jath'ibaye commented over his shoulder to Saimura.

"I thought sooner would be better than later." Saimura looked to the clay teapot and empty cup on the table. Kahlil recognized the scent of yellowpetal blossoms, so often used by northern physicians to ease pain.

"Should I have Addya bring up more tea?" Saimura asked.

"No." Jath'ibaye turned to face them. He focused his attention on Saimura, hardly glancing at Kahlil. "I'm fine."

Saimura nodded. "Has Ji spoken to you yet?"

"No, but I can wait till tomorrow." Jath'ibaye tied his hair back from his face. As he did, Kahlil noticed that he moved his left arm carefully, guarding himself from pulling a tender spot on the left side of his chest.

"I thought as much," Saimura said. "I couldn't find her anyway."

"She's probably still out digging up the garden." Jath'ibaye smiled slightly.

"Probably true." Saimura shrugged, and then to Kahlil's surprise, he simply walked away.

Kahlil wasn't used to seeing servants, not even house stewards, taking leave of their lords so casually. Jath'ibaye seemed unfazed by Saimura's presumption. He turned back to the blackwood cupboard and opened a drawer.

Kahlil waited, nervously watching Jath'ibaye's back.

His presence dominated the room. Even now, with his back turned, bent over a drawer, Kahlil could focus on nothing else. Physically, he was intimidating, taller than Kahlil, with a sharp, muscular body. Even pale and poisoned, he seemed like he would be a tough man to take on.

But he was more than a physical presence. He had destroyed the Payshmura and held back the armies of the gaunsho'im. As one of the rare few who had altered the world to his will, Jath'ibaye both fascinated and frightened Kahlil. Yet he seemed strong, quiet, and perfectly human. And that made him even stranger. Kahlil expected demons and gods to change the world, not mere men.

"So." Jath'ibaye straightened. Whatever he had been looking for he had either found or given up on. "You have something to give me?"

He turned but didn't look at Kahlil. Instead, he seemed to be taking in the measurements of his room. Again Kahlil noticed how pale and bright his eyes looked. But this time he knew why. It was the brilliance of a fever.

Kahlil dug the letter and box out of his satchel. He offered Fensal's seal but Jath'ibaye didn't seem to care about it. He yanked the small white box and letter from Kahlil's hands. With angry efficiency, he tore open the envelope and flipped the letter out and read. After a while he crushed the letter and dropped it to the floor. He tossed the box onto his bed, unopened.

"So," Jath'ibaye's voice was almost a growl, "am I supposed to take one look at you, fall to my knees, and hand you the keys to the kingdom? Is that it?"

Kahlil had no idea how to respond.

"I ...don't know. I didn't read the letter," Kahlil said. What was Jath'ibaye talking about?

"God," Jath'ibaye whispered, "even your voice ..."

He rounded on Kahlil, his expression cold and disdainful. "Well then, let's play our little drama out, shall we? Shouldn't you tell me your name?"

Kahlil stepped closer to the door. "Kyle'insira."

"Kyle ...of course!" Jath'ibaye's smile was hardly more than a flash of his white teeth. "Very clever. Go on. You have to have more lines than just that."

Kahlil stood silent. Until this moment, it hadn't occurred to him that when Jath'ibaye had looked at him with recognition, it might have been the crazed expression of familiarity that a fevered man had for his hallucinations.

"Stage fright?" Jath'ibaye demanded. "Or did Fikiri just tell you to stand there and bat your eyelashes?"

"Fikiri?" At last Kahlil had some idea of what to say. "No, I'm not with him. I've been sent to stop him—to save you."

"Nice delivery," Jath'ibaye replied. "Very believable."

"I'm telling you the truth—" Kahlil began, only to be cut off.

"I could kill you for this," Jath'ibaye ground out. "I should."

"But I'm not who—"

"Of course you're not," Jath'ibaye snapped. "You're just an innocent boy who wandered in looking like this and delivered me a bottle of poison." Suddenly Jath'ibaye caught hold of Kahlil's shoulders and pulled him close. His grip was hard and burning hot.

"If they told you I wouldn't hurt you, they lied," Jath'ibaye growled.

He was so close that Kahlil could smell the blood in his bandages. He wasn't about to stay here and find out how Jath'ibaye preferred to punish his enemies. Kindness to Fensal, duty to Alidas, and even his own curiosity weren't worth this. Kahlil jerked his arm back and slammed his fist into Jath'ibaye's wounded left side.

He felt the warm wet of blood soaking up against his knuckles. Jath'ibaye's grip loosened fractionally and Kahlil sprung back from him. With a flick of his hand Kahlil tore open an entry to the Gray Space, but it crumpled closed before he could step in.

Horrified, he looked back to see Jath'ibaye clenching his hand into a fist. Kahlil felt the air shuddering around Jath'ibaye. Somehow he had closed the Gray Space. True fear surged through Kahlil and his heart pounded like a wild thing kicking in a trap.

He lunged for the door, but Jath'ibaye sprang forward, again blocking his escape. Kahlil stumbled back, evading Jath'ibaye's grasp. Jath'ibaye stalked slowly after him. Softly, he said, "Didn't they tell you what I am? Didn't they warn you?"

The back of Kahlil's leg struck the bed.

Jath'ibaye dove forward and slammed into Kahlil, hurling him back onto the hard mattress and pinning him against the bed. He caught Kahlil by the throat. His fingers burned like heated irons against Kahlil's skin.

Kahlil fought against Jath'ibaye's grip, but his hands only tightened. He kicked Jath'ibaye's leg as hard as he could, but the other man barely seemed to register it.

Jath'ibaye leaned forward over him. His blue eyes burned like phosphorus. "Didn't they tell you that I am the Rifter?"

Kahlil's arms and legs began to tingle. He clawed at Jath'ibaye's tightening grip. He could put no force behind his kicks now. He gagged and gasped hopelessly.

"Do you understand what I could do to you?" Jath'ibaye whispered over him.

Kahlil's ears rang; his mouth felt numb.

Then, abruptly, Jath'ibaye released him and stepped back from the bed. Kahlil sucked in a desperate breath of air.

"Get out," Jath'ibaye said coldly.

Kahlil had already struggled to his feet. He stumbled toward the door.

"If I ever see you again, I will kill you," Jath'ibaye warned him.

Kahlil didn't stay to hear anything else. His mind burned with just one word, one thought.

Rifter.

CHAPTER TWENTY-THREE

Kahlil lay curled on the cool surface of the tiled floor. Nausea welled up in him, rolling and rising. His throat ached. Painfully, he swallowed.

The Rifter. After a decade of watching over John, how could he have let his true identity slip from his mind? He had bled himself nearly to death just to pursue the Rifter, just to kill him. How could he have forgotten?

He squeezed his eyes closed and pressed his face against the floor. He remembered the overwhelming feeling of guilt that had enveloped him when he had first tried to find the Black Tower of the Payshmura. Even then, he had known its absence was his fault, his failing. He had allowed the Rifter to escape, and now the Payshmura were no more.

The sacred convent of Umbhra'ibaye and the holy Black Tower had both been lost in an instant, as if devoured by the earth. Rathal'pesha and the city of Amura'taye had been consumed by geysers of molten stone. The entire northland, where he had grown up, rendered a shattered ruin in a day. Whole mountains had fallen, chasms of magma and steaming waters swallowing them. People had died, thousands of them, in the first disaster and then more in the following wars.

It all could have been stopped, but he had failed.

Maybe that's why he'd chosen for so long to forget.

Kahlil pushed himself up to his knees and lurched over the cold porcelain basin. His stomach heaved, bringing up nothing but bile. He coughed. There was nothing left in him to vomit up, but he couldn't stop feeling sick with self-loathing.

He folded back down against the floor.

He had wanted to forget. He had needed to forget.

That very first day when he had arrived in Nurjima he had known, somewhere deep in himself, that he had already been too late.

Now the solace of amnesia had been stripped from him. He remembered the torn envelope, the letter with its single word: Don't.

Don't fail.

Don't forget.

Don't let him live.

Only one word to obey, and he hadn't managed it.

Dayyid had been right: the taint in his blood, the weakness in his soul went even deeper than Parfir's blessing in his bones. They should have burned him along with his mother.

He'd been sick for hours now, purging everything from his body as if it could somehow empty him of his guilt. He leaned his forehead against the edge of the basin. Strings of his long black hair hung against his damp face.

"Kyle?"

He glanced up to see Fensal, and then hung his head back over the basin, glad of the predawn dimness. No matter how bad he felt, having a witness to his pathetic state made it worse.

"You've been at it all night. Are you dying?"

"I wish," Kahlil managed to croak.

A smaller figure stepped out from behind Fensal. Yu'mir stared at him with wide, worried eyes. Kahlil hung his head in shame, suddenly aware of how badly he stank. Though men in the barrack routinely witnessed each other's wretched states, it seemed somehow wrong to expose a woman to the sight of him.

"You should have called me sooner, Fensal." She crouched down beside Kahlil.

"You shouldn't be here." Kahlil's voice splintered as he tried to speak. His breath tasted of vomit.

"You're hardly in any condition to take me by force," Yu'mir said, misunderstanding his concern. "And I'm not too worried about falling victim to your seductive charms either."

He heard the snort of Fensal's repressed laughter.

"I brought whiteshell tablets." Yu'mir took a small paper packet from the pocket of her apron and placed it in his hand. "Do you think you can keep them down?"

He didn't know what he could keep down, or even if he wanted to keep anything down. A pathetic, tired part of him just wanted to die and have done with it. How hard could it be to simply die?

The moment the thought came to Kahlil, he rejected it.

He had failed. He had ruined the world. No amount of remorse would change that, and he had no right to expect the release of death. He had no right to dream of it, as he did each night. He deserved to feel bad and he deserved to suffer, but he didn't deserve to die yet. He had too many obligations.

Just sagging here, making himself sick like this, was both pathetic and self-indulgent. Only he knew of the world that might have been, of the world that had been lost. To everyone else this was simply life. Fensal and Yu'mir had their own concerns. Alidas had his. They were all present and real. Kahlil's guilt and sickness stemmed from an unalterable past and he needed to pull himself together and see to his present duties.

He opened Yu'mir's paper packet and dumped the chalky whiteshell tablets into his palm. They smelled of salt. Certainly a fresher odor than the one currently clinging to Kahlil. He swallowed them with a gulp of the cool water.

Yu'mir placed the palm of her hand against his forehead.

"I don't think you have a fever. Did you eat something bad?"

"Goatweed, I think." Kahlil took another drink of the water, using it to rinse his mouth out a little. "There was some growing in Jath'ibaye's garden and I was playing with it."

"I've never heard of it." Yu'mir glanced at the cup in Kahlil's hand. "Do you need more water?"

"Yes, thank you."

"It's no trouble." She took the empty cup and handed it back to Fensal. "Get him some more water."

"Me?" Fensal asked.

"Yes, you. You're in his debt," Yu'mir replied firmly.

"So you've told me," Fensal said. "But this is only going to last so long. I'm not going to be serving him hand and foot from now on."

Yu'mir rolled her eyes at Fensal's retreating back. She said, "He can be such an ass sometimes."

"He's not so bad," Kahlil told her, "especially if you ignore everything he says."

Yu'mir smiled. It made her look pretty. Not beautiful, she didn't have that kind of face, but she had a kindness to her expression that could make her quite pretty.

"Feeling any better?" Yu'mir asked.

Kahlil nodded. "I think the worst of it's over."

"So, goatweed?" Yu'mir asked. "What is it, exactly?"

"Just a plant." Kahlil leaned back against a tiled wall.

"I've never heard of it."

"Yes, you said that." Kahlil watched as she straightened her dress around her. He wondered if Fensal had the good sense to find her pretty.

"You look a little dazed," Yu'mir said. "Should you move back closer to the—"

"No." Kahlil shook his head. "I'm just tired. I think the tablets are helping."

"They usually do. If not, then dewroot will," Yu'mir assured him.

"You're quite the physician, aren't you?" Kahlil smiled. Fensal really should marry her, he decided. She'd make a good mother.

"It's mostly herbalism." Yu'mir dropped her voice a little. "That's why I'm curious about your goatweed."

"Oh." As his miserable nausea faded, Kahlil began to realize how exhausted he was. The bruises across his right leg and his throat throbbed with a dull pain in time with his heartbeat.

Yu'mir obviously waited for a better response.

"It's not as though I'm practicing witchcraft," Yu'mir suddenly explained. "Just teas and a few tablets like the ones I gave you. Nothing ..."

A shadow of worry crossed her face, though he was the last person she needed to fear. Her small concoctions of flowers and leaves were the soul of innocence. They were simple medicines, more cookery to them than power. Kahlil had seen true witchcraft.

"My mother was a witch." Kahlil didn't know why he said it, except that the knowledge had just come to him. "She taught me about goatweed, yellowpetal, and fire vines ..." He couldn't remember much else about her, except that they had burned her. He'd been young.

He closed his eyes. He didn't want to remember anything more. Not about himself or his life. He just wanted to slip away into the respite of a thoughtless, dreamless darkness.

"Kyle," Yu'mir whispered his name.

He could feel her hands against his forehead again and then touching the pulse at his throat. He must have fallen asleep for a few minutes. The silent dark had been so alluring.

"Kyle," she said again, "are you still awake?"

"I'm sorry. I'm not thinking very clearly." With an effort, he opened his eyes. "Have I told you that I think you'd make a good mother?"

"No." Yu'mir looked a little startled.

"Not for my children," Kahlil smirked at the impossibility of that, "for yours and Fensal's."

Even in the faint light Kahlil could see the blush that swept across Yu'mir's cheeks.

Then Fensal came through the doorway. For the first time, Kahlil realized that Fensal was only wearing his thin cotton underpants. The skin of his bare chest and arms looked blue in the cold morning light. He must have gone straight from his bed to get Yu'mir.

He had a clay cup in one hand and a pitcher of water in the other. He set the pitcher and cup down, then crouched beside Yu'mir. Next to her, Fensal looked rangy and unkempt. His brown hair stuck up in clumps from where he'd slept on it. Yu'mir's hair was pulled back into a smooth bun at the back of her neck. She'd probably been up for a few hours already, overseeing the morning baking.

"So, he's poisoned?" Fensal asked Yu'mir.

"I'm not sure." Yu'mir poured more water for Kahlil and handed him the cup.

He drank slowly, letting the cool liquid soothe his throat. The bruises Jath'ibaye had left on his throat were probably beginning to darken by now. They'd be black and yellow in a day. He didn't know how he'd explain them. Perhaps he'd be gone by then. Maybe sooner.

"Kyle." Yu'mir lightly touched his hand as he set the empty cup down. "Can you tell me more about the plant you ate? The goatweed?"

"It won't kill me," Kahlil assured her. "I just got some on my hands and forgot about it when I ate dinner. I wasn't thinking."

"I'll say." Fensal frowned at him, then looked to Yu'mir. "So, this goatweed will wear off eventually. It's not going to kill him, is it?"

"Why do you keep asking me?" Yu'mir asked. "I've never even heard of the stuff before now."

"It grows in the north, on scrub hills. Three gray leaves with orange tips," Kahlil said. "If the leaves are eaten they purge the body. Only goats and sheep can keep it down. It's an unpleasant plant, but the leaves alone won't kill a grown man."

"I'm just going to tell Desh'oun and the others that you're ill. Don't tell anyone else about this weed-eating of yours. It just makes us all look stupid." Fensal paused for a moment and then added, "Particularly you. It makes you look the stupidest."

"I won't do it again." Kahlil couldn't help but find Fensal's terrible bedside manner somewhat endearing.

"Stop lecturing him," Yu'mir said, "and get him to his bed. I have to go before the other runners see me here."

"Go, go." Fensal waved her away. "Thank you for coming."

Yu'mir smiled when Fensal turned his back to her. Then she slipped quietly away.

"Can you walk on your own?" Fensal asked.

"I think so." He stumbled out of the bathroom back into the quiet barrack. The canvas panels were still spread around the other runners' beds, creating an illusion of emptiness. Kahlil went to his own bed. He stripped off his thin, stinking underclothes and lay down naked. The cold sheets smelled clean.

Fensal followed him to the edge of his bed. Kahlil had expected that Fensal would just go back to bed himself, but then he realized that it was too late for that. Thin rays of dawn sunlight were already seeping through the small windows.

"How did the races go?" Kahlil whispered.

Fensal grinned and sat on the edge of Kahlil's bed.

"Good. The only one who came close to me was Nam. He's one of Jath'ibaye's runners. The bastard is a beast on hills. But I know the streets better. I took him at Baker Cross. He pulled off when he saw the trolley coming and I tore right past him."

"I'm sorry I missed it."

"There's always next year." Fensal rose. "I'm getting the rest of the men up now. You stay here and sleep. I want you well tomorrow."

He pulled the canvas panels around Kahlil's bed closed. Kahlil could hear Fensal rousing the other runners. It sounded like he was assaulting them with their pillows this morning. They groaned, coughed, and grumbled. Kahlil watched their blue-toned shadows jump and stretch across the white folds of the canvas panels. Fensal laughed at something. One of the younger runners started singing a song about his morning erection.

Kahlil rolled his eyes at the absurd lyrics.

He had allowed the Rifter to live, but the whole world hadn't been ruined for it. People still laughed and made their livings all across the country. These men didn't even know that their fates were meant to have been different. He wondered who they would have been if things had gone differently. If he had killed the Rifter, would it have changed their lives? Would some of them have become priests or heretics? Would there have been a new war?

There was no way for him to know.

Kahlil heard water running in the bathroom. The shouts and conversations sounded distant and dull. They grew softer and then fell into silence as the runners departed. Kahlil slept.

He dreamed of another room, one with the same strong smell of men, but higher walls and sharp northern light. He was sitting on a large bed, reading a book. A lean blond man sat on the edge of the bed next to him. He smelled like pine and rain. Kahlil could feel heat radiating from his body even through the heavy gray clothes they both wore.

Kahlil said, "You aren't supposed to be here."

The man smiled and said, "You haven't forgotten about the key, have you?"

Kahlil woke suddenly. Instinctively, he grasped Alidas' key, though he now realized that it had never been the key he had wanted it to be. Still, holding it reassured him.

The canvas panels twitched and Yu'mir peeked between them. Seeing that he was awake, she waved. The bright noonday light edged her brown hair in gold. Kahlil secured the blankets around his waist and sat upright.

"Feeling better?" Yu'mir asked.

"Yes."

Though they were alone, she looked nervous. Kahlil glanced down and noticed the folded piece of paper in her hands. She curled her fingers around it, but not enough to crumple it.

"Fensal's bed is to the left of mine." Kahlil pointed in the general direction.

Yu'mir lowered her face as a scarlet blush flooded across her cheeks.

"I wasn't ..."

"The note is for him, isn't it?"

Yu'mir nodded. "I wasn't going to wake you up to ask you, but I thought that if you were already awake ..."

"I'm awake."

"You don't think I'm being too forward, do you?" Yu'mir asked and Kahlil knew she didn't mean about waking him.

"Not at all. I left a secret note for someone myself. Yesterday, in fact." It seemed as if it had been weeks ago. "I won't tell anyone that I saw you here."

"Do you promise?"

"I swear," Kahlil assured her.

She rushed to Fensal's bed. Kahlil took advantage of the canvas panel hanging between them to get dressed. His clean pants were cold from hanging against the wall.

"Put it under his pillow," Kahlil advised. "Otherwise the other runners will see it and want to know what it says."

"They should mind their own business." Yu'mir hesitated at the edge of the canvas panels. "Are you getting dressed?"

"Yes, I'm nearly decent." Kahlil dug through the box under his bed for his spare shirt and some socks.

"Was it Wounin'an?"

"What?" Kahlil tucked his shirt in. The sleeves were too short for him, so he rolled the cuffs.

"The woman you sent the note to, was it Wounin'an?"

"Wou—" Kahlil began to ask who she was, but then he remembered the kitchen girl with the freckles. "No. Did she get a note as well?"

"I don't know. You two seem to flirt all the time."

"I don't think she's serious." Kahlil found his belt and threaded it through the loops of his pants.

"Why is it," Yu'mir asked, "that whenever a man isn't serious he says that he thinks the woman isn't?"

"An attempt at delicacy, I don't know. You can come in now. I'm decent."

Yu'mir stepped back through the panels. She frowned when she saw Kahlil lacing up his boots.

"You're not going out, are you?"

"I need to see if there's been any response to my note." Kahlil combed his tangled hair back from his face with his fingers. He probably still looked like hell.

"But you're supposed to be sick."

"I'm fine, thanks to your medicine," Kahlil assured her.

"Was that an attempt at flattery?"

"Did it work?"

Yu'mir sighed. "Fensal will be annoyed if he sees you running around the city. He gave you the day off to recover, not to chase some street girl."

"Street girl?"

"You know what I mean."

"A prostitute?" An undignified image of the fifty-year-old Alidas working a street corner came to his mind and Kahlil almost laughed aloud.

"Just because I'm a decent woman, it doesn't mean I don't know about the other kind." Yu'mir crossed her arms over her chest. "Is she very pretty?"

"No, not particularly," Kahlil answered.

"You're supposed to say that she's the most beautiful woman in the world," Yu'mir told him. "You're not going to get very far telling her she's not particularly pretty."

"That's not what's important between us." Kahlil pulled his coat from its wall peg.

"Is she pregnant?"

"Pregnant? No!" Kahlil gaped at her. He always forgot things like that. Wives, mistresses, children, all the domestic relations of other men's lives fell outside his experience. Pregnancy had a kind of irrelevance to his existance that surpassed even that of abstract math.

"You never know," Yu'mir told him.

"I know," Kahlil insisted. "I have to go if I'm going to get back before Fensal does."

"Fine." Yu'mir turned and started out of the room. "But if the baby's a girl you better name her after me."

Kahlil waited for her to leave, then stepped into the Gray Space.

A few moments later he let himself into Alidas' rooms.

Because of the weather, they were colder than before. The air felt crisp, despite the sun. He wondered if it would snow again.

"Is anyone home?" Kahlil called out.

No response. The rooms appeared to be the same as when he had left them yesterday, but the notes he had left were gone. He searched all three rooms but found nothing to tell him what response Alidas might have had.

Kahlil knew he shouldn't linger, but still he sat down on the corner of Alidas' bed as he had done the day before. He lay back and stared up at the ceiling.

What was he going to do when he returned to the Lisam palace? Still try to stop the assassination and save the Rifter?

More than a little irony in that.

Should he let Fikiri, Ourath, Nanvess, and Esh'illan all try their best to kill the Rifter? Only the key could truly kill him and as far as Kahlil knew Jath'ibaye was the one who had it.

They could all just go on without him while he lay on this soft bed.

He heard the click and groan of the front door opening.

Alidas stood in the doorway. The bright noon light at his back cast his features into deep shadow. Sweeping his eyes across the rooms, he caught sight of Kahlil. Brief surprise registered on his face as he stepped in and closed the door behind him.

"It's cold," Alidas said from the front room. "You should have started a fire in the wood stove."

"I didn't think I'd be here long." Kahlil became suddenly self-conscious about being caught lying in another man's bed. He sat up and joined Alidas in the front room.

"I just came to see if you got my note."

Alidas bent over the wood stove, feeding scraps of paper into the dull, glowing embers.

"I got it last night." He balled up a piece of paper from his pocket and tossed it into the growing flames. "There's a bundle of wood on the step outside the door. Grab it, will you?"

Kahlil found the scrap wood, untied the rope holding the bundle together, and handed Alidas a stick to add to the fire.

Already the first wave of heat radiated out into the room.

Alidas closed the grate and straightened up. "One of Nanvess' men came to the barrack asking about you."

"What did you tell him?"

"I told him that you left last month." Alidas shrugged. "You did."

"Did he say what they wanted me for?"

"To me?" Alidas asked. "They know I'm loyal to the gaunsho. They wouldn't tell me anything, but it wasn't hard to figure out."

"Nanvess wants me dead."

"I know." Alidas glanced to him. "You look pale."

"I was up too late last night." Kahlil watched Alidas' face for some notion of what he would want done tomorrow. Nanvess' involvement in the assassination complicated things.

Alidas observed the fire and after a moment said, "You should sit down."

Kahlil took a chair. As usual, Alidas remained on his feet, leaning against his desk. Kahlil supposed that Alidas only kept chairs for the sake of other people.

"I have a train ticket to Ris'ela. It's southeast in the Tushoya lands." Alidas glanced down at one of the books on his desk. "I know you don't know anyone there, but that might be an advantage. No one there will know you either. You can make a clean start of it."

"You want me to just leave?" Kahlil couldn't credit it. "But what about tomorrow? What—"

"An assassination attempt against Jath'ibaye is dangerous to the Bousim House," Alidas told him, "but division within the house is worse. Guansho Bousim is old and he knows he has lost much of his power to Nanvess' father. For the sake of uniting the entire Bousim House, the gaunsho will appoint Nanvess as his heir."

"But they don't know what they're doing. Jath'ibaye—"

"Kyle," Alidas stepped closer to him, "it isn't your concern anymore. You need to leave."

But Jath'ibaye was his concern, far more than Alidas could know. He looked up to say so just as Alidas reached out and brushed a strand of Kahlil's black hair back from his face, shocking him to silence. It was so unlike Alidas to touch him.

"You should have your own life," Alidas said. "For the last two years you've lived in secrecy, in isolation. You've had no friends, no family. No one."

"I had you, and I didn't need—" Kahlil cut himself off as he realized how pathetic he sounded. "You saved my life; I owed you the work."

Alidas watched the fire. His dark eyes caught its light and glowed like amber.

"I saved you because I knew I could use you," he finally said. "I saw the remains of the man you killed with your bare hands.

And I knew that if I could control you, I could bring the men I wanted down. I wasn't moved by kindness or even pity. I wanted your skills."

"And now that you've had them you want me to leave?"

"I want to give you your life back," Alidas said.

"In Ris'ela?" Scorn crept into Kahlil's voice. "What would a person like me do there?"

"Whatever you liked."

"I don't think I even know how to live like that. I've never—"

"I have orders to kill you," Alidas said flatly. He didn't meet Kahlil's eyes, but only glanced down at the pile of books on his desk.

"From Nanvess?" Kahlil asked, hopeful. Nanvess hadn't been named guansho yet. He still had to answer to his uncle's authority.

"From Gaunsho Bousim. The house must remain united." Alidas pulled the grate of the wood stove open. He threw in another scrap of wood, a piece of broken table leg. "That's why I bought the ticket for you. I was going to leave it here and hope that you had the sense to go."

"I see." Kahlil's stomach clenched and for a moment he thought he might be sick again. "So this is my fair warning, then?"

Alidas nodded. "If I see you again, I'll have no choice."

"I understand." Kahlil forced briskness into his tone. "You should probably have your key back."

"Yes, I suppose I should."

Kahlil unclasped the chain around his neck and slid the key off. For a moment he held it in his hand, feeling the warmth it radiated, before he handed it over. Alidas' concerns were matters of house loyalties and political stability. He was an excellent leader to his men and an honorable servant to his gaunsho. He would never involve himself in something he'd been ordered to disregard.

"What will happen tomorrow at the Bell Dance?"

"That depends on the men involved." Alidas dropped the key into his coat pocket. "If they kill Jath'ibaye, then we still have his followers to contend with. If they fail, then it could be easier or worse. It would depend on how forgiving Jath'ibaye is feeling. In any case, it's out of my hands."

Kahlil supposed that this was true. The Rifter was not a matter to force on Alidas. Nothing in Alidas' life or training would have prepared him to take responsibility for Parfir's destroyer incarnation.

"Will you go?" Alidas' question interrupted Kahlil's thoughts. He offered the train ticket.

"I'd be a fool not to." Kahlil managed a cocky smile as he took the ticket.

Alidas said, "I'm sorry that it turned out like this, but perhaps it's for the best. At least your life is your own now."

"Maybe so." Kahlil slid the ticket into his coat pocket. His life was his again. It was like inheriting a burning house.

"I should go and pack." Kahlil's voice sounded flat, mechanical. Alidas only gave a nod. They had already said goodbye weeks ago. Doing it all again just seemed pointless.

Kahlil let himself out and closed the black door behind him. It was getting late and dark clouds crawled across the pale blue sky. He flicked his fingers apart and stepped into the silent Gray Space.

CHAPTER TWENTY-FOUR

After weeks of morning frost and evening sleet, the warmth of the following day was surprising. Balmy winds twisted through the soft blue sky and sunlight poured down.

Street vendors came out in droves. Every corner Kahlil pedaled past burst with the scent of frying dumplings, the brilliance of paper flowers, and the sudden explosion of wings as pigeons took flight before his bicycle. The spring warmth drew crowds of people outdoors. Often, Kahlil had to swerve past some man—a shop clerk, tailor or banker—who had just stopped to stand with his face lifted to the sky, feeling the sun on his skin.

Clusters of wealthy women, clothed in richly embroidered dresses, emerged from the shelter of their homes as well. They traveled together like schools of fish, younger wives following the lead of the older ones, all of them keeping their children safely between them. Brightly-dyed honey candies flashed in the children's hands. Silver wedding rings and fine chains glittered across the women's fingers.

"Know what's new!" a young boy selling newspapers shouted. "Lisam runners menace the streets once again!"

Kahlil glowered at the boy from his bicycle. The boy grinned back at him.

"Jath'ibaye to attend Bell Dance," the boy called out. "Gaunsho Tushoya fears for the safety of his daughters! How safe are yours?"

Kahlil waited for the man ahead of him to lead his wives across the street and then he sped onward. Behind him, Kahlil heard the paperboy shout, "Lisam runners throw streets into chaos! What will be done? Read the paper and find out!"

Fensal had probably already bought the paper and clipped the article to add to his collection. He would have been disappointed to see how politely Kahlil waited at the street crossings, and how cautiously he rode around the potholes and mud puddles in the roads. But today Kahlil couldn't afford to damage the packages bundled up in the basket of his bicycle. He'd spent the entire day collecting each of those little prizes.

He had pedaled back and forth across the Blackbird Bridge twice. He'd searched through dozens of winding, narrow streets. He'd ferreted his way through storefronts and into the back rooms of tailors, cobblers, and countless laundry services all over the city. It had taken him hours of hunting, haranguing and no end of lies, but at last he had pieced together one of the uniforms that the servants and musicians would be wearing for this year's Bell Dance.

The shirt, pants, and jacket were all cut from soft white linen. A fine pattern of silver embroidery edged the jacket's cuffs and collar. There were also white gloves, socks, slipper-like shoes and a set of dull, gray cufflinks. Kahlil guarded the complete uniform as if it were blown from glass. One tear, one spatter of mud, one missing piece could ruin it.

He waited on a street corner while the trolley rolled by. Noblewomen peered out of windows. Some of the younger ones already wore their hair piled up in the elaborate braids and curls they would wear at the Bell Dance. Most of the noblewomen would be in attendance, as the Bell Dance offered a rare opportunity for unwed girls to assess the men who would one day become their husbands.

Kahlil guessed that for many of them the possibilities of what could happen, both beautiful and humiliating, were far more thrilling than the actual event would be. It was now, in the grip of anticipation that, flushed with excitement, their imaginations ran wild.

Anticipation meant something entirely different for Kahlil. It was something to suppress, an infection of anxiety that he couldn't allow to take hold. Two years of hunting men through the west dock slums had taught him not to think too far ahead of the moment.

He couldn't trust his past and he couldn't know the future. The present was really the only place for him.

The trolley trundled past, and Kahlil pulled his attention back to the street ahead. His eyes swept over the men there, and then he froze in place.

Nanvess Bousim stood directly across the street from him, chatting with another man. Both of them wore the deep green colors of the Bousim house and their black hair shone in the sun. Nanvess looked up and his gaze fell upon Kahlil without interest or recognition, the same way he might have noted a street sign. Then his attention returned to his companion. Both men stepped off the curb to stroll across the street toward him.

Kahlil swung off his bicycle and walked it across the street. It was hard to find the natural balance between staring fixedly at Nanvess and pointedly avoiding all eye contact. Kahlil focused his gaze on a cage of birds in the shop window directly ahead of him.

Nanvess came close enough for Kahlil to overhear his conversation.

"Would you want your sister to marry him?" Nanvess asked his companion. "I certainly wouldn't."

"But if Jath'ibaye were to marry into a gaun house, then he would have an incentive to protect the rights of the gaun'im," Nanvess' companion replied.

"I think that's assuming quite a bit about the man."

Kahlil was so close that he could smell Nanvess' thick anise cologne. He could have reached out and caught him by the throat. It would be so easy. With just a flick of his fingers and a sweep of his arm, he could drag a sheering edge of Gray Space through Nanvess' neck. Kahlil could almost feel the heat of dark blood gushing across his palm. He'd killed dozens of men the same way, with just a touch.

But killing Nanvess now would only scare his conspirators, forcing them to alter their plans for the assassination. Then he might never find Fikiri again. And Fikiri still had the yasi'halaun. More important than anything else was ensuring that he got the black blade back before Fikiri could use it. Kahlil's only sure opportunity to get it back would be tonight at the Bell Dance.

Kahlil swung back onto his bicycle and sped down the street. The sun was beginning to dip toward the western horizon. Lisam runners would be turning back to the palace for their meals soon. A fellow runner had already zipped past him. Kahlil and the other man exchanged quick waves. Kahlil allowed the other runner to outdistance him.

He coasted along Seven Palaces Road. Parks and stone statues blurred past. He wove between carriages and delivery wagons. In a few hours the streets would begin to fill with gawkers and newsmen. But for now, there were only subdued clusters of men and women basking in the fading sun and street vendors packing up their wares.

He turned off Seven Palaces Road and raced up the narrow street to the Gaunsho'im Council building. The building itself was only two stories high and comparatively small. There were no vast wings of suites, no private libraries or magnificent treasuries. Even the dark pines and twisting evergreen trees surrounding it were dwarfed. Their topmost branches barely cleared the walls surrounding the grounds.

Despite its diminutive size, it was not a building that could be overlooked, not even among so many palaces. Embossed gold gleamed across the domed roof. Detailed bas-relief wound down the marble walls, giving them the appearance of delicate lace. Bands of gold ringed the carved pillars in front of the massive ivory-inlaid doors. Polished golden tiles flashed from the steps leading up to the entry.

Kahlil rode around the wall, taking in the surrounding land and noting the positions of the armed guards. Their rifles weren't as powerful as the ones Jath'ibaye's sentries had carried, but they still looked lethal. The guards watched him from the stone walls as he pedaled past. He waved. None of them responded with anything but a scowl.

Another three guards were posted at the servants' gate at the back of the grounds. With their rifles and their gleaming gold-and-indigo uniforms they too presented an intimidating appearance. But Kahlil could see that they were more or less hapless in the midst of the intense activity all around them.

Streams of hired men hauled cases of fish, casks of wine, entire racks of roast dog, and bushels of southern fruits from waiting wagons. They grunted and heaved their loads through the gates and past the guards. Delivery boys from city shops darted between them with trays of brilliant candies, vases of cut flowers, and towering silver cakes. Staff from the council building, in blue and gold liveries, scurried from one point to another, shouting directions and attempting to check the deliveries and invoices.

"Lisam runner," Kahlil told a guard. "Deliveries for the steward." He pointed to a tissue-wrapped bundle in the basket of his bicycle. It contained his socks.

The guard just waved him in. Behind him, Kahlil heard tahldi and the creak of wooden wheels. He glanced back to see that several red, rented carriages had arrived. Musicians climbed out, most of them cradling or lugging instruments. Some were fully dressed in their white uniforms, but most still wore their street clothes. Immediatly, an argument started up as to who was responsible for paying the carriage drivers.

Kahlil caught the guard's momentary expression of tired exasperation. By the end of the night, the guards would certainly have seen enough men pass between them to forget his face.

Kahlil simply drifted through the back courtyard. The unyielding weight of his bicycle protected him from too many bumps and shoves. The air in the courtyard rolled over him as he walked. One moment he grimaced in the grasp of fish odors, then he pushed past a clot of delivery men and found himself plunged into scents of mulled wine and spring blossoms. Men shouted questions and orders all around him. Kahlil didn't think anyone really knew what was directed to whom.

He reached the racks behind the kitchen. He locked his bicycle next to three other delivery bicycles and then wandered into the council building with his clothes in his arms.

The interior of the building didn't pale in comparison to the exterior, not even in the back rooms. The trim over the doors was carved with twining ivy. Scattered between the leaves were gilded coins, each bearing the crest of one of the seven gaun'im houses. The Lisam bull glared down from a corner. Across from it, Kahlil recognized the crossed arrows of the Bousim house. Just faintly, above the ivy, Kahlil could see that there had once been another, larger symbol. He squinted up at the vague shadows and then realized that he was looking at the remnants of a Payshmura sun.

The council building had been constructed before the Payshmura had fallen. Now that Kahlil thought of it, he could see old remnants of their dominance all around him. As he wandered the halls, stepping past flustered staff and deliverymen, he noted the small, incised alcoves where dishes of prayer stones would have been placed. Now they were either filled by bowls of cut flowers or gilded tiles depicting the crests of the seven houses.

"What are you doing?" an older man suddenly demanded of him.

"Delivery," Kahlil answered.

The man rolled his eyes. Obviously most of the men pushing their way through the back rooms and halls had deliveries.

"Who is it for?" the old man demanded.

"A musician," Kahlil said. "I'm supposed to deliver it to his dressing room."

"His dressing room?" The old man scowled. "That's rich. They're all going to be using one room, the light-fingered little thieves." The man suddenly turned to the group of stocky deliverymen slouching next to the wine racks. His wrinkled face seemed to fold in on itself as he glared at them. "If you're done, don't just stand around taking up space! Get out!"

The men quickly retreated back down the hall.

The old man snapped his attention back to Kahlil. "The fourth door on the right."

"Thank you," Kahlil replied.

The old man had already turned away and was stalking toward a cluster of young men milling around two kitchen girls. Kahlil shook his head. He couldn't imagine being a house steward.

He found the room that had been designated for the musicians. Any decoration that could be removed obviously had been. The inlaid walls were bare, and even the flowers had been removed from the alcoves. None of the musicians had arrived yet. Kahlil stripped off his clothes and changed. He doubted that he would have an opportunity to recover his old clothes. Still, he folded them into a neat pile out of habit. He'd miss his coat and boots.

After that, he simply drifted through the council building, randomly carrying out instructions. He decanted a bottle of wine, removed and then returned a vase of lilies to an alcove. He avoided the steward, easily fading into the crowds of other men in white uniforms.

He accustomed himself to the layout of the building. Beyond the small back rooms stood a huge ballroom. There the screens that would hide the musicians had already been spread. Intricately carved chairs and tiny decorative tables had been placed along the left wall. A profusion of fresh flowers were scattered across the tables. The blossoms looked fragile compared to the huge shields and carved wreaths mounted on the walls. The polished floor shone brilliantly as it reflected the blazing gold and silver chandeliers overhead. A staircase on the the right wall led to the second floor but it had been chained off.

Kahlil doubted that Ourath or any of his conspirators would attempt anything here, under so much light and in such an open space.

Kahlil picked up a bouquet of spring buds and stalked purposefully past the other servants out into the gardens. The guards on the walls hardly took note of him.

A path of marble stones wound slowly up a slight hill to the west garden, the one Nanvess had mentioned. At the top Kahlil found a flickering stone lamp surrounded by dark pines. Yellow and red ivy vines cascaded over trellises. Between the trees, low shrubs hid the bare ground with dark winter-hardy greenery. Here and there tiny patches of red and violet spring flowers pushed through the dark soil.

Kahlil turned slowly around, taking in the deep shadows, the walls of ivy, and the thin, flickering lamplight. He couldn't have chosen a better place for an assassination himself. He was sure it would take place here. But he couldn't just wait around in plain sight. He turned back down the path.

He couldn't know where Fikiri would come from or when he would arrive, but Kahlil did know that one way or another Fikiri would have to get close to Jath'ibaye. So all he had to do was slip back into the council building and wait for Jath'ibaye; then Fikiri would come to him.

When he walked in through the back door, several women looked up at him. They were portioning out cutlets of dog meat into white dishes.

"Where have you been?" an older woman demanded.

"The steward sent me out to get some more flowers." Kahlil held up the bouquet of spring buds he had carried out with him.

"Forget that," the older woman told him. "The ladies are arriving and they aren't half-hungry. Take a tray and get out there."

Kahlil picked up a silver tray and strode out to the ballroom. The musicians had situated themselves behind their blinds and played quietly. Kahlil followed the other men in white uniforms, serving the exquisitely dressed gaun'im women at the tables.

As more gaun'im arrived, Kahlil's duties changed. He took out trays of drinks for the men and candies for the youngest girls. All of the noblemen came dressed in their house colors and carried at least one long string of fine silver chain. Though the chains were symbols of the wealth that they could offer to their future brides, Kahlil still found them sinister.

Esh'illan Anyyd arrived with several of his brothers and a particularly sturdy set of silver wedding chains. Draped over his silk clad arm, the chains just brushed his knee. No one else seemed to take any note of them. Ourath arrived with his three wives and his young son, all clad in the rich tawny colors of the Lisam house. Ourath's hair looked particularly red and his low voice seemed to brim with happiness as he spoke. He took a glass of wine from Kahlil without even sparing him a glance.

The music grew louder, competing with the rising hum of conversation. The heat from the lamps and chandeliers swelled with the warmth of so many bodies.

Several members of the Bousim family were announced, but Nanvess was not among them. Then the massive doors swung open again and a boy in blue and gold announced, "Welcome his honor, Jath'ibaye'in'Fai'daum."

Kahlil and every other person in the entire ballroom turned toward the door. Even the musicians seemed to pause a moment to steal glances at Jath'ibaye.

Unlike any of the gaun'im, Jath'ibaye had come alone. His wild blond hair blazed gold under the profusion of light. The blood red of his clothes declared his Fai'daum loyalty. He hadn't brought a single silver chain.

Kahlil thought he heard an audible sigh of relief from some of the girls near him.

As Jath'ibaye scanned the crowded ballroom, Kahlil bowed his head. He could remember too well how Jath'ibaye had picked him out even in the darkness.

Ourath broke away from his conversation with a Tushoya woman and her unwed daughters. He strode easily through the crowd, lesser gaun'im men quickly making way for him. He greeted Jath'ibaye with a smile and led him into the ballroom. Kahlil stepped back behind a vivid yellow bouquet as Ourath looked around for a server. At last he stopped a young man in a white uniform and took two drinks. Ourath handed one to Jath'ibaye and offered a toast of some kind.

They drank together and Ourath introduced several other gaun'im to Jath'ibaye. After a few moments, the room seemed to return to normal. More guests arrived. The ancient Bousim gaunsho shuffled through the doors, followed by his dozen wives. Steadily, couples began to fill the middle of the dance floor. Ourath escorted his first wife out for a dance, but afterwards he returned to Jath'ibaye's side.

Kahlil still hadn't spotted Nanvess when he noticed Ourath drawing Jath'ibaye away from the crowd toward the back of the building and the gardens. Kahlil set his tray full of iced fruit down and cut through the kitchen to the west garden.

Once outside, Kahlil raced up the hill, keeping to the side of the path where the deep evergreen leaves hid him. He waited for Ourath and Jath'ibaye. A few moments later they appeared, walking slowly along the path. Far behind them, Kahlil caught sight of Esh'illan.

As Ourath led Jath'ibaye closer, Kahlil moved farther ahead. Though now they were close enough that he could hear their conversation. Suddenly, Jath'ibaye drew to a halt.

"You shouldn't depend upon my affection," Jath'ibaye told Ourath. "It's not my strong point."

"No?" Ourath asked. "What is?"

Jath'ibaye didn't answer right away. Instead, he studied the knots of dark trees and undergrowth ahead of him. Kahlil stood still as a statue, holding his breath. Eventually Jath'ibaye turned back to Ourath and asked, "Are you sure this is what you want?"

Ourath flushed.

"Absolutely." He smiled at Jath'ibaye and this time the force behind it showed a little. "I know you'll want to see these herbs."

Ourath started forward, but Jath'ibaye caught him by the shoulder.

"I'm not a fool, Ourath. I know you're not planning on show-ing me any herbs up there." Jath'ibaye's tone was oddly gentle in comparison to his harsh expression.

"Really?" Ourath slid his hand around Jath'ibaye's, twining their fingers together. He lowered his head to brush his lips over Jath'ibaye's wrist.

"So I want to be alone with you." Ourath gazed up at Jath'ibaye. "You can't be disappointed, can you?"

Again, Jath'ibaye glanced to the shadows beneath the pine trees before looking back to Ourath.

"We could stop it here, now." Jath'ibaye spoke so softly that Kahlil hardly caught the words. "I wouldn't hold it against you. People make mistakes."

"What do you mean?"

"You're still so young," Jath'ibaye said. "You can't understand how badly this could end for you."

"How can you still think that I would regret being with you?"

Jath'ibaye just sighed heavily.

"Do you regret being with me?" Ourath suddenly demanded, his voice edged with what sounded like genuine anger.

"I regret using you," Jath'ibaye said at last.

Ourath glared at Jath'ibaye and smiled at the same time. "Well, come. Regret it one more time."

Jath'ibaye allowed Ourath to lead him along the path.

Kahlil rushed ahead of them, cutting through the trellises of ivy, while they took the curving path upward. When Kahlil reached the edge of the clearing at the top of the hill, he came to a halt. There was something different about the place now. Despite the warmth of the evening, a chill emanated from the center of the clearing. The tiny flame in the stone lamp flickered and spat. Kahlil hung back in the shadows.

Ourath and Jath'ibaye rounded the last curve in the path.

"Here." Ourath caught Jath'ibaye's hands and suddenly pulled him forward. It was clear to Kahlil that Jath'ibaye allowed this.

Coming up from behind, Esh'illan made his move. He swung the silver chains and whipped them around Jath'ibaye's throat.

Jath'ibaye shoved Ourath aside, pushing him clear. Then he caught hold of the chains at his throat and jerked Esh'illan off his feet. Esh'illan gave a startled yelp as Jath'ibaye swung him up like he was spinning a child and then hurled him to the ground.

Jath'ibaye's calm speed stunned Kahlil.

Then the scream of rending Gray Space split the air. In an arc of flame and searing cold, Fikiri appeared. Kahlil almost rushed him, but then he realized that Fikiri's hands were empty. The yasi'halaun was nowhere on him.

At the sight of Fikiri, Jath'ibaye's countenance changed utterly. The cold, almost bored expression that he had worn even while Esh'illan attempted to strangle him transformed into raw fury. Jath'ibaye kicked Esh'illan's prone body aside and launched himself toward Fikiri.

Kahlil caught a flicker of a smile from Fikiri as he backed away, drawing Jath'ibaye farther into the clearing.

Then Kahlil saw Nanvess, crouching in the deep shadows of the evergreens and holding the yasi'halaun. His green clothes melted into the surrounding leaves; his black hair dark as the shadows. He lunged for Jath'ibaye.

It was such a simple plan, Kahlil realized. Nanvess would feed the yasi'halaun on Jath'ibaye's blood before Jath'ibaye even registered his presence.

Kahlil threw himself into the Gray Space, passing straight through Jath'ibaye's body. He burst out directly over Nanvess. Instantly, he snapped his fingers apart and punched the razor edge of a Gray Space through Nanvess' throat. Nanvess' hot blood gushed over his hand and splashed up his arm. Nanvess crumpled to the ground.

Initially, Kahlil didn't even feel the yasi'halaun's smooth blade driven deep into his abdomen. Then sharp pain exploded through him. The blade pulsed inside him, tearing through muscle and drinking in his blood. He gripped the hilt with his bloody, slick hands and wrenched the yasi'halaun free.

Fikiri stood, staring at him in abject shock.

Jath'ibaye too stood motionless, blood dribbling from his neck where Esh'illan's chains had cut through his skin. His blue eyes were wide, his expression haunted.

Kahlil felt sickeningly cold. His entire body shook. He fought to remain on his feet.

Only Esh'illan seemed able to move. Kahlil saw him draw his pistol. Fikiri caught the motion as well and a look of fear passed over his face.

"Don't!" Fikiri shouted.

Jath'ibaye spun back just as Esh'illan fired directly into his chest. Jath'ibaye rocked slightly with the impact.

Then the entire earth seemed to shudder beneath them. The stone lamp split. From above them came a sudden, tiny white burst of light, like a streak of lightning, and then the entire sky darkened. Pale clouds writhed and blackened as if they were burning.

Jath'ibaye strode forward and gripped Esh'illan by the throat. With a vicious snap he twisted Esh'illan's head back. Esh'illan convulsed and then fell lifelessly to the ground.

Kahlil could see guards running up the path. The gunshot must have brought them. Jath'ibaye didn't seem to notice or care about them. His eyes blazed blue, inhumanly bright. He glanced over his shoulder to the empty space where Fikiri had stood, then he turned his attention to Kahlil.

Thunder crashed above them.

Jath'ibaye simply stood there, watching him as a dirty black rain began to slap down. Three guards came running with lanterns. Other people—curious guests and servants—trailed behind them.

Kahlil brought his hand up.

"Wait," Jath'ibaye whispered.

Kahlil tore open the Gray Space and stumbled into its lifeless depth.

CHAPTER TWENTY-FIVE

The dark cables and girders of the Blackbird Bridge blurred and wavered in front of Kahlil. Out of reflex, he reached for the railing to steady himself. His hand passed through. He staggered down to his knees.

In the colorless, silent realm of Gray Space, there was neither night nor day, and yet it seemed to be growing darker all around Kahlil. And colder.

He curled his hand over the wound in his belly. In the Gray Space, his blood shone glossy black. It spilled through his fingers and seeped across the entire front of his white jacket and pants. He could feel it soaking into his socks. If he had been outside the Gray Space, it would have been warm. It would have steamed against the night air.

Kahlil pushed himself back up to his feet. He couldn't stop, not here. Not yet. He concentrated. The black mass of the bridge whipped back behind him. Narrow streets blurred past. He moved through walls and gates.

Ranks of rashan'im on tahldi patrolled all streets. Word of the attack at the Bell Dance had doubtless traveled fast. Both Esh'illan Anyyd and Nanvess Bousim murdered. Alidas would be furious. There would be no refuge for Kahlil anywhere in the Bousim district of the city.

No. He needed to go somewhere else. Dim, tangled shapes washed past him. Kahlil shuddered. He could hardly recognize the haze of darkness and light all around him. Boats, perhaps. A wave of numb cold pulsed through him.

He should get out of the city. Go somewhere better. Somewhere warm and light. Somewhere like the apple orchards that grew around the convent of Umbhra'ibaye. They'd been beautiful. It would be so nice to go there and see them again. The trees would be blooming.

But he wasn't going anywhere, he realized.

He wasn't even going to be able to stay conscious much longer. Panicked energy burst through him. He had to leave the Gray Space before he was too weak to escape it at all.

He lifted his hand. He'd get out.

And what then?

Again his gaze fell to the black wound in his belly. It gleamed and dripped with a constant flow of black blood. Despite the muting numbness of the Gray Space, Kahlil felt the ache of it tearing through him. Outside the Gray Space it would be agony.

This wasn't a wound that a man recovered from.

Only the Gray Space had allowed him to bear it this long. Now the best of his strength had gone. He could hardly see, hardly move. He was dying.

He squeezed his fingers around the hilt of the yasi'halaun. It had grown heavier, fed by his blood. It almost felt warm against his icy skin. At least he had it again. He had accomplished that much. Neither Fikiri nor his lady would use it to open the Great Gate.

He closed his eyes. There was no point in keeping them open. Only a dull dark haze came to him now.

If he left the Gray Space, it wouldn't save his life. It would only mean that his last moments would be ones filled with the brilliant red of his own blood and shattering pain. He would leave a corpse for someone to stumble across. And the yasi'halaun would be lying there in his hand.

It was better to die here, hiding the yasi'halaun forever.

A tremor of fear still moved through Kahlil. He didn't want to die, but the choice wasn't his. The pain and cold melted into a consuming darkness that engulfed him, surrounding him in soothing emptiness.

CHAPTER TWENTY-SIX

A wrenching scream tore through Kahlil's insentience—the sound of Gray Space being torn open. Then blinding, burning light exploded over him. He wanted to flinch back from it, but he couldn't move. A weak rasping cry escaped him as the heat of living hands seared his frigid skin.

He tried to pull himself away. His body remained limp. He couldn't even make his eyes focus. All he saw were faint blurs of color—dirty red, pale yellow—then they were burned away by the sharp, blinding white light that poured down over him.

Reflexively, Kahlil dragged in a desperate breath of the hot air. It tasted of sweat, blood, salt, and animals. It was too much. Kahlil didn't want to take another breath, but his lungs demanded it. Agony flooded over him. It burst up from his abdomen and tore like lightning into his chest. Kahlil's throat tightened around a reflex scream. It came out as a dry hiss.

"He's still breathing." The man's voice was rough and low. Jath'ibaye's voice.

"It's too late." The woman sounded older. She spoke with a careful softness. "I'm sorry, Jahn, but he—"

"No! He won't die. I don't care what sorcery you have to use, Ji. Save him!"

Why would Jath'ibaye want to save him? What did he want? Kahlil tried to clench his hand, to feel for the yasi'halaun. His fingers barely twitched.

"I can't bear his wound. It was made by the yasi'halaun. It would burn me to ash before I could heal him," the woman quietly insisted. "I'm sorry."

"Then let me bear it."

"When the blood transfers, the yasi'halaun will feed—"

"I don't care," Jath'ibaye cut her off. "Just bring him back to me."

"Jahn, he's not—"

"Do it!" Jath'ibaye flatly commanded.

A shadow moved over Kahlil, blotting out the blazing light. A hand touched his cheek lightly. It was still too hot, and yet Kahlil didn't care. Even the terrible pain in his belly seemed somehow distant. Perhaps it was simply unimportant.

The shadow deepened, growing nearly black at the edges of his vision. Steadily, it curled in over him. A dull numbness crept in its wake. It came as a relief after so much burning and hurt.

Low words were muttered over him. Kahlil could not understand them anymore. They were just sounds, whispers and rumbles. It was so much easier to let them drift away.

"No," Jath'ibaye growled, "I won't let you go."

Kahlil wished he could laugh.

He was already slipping away, even within the grasp of Jath'ibaye's hands. It was like a magic trick, like stepping into yet another space, one that carried him out of his own body. It was a perfect escape.

If only he had figured this trick out sooner. It would have saved him so much pain. If only he hadn't been so terrified of this dead darkness. But it was nothing. Not pain, not fear. Nothing.

This, absence and silence, seemed to stretch out forever and through all time. It devoured his future and past, engulfed his present, and absolved all with an endless, soothing darkness.

《 《 《

Darkness.

And a slight rocking. But still dark—a soothing, cool dark. Then a creak, almost like the noise of straining wood. Faintly, almost imperceptibly, a scent of river water drifted over him.

He hadn't thought that death would be so much like being on a boat.

Kahlil cracked one eye open and saw polished wood and portholes. Instantly, he realized that he was aboard one of those narrow river clippers. He could tell just from looking at the close angles of the walls and the swift blur of water outside his round windows.

He pulled his other eye open and surveyed the tiny cabin. Apart from the bed that he lay in, it contained a small built-in desk and a chair, which Jath'ibaye occupied. His long, broad body looked absurd slumped in the frail chair. His chin rested on his chest, his wild blond hair fell over his face, and his breath rose and fell with the slow, steady rhythm of deep sleep.

Kahlil tried to sit up as quietly as he could. His muscles ached and resisted. His right hand bumped against something heavy on the bed next to him.

Sheathed, and resting on top of the blankets, lay the yasi'halaun. It had grown to nearly the length of his arm and its once black body now shone a lusterous gray. It had tasted the Rifter's blood.

"You're awake." Jath'ibaye's voice sounded rough.

Kahlil eyed him cautiously. The last time he'd been alone with Jath'ibaye the man had threatened to kill him.

"It's all right. You're safe." Jath'ibaye winced slightly as he straightened in the chair, then offered him a tired smile. His blue eyes were rimmed with red, his mouth almost colorless.

Kahlil arched an eyebrow. "You said you were going to kill me the next time you saw me."

"I never could have ..." Jath'ibaye's smile faded and his eyes sank to the floor. "The first time I saw you, you were in Fikiri's territory, and then you came to me with that letter and the poison from Ourath. I thought it had to be some trick of Fikiri's. I didn't know how else you could have come back."

Kahlil himself hadn't been sure how he'd come back from Nayeshi; he'd needed to and he'd been willing to die trying. He supposed that had been enough.

Kahlil pulled himself up a little in the bed. The profusion of pillows on either side of him made the motion awkward. He expected to feel a sharp complaint from the wound in his abdomen, but there was nothing.

"I came back on my own power, but I didn't do a good job of it. I was a mess for a while and the only work I could find was for the Bousim family." It felt strange and relieving to be able to say this, to tell someone and know that he would understand. "They wanted to avoid the conflict that an attack against you would cause, so they sent me to take a job as a Lisam runner to try and stop your assassination." Kahlil stared at Jath'ibaye, then scowled.

"Did you just tell me that you knew Ourath sent you poison and you still accepted his invitation to the Bell Dance?"

Strangely, Jath'ibaye smiled at this. He nodded without looking up from the floor.

"Did you want to be killed?" Kahlil demanded. He suddenly had an insight into how Fensal must have felt about him eating the goatweed.

"I have, from time to time, but no." Jath'ibaye stole a brief glance up at him. "Not now. I was just tired and it would have offered me an excuse to make a clean break from Ourath. It wasn't as if he could have killed me."

"You let him poison you because you thought it would be easier than breaking up with him? Do you have any idea how stupid that sounds?" Kahlil spoke before he could consider either the intimate nature of the subject or the presumption of his words. Jath'ibaye didn't appear to take any offense at either.

"Saying it out loud just now, I did notice that," Jath'ibaye admitted.

"Maybe you should talk things out a little more often." Kahlil felt oddly at ease with Jath'ibaye at this moment, almost as comfortable as he had felt when they'd shared a house. He could remember that now—their time together in Nayeshi.

He'd been so happy then. He remembered the strong smell of coffee and the absurd simplicity of their domestic troubles—a leaky faucet, no toilet paper, the odd smell the oven gave off when it was preheating. Kahlil recalled the sweet tang of an apple and sitting together in the dark, waiting for the electricity to come back on.

John, or Jath'ibaye as he now called himself now, hardly seemed to have changed at all. And yet, Kahlil knew that decades had passed since the Fai'daum leader he was looking at and the graduate student he remembered had been the same person.

"Do you remember our phone number?" Kahlil asked. "It started out 647…didn't it? I can't remember."

"Phone?" Jath'ibaye finally met Kahlil's eyes. "We never had a phone …"

"Sure we did. In Nayeshi we had a landline because you didn't like cell phones." Kahlil scanned Jath'ibaye's face for a sign of recollection.

He didn't know why he had expected Jath'ibaye to remember everything from those days. His own memory was hazy—to say the least—and it had only been two years for him. Jath'ibaye had fought wars and destroyed an entire kingdom since then. The seven arbitrary digits of a phone number probably had no meaning at all to him now.

He felt stupid for even bringing it up. There were so many other more important matters that they should have been discussing: the holy key, the yasi'halaun. But Kahlil had just woken up and he wanted to ponder something unimportant, something small and amusing, as was his habit.

Jath'ibaye's expression was a study in blankness, as if he were holding himself back from any reaction at all.

"You followed me from Nayeshi," Jath'ibaye said slowly.

Kahlil couldn't understand why the thought should have such a strong effect upon Jath'ibaye. Maybe it was just the distant memory of Nayeshi. How long had it been since anyone or anything had reminded Jath'ibaye of the life—the whole world he had lost?

"It was hard, but I managed it. Forget about the phone number. It's not important," Kahlil said. Then he didn't know what else to say.

Jath'ibaye pulled himself to his feet. His skin still looked unnaturally pale. Dark bruises ringed his throat and Kahlil could see the uneven, bulky mass of bandages beneath his clothes.

"So, you're still calling yourself Kyle?" Jath'ibaye asked, though he said the name strangely, as if the Nayeshi pronunciation caught in his throat.

"It's easy to remember." Kahlil shrugged, an awkward movement, as his recently healed muscles were still slow to respond.

Jath'ibaye gazed at him so intently that Kahlil felt an embarrassing flush begin to rise across his cheeks. Then Jath'ibaye looked away to the view out the tiny portal. Outside, dark blue-green waters swirled and twisted past.

Kahlil took it all in with a kind of stunned wonder. Even a day ago, he would never have imagined that he could have ended up here. Or with John, again.

"I should go above deck and tell Ji that you're awake," Jath'ibaye said suddenly. "She wasn't sure if you would pull through." He started for the door, but then turned back to Kahlil. "Do you think you can eat anything yet?"

"I can try."

"I'll find something easy to start with."

"Thank you," Kahlil responded automatically, but as he studied Jath'ibaye's stark figure and pale face, he did feel genuine gratitude and wonder.

He had come back to Basawar to kill the Rifter and instead the Rifter had saved him. Now the idea of killing John seemed laughably pointless.

He had never wanted to do it in the first place. He had liked John—more than liked him, if he was truly honest. He thought that he might even like Jath'ibaye if he got to know the man.

"Wait," Kahlil called just before Jath'ibaye stepped out the door.

"Yes?" Jath'ibaye asked.

"Thank you for saving my life." The words couldn't convey all of his relief or gratitude, but they were all he could offer at the moment.

"I wish I had." Jath'ibaye gave him another smile. He looked so exhausted and worn that the expression almost seemed sad. "You should thank Ji. She's the one who did the work."

"Oh, I certainly will." He wanted to say something else, something that would make up for reminding Jath'ibaye of the life he had lost. No comforting words came to him, so he settled for a question instead. He said, "Where are we going now?"

"Home."

"Home?" Kahlil echoed the word as though he had just learned it. He had no idea where home was anymore.

"Vundomu," Jath'ibaye clarified. He lingered, halfway out

the door.

"I see." Kahlil knew he could have asked another question and kept Jath'ibaye with him, but there was no point in it. It wouldn't accomplish anything. If Jath'ibaye was pained by the memories that Kahlil brought back, then he would want to be alone. He had always guarded his privacy that way.

Kahlil let him go.

CHAPTER TWENTY-SEVEN

John pushed the hair back from his face and drew in a slow, deep breath.

After two years in Basawar, he had grown used to the thin air and the hungry quality of the soil and stones. It felt comfortable to him. The wet earth moved beneath him, curling around his heels and squeezing between his toes. Pools of yesterday's rain had turned the sparring ground into a wallow. As he moved, the mud slithered and squelched beneath him, but he didn't feel as if he was slipping. Instead, it seemed that the soil accommodated him, shifting and folding to support him.

The priest opposite him charged. John swung to the side. Mud squelched beneath both their feet. John caught the other man's arm in a loose grip, and with the slightest nudge, threw him off balance. The priest flailed out, attempting to catch John and pull him down with him. John stepped back and the priest tumbled down into the mud.

From the sidelines, John heard Samsango's laugh. The old priest sat with several other ancient priests, watching the battle practice and quietly making wagers. Their faded gray robes seemed to melt into the pale stone steps that surrounded the arena. The thin morning sunlight gleamed across his bald head. John guessed, from the collection of polished stones in Samsango's lap, that he had won a fair number of wagers.

John gave him a jaunty wave before turning back to offer his opponent a hand up.

More than a hundred low-ranking ushvun, like John himself, were gathered on the steps of the arena. Normally, only the thirty men who shared the same dormitory practiced on the training grounds at the same time. Today, men from all of the dormitories encircled John in a sea of gray robes and black hair.

A year ago he would have found it intimidating, but now he knew all of them by sight, if not personally. And he knew that most of them cared little about the outcome of these individual tests. They each experienced their share of defeats and conquests. In their dormitory groups they practiced fighting together every day. They were more interested in the opportunity the gathering offered to chat and gamble.

Their subdued conversations produced a low soft hum. It was a rare, comfortable sound—like distant radio music or birdsong—in the isolating silence of the monastery. It offered John the sense of being at once surrounded by life and, at the same time, not having to be drawn into it.

Some of the priests had stripped down to just the thin pants they wore beneath their robes. Others were still dressed in their robes and coats, keeping warm while they waited in the shadows of the armory building. A few, like John and his opponent, were spattered and streaked with mud.

John steadied his opponent and watched him slog back to the steps. The other priest simply stripped all his clothes off and tossed them onto a step.

John scraped a dried spatter of mud off his shoulder and waited for the prior to decide who he would fight next.

Normally, with the grounds in such poor condition, the tests would have been called off. But today was special.

Today, they were being watched.

The highest-ranking priests in Rathal'pesha—the ushman'im and ushiri'im—were gathered on the walkways overhead to observe the tests. John easily picked out Ushman Nuritam; his long white braids were swept up in the wind and writhed like ribbons. Beside him stood Ushman Dayyid.

Dayyid's black coat formed a dark column behind Nuritam's frail figure. His thick black braids cascaded down his broad shoulders, too heavy for the breezes to lift. The natural northern softness of his features was undermined by his sharp nose and arched lips.

During the first weeks after John arrived in Rathal'pesha, Dayyid had gone out of his way to come down to the training ground and demonstrate the battle forms, using John as his practice opponent. John hadn't known anything about the handholds or stances, and Dayyid hadn't tried to explain them to him, either. Time and time again Dayyid had hurled him to the ground, twisted his arms back, kicked him in the ribs, and held him down with one foot placed over his throat.

And John knew that Dayyid had done it simply to show John and the other priests that he could.

After a week, John's mouth had been split and too swollen for him to eat without tasting his own blood. Samsango had given him a balm to deaden the pain of his beaten ribs and bruised back. When John asked what he had done to offend Dayyid, Samsango had told John not to take the thrashings personally. Ushman Dayyid always beat new priests as a forewarning against insolence. He'd assured John that if he didn't fight, Dayyid would eventually grow bored.

Samsango had been right. After two days of meeting limp resistance, Dayyid hadn't returned to the ushvun training grounds to abuse him further.

He saw remarkably little of any of the ushman'im or the ushiri'im. They kept to the upper floors of Rathal'pesha, practicing their divine rituals and using the Gray Space to speak to Usho in the Black Tower and the Issusha'im Oracles in Umbra'ibaye thousands of miles away.

Beneath them, the common ushvun'im saw to the day-to-day upkeep of the monastery. As an ushvun, John cleaned goat sheds, tended weasel coops, scrubbed statues, scrubbed floors, scrubbed walls, hauled urns of lamp oil, carried bags of raw taye, prayed until he could barely speak, and stood through icy nights of guard duty. He had worked in the kitchens, the gardens, the laundry, and the bell towers.

At first, the constant labor had left him too tired to think. He had staggered through his first month in an exhausted daze. Once, Samsango had found him passed out with his face nestled into a fetid weasel nest.

He had lapsed into strange fantasies of floor buffers and dishwashers. Memories of spray-on oven cleaner and laundromats had flooded him with deep homesickness.

Steadily, he had adjusted. He had grown used to handling the animals and learned shortcuts through the twisting, maze-like halls of the monastery. He had developed the ability to know which duties were important and which had been assigned to him simply because he was standing there. Most importantly, he had mastered the critical skill of appearing occupied with a duty when the prior was nearby.

Now, the mere sound of the prior's footsteps could wake John from a lazy doze and send him striding down a hall with an intensely focused expression. The prior seemed to judge most of the ushvun by the speed of their movements and the intensity of their expression. An open frown or scowl would result in a reprimand for a surly attitude, while grins, smiles or any wide-eyed expression of wonder were indicators of too much free time.

John had found that wearing a slight frown, narrowing his eyes, and striding with a fast, deliberate pace down a hall was exactly what the prior liked to see him doing.

Right now, the prior stood at the edge of the practice grounds, scowling. He was a small, plump man and his three honor braids always gleamed with far too much sweet oil. They seemed to slither down his back and often left a slight stain at the nape of his robes. Two silver flail-shaped pins on the shoulders of his robe indicated both his rank and primary pastime.

The prior swung his left hand into the air, calling a new opponent down onto the muddy training ground.

The new priest was a younger man John didn't know well. He scowled as his feet sank into the cold mud. John, in contrast, slid one leg forward slightly, feeling the soil roll across his ankle. He could already sense where the best footing would be found.

His opponent flipped his single black braid back from where it had hung over his shoulder. John's own wild blond hair was pulled back and tied with a strip of leather. Wisps of hair escaped and fell in his face. He tucked them back behind his ears.

He wasn't allowed to wear even a single braid yet. That would come after his initiation this summer. Until then, he was still just an initiate, a man of little importance and the butt of most practical jokes.

Even old, bald priests like Samsango technically wore honor braids. Samsango's were woven from goat hair and sewn to the shoulders of his robes. He had two, which placed him just below the prior in honor. But even without any, John's position was better than that of a priest whose hair had been cut.

For a year after his braids were shorn, a dishonored priest was treated with animosity and utter contempt. He received the most demeaning and dangerous work, often cleaning the latrines or replacing the cracked tiles of the steepest roofs. He ate the coarsest food, wore the roughest clothes, and slept beneath the thinnest blankets. He could be punished for any misfortune and had no right to speak in his own defense.

John knew now that when they had first met, Ravishan's short bristle of black hair had been a symbol of disgrace. Ravishan had been punished for some transgression against the Payshmura creed. John had no idea which one. The ushvun rarely spoke of the ushman'im or the ushiri'im. When they did, it was with awe and reverence.

There had only been a few nights, while John had been serving guard duties high on the walls, when Ravishan had managed to visit him. Their time together had been brief and precious. John hadn't wanted to ruin those pleasant few hours by asking questions that could embarrass Ravishan. Instead, they had talked about Nayeshi and shared gossip about their fellow priests.

John wondered if Ravishan was watching from one of the raised walkways. He thought he could see other dark forms on the farthest walkways, but he couldn't make out any faces.

The prior lifted both his tanned plump arms into the air and John's attention snapped back to the practice grounds and his opponent. The other priest crouched back into a defensive stance. The prior dropped his arms, and John charged forward.

John's opponent shifted to catch John's shoulder, but he moved too slowly. John spun, mud spattering up under his feet. He swung his leg up and hooked the soft back of his opponent's knee. The priest buckled back. John slammed his open hand into the man's chest and his opponent splashed down into the mud.

Cold spatters smacked across John's bare stomach and chest. It was fast and simple. John found he liked that about the Payshmura battle forms. The fallen priest swore, but accepted John's outstretched hand. John helped him back up to his feet. Behind them, John heard another short crow of triumph from Samsango.

"Good form, Jahn," Samsango called out. "Keep on your feet."

John wondered just what Samsango had bet on him. It couldn't have been much. None of the ushvun owned anything but their braids, razors, and a few polished prayer stones. Though, they often wagered their duties. It was a sort of gambling where everyone started out laden with obligations and then hoped to come out with none. No one ever struck it rich. Even the greatest winning streak never amounted to more than a day off.

John strode back to the left side of the practice ground.

The prior lifted his arms again. This time, it was John's turn to take the defensive stance.

His mud-caked opponent charged, throwing himself ahead with brutal force. John crouched and, as the priest sprang at him, John lunged into him. The smaller priest was jarred with the force of the impact. John caught him by the hips, then heaved him upward with all his strength. The priest's legs flew out from beneath him as he flipped across John's back and went down into the mud again. John pivoted to face the priest.

Still sprawled in the mud, he shook his head at John. His expression didn't seem so much angry as concerned. John helped him back up to his feet.

"You're too good for your own well-being, Jahn," the priest whispered to him. Then, he glanced up to the walkway above them. John followed his gaze to Ushman Nuritam's thin figure.

John frowned. Ushman Dayyid was no longer there.

The prior lifted his left arm, again pronouncing the test in John's favor. John's opponent wiped the mud from his body. Then he climbed up the stairs and back out of the filthy grounds. John watched him go.

Then, John saw the tall black column of Dayyid's figure advancing down the steps. The soft murmurs and quiet conversations that had hummed across the steps went silent. As John looked out over the steps, he took in row upon row of black braids as all the assembled ushvun bowed their heads.

Dayyid spared none of the priests a glance. He stopped beside the prior. The prior bent in half before Dayyid. Dayyid spoke softly over the other man's bowed head. John couldn't hear any of what he said. He only caught murmurs and pauses. The prior bowed slightly lower, his glistening braids spilling down over his face and sweeping against the stone floor. Dayyid turned with mechanical precision and strode back up the stairs.

The prior straightened. His round face was dark red from being bent over for so long. He scowled, seeing John looking at him. John quickly lowered his eyes.

"Practice is done for the day," the prior shouted. "Those of you who have been on the grounds, bathe and then attend your duties. Those who have not been on the grounds, go directly to your duties."

John trudged through the mud and started to pull himself up onto the stairs. His dormitory was in charge of the pine garden this month. With the weather turning warm, the soil would need to be turned and prepared for seeding. It was work that John enjoyed.

The prior held up his hand for John to remain where he was. John waited as the other priests filed out of the arena. Samsango milled on the steps for several minutes after all the rest had gone. The prior gave him a sharp, warning glare. With an apologetic shrug to John, Samsango left too.

Once they were alone, the prior said, "Ushman Dayyid has done you the honor of accepting you for his ushiri'im to practice their battle forms against."

A slightly sick chill slithered through John's stomach. He didn't want Ushman Dayyid practicing anything on him, particularly not battle forms.

"You will wash and then go directly to the golden chamber on the second floor. If Ushman Dayyid finishes with you today, you are to come back to me directly. I won't allow for any distractions or laziness."

John nodded.

The prior scowled. "Well, go! You don't want to keep Ushman Dayyid waiting."

"Of course not." John couldn't manage to force any enthusiastic inflection into his voice. His words came out flat and dull.

He climbed up from the grounds and took the long way around the armory. The baths were a series natural springs, which the priests had sheltered with tall, latticed stone walls. There were carved stone seats where towels and clothes could be left but no roof. Moss and lichen covered the rough stone floor.

John wasn't surprised to find Samsango waiting for him. The old man looked worried.

"You haven't been called up to serve the ushiri, have you?" Samsango asked.

John just nodded and stripped off his mud-caked pants.

"But you haven't even been initiated!" Samsango protested. "How can Ushman Dayyid even ask you to walk through the golden doors, much less fight with his ushiri'im?"

"I don't know." John had the feeling that Ushman Dayyid could do just about anything he liked, but he didn't want to say that out loud.

Other priests were in the bath as well, some of them barely bobbing above the water.

A few of them glanced up at John, but then looked away. Their expressions were too sober and their voices too low. Normally, one of them would have teased John, or smacked his bare shoulders with a towel. Instead, he received only a few pitying smiles.

"The prior should tell him he's made a mistake," Samsango announced from where he sat cross-legged at the edge of the bath.

"If the prior was going to say anything to Ushman Dayyid, he would have already done it," John replied.

John scrubbed at the dried mud on his legs. Then he dunked beneath the water, washing his face and hair. When he came back up, Samsango continued talking.

"It's not just wrong to do this to you, but it does the ushiri'im no good to practice against a novice. Ushman Dayyid should reconsider."

John squeezed the water out of his hair and tied it back away from his face.

"You think that's likely?" John asked.

Samsango didn't answer. His frown deepened.

"I wouldn't have encouraged you so much if I had known." Samsango's gaze dropped to his lap. "I would never have thought that you would be chosen. Who would have?"

"It's not your fault," John told him.

"But I feel bad for winning bets on you now," Samsango admitted.

"It's all right," John assured him. "Just tell me what it is exactly that I'm going to be doing."

"You will fight the ushiri'im." The wrinkles lining Samsango's mouth pulled into deep fissures as he scowled. "They use criminals while they're perfecting their open-handed blade work. But after that, they need opponents who are trained in the battle forms, so that they can hone their skills. It's an honor to serve them, but you ..."

"I'm going to get my ass kicked?" John supplied for Samsango and the old man offered him a grim smile.

"I'm afraid so."

John closed his eyes. Before Dayyid had made it his mission to subdue his insolent spirit, John hadn't known how it felt to truly be beaten. He had thought that he would have to be dying to hurt so much. Black bruises had decorated his flesh like tattoos. His ribs had ached each time he took a breath, his muscles trembled with each motion, and his split lips had cracked and bled when he spoke.

Each day had added injuries and pain. To be hurt that much that often changed a man, he had realized. It made pain the center of his existence, the one constant that he could not escape. Even when Dayyid finished for the day, the pain remained. It became all he felt and all each new day promised. It devoured any pleasure he might have found in his surroundings, leaving him with only dread.

But he had endured it, and it had ended.

His muscles throbbed with the physical memories of those days. He didn't want to go through that again. But his only other choice was to flee.

If he got up right at this moment and abandoned Rathal'pesha, he could avoid it. No one was going to chase a braid-less novice down the steps. But it would mean abandoning his hope of finding a way home. It would mean facing Laurie and Bill and telling them that this world would be where they lived from now on. Sickness would dominate the rest of Bill's life; servitude and repression, the rest of Laurie's.

He had brought them here. It had been his foolish mistake. He owed it to them to try and get them home.

"Well," John said, "it can't be much worse than last time."

"It will be much worse," Samsango protested. "This will be blade fighting. The Unseen Edge, the God's Razor, the Silence Knife. You don't even know what these things are! How can you hope to defend yourself against them?"

"With my battle strategy of running, hiding, and crying?" John suggested.

"No," Samsango said suddenly. "I will have to go and tell Ushman Dayyid that this is wrong."

This statement drew a startled gasp from the ushvun sitting close enough to overhear.

John said, "Ushman Dayyid has never struck me as a man who is open to criticism."

"No," Samsango admitted. "But someone should ..."

John could tell that Samsango was frightened. He was old, frail, and of lowly rank. Ushman Dayyid could snap him apart like pieces of kindling. Or worse yet, Ushman Dayyid could pronounce Samsango's criticism a transgression of his holy authority. The two rough braids sewn to Samsango's robe would be stripped away. Then it would be the duty of every ushvun to punish the old man.

Samsango was too old to do much work. Other priests often took his share. They respected the lifetime he had given to the monastery and went out of their way to look after him. He depended on the kindness and generosity of his fellow priests. A year of castigation, abuse, and deprivation would kill him.

"It's all right," John said. "I can do this."

"But—"

"I'm a tough young man." John pulled himself up out of the water. "I'm sure the first sight of me bawling and hiding behind furniture will disgust the ushiri'im so much that they'll just send me away."

Samsango laughed, but then shook his head. "Don't offend them. They carry the god's own bones."

"I won't." John took the clothes that Samsango offered him.

John forced himself to dress quickly. His body seemed to resist him. His legs felt heavy and slow. His hands wanted to become clumsy. He almost dropped his clean pants twice. Finally, with the slow, premeditated gait of a reanimated corpse, John started up the stairs toward the golden chamber.

CHAPTER TWENTY-EIGHT

John had been to the second floor before, but only to scrub the halls. He had never been through one of the ivory inlaid doors that ran along the left wall of the hall. He recognized a few written Basawar words now, but not many more than those that allowed him to distinguish a cask of wine from a cask of fermenting taye blossoms. Nothing so complex as this writing.

The ivory inlaid words that arched and curled over the black door panels fascinated him, in part because he couldn't read them. John traced the curving sweep of polished letters with his finger. Beneath them, gleamed the emblem of a book. John wondered if the symbols spelled out the word for library.

He knew better than to try to open the door. It would be locked. All of the doors on the upper three floors were always kept locked. There was just one door that he would be allowed through, the door to the golden chamber.

As John continued down the wide gray stone hall, gentle spring breezes drifted in through the windows that ran along the opposite wall. The deep quiet of these upper floors always reminded him of the ruins of an aging, abandoned palace in some forgotten empire.

With its locked towers and inner sanctums that slowly spiraled down and out into nothing but latticed, roofless halls, and moss-covered stone paths, the monastery seemed as if it were ever so slowly eroding back into the earth.

Only the scent of incense hinted at the presence of the men who inhabited this level.

John followed the hall as it opened into a raised walkway that arched out to another building. At its end stood a heavy black iron door that looked like it had been made to withstand gun blasts and battering rams.

Two silver Payshmura eyes stared down at John from above the doorway. Beneath them, beaten into the door itself, a tight gold script arched over a gold sun and a silver moon. The letters were unusually clipped and square. John didn't think he had seen that style of Basawar script before. Then, as he reached out to the heavy knob, he realized that the gold letters weren't Basawar at all. They were English. A little disfigured, but clearly English.

Through this door to a thousand more.

John read it and frowned. A thousand doors. He remembered the words from a Basawar prayer. Samsango had taught it to him while they had been hiking down the Thousand Steps to Amura'taye to pick up supplies. At the time John had hardly been paying attention. His thoughts had been more focused on his plans to visit Laurie and Bill in the Bousim house. Now he frowned, attempting to recall the words.

Parfir sleeps behind a golden door
His blessing opens a thousand more
His blood and bone, my sea and stone—

John's thoughts were broken by a sudden shriek.

At first he thought it was human scream, but it didn't sound right for that. It sounded more metallic and inanimate, like sheet metal rending apart. Then, a faint but familiar smell drifted over him.

It was the same smell his old computer used to produce when it began to overheat: burning ozone. But that couldn't be possible, not here. It had to be something else.

A moment later, the scent was lost in the breeze rolling across the walkways. John supposed he would find out what the smell was soon enough. Or he might find himself in such pain that he wouldn't care. Either way, he had wasted too much time already.

He pulled the heavy latch and swung the door open. A stronger wave of the ozone smell wafted over him. As John stepped from the outdoor glow back into a darker interior, he found himself momentarily blinded. The door fell shut behind him while he waited for his eyes to adjust. When they did, John realized that he stood in a dark hallway only a few feet from two black-coated ushiri'im.

Payshmura emblems of silver suns glinted on their high, straight collars. Both men were older than John. Their faces showed that strange, worn texture that John had noticed in many ushiri'im. They weren't tanned, wrinkled, or chaffed like the ushvun. These men's skins were pale and too fine, almost as if their features had been eroded to an unnatural smoothness. Eight black honor braids cascaded down their backs. They were each only one braid short of being first rank ushman'im.

John immediately bowed before them. "Ushman Dayyid sent for me."

"So he said," one of the ushiri'im replied. "It certainly took you long enough to get here."

"I'm sorry." John bowed again. "I was instructed to bathe."

"You'll be dirty again soon enough." The other ushiri smiled, but not kindly. "Come along. You've already kept the ushman waiting longer than he likes."

The first ushiri gestured for John to precede him down the hall.

The oil lamps gave a yellow glow to the inlaid writing on the doors they passed. John lowered his eyes. More and more of the words were in English. He had never realized just how difficult it was not to read words written in his native language. Just glancing at a few letters sent the words ringing through his mind instantly. *Holy ...Forbidden ...Sacred ...Eternal ...Divine.*

He read the words with the same reflexive quickness that his lungs drew in breath. Only keeping his eyes squarely lowered to the floor allowed him to maintain the appearance of ignorant awe that any other ushvun would have possessed. Maybe later, under better circumstances, he would dare to read the doors, but for now, he couldn't afford to act out of his place.

The ushiri ahead of John stopped in front of a door. John pulled to a halt behind him. Despite himself, John stole a glance to the letters on the door.

Golden Chamber, Burn and Shine.

The ushiri lifted his finger to his lips and John heard the hiss of a Gray Space tearing open. A chill seeped through the air.

The ushiri's mouth moved, his lips pressing words against his raised fingers. John couldn't hear anything, not even a faint whisper of breath. It was like watching television with the mute on. The ushiri's voice slipped into the Gray Space to be heard by someone else.

Then Dayyid's low voice split the air above them. "Bring him to me, and we will see."

Again, John thought he smelled searing ozone, but this time he was more disturbed to note a tiny flash of flame shudder through the air. It died in an instant, and John might have thought he hadn't seen it at all, if that burning scent hadn't lingered after it.

The door opened and the ushiri led John through.

The golden chamber was neither gold nor a chamber. It was a long, white training hall. The polished stone floor was covered with heavy, stuffed mats. Intense light poured in from windows cut in the upper third of the high walls. Lower on the walls there were iron racks holding spears, swords, axes, and other weapons John didn't even know the names for. Even a locked gun rack displaying a vast collection of rifles and pistols.

Directly ahead of John on a raised dais rose a huge iron statue of Parfir. John didn't think he had ever seen the god's face carved into such a proud expression. The only hint of his usual smile was a cruel upturn at the corners of his mouth. Two rows of ten ushiri'im, dressed only in their gray pants, stood with their backs to John. They had the builds of young men in their late teens and twenties. None of them wore more than seven braids. Most only possessed six.

Only Dayyid, standing at Parfir's feet, faced him.

The room felt weirdly cold and the smell of ozone caught in John's throat.

"And, at last, here he is." Dayyid gestured to John.

At once the gathered ushiri'im turned to face John. They moved with a tight militaristic precision that unnerved him. He almost stepped back from them, but he forced himself to hold his ground. He didn't want their first impression of him to be that of a cowering giant.

He straightened slightly and returned the uniformly cold stare the group gave him. For an instant, his eyes caught on Ravishan's face. His hair had grown out some, but not enough yet to braid. It hung around his face in silky strands. He'd grown since John had last seen him. The boyish softness had gone from his cheeks, and now even a hint of dark stubble shadowed his jaw.

Ravishan's dark eyes widened at the sight of him and John looked quickly past. As far as anyone here could know, this was the first time they had met. It was safer for him to meet Fikiri's surprised eyes.

Fikiri too had grown, but not so markedly. There was certainly a lot more meat on him now, but his proportions remained those of a boy, his feet and hands a size too large for his body. His dark blond hair was pulled back into five braids, and his right arm was swathed in white bandages. John gave Fikiri a brief smile and the young boy returned it, only for an instant, before schooling his expression back into the hard stare of an ushiri.

As Ushman Dayyid stepped down from the dais, the ushiri parted before him, then immediately closed ranks again. Dayyid stopped just out of John's reach. He turned slightly to address the ushiri behind him while keeping his eyes on John.

"This is Ushvun Jahn. He will be serving as our welter-body for today."

John couldn't help but steal a glance at Ravishan. He had no idea what a welter-body was, but the way that Ravishan's face went slightly pale assured John that it couldn't be good. Samsango had said that the ushiri would be training against him with blades. John's eyes drifted across the racks of spears, swords, and knives. They didn't just look painful. They looked deadly.

"We will begin with a demonstration." Dayyid held his right hand up. It was empty. A momentary relief filled John, but he didn't trust it. Samsango had been too upset for John to even hope that he would get out of the golden chamber without suffering.

"The Unseen Edge." Dayyid snapped his fingers apart and John heard the hiss of Gray Space tearing. "This is only the edge of the space. It is not open and does not lead to any destination, but it may still have a use."

Dayyid stepped closer. John frowned at him, unsure of what he should be doing. Then Dayyid swung his hand out toward John's shoulder.

Frigid, tearing pain slashed through John's flesh. He jerked back. A weird nausea pulsed through his whole body. He clamped his hand over his wounded shoulder to staunch the hot blood spilling down his sleeve. But the injury didn't alarm John as much as the sense of utter revulsion—a physical sickness—that came from touching the edge of the Gray Space.

Dayyid's dark eyes twinkled. He smiled at John as if he were just on the verge of laughter. To the ushiri'im, he said, "A long, thin cut is produced. It often hurts more than it harms."

Dayyid held up his right hand again. This time he flicked his first two fingers up and folded the rest down against his palm. Again, John heard the hiss and felt the chill of Gray Space shredding open.

Dayyid said, "The Silence Knife."

Animal panic shot through John. He suddenly wanted to run for the door. But he forced himself to stand his ground as Dayyid turned on him.

Dayyid jabbed his right hand at John's chest. Automatically, John blocked with his left arm and jabbed his right fist at Dayyid's throat. Sick agony tore through his left forearm, as if Dayyid had driven a stiletto of ice through the muscle. John jerked back out of Dayyid's reach. Blood poured from a deep puncture just above his elbow.

This time Dayyid wasn't smiling. His left hand was lightly pressed to his throat, where John's knuckles had grazed his flesh.

If he hadn't jerked away from the pain, John realized, he could have brought Dayyid down. The thought sent a warm rush through John's body.

If only he had held his ground.

Then what? Would he really have killed Dayyid? He couldn't do something like that. He wouldn't. It was just the rage of so much pain boiling up in him. John forced himself to lower his gaze.

To get through this day he would have to let his anger go.

John kept his eyes down. Dark rivulets of blood slipped down his trembling fingers and spattered across the white mat.

Dayyid began again, "The God's Razor—"

"Don't!"

John, and every other man in the room, instantly looked to Fikiri. Dayyid scowled at him.

"He's a good man." Fikiri's voice trembled and he dropped his gaze submissively to his own feet. "You shouldn't be hurting him."

To John's surprise, Dayyid's voice was soft, almost kind. "Fikiri, I am not punishing Ushvun Jahn. This is an honor for him. And I am not hurting him much. Certainly not more than he can endure." Dayyid glanced back at John. "Just a scratch and a pinch. Demonstrations always look far worse than they are. Isn't that right, Ushvun?"

John forced himself to smile. The last thing he wanted was to cause Fikiri trouble. He just had to get through this, he reminded himself. Just take what Dayyid dished out. It would be over soon enough.

He said, "I'm fine."

Dayyid continued, "It requires determination and great will to perfect your blade work, but it will be necessary if any one of you is to become Kahlil. I know this, and Ushvun Jahn knows this. For the sake of your education, Ushvun Jahn has offered himself to assist you all to learn. Now, it does him and you no good to refrain from practicing the forms of the sacred blades because you might spill a few drops of his blood. That is why he is here and why you are here. Do you understand, Fikiri?"

Fikiri nodded glumly.

"Very good." Dayyid smiled. It was a professional expression, one that conveyed pleasure in mastery more than any warmth. "Now, let us return to our lesson. The God's Razor is an extension of the Unseen Edge. It is formed when two or more ushiri'im or ushman'im create a field of unseen edges. I will need an assistant for this." Dayyid glanced over the gathered ushiri'im. For an instant, Dayyid paused on Ravishan.

If Ravishan felt any hesitation at the thought of slicing through John's flesh, it didn't show. He kept his expression as cold as the rest of the ushiri'im. He met Dayyid's eyes defiantly.

Dayyid moved on to Fikiri.

Fikiri tried to control his expression but his mouth was obviously pressed closed too hard and his pale brows crunched together in misery.

"Fikiri," Dayyid said, "this will be an excellent opportunity for you to better your skills."

"But I don't know how—"

"It's simple." Dayyid beckoned him forward. Then he said to John, "Since Fikiri isn't experienced, you should probably hold as still as you can while we practice."

For a few minutes John watched with a growing feeling of dread and sickness while Dayyid tutored Fikiri in opening an Unseen Edge. The rest of the ushiri'im watched Dayyid's instructions with rapt interest.

Except for Ravishan. His eyes seemed to be focused on John's bloody right hand. When he looked up to John's face, he seemed startled to find John looking back at him and a faint red blush spread across his face. John returned his attention to the lesson in progress.

"Very good." Dayyid nodded as Fikiri snapped his fingers apart and a Gray Space wrenched open with a shriek. John felt the air around Fikiri's hands writhing as if it were in agony. The sensation sent a shudder through him.

"Now, push the edge outward." Dayyid extended his hand and snapped another edge of Gray Space open next to Fikiri's. "Push and allow the God's Razor to spread."

Fikiri emulated Dayyid, but the action didn't seem easy for him. Sweat beaded his forehead and chest. Fikiri's arm trembled as he extended the edge of Gray Space. A noise like nails being dragged across sheet metal filled the room.

John found himself hoping that Fikiri would succeed, and at the same time, deeply worried about what would happen if he did.

Dayyid held his own broad, tanned hand out over Fikiri's and then lowered it, so that his palm just touched the back of Fikiri's hand. He spread his fingers over Fikiri's and a thin horizontal line of flames suddenly burst up midair. The thick smell of searing ozone washed over John.

Instinctively, John's arms came up, protecting his face and chest. Then the edge of the Gray Space hit him, ripping into the muscle just above his elbows. A choked gasp of pain escaped him. He wanted to scream, but he could hardly draw a breath. Nothing in his life had hurt like this. The edge ground through his skin and muscle like a saw blade.

It had to stop. Now.

John could see the thin, trembling edge of the God's Razor. It blurred into a pale line, turning pink as his blood spattered along its surface. It looked absurdly small, like a tiny fissure in the air. Like a thread that he could just grab and snap if he wanted to.

John wondered if he was in shock from the pain.

He watched, feeling almost like a distant observer, as his right arm dropped down and grabbed the God's Razor. He felt the jagged grinding edge of Gray Space bite into his palm, but the pain seemed muted and dull. His blood spattered up in a fine mist as he clenched his fist around the opening of Gray Space. He crushed it closed.

Fikiri staggered back. Dayyid gaped in abject disbelief.

John's entire body shook. He felt hot and strange. He swayed on his feet and barely caught himself from falling. Every single ushiri stared at him in shock.

Even Ravishan.

He shouldn't have done that. Whatever it was that he had done.

John turned his hand to look at his palm. It glistened like ground beef. Nausea welled up. John looked away from his ruined hand to the men in front of him. They all stood perfectly still, as if paralyzed. Then Ravishan bolted forward. He placed a hand against John's back.

"Sit down," Ravishan said. "You should sit down."

John sat on the ugly, blood-spattered mat.

He wondered why his hand and arms didn't seem to hurt so much now. Shock, he supposed. He tried to remember first aid procedures. Treat the wounds. Keep the victim warm and hydrated.

"It's just shock," John mumbled. His words sounded strange and garbled. He started to say that he thought he needed stitches.

Ravishan scowled at him and whispered, "Be quiet!" Then John realized that he had spoken to Ravishan in English and clenched his jaw shut. He had to be careful.

A moment later, Dayyid crouched down opposite Ravishan, scowling.

"You were a fool to grasp the God's Razor. Your hand should have been severed."

John scowled back at Dayyid, not trusting himself to speak yet.

"His injuries need to be treated," Ravishan said.

Dayyid narrowed his eyes at Ravishan.

"I know what needs to be done and what does not," Dayyid replied curtly.

"Then you know that he needs to be tended to." Ravishan stared straight into Dayyid's face.

John had the distinct feeling that the struggle between them could have been about anything. Effectively, treating his injuries had become secondary to the crisis of their opposing wills.

For the first time, it struck John how much Ravishan and Dayyid resembled one another, not just physically, but in their mannerisms. The inflections of their voices and their expressions mirrored each other. No wonder Dayyid became so infuriated when Ravishan turned a commanding glower on him. It was Dayyid's own glare.

The pain in John's arms grew duller and he wondered if Dayyid had been telling the truth when he had said that the demonstrations looked worse than they were.

He glanced down and noted that both sleeves of his robe were dripping out little droplets of red. In the cupped curve of his aching right hand, a dark pool of his blood steadily welled up. He could feel tiny streams escaping between his fingers and slipping down the back of his hand. The color was brilliant against the white mats and the dull gray of John's robe.

"Please," Ravishan barely whispered the words, lowering his head as he spoke, "please call for Hann'yu to treat his wounds."

Dayyid nodded and then stood. "Fikiri, go fetch Ushman Hann'yu."

John tried to stand and follow Fikiri, but Ravishan held him back. "Don't try to move too much. It isn't just your hand. You touched Gray Space. You could be hurt inside."

"I'm not. I'm fine." John was pleased to note that his voice sounded stronger and the Basawar words came to him easily. He gave Ravishan a reassuring smile. Then, without warning, his vision went white and he crumpled down to the mat.

Chapter Twenty-Nine

John didn't open his eyes. He lay still, hardly awake but listening. The softness of the mattress beneath him tempted him to return to sleep. An antiseptic smell hung in the air, reminiscent of a hospital emergency room but not quite right. Some botanical note, a hint of pine, instantly told John he was not in a hospital. Not anywhere close to home, but in some bed in Rathal'pesha.

He heard the rustle of robes nearby. There was another man in the room with him. John considered opening his eyes and stealing a glance to see who it was, but the movement seemed like an immense exertion. Maybe in a few minutes he'd wake up enough to do it.

A warm hand touched his forehead and then very gently pushed the hair back from his face. An instant later the hand was withdrawn.

John caught the distinct sound of a door opening and then the snap of boot heels striking the stone floor.

"Hann'yu."

John instantly recognized Dayyid's voice. He forced his eyes open just a crack.

He lay in a large room with tall, narrow windows. He counted five other beds, but only one seemed to be occupied and John didn't recognize the man in it. He appeared badly injured, his body forming the wrong curves and hollows beneath his blankets. A leg and part of his arm seemed to be missing, but John couldn't be sure. The indistinctness of the body, blankets, and pillows disturbed him.

He turned his attention back to the other men in the room. Dayyid stood to the right of John's bed with the painted red door behind him. Ravishan and another ushman stood a little closer to John on his left.

"So, will he live, Hann'yu?" Dayyid asked.

The priest standing beside Ravishan nodded. Like Dayyid, he looked to be in his mid-forties. His hair was walnut-brown and pulled back into eight braids. His gentle features reminded John of Samsango's. His skin was much darker than either Ravishan's or Dayyid's.

"He may wake up tomorrow or the next day." Hann'yu smiled at Dayyid. "He's surprisingly strong."

John wondered how they could not have noticed that he was, in fact, already awake and watching them.

"Can you rouse him sooner?" Dayyid asked.

"I don't see why I should. Is there some emergency?"

"Ushman Nuritam wishes to test his bones," Dayyid replied.

"Really?" Hann'yu's grin was positively gleeful. "So, you nearly killed an ushiri candidate?"

"We can hope. But I doubt he'll pass the test." Dayyid stepped closer to John's bedside and gazed down over him. "He looks more like the tainted remnant of some Eastern bloodline."

"Well, who knows." Hann'yu shrugged. "They say that even the sun started out as a blond boy from the east."

"Who says that?" Dayyid asked. His tone was harsh but his expression struck John as almost playful.

"Story books. Didn't you ever read any when you were a child?"

"Of course not," Dayyid replied. "I read only the holiest of the holy. My thoughts were never polluted by heresy or trash."

"Well, there's no point in being bitter now," Hann'yu responded. "I'm sure that your parents didn't mean to deprive you."

Ravishan, who had until this moment remained silent enough to be overlooked, coughed to cover a little laugh. When he raised his hand to his mouth, John noticed the edges of white bandages poking out from beneath Ravishan's sleeves. Dayyid glared at him and Ravishan bowed his head in quick supplication. When Dayyid turned back to Hann'yu, the lightness in his expression had completely gone.

"Can you wake this one, or not?"

Hann'yu shook his head. "Not so soon. Perhaps tomorrow. Right now I think he's lucky to have a pulse. We should let him sleep as long as he needs."

How could they still not have noticed that he was looking at them? John frowned, and then realized that he couldn't actually feel the muscles of his mouth move. He'd just thought of frowning, but his body had not responded.

Dayyid asked, "Will you be keeping Ravishan as well?"

"I might need him to bear another wound."

"What about Ashid?" Dayyid's tone softened. John followed Dayyid's gaze to the misshapen body in the other bed.

Hann'yu's gentle smile faded. Dayyid closed his eyes, head bowed.

"Does he know? Is he suffering?" Dayyid asked quietly.

Hann'yu shook his head. "No, he won't wake. Tomorrow he'll be in better hands than mine."

Dayyid remained still and silent, gazing at the white blankets. Then he turned back to John.

"See if you can get him on his feet soon."

"I will," Hann'yu replied, "but next time don't knock him off his feet so hard."

"I know." Dayyid started for the door. "But they have to learn somehow. The Fai'daum certainly aren't going to show them any greater compassion." He pulled the door open and disappeared into the dark hall outside. The door fell shut behind him.

John wanted to sit up and say something, but he couldn't seem to do it. He wasn't even sure that his eyes were really open now. When he concentrated intently, he could feel his lids pressed closed. He had to be dreaming then. It wasn't the first time that he had slipped into a dream that seemed so deeply real. Still, he found it strange that he would dream of this. Maybe he was catching snippets of some conversation around him and building these images. Even as he thought about it, the dream continued just as the real world would have.

Hann'yu drifted past the row of beds to a heavy, carved table laden with dozens of smoked glass jars. Farther back, John thought he saw a wide shelf stacked with even more jars as well as several leather-bound books. Hann'yu took a pen and started writing something.

"Do you think Jahn's bones will pass?" Ravishan glanced back when he spoke to Hann'yu, but remained at John's bedside.

"I don't think it matters." Hann'yu didn't look up from his work. "It's not as if he could take your place. I think Fikiri's the one you have to worry about."

"Fikiri's too scared to even walk through a Gray Space."

"He broke a prophecy." Hann'yu opened two of the jars and poured dark powders from them into a mortar. "Even the Issusha'im Oracles don't know how he did it. You shouldn't underestimate him."

Ravishan nodded and Hann'yu seemed to take this as the end of their conversation. He dropped some wilted clumps of leaves into his mortar.

"Maybe," Ravishan whispered, "it wasn't Fikiri who broke it." Ravishan's warm hand brushed John's forehead again. His fingers swept John's hair back from his face. Then Ravishan lifted his hand away.

The touch hadn't been more than a moment of contact, but somehow it soothed John. It eased him to know that Ravishan watched over him. John slid into a deeper rest. His vision dulled to shadow, and for a time, he simply drifted in a mist of sleep.

The next time an image opened up before him, John knew he was dreaming right away. He was moving up a white stone staircase, floating through heavy gold gilded doors and passing deep into forbidden chambers.

The air around him roiled with the smell of burning ozone. Plumes of pale blue-toned smoke hung like the suspended letters of a script he couldn't read. They twisted around him and broke apart as he swept through them. As he took in a breath, he felt an electrical sensation prickle his lungs.

It drew him, though he felt a little afraid of it. He passed through the final door and stepped into a vast, circular room. The air inside crackled. Thick clouds of bluish smoke hid the ceiling.

All along the curve of the walls were gold arches. They looked like doorways but only opened to flat expanses of solid wall. Though they appeared to be nothing more than decorative details, the doorways revolted him. He couldn't bring himself to approach them.

Overhead bolts of white light burst through the cloudy blue smoke. John caught the silhouette of something huge hanging just above him: a long spiral of human vertebrae strung together on red copper wires.

Dislocated arm bones jutted out, extending their fingers to other skeletal bodies. Ribs arched open, holding hipbones and femurs. There had to be hundreds of bodies woven together, flickering with tongues of electricity. Suddenly, the spinal column directly above John twisted and a yellow skull peered down. The jaws gaped over him.

"We smells its blood," the skull whispered. The finger bones began to tremble and clatter against each other. They twitched and tugged at the wires holding them as if struggling to pull free.

John jerked back, falling through the door behind him into a sudden darkness.

He bolted upright.

"It's all right." Ravishan gently caught his shoulders. He was still in bed at the infirmary. It was darker now, almost nightfall.

"Lie back down," Ravishan told him. "You're not well enough to be up yet."

"I'm fine," John answered, but he let himself be pushed back into the comfort of the pillows. He felt cold and slightly sickened. Ravishan smoothed the blanket over him.

John said, "Have you been sitting beside me all day?"

"No, I was standing most of the time, but then Hann'yu left and I took his chair. One of the ushvun'im came to see you."

"An old man?"

Ravishan nodded. "Bald, with two honor braids. Very few teeth. I don't think he told me his name."

"Samsango," John supplied.

"I told him that you wouldn't be up for another day." Ravishan leaned back in the chair. "You really shouldn't be awake, you know."

"I don't think I'm as badly hurt as you think I am. The cut in my palm was pretty deep but nothing life threatening." He felt a little embarrassed now, remembering how he had fainted from the injury.

"It's not the cuts that I'm talking about." Ravishan's dark eyes narrowed as he gazed at John. "Don't you know what you did?"

"I know I passed out. I think it must have been shock. But I'm fine now."

"You collapsed the God's Razor." Ravishan lowered his voice slightly. "You overpowered Dayyid and Fikiri."

"It could as easily have been something Fikiri did wrong." John didn't know why, but the speculation that he harbored some kind of strange power within him made him uncomfortable.

Ravishan scowled.

"It wasn't Fikiri," Ravishan said. "He can hardly open his own Gray Space, much less crush Dayyid's."

"So maybe it was someone else."

"Who?" Ravishan asked. "We all saw you do it."

"I don't know." John sighed, feeling tired again.

"It was you." Ravishan smiled at him. "Now Ushman Nuritam wants to test your bones to see if you are an ushiri candidate."

John didn't see any point in arguing about it. And he suspected that he didn't know enough about the Gray Space to win the argument anyway.

"So, what will this test entail?" John asked. He closed his eyes.

"Nothing much," Ravishan said. "A few prayers. You drink tea, open a Gray Space ...take off your clothes and dance—"

"What?" John opened one eye, and seeing Ravishan's grin, whispered, "It's not nice to tease the man from another planet."

"You have my deepest apologies." Ravishan stretched in the chair and yawned.

"Tired?" John asked.

"Tired and sore." He lifted his arms slightly so that the sleeves of his robes fell back, exposing his bandaged arms. He smiled proudly. "Hann'yu asked me to bear your wounds."

"What does that mean?"

"I give my blood in place of yours." Ravishan lowered his arms. "It lessens the extent of your injuries."

Like donating blood, John imagined. But there seemed to be far more bandages than a transfusion would have warranted.

John asked, "Does it hurt?"

"Not much." Ravishan shrugged. "You?"

"A little pinch in my palm, but that's about it." It was something of a lie, but John didn't feel like complaining.

"You should sleep," Ravishan told him.

"You as well," John replied.

"I'll be right behind you. Don't worry."

"Don't take too long," John said. "I'll be waiting."

Ravishan gave a soft murmur. His eyes were closed and his arms hung limply across his lap. Steadily, his breath slowed and deepened. John smiled, realizing that Ravishan had already gone ahead of him.

Chapter Thirty

The simple, bell-shaped cup in John's hand looked as though it could have been carved from alabaster or limestone, but it felt lighter than either. No mineral created that finely grained surface. Delicate ridges marked where a ligament had once attached, where the force of muscles had once flexed and strained. The cup had to be bone.

Heat from the tea inside lent a living warmth. John took a quick drink of the greenish tea, expecting the bite of daru'sira. Instead a weak, floral fragrance hung in his mouth. There was almost no taste, just a light scent after he swallowed.

A year ago he wouldn't have tasted anything at all, but he had somewhat adapted to the faint flavors in this world. He supposed that when he got back home everything would be too strong for a while. He tried to imagine what his favorite salsa would taste like now. For a moment, he drifted back to sharp searing tangs of lime and lemon suffusing earthy-sweet cherry tomatoes, fresh cilantro clinging to chopped red onion, and slivers of jalapeno pepper all bursting up like fireworks between the soothing, cool bites of cucumber.

He took another sip of the tea, hardly tasted it at all, then glanced up to see how the men around him were enjoying theirs.

Rows of ushiri'im and ushman'im knelt on either side of him, forming a neat corridor between him and the raised, gilded dais at the front of the room where Ushman Nuritam sat. It was easy to find Ravishan's shorter locks in the sameness of bowed heads and long black braids. Fikiri too stood out with his dark blond hair. Both knelt directly behind Dayyid at the edge of the dais.

Ushman Nuritam sipped slowly from his own white cup. His long white braids fell around him like cascading streams.

This room was small compared to the massive scale of the rest of Rathal'pesha, but still it seemed almost empty with few more than fifty men filling it. Sharp morning light diffused into a soft glow as it fell through the hundreds of sheet mica windowpanes. Carved vines climbed the stone pillars and twisted over each of the steps leading up to the dais. Behind Ushman Nuritam rose the huge figure of Parfir.

John studied the statue. As always, Parfir's body rose up in an amalgam of trees, leaves, flowers, and animal forms. His raised hands extended to the ceiling. His fingers became arched supports. His hair had been sculpted into waves with marble fish and water lilies braiding through them. The light barely reached the heights from which Parfir stared down over his assembled priests.

John squinted up into the dimness. The god seemed to offer him the faintest smile.

Ushman Nuritam lowered his cup and set it to his right. Not knowing what else to do, John emulated him. Ushman Nuritam nodded just a little. John hoped that it was a sign of his approval and not that the priest was drifting off to sleep. The old man almost always seemed to have a distant point of focus and often he seemed utterly unaware of his surroundings.

Ushman Nuritam's voice was not loud but it carried easily throughout the absolute stillness of the chamber. "Parfir bless us, for we are your loyal sons. And forgive us, for we are not so wise as you. Help us know your purpose for our brother Jahn. Help us so that we may serve you more perfectly. Help us so that we may defend your holiness."

"Bless us!" The words rose in a loud unison from all of the priests surrounding John. John only managed to come in on the end, calling out 'us.'

Dayyid rose, strode to John, and then crouched down in front of him. His expression conveyed nothing.

He opened his black coat to reveal a leather vest reminiscent of a gun holster. From this, Dayyid drew out two sheathed knives. The hilts of both were black. They looked just like the knives that Ravishan and the other ushiri'im carried. Dayyid placed both in front of John.

"Choose one," Dayyid whispered to him.

John regarded the identical knives. John frowned, realizing that he should have kept Ravishan up, asking him more about this test. He wanted to peer out at the ushiri'im and ushman'im to see if he could catch a clue from Ravishan. But there was no chance of that. Dayyid was watching him too closely.

There was no point in dragging this out. He simply reached for the knife on the right. Immediately he pulled his hand back. There was something wrong with that knife. The air around it shivered with a cold, electric sensation.

"Why didn't you take it?" Dayyid asked.

"I don't know," John replied. He didn't want to tell Dayyid more than he absolutely had to.

"Is there something wrong with it?" Dayyid asked.

"I don't know."

"There must be a reason you drew back." Dayyid leaned closer to John. "It is important that you tell us."

"This knife just feels ..." John paused, searching for a word that didn't betray his revulsion but still conveyed the sensation that radiated from the knife. "Powerful and strange."

Dayyid nodded slightly. "And the other blade?"

John reached out more tentatively this time. He picked the sheathed knife up and held it for a moment. It was carved from bone.

John said, "I don't feel anything from this one."

Dayyid stood and addressed Ushman Nuritam.

"Ushvun Jahn did not choose the blade bearing the curse."

"And yet he knew it?" Ushman Nuritam replied softly. "He felt it."

"Yes."

"Then, let us continue," Ushman Nuritam decided.

Dayyid carefully collected the knife and carried it to Ushman Nuritam, who slipped it into his robes. He wondered what exactly had been so disconcerting about that particular blade. He recalled a similar but much more intense revulsion when he had come across the remains of the Great Gate at Wolf Rock two years ago. Were there certain elements in the world of Basawar that were so integrally foreign to him, to his entire world, that they were inherently repulsive?

John examined the sheathed knife that he had chosen. What about it had differed from the other so greatly? His fingers slid across the clasp that kept it sheathed, but he stopped himself from drawing it. He had no idea how an action like that would be taken in the context of the test. He wasn't even sure how his last action had been interpreted. He seemed to have chosen the wrong knife, and yet Nuritam insisted that he go on.

John set the knife down beside his small white cup.

Dayyid strode back down from the dais. With a flick of his hand, he swept his long, glossy, black braids back over his shoulder. "Stand and approach," Dayyid told him.

John stood, though not as gracefully as he would have liked. His left foot had gone numb from sitting crossed-legged on the stone floor for so long. As he limped forward, John thought he caught a brief smile from Dayyid. It was gone before John could be sure it had been there, much less guess why. Perhaps it was simply an acknowledgment of the universal experience, which all priests in Rathal'pesha had, of having a foot go numb.

Dayyid said, "Close your eyes."

John's instincts rebelled at the thought of closing his eyes with Dayyid standing so near him. He lowered his lids but still peered through the shadow of his lashes. Again Dayyid gave him a brief, amused smile. John realized that Dayyid knew he was peeking.

"Now turn your back to me," Dayyid told him.

With great reluctance, John did as he was told.

From behind him came the nearly inaudible hiss of a Gray Space opening. John almost bolted back around as he felt the chill. In an instant it snapped closed again and another space opened. John held perfectly still, eyes pressed closed. He desperately didn't want a Gray Space to touch him again. But he could do nothing but stand here and wish.

John found himself willing away the Gray Space with the same intense concentration that he had called upon as a young child to destroy the monsters he imagined awaiting him beneath his bed. It was all he could do, and he hated it.

One space after another opened and closed beside and behind him. Each time, John felt the air writhe. Even after the spaces closed, a wounded feeling remained etched in his mind like the gashes a skate left in ice. The air seemed to be growing thinner and torn. It felt rough, almost ragged, as John drew a breath into his lungs.

Behind him, he could hear Dayyid drawing in deep breaths, as if he were winded. John wondered if the grainy, broken texture of the air bothered him as well.

John waited for another space to open but none did. All he heard was Dayyid taking in one deep breath after another. John opened his eyes a little wider. Rows of unfamiliar ushiri'im and ushman'im stared at John. John stole a quick glance to Ravishan but his head was bowed, hiding his expression. Fikiri's eyes were wide, his mouth slightly open in surprise. He turned back to Dayyid.

Instantly a Gray Space arched up over John like a mouth about to swallow him. A flare of repulsion, fear and anger rushed through John in a wave of heat.

"No!" John shouted. His breath burned as it rushed from his mouth. Dayyid shuddered. Flames seared along the edges of the Gray Space above John. Then, it snapped shut. John swayed on his feet, feeling dizzy.

Dayyid stood before John, breathing heavily, his pale skin beaded with sweat.

"Parfir has blessed you with strength, Brother Jahn," Ushman Nuritam said at last.

"Or there's witch's blood in your veins," Dayyid whispered.

John felt the blood draining from his face. He had been here long enough to know what the Payshmura did to witches. They flayed them alive or burned them on the Holy Road along with Fai'daum traitors.

"The test has not been as conclusive as we could have wished. We must discuss your candidacy," Nuritam declared from the dais. "Dayyid, Hann'yu, you will attend."

Dayyid nodded.

"All rise," Dayyid called out to the gathered ushiri'im and ushman'im. All fifty men in attendance stood.

"See to your duties," Dayyid ordered. "Hann'yu, please remain to attend Ushman Nuritam."

The other priests filed out. John watched them, wondering if he, too, should leave. Dayyid clamped a hand on his shoulder.

"I am sure you will want to stay to hear this out, Ushvun Jahn."

It was only a matter of moments before the chamber emptied. Dayyid led John up the steps of the dais. Hann'yu followed them. All three of them sat down on the broad step just below Ushman Nuritam.

Up close, Ushman Nuritam's skin looked like a veil of fine silk. John thought he could see the man's bones just beneath the surface. His gaze drifted past John and seemed to settle on the distant wall.

Hann'yu offered John a quick smile—nothing like the hard flash of teeth John so often caught from Dayyid. Hann'yu appeared genuinely friendly. He stretched his legs and massaged his ankles.

"Jahn, don't you think we should have cushions? They have them at the Black Tower in Nurjima and so do our sisters at Umbhra'ibaye. I don't see why we shouldn't. We're not fanatics like the Kahlirash'im in Vundomu, you know."

"I have spoken to the Usho." Ushman Nuritam nodded seriously. "He has approved the purchase of 400 cushions."

"Then we could add them to the supply list for next month." Hann'yu's smile widened almost comically. "My butt will be so happy."

Ushman Nuritam returned Hann'yu's smile in a wide grin that almost startled John. He had grown used to seeing the ushman'im with dour and distant expressions. At just this moment, Hann'yu and Nuritam seemed suddenly very human and approachable. It was a relieving sight after being attacked, cut, and put through an incomprehensible test. It offered John some small hope of being able to appeal to either of the two men.

Then John glanced to Dayyid. His expression remained cold, almost grim. And for the first time, John noticed that the insignias on Dayyid's collar and the style of his braids were different from Hann'yu's. Hann'yu wore emblems of suns on his collar where Dayyid wore a both a sun and a small crescent moon. Hann'yu's braids hung forward where Dayyid's were pulled back close to his skull and fell behind his shoulders.

"I believe we can discuss provisions later," Dayyid stated. "Right now, there is the matter of Ushvun Jahn's placement."

Again Ushman Nuritam nodded. "This is a difficult matter." He shifted slightly and looked at John. "You obviously are of an Eastern bloodline."

John nodded. He had no way of contesting the statement. He certainly wasn't going to tell them that he was from the bloodline of an entirely different world.

"So, it is not so surprising that you felt the power of the curse blade." Nuritam patted his robe, where he had tucked the knife away. "But you also seem to have some sense of the Gray Space. That would indicate that your bones may be blessed by the god Parfir."

"Or, it may simply be that he comes from a strong line of witches," Dayyid said. "An Eastern taint can remain strong through generations. Witch's blood is not the same as the god's bones."

"True." Ushman Nuritam nodded and gazed out at the panes of mica that filled the tall windows. "It is hard to know what should be done."

"Even if his power arises from an Eastern ancestor, that doesn't mean it can't serve the god." Hann'yu glanced to the small tray beside Ushman Nuritam. "Do we have any more tea?"

"No," Dayyid stated flatly.

"We should have made more." Hann'yu glanced to John. "Are you thirsty?"

It was a simple question and yet John wasn't sure of what to make of it. His life was being discussed. Whether he was thirsty or not seemed like an utterly insignificant and unrelated question.

Hann'yu nodded, despite the fact that John had said nothing.

"Dayyid," Hann'yu said, "have someone bring us more tea. I can tell that Ushvun Jahn is thirsty and confused. He doesn't even know what we're talking about."

"Of course he knows," Dayyid replied. "He's not an idiot."

"Well, perhaps we should let him have a little more say in the decision, then," Hann'yu remarked.

Dayyid shook his head but then glanced over to John. "Tell me, have you ever dreamed in another place? Have you ever felt that you have slipped through walls or doors into places you have never been before?"

"You mean, in a dream?" John asked.

"It would seem like a dream," Dayyid replied.

"I don't remember most of my dreams too well." John didn't want to tell too much. "But I may have had one like that."

"You may have." Dayyid shook his head. "There are already too many young men struggling as ushiri. I don't need another."

"Of course you do. Someone should take Ashid's place," Hann'yu answered.

"And follow him to his grave?" Dayyid demanded. "It does no good to have a hundred ushiri if they are all torn apart by the Gray Space. A taint of witch blood simply isn't strong enough to protect them in the Gray Space. They must have Parfir's blessings. They must carry it in their bones."

Hann'yu shook his head. "You see, this is why we need some tea. It would give us a chance to pause and think over each other's points."

Dayyid scowled. "I won't train him. The signs aren't sure enough. If he only has witches' blood, then the first time he enters a Gray Space, it will chew him to pieces."

"But if his bones are truly blessed and you don't train him, you may have passed over the Kahlil," Hann'yu replied.

Listening to the two of them, John suddenly realized he wanted Dayyid to win this argument. He didn't seem to be accusing John of being a witch, as John had feared. Instead, Dayyid seemed to be arguing that he couldn't withstand the Gray Space. A sick shiver wriggled through John's stomach as he recalled feeling the edge of a Gray Space against his flesh. He knew he never wanted to be inside one.

And suddenly, he remembered where he had heard the name Ashid before. He had been the mutilated ushiri in the bed a little ways from John's.

"Ravishan will be the one," Dayyid said. "His flesh may be sinful and his will wayward, but I know his bones are the god's own. He will be Kahlil."

"What of Fikiri?" Hann'yu suggested. "His bones broke a prophecy. He crossed death itself to be delivered to us."

"Perhaps, but it's too early in his training." Dayyid's assured expression wavered slightly.

"You see, you don't know," Hann'yu went on quickly. "Not one of us knows. The Kahlil could be a heretic's son or a gaun'im's by-blow. We can't afford to cast even one possibility aside."

"Ushvun Jahn is not even a possibility," Dayyid stated. "It would be a waste of my time and his life."

Hann'yu's smile flattened. "He has power. You couldn't even touch him in the test. How can you let such potential go untrained?"

"Moving through the spaces is not just a matter of power. There is a ..." Dayyid scowled as he tried to find the word. His fingers moved as if trying to pull the word from the empty air. "There is a particular character that a man must have. And Ushvun Jahn does not have it."

"How can you say?" Hann'yu asked. "You hardly know him."

"When he first came, I practiced against him on the ushvun'im grounds. He has no passion. No fury. He will take beating after beating without question. To walk between the worlds a man must fight. He must struggle even when he may be beaten. That is not Ushvun Jahn's nature. If a Gray Space closes on him, he would simply allow it to devour him."

A small, egotistical part of John wanted to tell Dayyid that he had no idea what he was talking about. But John kept his mouth shut. If Ushman Dayyid thought he was weak-willed, so be it.

"With all respect," Hann'yu replied, "you're only describing men who share your own nature, Dayyid. But you, yourself, could not become Kahlil. Despite your devotion and your fearless nature, you failed that test. So, it could be argued that you do not know what qualities are required for a man to become Kahlil."

As Hann'yu spoke, John could see a dark flush spreading across Dayyid's tanned face. Ushman Nuritam shook his head.

"I have heard enough," Ushman Nuritam said softly. "Thank you both for arguing the matter before me."

Both Hann'yu and Dayyid bowed their heads.

Ushman Nuritam turned to John. "It seems that you have great potential, Ushvun, but perhaps not among the ushiri'im. I am sorry."

A wave of relief rolled over John. He didn't think he could have stood another assault from Dayyid, much less having to train under the man every day. John noticed Dayyid's slight smile and Hann'yu's sigh.

"If I may make a request." Hann'yu kept his head lowered.

"Go ahead," Ushman Nuritam said.

"At least allow Ushvun Jahn to be trained under me. I could use him to bear wounds, if nothing else."

Ushman Nuritam nodded. "Of course. Ushvun Jahn, you will be given the honor of serving Ushman Hann'yu in the infirmary."

"Thank you." John lowered his head to the stone step. A queasy feeling was already seeping through him. Bearing wounds. He wondered if he had just gotten a better, or worse, appointment.

"So, now we should have our tea," Hann'yu suggested.

Ushman Nuritam nodded slowly and somberly.

"If you could excuse me," Dayyid said, "I must return to the ushiri'im. We will have to break in a new welter-body."

"Of course. You are excused, Ushman Dayyid." Ushman Nuritam smiled at him. "May Parfir walk with you."

"And with you," Dayyid replied. He bowed to both Ushman Nuritam and Hann'yu, then quit the chamber.

John remained on the step, apparently forgotten, while tea was sent for and then brought. Ushman Nuritam discussed the division of tithes and how much would be allotted to Rathal'pesha as opposed to the holy fortress of Vundomu. As Hann'yu nodded and listened, he passed John a cup of tea with the ingrained politeness of the Basawar nobility.

The irrelevant conversation felt restful to John after so much intense focus on himself and his training. He relaxed on the lower step, only half-listening to the discussion concerning southern nobility and rumors of their secret fundeding of the Fai'daum. Then the conversation turned to the vague prophesies surrounding the Rifter. It was good to hear about things that had nothing to do with him for a while.

CHAPTER THIRTY-ONE

A month later, John had learned his way through the twisting halls of the higher floors. These days he spent most of his free hours in the library attempting to reclaim the prowess literacy offered.

This morning the yellowed panes of sheet mica in the skylights turned the harsh light soft and golden. The heavy hand-bound books filling the shelves and lining the walls added insulation against the cold that would have otherwise crept up through the stones. The books themselves all seemed infused with a scent of incense, and perhaps in a few volumes, just the hint of fires. It made him feel drawn into autumn.

Paging through a strange-smelling old book under the warm light reminded John of returning to school after the summer break. But of course, here in Basawar, all his associations were wrong. It was spring, and there were no summer vacations or post-graduate classes. Here, no one had even heard of ecology, much less an ecology degree, and John was far from a scholar. He could hardly read.

Ravishan rocked his stool back onto two legs and peered over John's shoulder.

"Par. Fir. Ati. Hyy. An. Pahr." Ravishan gave the sound for each of the letters as he pointed to them. "Parfir'ati hyy'an pahr."

Parfir brought rain. John understood the spoken sentence perfectly.

John traced his fingers beneath lines of faded brown symbols. One after another, they flowed and arced together into the long sentences that filled page after page of the aged book in front of him. He knew most of the letters now. Hann'yu had insisted that he learn them and John had been happy to. But it was frustrating to have to go so slowly, sounding the words out like a child.

"It's boring stuff," Ravishan commented. "Parfir creates earth and air and water and then gives them all life by pouring pieces of himself into each of them. His blood, his skin, his flesh, and his tears. All that, until the world is alive and he's just ...I don't remember exactly. An eyeball, finger bones, and some ribs, and I think some teeth."

John glanced down at the page. He thought he recognized the word for eye. It even looked a little like an eye, with a circle and a single dot in the center.

"Then the first empire of demons arises and Parfir creates the first Rifter from what remains of his body, except one finger bone, which got lost." Ravishan tapped the small, brown illustration at the bottom of the page. "The Rifter slaughters them all."

It was of a woman with long, wild blond hair and wide staring eyes. The ground buckled and split beneath her feet and bolts of lightning cut the air above her head. She vaguely resembled Laurie.

"But the Rifter, the sacred destroyer, was made too well, made too strong, and Parfir's own body shuddered as she walked across his back." Ravishan shrugged. "The same story everyone knows."

"I don't know it."

"Really?" Ravishan sat all four legs of the stool firmly on the ground.

"Really."

"They don't speak of Parfir's sacrifice in Nayeshi?" Ravishan asked.

"They don't even know about Parfir in Nayeshi."

"Such a strange place." Ravishan leaned closer and studied the picture. "I can't imagine what that would be like."

"When you become Kahlil, you'll see it for yourself," John told him.

Ravishan radiated pleasure at John's words.

It struck John that Ravishan had a disarmingly handsome smile, and then John recalled that he had thought the same thing the last time Ravishan had flashed him that charming grin. He supposed it wouldn't have had such a strong effect back at home, where dental care and toothpaste were common. Here it was different.

Ravishan's white teeth shone like pearls in contrast to his tanned skin. His eyes caught the afternoon light, glowing gold.

"When I am Kahlil," Ravishan whispered. "I like the way that sounds."

John smiled. When Ravishan was Kahlil, hopefully he would help John, Laurie, and Bill get back home. But that was probably still years away. John returned to learning his letters, but found himself distracted by the illustration of the first Rifter.

She reminded him of Laurie more each time he looked at her. The small mouth, the thin body, it resembled her in that simple but clear way that some police sketches seemed to exactly capture a suspect.

"So, my guess would be that Parfir has to destroy the Rifter." John skimmed the page, picking out words that he recognized and skipping those he didn't.

"Parfir can't destroy the Rifter. They're made of the same body, just as the living world is. They are all one divinity." Ravishan smiled. "That's why the Payshmura were created. One holy man found Parfir's single finger bone and it guided him. He created a poison to calm the Rifter, and when she slept, he cut off her leg, then used her own hungry bone to bleed her until she couldn't fight."

Ravishan leaned close to John and ran his finger under a line of gold script. "From Parfir's single remaining finger bone, the first priest forged a golden key that could open the Rifter's death. And from the Rifter's own blood-soaked thigh bone, he carved the first yasi'halaun."

John studied the words, sounding them out under his breath as Ravishan read.

"The yasi'halaun?" John asked. "It looks like one of the knives I was offered at the test."

"Yes. All our curse blades are carved to resemble the yasi'halaun. But the divine blade must be carved by the Kahlil from one of the Rifter's bones. Right now, the Holy Kahlirash'im guard the sacred bone at their temple in Vundomu. When I become Kahlil, I will bring the bone back to Rathal'pesha." Ravishan flipped ahead in the book, then stopped on an ornately decorated illustration of two black knives and one long gray sword. Golden words were written in minuscule script around all three.

"This is just a curse blade." Ravishan tapped the first black knife in the picture. "They're made from bone like the yasi'halaun but just animal bones, so they aren't all that powerful. Really, any blade made from bone can be made into a curse blade. All the ushiri'im have them. Even you carry one, though yours doesn't carry a curse."

"The knife I chose in the test?" John asked and Ravishan nodded. John was glad that his knife wasn't cursed. It now hung in its sheath from his belt. He had grown accustomed to the way it swung against his thigh when he walked.

Ravishan briefly drew his own black blade from its sheath. "You can place any kind of curse on a blade. 'Burn the blood, silence the cries. Sear the flesh, blind the eyes.' Then when you use the blade on an enemy, the curse infests them."

"Infests them?" John asked.

"Well, it kills them." Ravishan shrugged. He slid his knife back into its sheath.

"You're sure the wound doesn't do that?" John asked.

"I'm sure it doesn't hurt. But the wound doesn't need to be fatal. If you can cast a curse, then all you need is to draw blood. Your enemy won't be able to escape it."

John didn't respond. He wasn't inclined to believe in curses, but he also wasn't inclined to believe in gateways to other worlds or men who traveled through the Gray Space. He'd been living around too many things that he wasn't inclined to believe in to feel completely secure in his skepticism.

"And this second black knife is the yasi'halaun?" John thought he now recognized the symbols that made up the name.

"Yes." Ravishan smiled at the drawing. "The Kahlil carries both a curse blade and the yasi'halaun."

John nodded. He remembered the knives that Kyle had carried. He glanced down at the drawing again. This time he studied the long gray sword. Kyle had carried one like it as well.

"Nayeshi'hala," John sounded the name out, recognizing the words as he heard them. The key to Nayeshi. John looked to Ravishan. "The key to my world?"

Ravishan nodded, as if this were common knowledge. And John guessed it was, here in the libraries of Rathal'pesha.

"When the yasi'halaun drinks the blood of the Rifter, it grows into the Nayeshi'hala. That, too, is carried by the Kahlil." Ravishan beamed at the picture.

"It drinks the Rifter's blood and is made from her bones?" John asked.

Ravishan nodded. "Exactly."

"And the Rifter is ...who?"

Ravishan frowned at him as if the question didn't make sense. "The Rifter is the Rifter, the destroying aspect of the divine Parfir."

"But ..." John tried to think of another way to get his answer. "How does the Rifter end up having her bones carved up and her blood drained?"

"First, the Rifter must be poisoned. Then the blood is fed to the yasi'halaun. Then the golden key opens the Rifter's death. Once the Rifter is dead, the bones are taken and another yasi'halaun is carved."

Ravishan's description sounded like some kind of terrible ritual sacrifice. And it still didn't tell him what he wanted to know.

"They don't just pick some woman to be the Rifter, do they?" John asked at last.

Again Ravishan paused a few moments, looking at him as if he had asked something completely bizarre, almost incomprehensible.

"No, the Rifter is Parfir's own flesh, not just someone who can be appointed. If the Payshmura could just choose a Rifter, then they would be rid of the Fai'daum already."

"Oh." John frowned. There was something he failed to understand about the Rifter, something that made his questions seem absurd to Ravishan. John flipped back to try and find his place in the book.

He turned page after page, scanning the black, brown, and gold illustrations for a familiar image. Absently, he wondered if numbering pages had just never occurred as an idea or if somehow the Payshmura had deemed it sinful. So far John hadn't encountered a single page number in any of the massive texts he'd thumbed through.

Ravishan too apparently had other things on his mind. He asked, "Is Hann'yu sending you down to Amura'taye for supplies?"

"Yes, I'm going down with the other ushvun'im tomorrow."

"Do you know where Candle Alley is?" Ravishan lowered his voice to a whisper. John stopped scanning the book.

"I could find it. Do you want me to bring something back for you?" John lowered his voice as well as a reflex.

"No, I want to meet you there tomorrow night."

"Why?" John asked.

"There are things we can't talk about here." Ravishan glanced over the two empty tables behind them and then studied the rows of shelved books. John followed his gaze. There didn't seem to be anyone else in the small room with them, but John couldn't know for sure. There was always the possibility of some ushiri watching from the Gray Space.

John wondered what it was that Ravishan needed to tell him in strict privacy. Was it about Nayeshi? Something Ravishan had overheard Dayyid mention? Or perhaps it had to do with the nun at Umbhra'ibaye who Ravishan secretly spoke to.

Ravishan whispered, "After seven bells. There's a stone wall at the end of the alley."

"I'll be there," John agreed.

Ravishan smiled.

"You won't get into trouble, will you?" John asked quietly.

"Not if I don't get caught," Ravishan replied easily.

John thought of cautioning Ravishan, but he heard the soft whisper of the door opening behind the two of them. Ravishan instantly spun around to see who had entered. John restrained himself. He kept his eyes glued to the book in front of him. Nothing seemed more conspiratorial than two people simultaneously looking up in sudden, startled silence.

"So, this is how Rathal'pesha is written?" John ran his finger over the sweeping script.

"Uh—" It took Ravishan a moment to refocus on the book. "Yes, that's it."

"The reading is going well, then?" Hann'yu asked from behind them.

John turned back, as if he had just realized that Hann'yu had entered the room. "Not as well as I would like, but I think I'm improving."

"Good." Hann'yu walked to their table. To Ravishan, he said, "Ushman Dayyid must be expecting you at practice, don't you think?"

"I just stopped in to have Ushvun Jahn look at my arm." Ravishan pulled himself off the stool. "It's been hurting lately."

"Yes, I've noticed you've had a sudden rash of injuries." Hann'yu nodded, barely concealing his amusement. "You've been in to see Ushvun Jahn almost every day for the last three weeks. I hope you aren't dying."

Ravishan flushed. "No, I just ..."

"Yes, yes." Hann'yu waved aside anything else Ravishan might have said. "You really should get to practice."

"Of course." Ravishan bowed deeply to Hann'yu and gave John a slight nod. "Thank you for your time and skills." Then he quickly slipped out of the room.

Hann'yu watched him go and then addressed John.

"I hope you won't take this the wrong way, but he likes you quite a bit."

A wave of guilty dread rolled over John. He didn't want this to be the moment when Hann'yu warned him against getting too close, being too friendly. His skin suddenly felt slightly too hot and his palms went clammy. It was a guilty reaction, and he knew it. He said nothing and simply continued to gaze at Hann'yu as if the comment had been no more than a mention of the weather.

"It's good to see," Hann'yu continued. "I don't think he's ever made friends with any of the other ushiri. He's so much better at controlling the Gray Space than most of them and too proud of himself for any of them to like him."

"He's not a bad kid." John shrugged, hesitant to be drawn out any further.

"He's hardly a kid at all anymore," Hann'yu said. "When I was first sent here five years ago, he was scrawny, awkward, and so brittle. You wouldn't have recognized him. I used to worry that he'd just come apart one day."

"But he's gotten better?"

Hann'yu sighed. "I think having a friend has helped him greatly. It's brought a value to his life other than becoming Kahlil. I was worried for a while that if he failed it would kill him. When Fikiri came ..." Hann'yu shook his head. "I suppose I'm just trying to thank you for befriending him. I hope it isn't too much of an annoyance to you."

"No, not at all." John knew it was as important to conceal his pleasure as it was to hide his earlier alarm. Yet he couldn't help but feel happy to know that he had bettered Ravishan's life. "It's nothing, really."

John flipped through the book and found that he was once again looking at the drawing of the first Rifter. Her wide eyes and tiny pinprick pupils stared out in an expression that struck John as more horrified than wrathful. She appeared to be shocked that the world was crumbling beneath her feet.

Hann'yu glanced to the book and rolled his eyes. "Dull, isn't it?"

"It's not too bad," John replied.

"There must be something better here." Hann'yu studied the spines of the books on each of the shelves. "If we were in Nurjima, we could just walk down the street to a bookshop. Have you ever been there?"

"No. I've heard about it."

"A den of sin and revolutionaries." Hann'yu smiled as he spoke. "It's a beautiful place."

"Sounds like you miss it."

"I do, but politics won't allow me back," Hann'yu answered.

"I see." John returned to the book. He sounded out the words under his breath, slowly piecing together sentences as if he were reassembling the splintered remains of an ancient fossil.

"Parfir is the water, the air, and the land," John mouthed to himself. "He smiles, and the rain is gentle, the sun shines, and the fields prosper. But his rage is the Rifter bringing floods, fires, and chasms."

"You don't ask many questions, do you?" Hann'yu asked.

"Pardon?" John glanced up in confusion, his thoughts still occupied by the Rifter.

"It's nothing," Hann'yu answered. "I am simply surprised that you didn't ask me more about it. I think every other priest in the entire monastery has pulled me aside at one point or another to ask why I was sent from the Black Tower. Most of them seem to think I'm reporting back to the Usho."

"I guess that might follow." John knew that the Usho was the highest-ranking ushman in the Payshmura church. Their Pope, he supposed. But that was about all John knew of the subject.

Hann'yu smiled. "You couldn't seem to care less."

"Should I care?"

"No," Hann'yu replied. "I'm just not accustomed to such honest indifference."

"Well," John offered, "you can tell me all about it if it would make you feel more comfortable."

Hann'yu chuckled. "You're too amusing of a man to have to read that tired old rag. Let me see if I can't find something more diverting."

Hann'yu wandered back between two rows of towering shelves. John heard him climbing the rolling ladder that offered access to those books shelved up against the ceiling.

"You know," Hann'yu called back to him, "looking at the books here you'd think that there was no such thing as literature at all. Holy text, holy text, appendix to a holy text. And ...oh. Well, this isn't too bad. *A History of the Practitioners of the Forbidden.* Ah, and this as well. Not as bad as I thought. Oh, this doesn't belong here at all!"

John heard Hann'yu rustling through the books.

"Jahn," Hann'yu called him, "come here and take these. I can't carry them and get down the ladder at the same time."

John put his own book aside and took the small stack of books that Hann'yu handed down. Two were the heavy leather-bound volumes that John had expected. Brass clasps held them shut, and silver work had been inlaid across their covers and spines. The third volume was startlingly different.

John stared at it in disbelief. The cover was glossy, the binding supple and cheap. The title, *Dan the Milkman,* was written in the cheery typestyle of so many American children's books. There were deep gouges in the cover, and as John opened it, he could see that the pages had faded badly. He could hardly read the name printed on the flap. John squinted at the awkward pencil marks.

This book belongs to Kyle Harris. Please return if lost.

Kyle's book was beyond lost, John thought.

"Strange, isn't it?" Hann'yu asked. John almost jumped at the sudden intrusion into his fascination.

"Yes," John answered. "What is it?"

"A thing most rare." Hann'yu smiled. "It's a text from the world of Nayeshi."

John didn't know how to react. It was a children's storybook, probably printed sometime around World War II, judging from the look of the illustrations.

"I've seen copies of it," Hann'yu said. "But I never imagined that the original would just be filed with the rest of the books here." Hann'yu gazed down at the book with a warm, nostalgic expression. "I learned my first holy words from this book."

Carefully, almost tenderly, Hann'yu turned the pages of the book.

"His name is Dan." Hann'yu said the English name with a mechanical exactness. Then he smiled at John. "The book tells the story of how every morning, before anyone else rises, Dan visits the houses of good children, leaving gifts of sweet milk and cream."

It was an entirely different impression of a milkman than John had ever had. He sounded more like a kind of Santa Claus than a distributor of dairy products. But it did offer him a hint as to why all the ushiri'im were taught to claim they were milkmen. And also why Kyle had claimed his name was Kyle. For a brief moment, John wondered what would have happened if the book had been something like *Pirate Pete* or *Heather Has Two Mommies.*

Hann'yu closed the book gently. "I'm sure it was put here by mistake. It should be up in the holy cases." He gazed at the beaten cover a moment longer and then glanced up at John. "It looks like nothing but scribbles to you, doesn't it?"

"Pretty much," John replied.

"Maybe someday you'll learn to read it. For now, let's stick to simpler things." Hann'yu picked up one of the leather-bound Basawar volumes and handed it to John. "*Practitioners of the Forbidden.* Don't let Dayyid catch you reading it."

"I won't." John took the book with a feeling of slight dubiousness as to its contents. He didn't imagine that any of the 'practitioners of the forbidden' managed to live happily ever after.

"And speaking of reading." Hann'yu reached into the folds of his robe and produced a scrap of paper. "These are the herbs that I'll need you buy when you go down to Amura'taye. Can you read all this?"

John slowly sounded out the names of the plants.

"Good." Hann'yu handed him the list. "Then I'll leave you to it."

Hann'yu picked up the other two books. John thought he glimpsed the words: Tales of Tempting Women. Hann'yu grinned at him and said, "I may have to watch out for Dayyid myself."

After Hann'yu had gone, John pushed *Practitioners of the Forbidden* aside and returned to his original study. He flipped through the heavy pages, catching whiffs of incense, until an illustration caught his attention.

John knew it had to be the Kahlil. The dark-haired man glared out from the page with a ferocious intensity. The black tattoos above his eyes seemed to glare as well. He held a short black knife in each hand and the hilt of a gray sword could be seen rising from over his left shoulder. Ragged white bandages waved from his right arm like banners.

John leaned closer to read the minuscule gold letters that surrounded the figure.

Kahlil. He who crosses the worlds. He who hunts the Rifter. He who receives the golden key. He who unleashes the Rifter. He who spills the sacred blood. He who slays the Rifter. Blessed three times. Flesh, blood, and bones.

John read the words two more times, slowly absorbing them. Everything he had been reading, the conversations he had overheard, the images he had seen, they all clicked into place.

His roommate Kyle had been the last Kahlil, and he had been on Nayeshi hunting for a Rifter. The memory of how intensely Kyle had stared at Laurie washed over John. Kyle had asked her if she was a witch. He had felt that she had power, real power, while John had just thought her deluded.

Anxious tension gnawed through John's muscles.

Kyle had to have recognized Laurie as a Rifter that first morning when they'd met. He had even managed to send her back to Basawar. But something had gone wrong. John guessed it had to do with the key he had taken from Kyle. Guilt still nagged at John for the theft. Now, it seemed a far worse transgression. Kyle, the last Kahlil, had ended up torn to pieces in the White Space between worlds.

Now, the priests at Rathal'pesha were desperately attempting to train another Kahlil to find a Rifter to destroy the Fai'daum. And completely unbeknownst to them, their Rifter was already here, living at the very foot of their monastery.

John didn't want to think about what the Payshmura would do if they found her. But he had read the words. He had seen the images. They would use her to destroy their enemies and then they would poison her, bleed her, and murder her. Then they would retrieve her bones to carve another yasi'halaun, find another woman, and do the whole thing again.

John laid his head down against the cool surface of the table. He wanted to be wrong. But it all made too much sense. He would have to tell Bill and Laurie as soon as he got to Amura'taye. They needed to be warned.

Ironically, he remembered arguing with Laurie about the reason for the three of them being transported to Basawar. He had said that it was a mistake. She had insisted that there was a purpose behind it. Now, John knew that Laurie had been right. And as much as she liked being right, John doubted that she would take much consolation in this particular victory.

What an awful thing to have to tell someone: you're the Rifter, the living incarnation of destruction, desolation, and death. He couldn't even imagine how much worse it would be to be told such a thing.

CHAPTER THIRTY-TWO

Laurie leaned onto her elbows, resting her chin on her cupped hands. The bands of silver rings and fine chains that linked her fingers gleamed in the afternoon light. Her long, pale hair had been drawn up from her face in twisting braids. Silver beads, like those Lady Bousim and her maids wore, decorated her hair.

"The Rifter," Laurie whispered. She laid her hand on Bill's arm.

Bill's black hair shot out around his face like an ink spill. His skin was the color of wax. He said nothing, just frowned, and took a deep drink of his tea. The last two years had altered Bill deeply. He had recovered some of his strength and could move without struggling for breath, but he was still weak. John rarely saw him laugh or joke in public. He was only slowly drawn out by these quiet, private conversations.

"That sucks," Bill said at last.

John nodded.

Outside he could hear a kitchen woman shouting at a Bousim rashan for stealing a taste of the evening meal before it was finished. He picked out the sound of children's voices as well, loud and high-pitched but farther away. These were sounds that John never heard in Rathal'pesha. Even the season seemed different here. Protected from the harshest winds by the mountain, a gentle warmth hung over Amura'taye. The scents of blossoms filled the air, while up in Rathal'pesha frost still came at night and the wind remained frigid.

A breeze curled through the open window, brushing aside the thin green curtains. Two stories below, red and yellow spring blossoms colored the garden. Bright green ivy wound up the wall enclosing the Bousim house and grounds.

Most of the buildings of Amura'taye were yard-less stone structures, hunched close together along narrow lanes and alleys that wound crookedly through town. John watched as a herd of tiny black goats hurried up the muddy street outside the Bousim compound, darting between wagons and among the bicyclists who pedaled along the rutted streets.

"Are you sure?" Laurie still hadn't lifted her hands away from her small mouth.

"I don't know, but it seems very likely." John absently swirled his tea, feeling the liquid within the cup curl into a tiny vortex.

"Destroyer of worlds?" Laurie's eyes widened. "Does that sound at all like me?"

John sighed. He wished someone else could be telling her this. He was already tired from the early morning trek down from Rathal'pesha. He didn't know if he had the strength to argue.

"I thought it was a myth, like some kind of personification of an earthquake or something," Bill said.

"I thought the same thing at first, but training with the ushiri'im convinced me otherwise. These men aren't crossing through Gray Space and tearing themselves apart in pursuit of some philosophical concept. They are hunting a living person. The Rifter is real."

"And a guy," Laurie suddenly broke in. "The Rifter is supposed to be a man, right? Lady Bousim said as much."

"The one who destroyed the Kingdom of the East was a man, but there isn't just one Rifter," John replied. "As far as I've read, there have been five Rifters, two men and three women. Each of them were brought from Nayeshi by a Kahlil."

"But then it could be any one of the three of us, couldn't it?" Laurie glanced to Bill, again plainly seeking his arbitration, as she often did.

"Maybe, but if it was John, then why wouldn't Kyle have brought him back right away? He wouldn't have shacked up with his destroyer-god for months just to hang out with him, would he? And as for me, behold my awesome might." He gave a brief, dry cough. "I'm not shattering this world anytime soon."

"You're the one who has power here, Laurie," John said.

"But I'm not evil." Laurie glared at her clay cup. A wisp of steam rose off it and John wondered whether the intensity of her emotion had caused it.

"I don't think any of the Rifters were," John replied soothingly. Laurie turned her glare on him. "They tore apart whole kingdoms!"

"But I don't think they did it on purpose. The Payshmura used them. They set them off somehow."

"Like bombs?" Bill asked.

"Not literally. They didn't explode," John replied. "But two of the pictures I found showed the Rifters wounded and all of them looked scared." John shook his head. "I don't know. I'm piecing all this together from what I can read and some drawings. I could be completely wrong. But I thought you should know. You should be careful and not light any more fires or do anything else like that."

Laurie and Bill shared a cagey glance that sent a thrill of alarm through John.

He said, "You haven't been doing anything, have you?"

"No," Laurie said quickly.

"Yes," Bill admitted.

Laurie shot him a reproachful look and Bill shrugged.

"They've been practicing witchcraft," Bill whispered, leaning in close. "Laurie, Lady Bousim, and Ohbi."

"But nothing that would blow up the world," Laurie insisted. "Just healing spells for Bill and small things like that."

"At the foot of Rathal'pesha, you're practicing witchcraft?" John shook his head in astonishment at their recklessness.

"We're careful," Laurie assured him.

"You'd better be. You know what they do to witches here?"

Laurie leaned back and crossed her arms over her chest. "It's not as though Bill and I have been drifting along in dreamland while you are figuring everything out. There's a chance that I could find a way home for us through my spells. Have you thought of that?"

"If you did, it would be great." John wasn't about to be drawn into an argument over what Laurie was or was not allowed to do. "Just don't get yourself killed trying."

"I won't," Laurie said flatly.

John nodded. He'd told her what she needed to know. He wasn't going to get any further when it came to warning Laurie. She'd just think he was being highhanded and resist his advice. He knew her well enough to recognize that set expression she wore.

Living in Basawar had only made her resent being told what to do even more than she normally had. John couldn't blame her. As a woman, the culture didn't afford her much respect. Even with her relatively elevated status as Lady Bousim's attendant, Laurie didn't have the right to venture outside the Bousim grounds without a male escort. She couldn't carry her own money and she couldn't be out past six bells when the sun began to set.

John sipped his tea. It was a refined drink, like the best served in Rathal'pesha, and so didn't have much taste at all. The same held true for most elite foods. He could hardly taste them. Rough taye and the game meats, considered the coarsest peasant fare, were the foods he liked best. They had the strongest flavors.

He drank a little more tea anyway, just to fill the time and allow Laurie to relax.

"How have things been with Rasho Tashtu?" John asked finally. The last time he'd spoken with Laurie and Bill they had been having problems with the commander of the rashan'im.

John only vaguely remembered Tashtu. His broken nose and black beard had dominated his face. His body had seemed heavy with both hard muscle and fat. Apparently, he had taken offense to the fact that Laurie had chosen to marry Bill, whom Tashtu deemed a sickly weakling, and decided that a course of harassment would convince her to take up with him instead.

John had spoken to Pivan about it, but there wasn't much Pivan could do to curb the commander's comments or leers. Though Pivan had assured John that he would never allow Tashtu to act on either.

"He's been better lately," Bill answered. "He's still a huge asshole. But now that I can walk, he's had to really cut back on calling me a worthless cripple."

"I wanted to curse him but Lady Bousim thought it would be too obvious." Laurie sighed. "I still think most of the women in this town would be relieved if the man fell off a cliff."

"Most of the world would be relieved, but it's not something you should get involved in," Bill said. "Dropping the bastard off a cliff is a just something we have to hope the drunk fuck will do to himself. Maybe we could shove him a little, but no more than that. One little shove …maybe throw a rock down after him…but that is absolutely all."

Laurie caught Bill's hand and gently squeezed it. "You say the nicest things."

"I just want to share your beautiful dream."

John looked past them out the window as they kissed. He was glad that they had each other. It seemed to keep them both safe and sane, but moments like this brought his own solitude to the fore. It had been two years …no, even longer. Nearly three years since he'd been with anyone.

The little black goats were back, scampering across the busy street. John wondered if anyone owned them. Were they just feral things, like alley cats, being adopted or abandoned according to the whims of children and lonely old women?

Bill said, "Forget Tashtu. It's that sweet talker, Fikiri, who I'm more worried about."

Laurie laughed in that odd, silent way that Lady Bousim and her maids laughed. It was like seeing the image of pleasure without the sound.

John had only been half-listening, not quite sure if the words were meant for him or Laurie alone. But that name caught his attention.

"Fikiri?" John asked.

"Lady Bousim's son," Bill said, as if he would need to explain that to John.

"He has a little crush on me." Laurie smiled. "It's pretty harmless. He sneaks down from time to time to visit his mother. He always brings me a cookie or something."

"Last time I taught him a couple dirty jokes to ease those lonely nights up on the mountain," Bill added.

"How does that exactly help?" Laurie asked.

Bill shrugged.

There was no way Fikiri could just walk down from Rathal'pesha without being missed. The trip down lasted hours and getting back up took nearly a full day. He had to be moving through Gray Space, which meant he had been hiding that ability from Dayyid.

"He's a nice kid," Laurie went on. "He's got a lot of potential."

John just nodded. He saw nothing wrong with what Fikiri was doing. But if Dayyid discovered it, John imagined, he'd be furious.

"He can do incredible spells with water." Laurie poured more tea for Bill and glanced to John's cup.

"He's practicing witchcraft with you?" John felt a rush of horror at the thought. He could see Fikiri creating a direct route for Dayyid to discover all of Laurie's transgressions against Basawar law.

Laurie frowned at him. "Is there something wrong with that?"

"He's a teenaged boy—" John began.

"It's not like we're corrupting him," Laurie snapped. "What do you think we do, dance naked and hold orgies?"

"I'm not accusing you of anything like that," John replied. "I was going to say that Fikiri might not be the most reliable confidant, if you want to keep all this secret. Boys like to brag, and they make mistakes. If he gets found out, then all of you could be discovered."

"It was only once." Laurie glared at him, as if expecting him to challenge her. Bill just shook his head weakly.

John's cup was nearly empty. He drained the last of it and then shook his head. "I'm not saying anything right today. I just want you both to be safe."

A week ago, he had been looking forward to seeing his friends. He'd thought of all the things they could talk about that none of them could mention to anyone else: washing machines, television shows, band aids, popcorn. He'd remembered earlier times, when they would all three laugh and joke together. They had been relaxed in each other's company.

But that had been an entirely different world, and it had been years ago. Basawar had changed all three of them. With everything she was and everything she did being wrong here, Laurie had grown to expect condemnation and offhanded dismissal. She had become angrier than she ever would have been and more defensive.

Weakness and illness had drained Bill to a mere impression of the brash man he had once been.

It was harder for John to recognize the changes in himself, but he knew they were there—signified, or maybe even caused, by the nightmares that haunted him. He dreamed of the dark chambers high in the monastery, where doorways led nowhere. He saw a room full of mutilated bodies, skinned, but still struggling. Their slick bones writhed against bindings of red wire while they whispered threats into his sleep.

These certainly weren't dreams he'd had before this.

Outside the town bells rang out low and loud. Five bells. It would be getting dark soon.

"I should get going soon," John said at last. "I have an entire list of medicinal herbs to purchase for Hann'yu."

"You just got here," Bill said.

"I'm sorry, but—"

"Did he tell you where to buy the herbs?" Laurie asked.

"No," John replied. He couldn't imagine why it would matter.

"Dahl'ami sells the best herbs." Laurie leaned forward slightly "She and her husband live close by. You could stay a little longer ..."

"I would, but I have to find a place called Candle Alley as well. It might take me a while."

"Bati'kohl knows the entire city. He could take you there." Laurie refilled his cup.

"Candle Alley?" Bill raised an eyebrow. "Why?"

John didn't know why, but he hesitated in answering the question. It wasn't as if Bill or Laurie were going to inform Dayyid. "I promised Ravishan that I'd meet him there."

"Now who's taking chances?" Laurie asked.

John scowled at her. "It's nothing like that. He has something he needs to tell me privately."

"What do you think that's going to be?" Laurie asked. Bill let out a weak snicker.

John said, "If I knew, I wouldn't need to be meeting with him to find out, would I?"

"It's going to be David Lewis all over again," Laurie pronounced.

For several moments, John had no memory of anyone named David Lewis. Then, with sinking dread, he remembered. It amazed him that Laurie could so quickly recall an incident that had taken place in the third grade. He didn't think that he would have remembered David Lewis without her prompting, and he'd been the one who had been caught kissing the boy.

"I'm serious," Laurie went on. "Ravishan likes you way too much."

"He's just lonely," John assured her.

"Lonely, handsome, and completely infatuated with you," Laurie replied. "You're a total sucker for that kind of thing."

"I am not." John felt his face flushing.

"You are," Bill concurred.

Laurie pressed on. "What about that other guy ... Anthony Salazar. That was the same thing."

"Anthony Salazar?" John didn't have to dredge the archives for that name. He had broken two bones in his right hand by punching Anthony Salazar in the mouth. Anthony had lost a tooth and sported a lip the color of an eggplant for a month.

"The one who got expelled for trying to burn down the school," Laurie prompted.

"Hey, I remember him." Bill narrowed his eyes at John. "You and him?"

"Are you kidding? No," John said firmly. "He was getting girls pregnant in the fifth grade."

"Maybe I've got the name wrong." Laurie frowned. "But there was some kid that almost got you thrown out of school ..."

"That was Anthony Salazar," John said. "We were both suspended for fighting. We weren't boyfriends."

Laurie studied him intently over the edge of her cup. "Are you sure?"

"Positive."

"I don't know if I believe you. There was always this weird tension between the two of you," Laurie said.

"That was seething hatred, utterly free of homoerotic underpinnings."

Laurie scowled, though not with any real anger. John could see that she was enjoying needling him. "Yeah, but what about David Lewis?"

"What about him?" John said.

"You totally got caught." Laurie jabbed a delicate finger at him. The silver chains on her rings tinkled against each other. "Full on, sucking face with David Lewis in the tunnel slide."

"Yes. All right, I admit that I got caught with David Lewis." How could this incident still embarrass him almost two decades later?

Laurie grinned.

"Wait." Bill suddenly straightened up. "That wasn't the same David Lewis from high school, was it? The guy who stuffed me in my locker?"

"Yeah, that was him."

"Talk about overcompensating," Bill said. "He didn't even have a neck. Tell me he had a neck when you kissed him."

John laughed. "In third grade he had a neck."

"Good. I mean, it's none of my business, but I'd hate to think of anyone I knew dating no-necks."

"Have no fear," John assured him. "I have no intentions of dating the neck-less."

"No, you're going to end up dating teen-priest." Laurie smiled and threw back her tea like it was a shot of whiskey. John imagined that she rarely had an occasion to tease anyone anymore.

"So, how old is Ravishan now?" Laurie asked. "Sixteen, seventeen?"

"Nineteen," John supplied flatly.

"Nineteen," Laurie repeated. She looked meaningfully at Bill. Lewd jokes were normally his specialty, but this time he passed.

Bill said, "I know this is off topic, but when we get back home, what are we going to tell everyone? I mean, we've been gone two years now."

"I don't know." John hadn't dared to think that far ahead.

"Alien abduction," Laurie whispered. "We could make millions on talk shows."

Bill smiled. "Hey, yeah, we could sell the rights to HBO or some place and have one of those cheesy docudramas made about us. I'm kinda seeing myself, played by a buff male model, running in slow motion. Then a silver-suited ninja-alien leaps out. We fight. More ninja-aliens materialize all around me. I go into this super-powered spinning kick and knock off all of their heads. As their decapitated bodies slump to the ground, I growl, 'Probe my ass, will ya?!'"

John just stared at Bill for a few, stunned seconds. Then he said, "You really have a rich fantasy life, don't you?"

"You have no idea."

"Do you think I could be played by a Black woman?" Laurie asked.

It was the kind of question he would have expected from the Laurie he had known two years ago: simple and at the same time utterly inexplicable.

"I think the writers would give me more sassy lines if I were Black," Laurie explained.

"Like, 'Probe my ass, will ya?'" John asked, deadpan.

"Hey, my line is plenty sassy," Bill protested.

"It would definitely get you a date with David Lewis." John allowed a note of snarkiness into his voice.

"Laugh all you want," Bill continued. "Just wait until it's splashed all over McDonald's collectable toys and cups. Children, women, and men all around the world will be asking for the 'Probe My Ass, Will Ya' special."

"I can just see the relish with which employees will ask, 'Can I supersize that for you?'" John replied.

Laurie laughed out loud and then clapped her hands over her mouth. John smiled. It was good to hear her really laugh, even for a few seconds.

Bill went on, building larger and more absurd fantasies on the theme of their disappearance and return home. None of the stories touched on the ugliness of their real lives. Laurie's repression, Bill's illness, and John's isolation were all outside the realm of their new fantastic adventures.

Instead, they were played by beautiful movie stars, made millions, and received Nobel peace prizes. They took over several tropical islands, were inducted into a secret ninja clan, learned to fly and to communicate with dolphins. Laurie became a goddess with millions of followers. Bill usurped leadership of the ninja clan, and John had a brief but beautiful relationship with a brave super-intelligent dolphin.

When six bells rang out across the city, it all came to an end. Reality washed back in over them. The sky was going dark, and John couldn't stay any longer. He drank the last of his tea, glad he hadn't left earlier and disappointed that he had to leave now.

When he stood, Laurie hugged him fiercely.

"Be careful," Bill said quickly.

John nodded. "You too. Take care of each other."

He hated saying goodbye, and he hated leaving. It always felt like it could be forever.

CHAPTER THIRTY-THREE

Rough stone walls pressed close and rose up over John's head. He could only see a thin strip of night sky directly above him. Everything else was compressed into a jumble of dark shadows that briefly burned away before John's lamp, then closed in behind him.

Within the tight confines of the winding alley, his senses narrowed to the feel of old thatching beneath his feet and the smells of urine and soured human sweat that emanated from the humid alcoves. When his lamp revealed the half-naked forms of couples, John averted his gaze and hurried past.

Bati'kohl had given him directions to Candle Alley but refused to go there himself. It wasn't the kind of place a young boy from a good house went.

A lone girl looked up at him as his lamplight fell across her. Her black hair hung in strings over her emaciated arms and small, bare breasts. With a listless wave, she beckoned him to enter the dank alcove where she lay. John could see dark stains on the blanket beneath her. The girl's head dropped back to the ground. She seemed hardly awake as she mumbled, "Come on in."

She spread her legs.

John walked on quickly.

Other men wandered through the narrow lane. Some carried lamps. Most had only cheap tallow candles. There seemed to be an unspoken order to their pacing. None of them walked close enough that the lights they carried illuminated another man's features. When they passed going opposite directions, each averted his eyes and said nothing.

Only once, as John passed by, did another man reach out and brush his hand across John's hip in clear invitation. John offered no response, and an instant later, the other man was swallowed by the darkness as he disappeared into one of the alcoves.

John didn't like to think of Ravishan even being in a place like this, let alone cruising here. He thought that it might even come as a relief to discover that he'd gone to the wrong location entirely.

He reached the wall that sealed the narrow lane off. No one waited for him. John lifted his lamp to scan the partially collapsed wall. Stones had fallen, or been pulled from their mortar, creating a gap that a slim man could squeeze through. John stepped closer to the crumbling space.

"Up here." Ravishan's voice sounded in the darkness. "You should put out the lamp."

John blew out the flame and waited for his sight to adjust.

It was always remarkable to him how much he could see in the dark here. With the lamp lit, his eyes never adjusted and so the shadows remained impenetrable. But as his pupils widened, he realized that he could make out the wall quite well.

Higher up, the wall was thick and wide, and the broken spaces where the stones had fallen away formed rough steps leading to the very top. Spindly saplings had taken root on several of the steps and they created even darker shadows than the night offered. Small pale flowers drooped from several branches.

Ravishan lounged against the slender trunk of one of the saplings near the top. His dark hair looked wet and John guessed that he had just washed it.

John started climbing. The air was cooler beneath the young trees. The flowers gave off a faint honey-like scent. It almost masked the dank, humid odors that emanated from the alley below.

"I thought you might not come," Ravishan said.

"I told you I would."

"I know." Ravishan smiled briefly at John, then glanced anxiously away. John wondered what was making him so nervous. Obviously not something that was easy to talk about, otherwise he would have come out with it already.

John frowned as Ravishan pulled several weeds out from between the stones of the wall.

"Their roots break the mortar apart." Ravishan gazed intently at the small plant in his hand. Then he threw it aside. "I suppose the trees do worse."

John could have told him that it was the smaller plants that made the first inroads through which the trees' roots would spread, but he knew it wasn't important. They weren't here to talk about mortar erosion.

"There was something you wanted to tell me," John said.

"There was." Ravishan leaned back, letting the young tree take his full weight. He stared upward. John followed his line of sight up between the spindly branches of the tree to the dim stars.

"But now that you're here ..." Ravishan shook his head just a little. "I'm not sure."

John frowned but didn't say anything. He wondered if Ravishan was trying to tell him goodbye. The awkwardness of the exchange reminded him of the uneasy farewell he'd exchanged with his brother when he'd come to visit John against their father's wishes. It had been the last time they'd ever spoken to each other.

Had Ravishan finally decided to escape from Rathal'pesha? John dropped his gaze down to his hands. He didn't want Ravishan to leave.

"When you think of someone in your mind," Ravishan said softly, "they are exactly as you think they are. You think they're kind, and in your mind, they are kind. But then you encounter them in the flesh, and you realize that perhaps they could be different." Ravishan looked at John for a quiet moment before going on. "Right now, you and I exist in each other's minds. Perhaps you have an idea of me, and I have an idea of you, but we haven't tested those ideas. Do you know what I mean?"

"I think so." John nodded. He just wasn't sure where Ravishan was going with the conversation. He wondered if Ravishan was simply trying to avoid saying anything.

"Right now, I think you like me." Ravishan quickly looked back up at the stars. "And I don't want you to change your mind. So I don't want to tell you something that will make you think I'm not the person you like."

"So, you've changed your mind and you don't want to tell me?" John asked.

"No." Ravishan sighed. "I want to tell you. And at the same time, I don't want you to know."

"Well, that's a quandary," John said. "It's going to have to be one or the other."

"I know," Ravishan said.

"I suppose it all depends on how much you trust me," John said.

Ravishan gazed up at him from beneath heavy lashes. "I trust you."

"Then you should tell me."

Ravishan straightened. John could see the pulse hammering along the curve of Ravishan's throat. His hands shook and his dark eyes went wide. Suddenly, he looked away from John down to his feet.

"I can't say it when you're watching me." Ravishan flushed. John could clearly see the dark color spreading across his cheeks.

John realized that Laurie had been right and he was a complete idiot. And if this truly was David Lewis all over again, John knew exactly what would happen next. Ravishan would ask him to close his eyes and then kiss him.

"Ravishan." John's voice felt suddenly rough in his throat. His skin felt hot. "You know that this isn't safe for either of us."

"I know," Ravishan whispered.

John could smell faint hints of sweat and incense on Ravishan's skin. A deep, primal part of him longed to draw in more of Ravishan's scent, to taste him.

"Close your eyes," John told him.

Ravishan hesitated for a moment, then obeyed, his head tilted back just slightly, his lips barely parted.

As he leaned close, John whispered, "Just this once." He felt the heat of Ravishan's breath. Then, very gently, John kissed him.

Ravishan's lips parted beneath his and John automatically deepened the kiss. Ravishan's mouth tasted sweet and felt burning hot. Hungry desire throbbed through John's body. He hadn't expected Ravishan to give himself so well.

John's hands instinctively slid down the curve of Ravishan's back and around the stiff leather edge of his belt until his fingers touched the cool metal of Ravishan's belt buckle.

Ravishan trembled against him and arched into John's hands, his skin radiating heat even through his heavy clothes. The scent of him, the taste of him, the feel of his strong body—it was every-thing John had been deprived of for years. The intensity of his own arousal alarmed him.

They were courting death doing this.

John pulled away. If he didn't stop now, he wouldn't stop at all. He knew that much about himself.

Ravishan started after him, but John placed a restraining hand against his chest.

"We can't." John's voice sounded hoarse even to himself.

"But you said this once." Ravishan's hands slid along John's arm, stroking the tender skin of his wrist and elbow. Shivers of pleasure whispered through the muscles of his arm and spread through his chest.

"I meant just one kiss." John could hardly catch his breath. His entire body burned and he ached to pull Ravishan against him again.

"Couldn't we be… together just once—"

"It's never just once." John knew better than to hear out any argument, since he already wanted to give in. He stepped out of Ravishan's reach. "Neither of us can afford to start this. Not here. Not now."

"But you liked it." Ravishan pursued him, pressing close enough for John to feel his breath tickle his ear.

"Of course I liked it. That's the problem." John dropped his voice to a soft whisper. "I like it. I like you. If we got started, I wouldn't want to stop. And that could get us both killed."

"I would be willing to die, if I could be with you," Ravishan whispered.

John knew the words were meant to be arousing, to show John how deeply Ravishan longed to be with him, but they only revealed the innocent arrogance of his youth. He wasn't consider-ing actual death.

Ravishan plainly envisioned himself as a character in some ancient, tragic, love poem. But John could too easily imagine a real execution, so Ravishan's words sent a spike of cold dread down his spine. The thought of Ravishan bound and burning on the Holy Road destroyed John's desire in a moment.

"I will not put you in that kind of danger," John said flatly.

"I don't care," Ravishan insisted.

"I do!" The words came out harsh and angry. John didn't mean them to, but he needed Ravishan to stop tempting him. "You don't endanger the life of a man you care about just so you can get laid. How selfish can you be?"

Ravishan recoiled as if he had been physically struck. The color drained from his cheeks and mouth. His hands dropped to his sides.

"I'm sorry," John said. "I shouldn't have ever kissed you."

"I wanted you to." Ravishan hung his head.

John wanted to comfort him, but he couldn't afford to do that right now. He said, "I'll see you tomorrow at Rathal'pesha."

Ravishan only nodded.

John turned and climbed down the broken wall. He wanted to look back to see if Ravishan still stood there watching or if he had already gone, but he didn't. He kept his eyes on the muddy, torn ground ahead of him, steadily retracing his path back out of Candle Alley as if by finding his exact footsteps he could take the entire night back.

To Be Continued …

Titles, Ranks, and Terms of Address

Usho—Leader of the Payshmura Church.
Kahlil—Holy Traveler and Companion to Parfir.
Ushman—High Ranking Clergy; often in a position of great responsibility.
Ushiri—Talented Priest studying to become Kahlil'im.
Ushvun—Priest.
Ushvran—Nun.
Kahlirash—Military sect devoted to Parfir's destroyer incarnation.
Gaunsho—Lord of one of the seven noble houses.
Gaunan—Nobleman.
Gauniri—Noblechild.
Gaunvur—Noblewoman.
Gaun'im—Nobles (as a group).
Laman—Scholar, Doctor or anyone learned.
Lamiri—Student.
Rasho—Military leader, particularly cavalry.
Rashan—Soldier.
Vunan—Common man.
Vuran—Common woman.
Shir—Animal; derogatory when used to address a human being.

Characters from Kahlil's Story

Alidas—Captain for the Bousim in Nurjima; partly crippled.
Desh'oun—The house steward in the Lisam Palace.
Saimura—Jath'ibaye's house steward in Nurjima.
Esh'illan Anyyd—A young gaunan allied with Ourath.
Fensal— A Lisam runner.
Fikiri Busim—An ushiri from the fallen Payshmura Faith.
Ji Shir'korud—Dog demon; called Jath'ibaye's bitch by some gaun'im.
Jath'ibaye—Leader of the new Fai'daum kingdom.
Joulen Bousim—Bousim heir after Nanvess. Currently serving military duty in the northmost Bousim holdings.
Kahlil— Kyle'insira also called Kyle.
Mosh'sira'in'Bousim—Gaunsho Bousim; aged and weak ruler.
Nanvess Bousim—A gaunan; named the Bousim heir for political reasons.
Nivoun Bousim—Nanvess' father; highly ambitious for his son.
Ourath Lisam—Gaunsho Lisam.
Parfir—God of the banned Payshmura Church, his worship is now forbidden.
Yu'mir—A servant woman in Lisam Palace.

Characters from John's Story

Ashan'ahma—An ushiri studying at Rathal'pesha.
Alidas—A rider for the Bousim family; partly crippled.
Amha'in' Bousim—Lady Bousim, 3rd wife, exiled to the north.
Bati'kohl—A servant of Lady Bousim; brother of Ohbi.
Bill—Called Behr in Basawar.
Dayyid—Second ushman at Rathal'pesha.
Fikiri Bousim—An ushiri candidate; son of Lady Bousim.
Hann'yu—An ushman exiled to the north— specializes in healing.
Inholima—Spy in Lady Bousim's household.
Issusha'im—The Payshmura oracles.
Ji Shir'korud—Dog demon; one of the Fai'daum.
John—Called Jahn in Basawar.
Laurie—Called Loshai in Basawar.
Mosh'sira'in' Bousim—Gaunsho Bousim.
Mou'pin—A rider under Pivan.
Nuritam—The ushman at Rathal'pesha.
Ohbi—A loyal servant to Lady Bousim.
Parfir—The earth god.
Pivan—The second in command of the Bousim rashan'im.
Rifter—The destroyer incarnation of Parfir.
Ravishan—The most promising of the ushiri at Rathal'pesha.
Rousma—Ravishan's sister.
Sabir—The leader of the Fai'daum.
Saimura—Ji's son.
Samsango—An elderly priest at Rathal'pesha.
Serahn—Powerful ushman in the Black Tower of Nurjima.
Tashtu—Pivan's commander.
Wah'roa—Leader of the kahlirash'im at Vundomu

Dictionary of a Few Useful Words

and — iff
animal/it — shir
asshole — wahbai
bark (tree) — istana
bee (honey) — behr
best — sho
black — yasi
blond hide — jahn
blood — usha
blue — holima
bone — sumah
bones (holy) — issusha
book — lam
brothers — ashan
but/however — hel
chasm — kubo
city — tamur
cold — polima
dead — maht
death-lock key — maht'tu hala
deer (mount) — tahldi
delicious — mosh
dog (domestic) — kohl
dog (wild)/wolf — sabir
exhausted — renma
fast — sam
fire — daru
food — nabi (grain)
friend — pashim
from/of — in
fuck — faud
goat — fik
good/ pretty — domu
grain plant — taye
green — ibaye
harm — ratim
hawk — alidas
hill — rousma
holy — ushmana
hot — niru
how/because — ahab
idiot — bai
joy — amha
key — hala

knife — halaun
lazy — pom
little/diminutive — iri
lock — tu
lost — gasm'ah
love — mohim
man/male — vun
meadow — pivan
meat — nabi'usha
medicinal tree — yasistana
monastery — ushmura
money — jiusha
mountain — rathal
no — iss
noble — gaun
none — illin
orchard — umbhra
peace — tumah
place — amura
quiet — itam
rain — parh
red — daum
river — fai
road — nur
run — sango
sacred books — ushmana'lam
sacred drink — fathi
same — kin
shit — jid
similar — ro
sky — loshai
snow — pelima
solitary — jath
speak — vass
spill — ra
spoil — lafi
still — tash
stop — nahara
strike — bish
terrible — tehji
time/year — ayal
to be lost — gasmya
to drink — siraya
to eat — nabiya

Dictionary of a Few Useful Words

to harm — ratimya
to kill — rashiya
tree (fruit) — isma
tree bark — istana
ugly/bad — mulhi
unholy/unclean — korud
water/drink — sira
weasel — ganal
what — bati
when — bayal
where — bamura
white — pesha
who — ban
why — bahab
wine — vishan
witch — tahjid
woman/ female — vur
gold/yellow — jima/ ji
yes — du

PRONOUNS

he/him — vun
his — vun'um
they(all male) — vun'im
she/her — vur
hers — vur'um
they (all female) — vur'im
they(mixed) — pun'im
theirs — pun'um
I/me — li
mine — li'um
we/us — li'im
ours — lim'un
you — yura
yours — yura'um
you (plural) — yura'im
yours (plural) — yura'un
it — shir
it (plural) — shir'um

DECLENSIONS AND CONJUGATIONS

positive — dou
negative — iss
question — sa
object of action — hir
source of action — ati
one who does — hlil
plural — im
possessive (singular) — um
possessive (plural) — un
future tense — ad
past tense — ah
present tense — ya
(Ya literally means 'to do' or 'to be'.)
possible — at
hoped for (future) — atdou
hoped against — atiss
command form — hi
gerund — yas
adjective — an
adverb — al

ACKNOWLEDGMENTS

Far too many people for me to list on a single page—or even two—have helped me and offered their support throughout the ten odd years that it took for The Rifter to go from an idea to a digital serial and then into print.

The wonderful Rifter Goodreads group alone deserves their own index of kind deeds done. They made an otherwise nerve wracking year into a joy. (I still hum "On A Boat" to myself when I'm writing now!)

Here, however, is a short and by no means complete list of people who made all the difference to me and this book: Nicole, Melissa, Josh, Gavin, Michael, and Alan.

I am deeply grateful to you all.

ABOUT THE AUTHOR

Ginn Hale lives with her wife and two lazy cats in the cool green shadow of Mt. Baker. A proponent of animal welfare, she is a supporter of Best Friends Animal Society and has recently become involved in New Moon Farm's Goatalympics—a fund raiser for goat rescue.

Her publications include *The Lord of the White Hell* series, *Wicked Gentleman*—and as coauthor—*Irregulars* and the *Hell Cop* books.

The Holy Road

Book Two of the Rifter

March 2013